THE SCHOOL FOR HUSBANDS

Sophie's marriage was perfect. But now it's all gone wrong. Mark works late; she's left with the baby, domestic drudgery, her own career to keep on the go and a feeling Mark's up to something. When, one night, he fails to come home it's the last straw.

She wants a divorce but he doesn't. He hasn't been unfaithful, just thoughtless. Desperate to save his marriage, Mark enrols at the 'School for Husbands', which does what it says on the tin. But will its intensive and unusual tuition be enough to reunite him with Sophie? Especially now an eligible millionaire is after her...

THE SCHOOL FOR HUSBANDS

Wendy Holden

WINDSOR
PARAGON

First published 2006
by
Headline Review
This Large Print edition published 2007
by
BBC Audiobooks Ltd by arrangement with
Headline Book Publishing

Hardcover ISBN: 978 1 405 61668 3
Softcover   ISBN: 978 1 405 61669 0

British Library Cataloguing in Publication Data available

To JM, AAM and IM

Printed and bound in Great Britain by
Antony Rowe Ltd., Chippenham, Wiltshire

CHAPTER ONE

Sophie twisted round. Relief flooded through her. People had turned up. More guests were coming into the church all the time. Everyone had dressed up too: the men fresh in pale summer suits; the women pretty in floaty florals. Some, even more gratifyingly, had gone as far as hats, which looked sharp and colourful against the soft mediaeval stone of the walls.

Her mother's hat, as expected, was the biggest of all; a huge confection of gold gauze. It seemed to Mark, next to Sophie, that it filled the whole church. Any objection he had had to the 'proper christening' his wife had wanted for Arthur had stemmed less from doubts about delivering his son into the hands of the Almighty than delivering the party into the hands of his in-laws. But Shirley and James lived in a postcard-perfect village. The Dower House had a big garden and they were able to fix it with the vicar. So the venue had been unarguable.

Most of the rest of it, unfortunately, had been very arguable. That Shirley intended the occasion to be the big wedding reception they—and more significantly she—had never had was obvious from the start. His mother-in-law, Mark knew, had never forgiven him for depriving her of her big-hat moment as Mother of the Bride by insisting on a register office followed by a small lunch.

But nothing was to be small now, apart from Arthur of course, though the vast christening robe Shirley had bought for her grandson went some

1

way to addressing even that. Mark looked down at his son in his wife's arms, swathed in acres of fake-ancestral frills. He wondered whether Arthur's unusual calm was due less to a sense of occasion and more to a sense of being smothered.

Mark felt smothered himself. Shirley and James were paying for the celebrations, admittedly. They had absolutely insisted, and his and Sophie's financial circumstances did not constitute a contrary argument. But even so, did Shirley's arrangements have to be so relentlessly unheeding of anything he or Sophie had wanted? What he had mainly wanted was to keep it simple. Sophie had wanted to keep the peace. Shirley, however, had wanted fleur-de-lis cocktail napkins, a marquee festooned with ivy, and luxury portaloos with mahogany seats and carnations in the cubicles. She had converted their plans for sandwiches (plain beef or egg) into poached salmon on thyme ciabatta or roasted Mediterranean vegetables on tomato bread. Thankfully, he had got wind about the string quartet in time.

'I was thinking more along the lines of a brass band,' he had told Shirley. In actual fact he didn't care what the music was, but he was damned if Shirley was getting her own way in everything, paying for it or not.

His mother-in-law had frowned as much as facial surgery would allow. 'Rather common, don't you think?'

Her gaze had lingered on him meaningfully. Mark was aware that his mother-in-law considered him a less-than-perfect husband for her daughter. Or a less-than-perfect son-in-law for herself, which was possibly a slightly different thing.

He had not particularly expected to win the brass band argument, but Sophie's father James, a retired corporate accountant who generally gave way to his his wife in all things, had most unexpectedly lit up at the suggestion. Sophie, too, had lent her support. So a brass band had been duly engaged and briefed to play 'Oh I Do Like to Be Beside the Seaside', 'Knees Up Mother Brown'—which, as Mark pointed out, had particular relevance given Sophie's married surname and Arthur's recent birth—and other jaunty Edwardian ditties.

Shirley had hit back with the flowers. Examining them now as she sat in the church, Sophie tried to persuade herself that her mother's 'statement' gladioli and gerbera weren't garish in the least and worked just as well as the simple summer country flora she and Mark would have preferred.

But the weather was wonderful, which was infinitely more important. The saints, sinners and coats of arms glowed richly in the stained-glass windows as the sun outside gathered momentum. Watching various members of the congregation bow their heads as they sat down, Sophie realised guiltily that she had prayed for good weather far more fervently than anything else. She had consulted the BBC's five-day weather forecast on a daily basis; latterly, almost hourly, much to Mark's amusement.

Frankly, she could have done without him laughing. Much as she loved Mark, and she truly did, Sophie could not help feeling unsupported at times, now being one of them. Organising— or, more accurately, organising her mother

3

organising—an event on the scale the christening had become had sent her stress levels soaring. New problems seemed to emerge every day, none of which Mark had been particularly helpful in solving. She accepted that he had been very busy with work—his job was new, he had to prove himself, and their financial circumstances were straitened. But even so, he could have been more diplomatic with Shirley and more constructive about the crucial question of godparents.

In the end it had been Sophie who had decided that what they needed was one reliable, steady godparent and one exciting and influential one. 'That way we cover all bases,' she had explained to Mark.

Cecily was the reliable one. An old university friend of Sophie's, she was single, childless and a primary school teacher. 'Cess'll have time for Arthur because she doesn't have children of her own, and she'll be able to tell me whether he's reaching his milestones or not.'

'And confirm he's an undoubted genius at five months, too,' joked Mark, effortlessly guessing his wife's unspoken agenda. 'But are you sure she does organised religion?'

'Absolutely. She's very interested in religion. Has to be. Her school is in one of the most deprived areas of London, ninety-nine per cent Muslim, I think she said.'

Mark nodded. 'But isn't she a bit—well—alternative? You didn't speak for weeks, remember, when she found out you were putting Pampers on Arthur.'

'Oh, she's got over that now. And anyway, it will be good for Arthur to have a godparent who can raise his social consciousness. He needs to realise there are other people out there apart from middle-class kids like him.'

'I suppose so.' Mark decided not to point out that their street of gentrified terraces faced one of the largest council estates in South London.

'Good. That's decided then.' Sophie smiled.

For the exciting and influential godparent Sophie chose a former work colleague whose father was a frozen-foods tycoon. His revelation that Arthur would be one of his ten godchildren and not, as she had thought, the special one and only, was a disappointment.

'Of course,' she had grumbled to Mark, 'the others only asked Richard because he's got no children, a rich father and good contacts.'

'So why else did *you* ask him?' Mark had teased.

'Because,' Sophie flashed back, 'Richard's the one who'll take him out and buy him champagne cocktails and tell him about girls.'

Shortly after this exchange, Richard texted to say he had come out and was going to New York to live with his boyfriend. It was the text that hurt. Sophie withdrew the godparent invitation and announced they must find someone else to fulfil the fun and influential brief.

'But who?' Mark had asked.

It was a good, if difficult, question, and one, again, which seemed to fall to Sophie. The problem was that every other suitable male of their acquaintance was married with children of his own and no spare capacity, financial or spiritual, to take an interest in someone else's offspring. As the date of the christening neared, Sophie was even considering asking the postman. He was pleasant,

5

friendly, clean and childless, although, as he had a girlfriend, there was no guarantee this would continue. Still, he was better than nothing.

In the end, help had come from a most unexpected source.

Her mother had taken to ringing Sophie about the party on an almost daily basis. 'Cambozola!' Shirley declaimed dramatically as Sophie picked up the phone one morning.

'Sorry?' Sophie frowned. What language was being spoken? 'Who *is* this?'

'Cheese, darling. We need to decide.'

'I don't care, Mum,' Sophie groaned. She was by now wondering whether the nice man in the newsagents had spare godparental capacity. After all, if it was contacts in the media she was wanting . . .

'Still no luck with the replacement godfather, darling?' Shirley enquired, divining the reason for her daughter's lack of interest in dairy products.

'Not as such.'

'Well you'll never guess who I bumped into in town today!' Shirley exclaimed. 'Margaret Sharp!'

Her mother was right; Sophie never would have guessed. While Shirley meeting this mother of an old boyfriend was not improbable—they lived in neighbouring villages, after all—the warmth with which she spoke of it was astonishing.

'Margaret! But I thought you didn't like her. You used to say she was common when I was going out with Simon.'

'That was nearly twenty years ago.' Shirley sniffed. 'People change.'

Sophie considered. She remembered Margaret Sharp as a dumpy woman who worked in a factory

6

and had a face like an anxious hamster. Short of her suddenly becoming the Duchess of Devonshire, it was hard to imagine how she could possibly have changed enough to interest her mother.

'Simon's doing awfully well now,' Shirley added casually. 'He's a millionaire banker with a manor house in Hertfordshire.'

'*Simon* is?' Sophie exclaimed. 'I mean, I knew he was a banker, but—'

'Heated swimming pool as well!' her mother interrupted. 'You see what you missed!'

Sophie's hackles rose. 'Mum! Simon was twenty years ago. We hardly went out for more than a month. And you didn't like him anyway. You used to say he was a spotty oik.'

'As I say,' Shirley said breezily, 'people change. Do you ever hear from him, by the way?'

'He still sends me a birthday card.' Sophie had never been quite sure why. She suspected the date was on his secretary's database.

'Mmm.' Her mother was silent for a few moments. 'Well, seeing Margaret gave me an idea. It's the obvious answer to your problem.'

'What is?'

'Simon's *perfect* godfather material.'

'*Godfather* material!'

'Well, why not?' her mother challenged. 'He's rich and successful and a wonderful role model. Arthur needs good role models.'

'Are you saying,' Sophie asked touchily, 'that Mark isn't a good role model?' But why ask the question? Of course her mother was saying that. Mark was a book salesman and Simon a millionaire. 'It's not all about money you know,'

7

she grumbled.

'Well, most of it is. And it's Arthur you're thinking about here, anyway. Simon's rich and successful, he's someone you're still in touch with and someone who could help Arthur a lot in the future. And frankly, darling, isn't time running out?'

*   *   *

The vicar had now arrived. A woman vicar, whom Mark had liked from the first meeting. She was laid-back, friendly and obviously hadn't minded his uncertain approach to Believing. She had also turned out to be a Merseysider, with an interest in Liverpool Football Club as well informed as it was unexpected.

The organist, an old lady whose style Mark appreciated for its clear Les Dawson influences, struck up a tune that emerged, after a few confusing seconds, as 'Jerusalem'. This being the cue, Mark, Sophie, Arthur and the godparents moved forward to the font.

They made an arresting group. Cess, who was no lightweight and whose clumsily bundled-up hair was dyed a brilliant red, was dressed for the occasion in a hot-pink sari. This not only made her pink face look puce by comparison, but also clashed, Sophie feared, with her own flowered wrap dress. Thank goodness Simon and Mark looked properly sober. Simon in particular looked perfect.

About this, Mark was less sure. Simon Sharp had apparently been Sophie's boyfriend when they were both eighteen. Although, frankly, it was difficult to imagine the tall, grave Simon as a teenager.

He seemed focused and controlled to a rather scary degree; polite but uneffusive. His face was flat and masklike and his eyes were watchful. The feeling of standing in front of him was, Mark thought, that of standing before an open freezer door.

'He's not much fun, is he?' Mark had objected. 'You wanted someone fun and influential to be the other godparent.'

'But Simon *is* influential,' Sophie argued. 'Just think how useful he'd be if Arthur ever wants to go into the City. Or law. I think Simon has lots of legal connections as well.'

Mark raised his eyebrows. Admittedly, Arthur was only a few months old, yet already possessed of the kind of volcanic temper that sat ill with a career at the Bar. Unless, that was, as a defendant.

'And Simon's single, and doesn't have any other godchildren,' Sophie added.

'Yes, but what does that say about his ability to form relationships? Like I say, he's not much fun, is he?'

'Look, we're not choosing a godparent for ourselves, we're choosing one for Arthur. Anyway, there is something fun about him.'

'What?'

'He's very rich, according to Mum. He has a manor house in Hertfordshire with a heated swimming pool.' Sophie felt a twinge of guilt at using the argument that had so annoyed her coming from Shirley. But of course—to a certain extent—money did matter. As, she suppressed a sigh, did the lack of it.

'Good for him.' Mark was unimpressed. In his pool, in his manor house even, Simon Sharp was still Simon Sharp. And it would take more than a heated swimming pool to warm a cold fish like that up.

Mark had eventually agreed to Simon because he could not imagine why anyone, least of all a busy banker, would want to be godfather to the child of someone he had not seen for twenty years. He had not expected Simon to accept the invitation. When he had, and with alacrity, Mark had assumed, slightly contemptuously, that their teenage relationship had meant more to Simon than it had done to his wife.

Watching Simon Sharp now, holding Arthur at the font, Mark tried to imagine him married to Sophie. He wondered what his blonde, vivacious wife had seen in this feelingless waxwork. On the other hand, as Sophie had said herself, an alternative evening's entertainment at the time had been sitting in front of *The Two Ronnies* with her parents. Mark could just imagine it: James snoring in his armchair and Shirley not getting the jokes.

Glancing at Sophie, listening intently to the service, her straight features lit in a shaft of colour from the windows, he felt a rush of pure love. How wonderful that Sharp hadn't got her first. That they had found each other. That she had married him. And now that they had Arthur.

Watching Simon Sharp now, holding Arthur at the font, Shirley tried to imagine him married to Sophie too. She found it a great deal easier than Mark had. *My son-in-law the millionaire financier. My daughter's mansion in Hertfordshire with the heated swimming pool.* What wouldn't she give to

10

be able to say that to certain villagers, especially Venetia Bothamley-Tartt! *My daughter the sub-editor and my son-in-law the book salesman living on Verona Road, South London* somehow lacked the same ring.

She looked fondly at her grandson—such a gorgeous little boy, such a beautiful christening robe, such a shame his father was . . . well. Shirley heaved a sigh so powerful it sent waves across the water in the font. The main chance may have been missed but at least she'd roped Simon in as godfather. Not all had been lost.

Watching Simon Sharp now, holding Arthur at the font, Sophie's main emotion was gratitude. He had responded to her nervous invitation to be a godfather with an eagerness she had not expected after the near-two decades since she last saw him. A gratifying contrast to the deeply unworthy Richard. And as she had only spoken to Simon on the phone about the christening—some crucial takeover had impeded meeting in person—she was unprepared for how much he had changed physically. It was amazing. He actually looked as if he lived in the same space-time continuum as everyone else these days.

Gone was the side-parted, short fair hair of 1986 and the accompanying paperweight glasses. Unencumbered by optical real estate, Simon's face looked surprisingly regular. Handsome, even, although not, she thought, sliding a glance at her husband, anything approaching Mark's blend of dark-haired, crumpled glamour. As Mark caught her glance and flashed a smile, her heart compressed with love. She had a handsome and loving husband and a beautiful son. She was the

11

luckiest woman in the world.

The last hymn, 'Dear Lord And Father Of Mankind', struck up, and Sophie sang heartily. Happiness poured into her like the sun through the stained-glass windows. The stress of the last few weeks was fading. All they had to do now was go and drink champagne in her parents' garden. Everything was perfect.

CHAPTER TWO

Simon Sharp watched Shirley proudly parade The Dower House lawns with her grandson. As she smiled and waved at him over the hatted heads he nodded briefly back. Her new cordiality towards him did not fool him in the least. Years ago it may be, but he had not forgotten her hauteur when he had dared to pay court to her daughter. The exclamations of amused surprise when he shovelled his peas in, tines-up. The polite and repeated enquiries as to where exactly in the council estate his home was.

He watched as she struggled to extract a high heel from the lawn without falling over with the baby. Silly woman, always had been mutton dressed as lamb. And more so than usual today, with that tiny skirt and huge, ridiculous hat.

Being asked to be godfather to Arthur had been a surprise, but not a shock. It was obvious that the reason was money just as soon as Sophie confessed it had been her mother's idea. Normally he would have said no; Sophie, after all, had been a summer romance a million years ago. The reason she had

had virtually no successors was less because she was the love of his life than because the real love of his life was money. Simon had little interest in anything else, and no interest in anything that got between him and the making of it, as a woman might.

His job, and the accumulation of wealth that it afforded, were Simon's entire focus. Within the international bank where he worked he had risen higher and higher and grown richer and richer. There seemed no obstacle to his getting higher and richer still. Until, that was, the recent, dramatic boardroom coup in which Isaiah and Abel Wintergreen had taken over.

It was a typical move by the Wintergreen brothers, who liked to strike fast, hard and unexpectedly. Within corporate financial circles their boldness and brilliance was legendary. Each company they acquired flourished, and it was expected that Simon's already successful bank would now out-perform itself several times over. The opportunities that lay before Simon therefore looked considerable. Within his grasp was the prospect of acquiring wealth beyond even his dreams of avarice.

Only one thing stood between Simon and this happy outcome. It was, however, a considerable thing. The Wintergreens hailed from one of the poorest parts of the American Deep South and were passionately proud of their roots. This expressed itself in a number of ways. For a start, the Wintergreens spurned suits and ties, preferring cowboy boots and check shirts. They also held firm and unbending views about family life. Both Wintergreens had been married since age

13

seventeen and they had eight children each. It was rumoured—and the rumour seemed to be backed up with fact—that only employees who were married parents were promoted within the company.

This rumour unsettled Simon considerably. Not only did he not have a wife or a family, he realised that he didn't even know any children. While his colleagues frantically framed and displayed on their desks every available image of their offspring, Simon's workstation remained incriminatingly empty. Into this difficult situation, and the dire threat it posed to his future, Sophie's invitation to be a godfather had appeared nothing less than a miracle. Arthur might not be a son, but a godson was better than nothing. He was, at least, something to put on the desk.

Simon now slapped his pockets for the hi-tech, super-slim, wildly expensive camera he had bought for the christening. As he framed a shot of the distant Arthur, still being shown off by his grandmother, a large figure in pink blundered into the picture. A split second later, Cess collided with him heavily.

'God, sorry,' she gasped, retrieving her mobile from the grass. 'Didn't see you there. Just taking a few snaps on my phone. Thought it would be good for a project on Ceremonies we're doing at school.'

'Oh,' said Simon, utterly uninterested.

'We never got properly introduced in the church, did we? I'm Cess. Godmother.'

'Cess,' repeated Simon, faintly. 'I'm Simon.'

'I've heard about you. Banker, yeah?' She eyed him challengingly. 'D'you think they should drop the debt?'

'Certainly not,' Simon said immediately. The more debt there was the better. Debt meant interest and interest meant profits.

'Hmm. Suppose a City breadhead would say that. D'you think this is Fairtrade champagne?' She brandished a near-empty glass in front of him.

'I have no idea,' Simon said coldly.

'Well, whatever, I've drunk too much of it,' Cess remarked cheerfully, stumbling off.

Elsewhere in the garden, Sophie tried to hold a conversation with an old friend while simultaneously holding Arthur, with whom she had just been reunited. 'He's awfully squirmy, darling,' Shirley had announced, shoving the thrashing bundle back in her arms.

Sophie looked around for Mark. There he was, in the middle distance, with a group of their friends, throwing back his head to laugh between sips of champagne. She hadn't had a glass at all yet. A quiver of exasperation ran through her. Surely it was about time Mark looked after Arthur?

'When was it you said you were going back to work?' Juliet drawled.

'When Arthur's six months, at the beginning of September. About a fortnight from now, in fact.' Sophie felt a charge of excitement at the prospect of picking up her work bag again, of clacking smartly out of the house in high heels and fitted clothes. How different it would feel from lolloping around in flip-flops and slobwear.

'Rather you than me,' Juliet yawned. 'I couldn't face work after I'd had the kids.'

Sophie suppressed a smile. Juliet couldn't face work before she'd had the kids either. After

15

university, which was where they had met, Juliet's working life had consisted of one half-hearted attempt to start up a luxury mail-order food business. Since Cassandra and Orlando had appeared, she had retreated into the luxurious languor of her husband's ancestral home in Wales.

Yet Sophie did not envy her. It would be nice to be rich, certainly; nice not to have to walk the financial knife-edge in which Mark's unexpected recent redundancy had resulted. But be married to the boorish, red-faced Harry instead of Mark? Not nice. Not at all.

Besides, quite apart from the financial imperative, Sophie had never seriously entertained not resuming her career. While being at home with Arthur had had its positive aspects—him, most of all—she had known full-time motherhood would eventually pall. As her maternity leave had drawn to a close, she began once more to hear the call of the world, the pull of work and proper waistbands.

Just for now, though, she was hearing the call of alcohol. Urgently. Out of the corner of her eye she saw Mark drain his glass and pick up another from a passing tray.

'Look,' she said to Juliet, desperately. 'You don't think you could go and get me a—'

'Oh God. Look at them. Cassie! Lando! Where's that bloody nanny of theirs?' Juliet dived after her children.

Something tall and grave now loomed at Sophie's side. 'I've brought you a drink,' Simon Sharp announced.

'How absolutely lovely of you!' Sophie seized the longed-for glass and smiled while Simon pointed a miniature digital camera. Her smile widened as his finger pushed the button. How very sweet of him to want to take so many pictures of his godson. Touching, too, how concerned he seemed to be to get absolutely the right shot. She stared at the camera lens zooming in and out. It looked very expensive, but what about Simon didn't? His suit was unmistakably cashmere, while his skin had an expensive, Jermyn-Street-wet-shaved look, very different from the patchy, snatched affairs that haste forced upon Mark.

'Awfully sorry to hear about Mark's job,' Simon murmured in his rather nasal voice.

Sophie coughed into her glass. 'Sorry? How do you mean?'

'Him being made redundant and everything.'

'He got a great new job, straightaway,' Sophie said defensively. Who, she thought furiously, had been so indiscreet as to let slip to Simon Mark's recent, brief professional setback? Her eye caught her mother, bustling after a caterer carrying a tower of profiteroles. 'Make way for the *croquembouche*!' Shirley was trilling.

'Your mother never mentioned he had a new job,' Simon remarked.

'I don't suppose she did. But in fact he's just started as sales director designate of a new publishing company.'

'Designate?'

'If he does well, he gets the job permanently. And he *will* do well,' Sophie said loyally.

'Does it pay well, though?'

Sophie started at such frankness. On the other hand, Simon was clearly taking his financial godparental duties very seriously, to judge by the large cheque that had been paid into the bank

17

account he had opened for Arthur at Coutts. That their son had more expendable capital at the age of five months than they had at a combined age of over seventy, had been a sobering realisation.

'Not bad,' she said, which about summed it up. Mark's new company was small and unestablished. Making it big and established was his challenge. Then he would reap the rewards.

Simon felt scornful. No doubt the husband was making peanuts; he knew from his own experience recruiting redundant staff how pathetically grateful they were to have a job again. Their willingness to accept tiny wages was something he had exploited several times in the past. He watched Mark laughing in the sunshine and wondered what on earth, given his obvious poverty, he had to be so happy about. Being content without several million in the bank was inconceivable to Simon.

Emboldened by champagne, Sophie decided it was her turn as question master.

'Never married, then, Simon?' she asked playfully.

'Er, no.' Simon's heart was pounding. He was prepared for such questions in the bank, but to be cross-examined on this most sensitive of subjects amid the bright sunshine of a christening party was a horrible shock.

He kept his shock concealed from Sophie, however. The champagne on her empty stomach made her merry enough to probe further.

'But you'd make someone a lovely husband,' she teased.

'I never found the right girl, I suppose,' Simon muttered. 'No one quite measured up to you, you see,' he added lightly.

'Oh Simon!' Sophie burst out. 'As if!' Slightly embarrassed, she sought to change the subject, as he had intended her to.

'I'm going back to work soon,' she told him excitedly.

CHAPTER THREE

Sophie's first shock at returning to work was that the desk had changed completely. Gone was the former chief sub-editor Anne, a spirited brunette with a union-leader streak who had fearlessly defended her staff against what she considered the more unreasonable demands of management.

This was a sinister development. Besides being a solid colleague, Anne had several children and defended fiercely her right to get home on time to see them. Sophie had been counting on her sympathy in the nursery-to-work struggle, not to mention vice versa—journeys which had turned out to be far simpler in theory than practice. But Anne, Sophie now gathered, had objected to late working hours once too often and consequently had trodden the time-honoured route to Human Resources, the exit door and a jobshare on *Sedimentary Geology Monthly*.

But if none of that boded well for Sophie, Lisa boded even worse. Lisa was Anne's replacement; a man- and marriage-hating fortysomething whose attitudes seemed rooted in her own lack of success with the opposite sex. Some of which, Sophie suspected, might be down to her appearance. Her violently black-dyed hair and bright orange foundation were strikingly peculiar, especially when teamed with pearlised lipstick. But there was nothing funny about working for her.

This morning, as all mornings, Lisa stared meaningfully at the office clock as Sophie entered. It was a gesture designed to eliminate the possibility Sophie could be unaware that she was arriving fifteen minutes late.

'I'm sorry. I'll make up for it in my lunch hour.' Sophie gasped her apologies with what breath she had after sprinting up six staircases. She had lacked the time—or nerve—to wait for the lift.

Lisa's eyes were merciless and cloggy with mascara. 'You're already making up in your lunch hour for yesterday and the day before.'

Sophie dipped her head to disguise the fury in her eyes. *The bloody bitch.* Then a wave of misery engulfed her as she remembered Arthur at the nursery that morning, wailing and clinging to her legs. She sought relief from both emotions by throwing her belongings under the table with force.

'Ow,' yelped Penny, Lisa's deputy, as Sophie's bag impacted on her calf. She glared at her colleague. Sophie muttered an apology, but secretly wished she had hit her harder. Penny was just as bad as Lisa, if not worse.

Sophie had originally been furious that Lisa had ignored her own right to promotion. But now the full horror of her new boss was evident, Sophie was relieved not to be immediately under her. Penny, at any rate, was Lisa's natural partner, as sour and sarcastic as she was, and almost as frightening to look at, with burgundy spiked hair and stern, metal-rimmed spectacles. She too was single, and seemed to reserve her special ire for married women and mothers.

'What do you call an intelligent, good-looking, sensitive man?' she would call to Lisa. 'A rumour!' And the two would crack up.

'What's the fastest way to a man's heart?' Lisa would rejoin. 'Through his chest with a sharp knife!'

'Ha ha.'

Sophie never reacted to these exchanges and tried not to listen to them. It was clear that their intention was to hurt and mock a happily married woman. She resolved to appear happier and more married than ever, although for various reasons this had seemed difficult of late. She put it down to readapting to the job. For it was not only the personnel who had changed. The workload had too, since the magazine's format had altered. This had been another surprise.

The publication's previous focus on celebrity lives had shifted to an emphasis on what the magazine's editor called 'zeitgeist touchstones'.

Lisa, who had the editor's ear, translated this for her underlings as 'features exploring emotional scenarios calculated to strike a chord with the mostly female readership'. The editorial meetings in which the scenarios were decided were a fascinating fast-forward through staff members' private lives. The deputy editor's suggested 'Successful, Divorced, Single, Am I Scary Or Something?' had precipitated mass staring at the carpet, while the apparently happily married chief designer's 'When He Comes Back', had left the editorial meeting quietly staggered; no one having known he had left. 'When Your Mother Takes

Over Your Life', meanwhile, had come from a very cool, very big and very macho man from the production desk, whom no one had previously imagined labouring under the maternal yoke.

While Sophie was as interested as anyone in these developments, the change of editorial tack made extra demands on her. To give weight to the pieces it was, for instance, necessary to secure several quotes per article from various relationships experts. The most eager to provide quotes, Sophie had found, was a media-friendly American marital therapist called Martha Krankenhaus. She was strange, of course. They all were. But at least she answered the phone.

Sophie braced herself to call her now. Scientific input was required for 'Why Do Men Find It Hard To Talk?', suggested by the manically garrulous picture editor.

'Dr Krankenhaus,' Sophie said, as the relationships expert picked up in New York.

'Dr *Martha*. Dr Krankenhaus is too alienating.'

Sophie sighed. She found the doctor alienating whatever she was called. The touchy-feeliness of her manner was rivalled only by the convoluted nature of her pronouncements.

'Why do men find it so hard to talk, Dr Martha?' Sophie's fingers hovered over her keyboard in the hope of catching some of the torrent of words she knew would follow. Dr Martha certainly did not find it hard to talk. Far from it. Five minutes later, she was still going strong.

'. . . the syndrome presenting as male speech inhibition is often best approached through promoting self-esteem and a sense of self-worth by assisting patients in learning how to participate in

22

creating situations fostering physical, emotional, sexual, psychological, and spiritual safety and growth, and aid-assisting patients in the development of coping mechanisms. OK?'

'Thank you, Dr Martha. That's . . . er . . . great.'

Another of Sophie's new areas of responsibility was coaxing the weekly page of predictions out of the astrologer. This was a redoubtable, violently groomed female named Marjorie Starr, the top of whose head featured an auburn tsunami of hair as high as her face was long.

Sophie, wresting this week's prediction from the fax machine at teatime, had no need to read her own fate. This page always took hours and she was going to be late. Racing through the star signs checking for errors, she tried to block out Lisa and Penny.

'A couple are lying in bed,' Penny snorted. 'The man says "I'm going to make you the happiest woman in the world." The woman says, "I'll miss you." Ha ha!'

'Hee hee,' spluttered Lisa.

'People with children,' Penny added indignantly as Sophie finally threw on her coat, 'think the whole world revolves round them. Leaving early to go to the nursery! What about us?'

Lisa's eyes blazed. 'Absolutely. What if I wanted to go early because of my line dancing or my cats?'

Sophie, leaving, silently sent her every sympathy. Line-dancing. Cats. What a life. She wouldn't change hers for anything, really she wouldn't. But there were some things that could be easier.

She clattered at ankle-breaking speed down the escalator at the nearest tube station, praying, as

23

she shoved on to the crowded platform, that there would be a train, that she would be able to get on it and that, once she had, it wouldn't stop except at stations. It was the only way she was going to make Little Explorers on time.

Sophie had once read a parenting book advising that, before collecting one's child at nursery, the mother should take five minutes to de-stress and re-energise. 'Sit in the car, shake off your office mood and refocus on that huge cuddle you're about to share.' It made Sophie laugh—hollowly—now to remember how seriously she had once taken this. The huge cuddle was indeed her priority; seeing Arthur's big smile and folding his little body into her arms was always the best moment of the day. But any possibility of a spare five minutes to stand outside and think about it had been lost in the tunnel between Charing Cross and Kennington. And earlier in the tunnel between Aries and Virgo.

Ten minutes later, Sophie rattled Arthur in his buggy down the nursery pathway. She was anxious to get off the premises as quickly as possible. The Little Explorers manager had made it clear that, with a waiting list like hers, she had no need to or intention of tolerating consistently late parents. The thought of adding the finding of a new nursery to her other challenges made Sophie feel nauseous.

'Hello, there!' A friendly voice rang out from the car park. Raising her eyes from the floor where she habitually focused them, Sophie saw a smiling blonde woman packing her child into a silver estate.

It was Helen, one of the friendlier mothers.

24

Sophie had, when Arthur began at Little Explorers, entertained hopes of enlarging her circle with an influx of young local women in similar circumstances to her own. However, these had not been realised. While most of the women delivering their children to Young Explorers seemed round about the same age as her, they were not particularly friendly. Knots of two or three sometimes stood about chatting before remounting one of the gleaming four-wheel drives crowding the car park, but Sophie had not managed to get more than a distracted grimace out of most of them. She could imagine why. The other mothers were an intimidatingly glamorous bunch with an unofficial uniform of swayingly high heels, tight designer jeans and shaggy jackety things over clingy T-shirts with appliquéd cupcakes on the tightly defined breast area. The effect—from the back at least—was sixteen. The front could be another matter, but it was always very well groomed and involved a lot of make-up.

Sophie, by contrast, spent most work lunchtimes with eyes on the distant doors of Boots rather than searching trendy clothes emporia. Sacrificing style for speed had resulted in some rather odd outfits, which was why everything she bought these days was either navy blue or black. You might look like a member of the Salvation Army, but at least nothing clashed.

Most of the glamorous mothers didn't seem to work, but those who did seemed to have glamorous jobs too. One was supposedly a successful novelist. Another was a BBC producer and another an actress. Yet another seemed to work in fashion PR: 'The paparazzi are a nightmare for Kate at the

25

moment,' Sophie had heard her gasp into a cutting-edge mobile one morning.

Only Helen, the smiling blonde, seemed a normal sort of mother. If she happened to know Tony Blair personally or was appearing in the next Jane Austen multiplex-filler, she at least kept it to herself. Sophie had, during Arthur's first week at Little Explorers, walked part of the way home with her and discovered with pleasure that Helen's house, in Illyria Avenue, was a mere few streets from hers in Verona Road. The possibility of walking home together most days, however, faded after Helen explained that she usually drove. 'My husband has the car today.' She smiled. 'We share it.'

'Oh, right.' It had never occurred to Sophie to ask Mark to share theirs. He had never offered either.

She yearned to have Helen for a friend. She was kind; so normal and relaxed after the tense atmosphere of the office. Her son, Teddy, a solemn-faced boy with hair so white it had a bluish tinge, seemed nice too.

The only problem was that Arthur didn't appear to agree. Each evening the nursery handed to the collecting parent a report containing such details as what their child had eaten that day, what his sleep times were and who he had played with. Arthur's list of preferred playmates never included Teddy, and presumably Teddy's never included him. While this lack of concord between their offspring did not necessarily end all hope of friendship with Helen, it inhibited, Sophie felt, the next logical step in its development.

Given the mutual lack of interest, it might seem

excessive to invite Teddy to Verona Road to play with Arthur. It seemed unfair, Arthur preventing her making even one friend while she gave him the chance to make so many. But of course, Sophie reminded herself, one did not enter motherhood expecting rewards.

Not that sort of reward, in any case. The rewards of parenting were, of course, in the joy of watching and helping, with one's husband, the development of one's wonderful child. Sophie firmly pushed from her mind the thought that Mark's involvement in the helping and even the watching had lately been less than it might be. His new job seemed all-consuming, although he rarely talked about it. And she didn't ask. Her own work occupied quite enough of her thoughts.

Having waved off Helen, Sophie tried not to think about the two hours of mayhem that awaited her on arriving home. Arthur's evening ablutions had, with her return to work, taken on a new and hideous pattern.

Bathtime, when they had both been at home all day, was a relatively relaxed affair. She had not expected it to change much, but it had. Now that she was tired from the office, and Arthur from nursery, the whole business was not dissimilar to trying to bath and put a Babygro on a strong and uncooperative dog.

She passionately hoped Mark would be home before her tonight to help with the struggle. While he had been punctilious about this when she first returned to work, his attendance record had slipped slightly since.

But surely tonight, with her more tired even than usual, he would be there. She pictured raising

27

her key to the front door, only to find it already open and, at the end of the long passage inside the front door, Mark's tall, reassuring form silhouetted against the glass sliding doors leading into the garden from the kitchen. He would call out a cheery welcome, ask if she wanted a cup of tea or something stronger (something stronger, definitely). Having fixed this, he would stride down the passage, hand her the drink, unbuckle Arthur, swing him up the stairs and start running the bath. Sophie, meanwhile, would shuffle exhaustedly into the sitting room and collapse on the sofa, thanking God for gin and good husbands . . .

But as she turned the corner into Verona Road the parking space on the kerb opposite their house was empty. Yet again, she was on her own.

CHAPTER FOUR

Mark revved impatiently at the red light. He was late home and it was all Lance's fault. The managing director, clearly still under the influence of lunch, had lurched into his office and embarked on one of his 'little talks' just as Mark was trying to leave.

Possibly, in the past, Mark would have pointed out his dilemma and left anyway. But that was before the redundancy, which had been a shock to his system and bred in him a fear of the same thing happening again. He was grateful to have been picked up by Charlatan, even though the fledgling publishing house clearly had a long way to go. And he, sales director designate, was the one supposed

28

to be taking it there.

'We're new, we're exciting,' Lance had repeated to him tonight, his foxy eyes alight with ambition. 'That's what the name's all about. Charlatan— humour, audacity, a twist of danger, expect the unexpected. All that stuff.'

Mark had nodded soberly. He had certainly expected the unexpected when it came to his staff. He had expected twice the number, which was unexpected news to Lance, or so he made out. Mark had used the 'little talk' as an opportunity to raise the subject again.

'No can do, old chap,' Lance had drawled, pulling at his Jermyn Street cuffs. 'We simply don't have the dosh. You know how things are.'

Mark did know how things were. Publishing in general was suffering and sales were down across the board, which was what had caused his former firm to 'release him', as they had put it. Charlatan's fortunes depended entirely on the success of its autumn publishing list, whose twin jewels were a novel and a non-fiction self-help book, each of which had involved a large advance for the author. This 'investment' had to be recouped, and with profit on top.

It was, Mark knew, up to him to come up with a strategy to shift the volumes required. He had done his best, but the Charlatan sales team was inexperienced, small and understandably cowed by the task of aggressively pushing the firm's titles in an unprecedentedly competitive market.

'You've just got to make the best of it, I'm afraid,' Lance warned amid whorls of blue smoke from his cigar.

When, finally, they reached the car park

together, Lance paused briefly beside his Aston Martin. 'I do have one piece of good news for you, old chap. I've hired a fantastic new PR manager. Name of Persephone. Brains on stilts, and,' he slid Mark a knowing glance, 'rather nice stilts as well. Should help you no end.'

Now, delayed at a traffic light, Mark brooded on this intelligence. The PR appointment really was good news. Charlatan was desperately in need of someone competent to handle relations with the media and work with Mark's sales team on the various promotions.

He drove along, the cheerful neon lights of passing shops sliding over his face and lifting his spirits slightly. At least the advent of Persephone was something positive to tell Sophie. This would be useful, considering the mood she would undoubtedly be in when he got home.

He sighed. Sophie seemed in a permanent strop these days. She was tired, he knew, but he wasn't exactly buzzing with energy himself. Besides, how hard was it, checking pages on a women's magazine? A damn sight easier than trying to persuade some ballsqueezing book buyer to up their order, that was for sure. And he couldn't lose this job. He had to make a go of it, get the designate bit removed from his title. And he would, Mark vowed to himself with a sudden surge of confidence. And once he had, everything would be fine.

As he approached Verona Road, he began to feel defensive. He *had* intended to get back early, but what could he do when his boss demanded a meeting at the last minute? Besides, just how difficult was it, washing Arthur?

Bathtime that night had been worse than Sophie ever remembered it. Arthur, whose emerging teeth now necessitated some attention with a toothbrush, resisted her efforts to insert it into his mouth with physical and oral power of a stupendous nature. Her ears ringing, Sophie struggled with her kicking, screaming, sweating son, expecting any time to hear the police or the neighbours banging on the door.

Finally, with superhuman effort, she managed to imprison Arthur in his cot. She stared at him through the bars with the mixed fear and relief of one who has caught and caged a dangerous fugitive. Arthur's roars of fury at his incarceration echoed loudly after her down the stairs.

Alcohol. Strong alcohol. That would calm her resentment and her shredded nerves.

Crouching down, she rummaged in the bottom of a cupboard. There had been a bottle of gin there recently. Somewhere. Increasingly frantically she rattled among the bottles of ginger wine, advocaat, things nobody drank ever, desperate for a glimpse of that cheerful red and yellow label. Determinedly she pushed to the back of her mind any idea it might have been among those in the recycling box on the council's bottle collection day. She couldn't have finished it already. She needed it, needed that cold, powerful, fizzing kick followed by that epidural soothing.

The bottle, however, wasn't there. Crushed with disappointment, debased by shameful alcoholic longing, Sophie crouched on the unswept kitchen floor tiles, gazing at the crumbs in despair.

Into this miserable scene now intruded the sound of a telephone. Sophie leapt up, energised by sudden terror. Not until now had it occurred to her that Mark might not be home because of an accident.

It was her mother. As of course, Sophie should have known. Shirley had a knack of phoning when her daughter was at her lowest ebb.

'What's the matter?' Shirley asked. 'You sound completely fed up.'

'Bit tired, that's all. I've just put Arthur to bed and he's been, um, a bit difficult.'

'Mark's not home yet?'

'No . . .'

Shirley exclaimed in annoyance. 'Doesn't he realise how tiring it is for you, adjusting to work so soon after having a baby?'

'Er, yes, of course he does, but . . .' Sophie said automatically, while wondering whether he did, really.

'I mean, ideally you shouldn't be having to go to work at all,' Shirley grumbled. 'I never had to; thankfully your father earned enough—'

'I *want* to work, Mother,' Sophie interrupted, trying to sound as if she meant it. Which she did, of course—in theory. She didn't want a day of Lisa, Penny, Dr Martha and Marjorie Starr, obviously. But she wanted a life outside the home, not to mention any opportunities that her present job would lead to. Hopefully. If she stuck at it.

'If you say so. Anyway, darling, what I was ringing to tell you is that I'm coming down next week. To see my secret weapon.'

Shirley's secret weapon was a Harley Street

surgeon called Dr Carmichael who injected her forehead at regular intervals. She had discovered Botox comparatively late in life, but had embraced it with enthusiasm, much to Mark's disgust. 'Does she have any idea what that stuff *is*?' he complained to Sophie, who had shared his revulsion. But recently, seeing back-to-work stress added to the up-all-night look of her face, she was wondering about Dr Carmichael herself.

'I'll be popping into Selfridges as well, to see what the new collections are like. I *know*,' Shirley added as an idea struck her, 'let's meet for lunch in the Oyster Bar.'

'I'd love to, Mum.' Sophie struggled to sound patient. 'It might be a bit tricky timewise though.' Making up for a week's worth of late arrivals and going to Oxford Street for a shellfish lunch could well be a challenge.

'Have you seen Simon since the christening?' Shirley wondered.

Sophie frowned. Simon? She hadn't given him a thought for weeks.

'Darling!' Shirley chided. 'Now he's Arthur's godfather you should see him more often. Keep in touch.'

'I suppose so.' Sophie noted that her mother's concern that Arthur keep in touch with his godparents did not extend to plainer, poorer Cess.

'I know!' Shirley exclaimed. 'Now your birthday's coming up, it would be the perfect occasion to invite him round. He could see Arthur. He is his godfather, after all.'

'Mum! I haven't even *thought* about my birthday. I haven't had time.'

*   *   *

When Mark finally came in, Sophie was standing beside the cooker trying to summon up the strength to use it.

'Hello, darling!' he called loudly, hoping to steamroller any ruffled feelings with the sheer force of his greeting.

'Where've you been?'

'Meeting with Lance,' Mark groaned.

'What, right at the end of the day? Couldn't you say you had to go?'

Mark sighed. 'Look, I've only been in the job five minutes. I have to show willing.'

The row to which they were dangerously close would, Sophie realised, help nothing. She forced a smile.

Mark grasped the olive branch with relief. 'Don't worry,' he assured her. 'Things will pick up once we get the autumn list launched.'

She tried to respond to the optimism lighting his tired face. ''Course they will,' she said supportively.

'*Red Hearse* should fly out of the shops,' Mark added confidently.

'Is that the one about Stalin?'

'About an aristocratic Moscow family living under Stalin, yes,' Mark corrected gently.

Sophie smiled. 'I should read it. Now that I'm living under Stalin myself.' She pointed at the ceiling and Arthur's bedroom directly above it.

From the entrance to the kitchen she watched Mark collapse on the sofa and let briefcase, coat and copy of the *Evening Standard* spill all over the sitting room's oak floor.

She struggled with more annoyance. She had just, on bended knees—agony on a wooden floor—cleared away the toys Arthur had thrown everywhere. And now Mark had walked in and thrown down his own.

'Christ, what a day,' Mark groaned, covering his eyes with his fingers.

'Mine's not been all that great either, actually,' Sophie remarked softly. 'Lisa was in a foul temper all day and Penny was vile.'

Mark made a dismissive gesture. 'They're just a pair of bitter old bags. You should ignore them.'

'Well, I can't when I sit opposite them all day. At least *you're* able to move about. Go to meetings and things.'

'Meetings!' Mark looked at her in amazement. 'Have you any idea how boring most of the meetings I have to go to actually are? I have to kick myself under the table sometimes, just to keep awake.'

'Yes, and trying to keep awake wouldn't be anything I'd know about, obviously,' shot back Sophie furiously.

They stared at each other in dismay. What had been chiding and then bickering had somehow become a full-blown argument.

Sophie fought once again to claw them back from the brink. 'My birthday's in a few weeks,' she muttered, reaching into the fridge for some rocket that looked even more exhausted than she felt.

Mark tried not to look shocked. He had never forgotten her birthday before, ever. Thank God she had reminded him.

Sophie had not seen his evident surprise. She was now uncorking with relief and delight a whole

35

bottle of Pinot Grigio found lurking most unexpectedly in the salad box. As she poured the greenish-yellow liquid into glasses, she smiled. Her birthday had always been memorable. A real occasion.

Images of past, perfect joy now sprang to mind. There had been that afternoon at Scarborough, the birthday they had rented a cottage on the North York Moors. The weather had been wonderful and windblown. They had got rained on at the beach and eaten fish and chips in newspaper while balancing scalding cups of takeway tea. Mark had looked hilarious in a hideous orange cagoule, borrowed from the cottage. They had sheltered from the rain in a shop selling everything from sticks of rock to firelighters by way of naked-women aprons with revolving tassels on the breasts. It had seemed, even at the time, to be the sort of fun money couldn't buy.

Then there had been the birthday weekend at the country house hotel in Wales. The glamorous-sounding set of rooms Mark had booked turned out to be a converted attic, whose low ceilings and cross-beams proved impossible for someone of his height. After several stunning blows to the head he had simply dropped to his knees and shuffled about on them whenever he was in the room. They had spent all weekend laughing about the Toulouse-Lautrec Suite.

In the sitting room Mark was dozing. Sleep was already pulling him far away. As Sophie came through with two glasses, he woke with a start.

'What shall we do this year, anyway?' she said, her face bright with happy memories. She imagined that, like her, he had been reminiscing fondly for the past few minutes.

'About what? Oh, your birthday, of course, absolutely, yes . . .' Mark forced his eyes open. 'Well we could go out . . .'

'Ye-es,' Sophie said doubtfully. Arranging a babysitter always seemed more effort and expense than the night out itself. And then there was all that ringing them up between courses. Hardly relaxing.

'What about a dinner?' she suggested. 'We could ask some people.' Her mother's idea wasn't such a bad one. Something festive would happen, but in the safe confines of home.

Mark looked at her blearily. A dinner? He could not envisage making social arrangements. He had no plans beyond bed. 'What people?' he asked suspiciously.

A brilliant idea had just struck Sophie. Incredible that she had not thought of it before. Not just Simon, but Cecily too! She should invite them round *together*! What had Simon said about not finding the right girl? Two lonely people . . . and Arthur's two godparents, no less.

'Why don't we have Simon and Cess?' she suggested brightly. 'It would be lovely for Arthur. And it would be great to get those two together.'

Mark could not believe it. Sophie wasn't just planning a dinner, but a matchmaking dinner. He fought the urge to point out that two less obviously compatible people than Simon and Cecily he had yet to meet. One was a right-on headmistress, the other a money-making machine. But he could see from Sophie's excited face that she was set on the idea. And it was her birthday, after all.

'Great. Yes, fine. Wonderful. Well, I'd better

polish my anecdotes if Simon's coming round. You know what a laugh a minute he is.'

'Don't be horrid,' chided Sophie.

*　　　*　　　*

After supper, Mark remembered what he had been meaning to tell Sophie all along. 'Lance had some good news for me,' he announced from the sofa.

'Pay rise?' Sophie murmured from the opposite chair where she was trying to focus on a novel. She was fifty pages into it but had no idea what it was about.

'Almost as good,' Mark twinkled. 'A new PR manager. Name of Persephone.'

'Oooh,' Sophie teased. 'No wonder you're pleased. Sexy brunette with a posh drawl, is she?'

'What are you saying? As if I'd ever look at another woman.'

Later, in bed, he pulled her towards him. He had always been a passionate lover and Sophie equally ardent, although, for her, the birth of Arthur had brought in its wake both dragging tiredness and the continued, inhibiting presence of wobbly flesh upon which she shrank to feel his fingers. Tonight, however, they seemed to have recovered something of their old heat. Perhaps, Sophie thought, snuggling happily afterwards against the warm plain of his back, it was the near-row that had done it. Perhaps they should row more often.'

CHAPTER FIVE

On the morning of her thirty-seventh birthday, Sophie glanced critically at her naked body as she stepped out of the shower. The bathroom mirror, bought in the days she and Mark had the time, energy and personal freedom to trawl markets and antique shops, had originally formed the back panel of a display cabinet in the Natural History Museum. It was perhaps because of this that Sophie always felt rather like a specimen looking into it, and not the best of her kind at that.

She eyed the scales under the sink with distrust. The universal law that one always had more pounds than one thought on the scales and less pounds than one thought in the bank was something she did not want confirming on her birthday of all days.

Mark burst into the bathroom behind her and started to scrabble wildly about for his toothbrush. 'I've put weight on, haven't I?' Sophie sighed, looking appealingly at him in the mirror so he could deny it.

Mark, however, did not meet her eyes. Having secured the toothbrush, he was now busily hunting for the paste. 'Mmm,' he muttered distractedly.

Shock shot through Sophie. Was that agreement? He was telling her she was fat? On her *birthday*? Fire leapt in her eyes as they alighted on the tube of toothpaste he clutched in his hand. 'Why don't you ever put the cap on the toothpaste?' she snapped. 'I'm always asking you and you never take any notice. It's always disgusting and crusty and horrid round the end and all squeezed and bent over in the middle.'

As she slammed out, Mark stared after her in bewilderment. It wasn't even eight o'clock and he had made a fatal mistake already. What exactly had she asked him? Sophie was a minefield at the moment. You tiptoed around but things could explode without warning.

Cleaning his teeth, Mark returned to his original concerns. Lance was putting ever tighter thumbscrews on about sales figures and the need to pull ahead of their rivals. Nothing, Mark knew, would help with both situations more than a couple of additional staff. Staff with brains. But Lance was deaf to his pleas and the new head of PR had turned out to be not the saviour he so longed for, but a complete liability.

He scrubbed more violently at the thought of Persephone. She was absolutely bloody useless. He had found out the hard way that to leave a single book launch party or author signing session in her exclusive care was asking for trouble. Persephone's success with the media, meanwhile, was illustrated by the complete absence of Charlatan authors from the publicity spots where rival companies' writers constantly appeared.

Persephone. Alwaysonthebloodyphone would be a better name for her. Making vital-sounding calls on her mobile—to her hairdresser, drug dealer, dog-groomer, Mark could only guess—seemed to take up her entire day. 'Yah. Yah,' she would honk tensely into her elaborately complex receiver, eyes snapping urgently about in every direction apart from Mark, the author she was meant to be accompanying or the bookshop

40

manager she was meant to be charming.

Wave after wave of annoyance swept Mark as he thought about the PR manager. Her appointment had added more work to his load, not less. To his wish list of having at least two more sales people Mark added the fervent desire not to have Persephone.

*　　　*　　　*

That evening, Sophie reflected miserably that the bad start to her birthday had rather set its tone. Here she was, bathing Arthur on her own as usual, and with the usual struggles and screams. Meanwhile downstairs, with the guests expected within half an hour, the dinner party food slumped unpacked in its supermarket bags on the unwiped and cluttered kitchen work surfaces.

And yet getting it there had been a heroic achievement. The agony of hauling two chickens, a tarte au citron, courgettes, aubergines and tomatoes, plus three bottles of red and one of champagne, across London at rush hour on the Tube was forever branded into her brain as the bag handle marks probably were into her palms.

Then there had been the toe-curling half hour before lunch when, according to the inflexible rites of office birthdays, she had been forced to stand round the photocopier drinking cava from plastic cups and making small talk with the editor's secretary. 'I always feel that, after a certain age, birthdays are more about drowning one's sorrows than celebrating, don't you agree?' Penny had asked her. Sophie had then been presented, by the editor on behalf of everyone, with some skin serums made from bee stings that she suspected had been languishing in the beauty cupboard. She had accepted it graciously, despite the fact that going about with a face full of venom had seemed like an odd idea. On the other hand, Lisa did it every day of her life.

At the nursery, Helen had wished her a happy birthday and Sophie was seized with the sudden wish to ask her to her birthday dinner. On the other hand, the dinner had a purpose, and rather a private one at that. Simon might fall in love with Helen and not with Cess as intended. There was also the problem of their children's mutual lack of interest. Arthur's report balloons still bore no sign of Teddy.

'Oh, *Arthur!*' Sophie shrieked now as a great wall of tepid water rose up from the bath and soaked her.

'Is that you, Sophie?' came Simon Sharp's voice from the bottom of the stairs. Sophie gave a small scream of horror. She must have left the front door open in her rush to get ready. And he was early. Almost thirty minutes. Unbloodybelievable. 'I'm in the bathroom,' she gasped. 'Bathing Arthur.'

As Simon's grave face appeared round the door Sophie tried to scrape together some semblance of control. This was as shortlived as the time it took Arthur to lob a large piece of foam slap bang in her face. In addition, she was horribly conscious of her nipples poking through a damp, clinging T-shirt demanding 'Where Have All The Good Men Gone?' At the time Mark had bought it for her it had seemed like a joke.

'Hi, Simon!' she gasped, blinking the soap away and deploring her wild-haired, wet-stained,

42

generally scrunched-up state. She had not seen her make-up bag since seven-thirty that morning and a glimpse was all it had been in the end; some more pressing matter driving out of her head the need for mascara and lipstick. Until she was halfway to work and had caught sight of a frowning, aged woman in the mirror of a Photo-Me booth at Oxford Circus and realised in horror it was herself.

'Hello,' Simon replied in his toneless voice.

As at the christening, he looked impeccable, shoes polished to glossy perfection, not a hair on his head out of place. A silver cufflink gleamed from a brilliantly white cuff as he raised a long arm. An enormous Jo Malone bag dangled on the end of it.

'Happy birthday,' he pronounced.

'Oh, Simon! *Thank* you!' Sophie exclaimed excitedly. 'I love Jo Malone.'

As he looked impassively around, she was aware that her bathroom belied this interest in luxury. An over-bright bare bulb pitilessly illuminated the fact that the walls were acned with damp and some of the tiles had peeled away. The décor had always been a patch-up job; when they had moved in, Mark, in lieu of replacing the whole lot, had tried to tone down the prosthetic pink of the sixties' bathroom suite by painting the walls green. It had only made things worse.

Arthur, in the bath, was staring suspiciously at the newcomer. 'Darling!' Sophie gasped with anxious brightness. 'This is your godfather, Simon!'

Arthur looked unimpressed. Simon, meanwhile, was plunging a hand into his suit pocket. 'I brought this for Arthur. I thought he might like it.'

43

'Uh, uh,' bleated Arthur from the bath, waving a wanting hand at the smartly wrapped box now being produced.

Sophie removed the ribbon and lifted the box lid to reveal a heavy silver teething ring. 'Fantastic,' she said quickly, trying to suppress the images of Arthur hurling it at everything from the TV to the glass door that led into the garden.

'Mark not home yet?' Simon asked, effectively stamping out what remained of Sophie's spirits.

'He'll be back soon.' She tried to sound at ease, despite a throat suddenly rigid with tension. It was infuriating and hurtful that Mark was not here and it was her birthday and she had everything to do.

Then luck intervened. The doorbell rang. 'Simon, you couldn't possibly go down and let in . . . Cecily, could you?' She decided to give Cess her full name. That way she sounded glamorous, at least.

'Of course.'

'Thanks.' She smiled at him gratefully, stirring the water frantically. She wasn't entirely sure Arthur hadn't done something unfortunate in the bath. But if the water was moving fast enough no one could see what was going on. It was the philosophy behind a thousand hot tubs. 'You remember Cecily from the christening, of course. She's your fellow godparent. The mother to your father. As it were.' Simon left the room in silence.

With him gone, and occupied, she started to feel more relaxed. The way was now wide open for her to get ready and for Simon and Cess to get to know each other. As Mark had pointed out, not terribly helpfully, they had hardly spoken at all during the christening party. Well, now they could

44

make up for lost time. Really, the longer she left them alone the better. It was curious, how this plotting cheered her up, as if scheming a happy union for the godparents compensated for the increasing shortcomings of her own. Just where the hell was Mark? He'd better have a *bloody* good excuse.

She herded Arthur through the final stages of bedtime, singing 'Old MacDonald' determinedly as he bellowed all the way into his Babygro. Yet she could not help noticing, in the short intervals between yells, that the sound from downstairs was not the low murmur of interested verbal exchange. It was silence. At one stage she crept to the top of the stairs to hear Simon ask Cess in a tight voice where she lived in London.

'Peckham.'

'I see,' said Simon. 'Isn't that supposed to be rather violent?'

'Well, sure, it's got its problems but it's a really fantastic, lively, multicultural area with a lot of heart,' Cess said defensively. 'Where do you live, anyway?'

'I divide my time between a flat in Knightsbridge and a country house in Hertfordshire.'

'How can one person justify all that real estate?' Cess demanded angrily.

Sophie speeded up her mascara application.

'You could open the champagne if you like,' she shouted down the stairs.

Where *was* Mark? She mourned his absence all the more for knowing what his easy, charming presence could bring, particularly to situations like the one currently unfolding in the sitting room.

Why was he not here? How could he let her down like this?

A cork popped joylessly into the downstairs silence.

Footsteps came to the bottom of the stairs.

'These bags in the kitchen,' Cess called. 'Why don't I unpack them, maybe get some of the food on the go? Save you time, as, um, Mark's not here yet.'

Sophie groaned. As if she needed this pointing out.

'I mean, we're just sitting here,' Cess continued, rubbing that in, too. 'We may as well do something useful.'

*   *   *

When, ten minutes later, Sophie came down, Cess, dressed for the occasion in a yellow African print dress teamed with a pair of bottle-green leggings, had unpacked the bags. 'This chicken is *not* free range.' She waved the raw and naked fowl accusingly at Sophie.

'Oh isn't it? I meant it to be.' Sophie glanced distractedly around for Simon. Had he left? she thought with a clutch of horror. Oh no, there he was. In the sitting room, buried behind the *Evening Standard*.

'The road to hell,' Cess warned sternly, still gesturing with the bird, 'is paved with good intentions. You have no idea what sort of a life it's had. And is this smoked salmon farmed?' She held up the packet.

Sophie strove to be patient. She didn't know, God forgive her, but actually she didn't care, and

46

at this rate the only thing Cess would pronounce fit to eat were some old chickpeas at the back of the cupboard. It was all going so horribly wrong. Cess and Simon obviously hated each other, the food was unconscionable and there was still no sign of Mark.

'Just when is Mark coming?' Cess demanded. 'He's a very long time.'

'Yes, he is,' Sophie muttered miserably.

'Honestly, you'd think, on your birthday.'

'Yes you would,' Sophie whispered, close to tears.

'Well, you *would*,' Cess thundered. 'Wouldn't you?'

Sophie bit a suddenly trembling lip.

'Men!' Cess huffed, rolling a baleful eye in the direction of Simon in the sitting room.

*   *   *

Cess served the starter. The suspected farmed salmon had been disposed of and replaced with some squashed watercress. As Sophie searched for topics to light the conversational blue touchpaper, Cess launched into a rant about the evils of the supermarket company currently trying to buy up and develop her school's playground. This lit a fire rather different from the one Sophie was intending. 'It's enterprise,' Simon stated. 'You can't argue with that.' Cess did, however, and at some length.

'That was delicious,' Sophie said to Cess as she put her fork down later. In fact, her stomach was churning so much she could barely eat. She had tried Mark on his mobile a total of ten times. And was increasingly certain something terrible had happened. Should she, she wondered wildly, start calling the hospitals? The police? Then she imagined Cess upbraiding her for wasting valuable community resources and decided to wait just a little longer.

'Surely it's normal for him to work late anyway?' Simon suggested.

Cess served the chicken, muttering darkly as she did so about its credentials. Sophie picked at it, draining glass after glass of red wine, while Cess and Simon resumed the row about the supermarket. Sophie had long since ceased to care that romance was evidently not on either of their minds. All she hoped now was that they would not come to blows. Arthur's godmother accusing his godfather of being a vile fascist capitalist pig was all she needed to make her Unhappy Birthday complete.

Sophie herself served the pudding, drunkenly sticking the candles in the tarte au citron, which had, not inappropriately, cracked across the middle. She brought it to the table still in its foil container and threw a bundle of forks down to accompany it. What was the point of plates? What was the point of anything?

Simon, serious-faced, lit the candles and they sang 'Happy Birthday'. Before the end Sophie, eyes glistening, begged Simon to open more champagne.

'There isn't any,' he informed her gravely.

This breached the levées. Sophie sobbed harder. She lifted her red, tear-swollen face. 'I'm sorry,' she gulped unsteadily. 'I'm afraid it doesn't look as if my own husband is coming to my own birthday party.'

This was the scene that greeted Mark when, at a quarter-past eleven, he finally came through the door.

CHAPTER SIX

Earlier that evening, some twenty minutes before the signing session with Charlatan's most important author, Mark arrived and parked outside the bookshop. He had a niggling feeling he had forgotten something, that there was something else he was meant to be doing. After some minutes of unilluminated thought he dismissed it on the grounds that, these days, he always felt vaguely guilty about something. His wonderings were soon replaced with irritation. It was ridiculous that he, sales director designate, should be the one checking that there were pens, that the author had a chair, that all was in order for the signing. It was supposed to be the job of the head of PR.

It had, however, become increasingly clear that leaving any of the company's authors, let alone Alexander King, to the tender mercies of Persephone was a risk. King himself had called Mark in a fury the previous afternoon. He had apparently spent twenty minutes at a signing in Waterstone's trying to attract the PR manager's attention because his pen had run out. But Persephone had been on the phone.

To be strictly fair, Mark knew, Persephone had contributed ideas to the Alexander King campaign. It was just that none of them was any good. The

49

worst was the suggestion that key bookshops be persuaded to display a full-sized funeral hearse, sprayed red and with a coffin in the back crammed to spillover point with copies of the novel.

'Oh, you don't think so?' she had said, crestfallen, as Mark had turned on her an underwhelmed face. 'You don't think that would be really cool?'

'I think it would be really offputting,' Mark told her through gritted teeth. 'And just a *tad* over-literal as well, because the red hearse of the title *isn't* a hearse, as such. It's a metaphor for the death of civilisation, which is how the people in the book see Stalinist rule.' As you'd bloody know, if you'd read it, he silently added.

Mark felt he had no option now but to supervise this King signing. The bookshop involved was one of the biggest national chains and a crucial customer. Upon the success of the autumn list, top of which was *Red Hearse*, rode all his chances not only of promotion and job security, but of straightening out the mess he was in at home. Work-life balance? There wasn't a balance, frankly. The very scales had fallen to pieces.

Yet his hard work was paying off, at least. His sales strategy had been a success. Despite Persephone's efforts to sabotage it, *Red Hearse* was doing well, much better than he ever could have hoped. Once the campaign was over he would have a powerful hand with which to arm-wrestle Lance into strengthening his sales team, giving him a deputy who could help share responsibility for absolutely everything.

He entered the shopping arcade and strode into the branch of the big chain bookstore. While King, as expected, was not there, Persephone completely unexpectedly was—early for once, if, naturally, glued to her mobile. Mark turned his attention to the display of Alexander's books, which the manager had promised would be big and impressive.

A jolt of pure horror went through him. He stared. He simply could not believe it.

Ranged before Mark, flanked proudly by the bookshop assistants, was a whole wall of copies of *Red Hearse*. Their covers bore the large round discount stickers so beloved of the big book chains.

'Why did you stick them *there*?' he gasped at the nearest assistant.

She gestured towards Persephone, still yacking on her mobile. 'She told us to. Said it was the most obvious place.'

The stickers—there must have been two hundred in all—had been securely adhered to the first two letters of the second word of the book's title. Meaning that Mark now found himself staring at a solid mass of novels bearing the title *Red Arse*.

He turned from the display and strode over to Persephone. 'It says *Red Arse*,' he pointed out heavily when, after a few more twittering minutes, she eventually gave a breathy '*Ciao*.'

Persephone stared blankly at the wall of novels. Then she clapped her hands. '*Red Arse*. Tee hee.' She broke into a silvery peal of giggles.

Mark was already on his knees, pulling the books out of the display shelves and peeling the stickers off. They had, he calculated, about two minutes before Alexander King arrived.

He now shelved his intentions to go home, and

decided to stay for the entire signing. It seemed wildly irresponsible to do anything else. So far, no thanks to Persephone, everything, including sales, had gone according to plan with this novel. Nothing could be allowed to go wrong now. Sophie would understand. He wished he dared slip out and phone her, but all hell might break loose, and besides, his battery was flat.

After its potentially fatal start, the signing proceeded smoothly. Finally in the car on the way home, Mark allowed himself to think of his family. They deserved a treat, Sophie and Arthur. Once this crop of books was successfully launched, they'd all go away together somewhere wonderful. One of those luxury resorts with nannies to look after Arthur, leaving himself and Sophie plenty of time to lounge around in the pool with its swim-up champagne bar.

Glowing with this thought, he parked happily outside the house. Walking up the path, he was surprised to see the light on in the sitting room. Sophie was not in bed as he had expected. He felt a clutch of fear. Had something happened?

The clutch tightened and twisted as he walked into his hall to hear the sound of sobbing. Sophie sobbing. And then, like a fist in the stomach, came remembrance. 'Oh my God,' Mark gasped, bounding into the kitchen to see his wife in tears at the table, with Simon Sharp sitting next to her. Of course. Her birthday. The dinner.

*   *   *

The next few days for Sophie passed in a miasma of misery. The embarrassment of the birthday

52

evening stung and burnt. For all Mark's desperate apologies and obvious remorse, she felt as if a bridge had been crossed. He had never, ever forgotten her birthday before, no more than he had forgotten Christmas. She would never dream of forgetting his. Along with her own and Arthur's, the date was tattooed on her heart. But not on his, obviously.

A fortnight into her thirty-eighth year, Sophie was still feeling bruised. Despite her efforts to do as Mark begged her and forgive him for the birthday disaster, accepting it as an oversight that would never be repeated, there had been another argument the night before. The dinner party had not been the ostensible reason—she had privately vowed never to mention the painful subject again—but the resentment she still felt had certainly fuelled the disagreement.

Evenings, Sophie now found, were dangerous times for her and Mark; the time when sparks of ill temper were most likely to burst into a full-blown, flaming row. It was relatively easy not to row in the morning; sleep may have been scant, but what there had been was fresh in the memory. One felt as rejuvenated as was possible under the circumstances and there was too much else going on anyway.

In the evening, however, after a long day being stretched like a sail opposite the soul-battering buffets of Lisa and Penny, she felt weaker, weepier, angrier. She was so tired it hurt; her eyes were aching and hard. So when Mark had come in an hour later than she was expecting, the evening—what was left of it—was already off to a bad start.

Things had veered further into the danger zone over dinner, when Mark had muttered about it being, yet again, a ready meal. Sophie had stopped this one dead in its tracks. 'If you want home-cooked food, *you* cook,' she challenged, knowing that he couldn't. And she wouldn't—not any longer. Why bother? If God had meant hard-pressed working women to cook, why had He invented M & S salmon and broccoli pasta? No effort, hardly any washing up and three out of five recommended daily vegetable portions.

A bottle of Côtes du Rhône later, they were snuggled up on the sofa, the evening's initial irritation a distant memory. Sophie had finally, gratefully collapsed on the sofa and Mark, having drawn the usual blank with Sky, was rummaging through the DVDs. It struck her that he was flicking through the boxes violently and muttering under his breath. 'What's up?' muttered Sophie, lifting her head.

He looked at her, dark eyes accusing. 'Well they're all over the place, these DVDs. I've just opened *Kingdom of Heaven* and it's got something called *Hats Off To Oswald* in it.'

She blinked. 'Oh yes. We were watching it earlier. Arthur loves Oswald.'

'I was expecting Jeremy Irons.' Mark looked at the small coloured disc in his hand. 'What I get is a blue octopus in a bowler hat.'

Sophie felt irritation rise. She bit back the suggestion that if Mark felt so strongly about her disc librarian skills he might care to come home and attempt to entertain Arthur in that friable half hour before his bath time. 'They've just got mixed up, that's all. When I take a DVD out I put it in the

54

box belonging to the one I've just put in—'

'Why don't you just put it in the right one?'

'Because,' Sophie strove to remain reasonable, 'as I've just explained, that has got the one in that I took out to put the new one in.'

'So where's *Kingdom of Heaven* now?' Mark felt exhausted and annoyed. He wanted to be taken out of this small room, away from this situation, away from the day he had just had. He had been counting on Jeremy Irons and his Crusader companions to do just that.

Sophie shrugged. *'Peep Peep Hurray.'*

'What?'

'It's a Thomas The Tank Engine DVD. Arthur's potty about it.'

'Potty,' Mark muttered as he located the case with the manically grinning blue engine, 'is the word. And actually,' he added sulkily, *'Kingdom of Heaven* isn't here anyway. *Spinal Tap* is.'

'Oh yes. That's right. *Kingdom of Heaven*'s in *Bob the Builder.'*

Having finally located the sought-after disc, Mark gave an exasperated sigh. 'That is such an annoying habit of yours.'

Sophie, finally, had had enough. 'Annoying?' she exclaimed, sitting bolt upright against the sofa cushions. 'Would you like to hear about all the things that annoy me about you?'

Mark could have kicked himself. She was standing before an open goal and was poised to shoot straight in. Hurriedly, he attempted some diversionary tactics. 'If you mean the birthday party, we've talked about it. You know how sorry I am . . .'

'No, I don't mean that.' A choking sensation was

55

filling Sophie's throat, a feeling of blockage, as if a great many things were struggling to get out. 'God, I mean, where do I start? The birthday party, well, yes, that was bad. That was awful. But it's not just that. There are all the other things too. The way you never help with Arthur—'

'Well I'm never here. Because of work,' Mark defended, rattled and panicking. He could sense the dam had been breached.

'Well you are here sometimes,' Sophie thundered. 'Night, for example. And you just sleep through when he cries.'

'Because I'm so tired,' Mark offered, realising, even as he spoke, that this was probably not the excuse best calculated to win over Sophie.

Sophie, however, was now on a roll. Of blame, Mark realised ruefully. 'But it's not even the fact you never get up when Arthur cries. It's . . . oh . . . millions of things. The way you leave wet towels on the bed. The way you never unload the dishwasher, just dump more dirty plates on top of it. The way you never shut cupboard doors or put lids back on anything, or put things back into the fridge. The way you never replace the binbag in the kitchen bin when you take it out, so whenever I put anything in it just falls straight on to the floor. The way you never put the loo seat down, or replace the roll when it runs out. The way your idea of cooking is to put something on the stove, turn the ring up full blast and then walk off and let it burn . . . Aaargh!' Sophie cried, crowding her hands to her head as the frustrations pressed in.

All the small things, she realised, all the unimportant things, yet together, how important they seemed. And what damage they had done. It

56

was as if all the annoyed thoughts she had had over the years had worn their once-solid love away like wind and rain wore stone.

The way Mark threw his coat on the kitchen table instead of hanging it up. The way he left small piles of coins in heaps all round the house for Arthur to pick up and put in his mouth. The way he never seemed to want to talk to her. One night recently, in fact, she had decided to leave it, to let him speak first, to see just how long it took. Incredibly, between the arriving-home salutations and his first subsequent remark, forty-five minutes elapsed. 'We've run out of milk,' Mark had eventually observed, opening the fridge door.

At the end of her speech there was a long silence. Then, through his shock, Mark tried to defend himself. 'But I'm not useless,' he muttered miserably. 'I can change Arthur's nappy without being asked. And I do my share of the dusting.'

'You do a bit of cleaning once a week, yes. But who cleans the bathroom floor every single time either of us has had a shower and after Arthur's baths? *Me*.' Sophie took a deep breath. She was a hair's-breadth away—a hair-in-the-bath's-breadth away—from launching into yet another rant, but wanted to rein herself in. Because Mark did not understand—that was obvious. He had no idea of the extent to which she was giving her all as a mother, putting everything into being patient and loving with Arthur and never, ever losing her temper with him. No idea, either, about the frustrations of work, the goading of her colleagues, the stress of the deadlines both of the magazine itself, and of getting to the office and leaving it on time. Was it so astonishing there was bad feeling about?

Mark was looking at her musingly. 'I've been thinking,' he said gently.

'Yes?' Sophie's voice leapt with hope. Was he about to absolve her with understanding, saying that he quite understood she was worn out and depressed, with subzero self-esteem and desperately in need of love and reassurance? That she mustn't worry and he didn't blame her in the least?

'Er—don't you think you're making a bit of a meal of this work-and-life juggling thing? If you were a bit more efficient and a bit more ruthless . . .'

'What?!' Words rained once more from Sophie's angry mouth. Hailed, really.

*   *   *

Hurt, Mark had wandered away to lick his wounds. He felt the same as Sophie in every way. He never got any credit either. And a bit of appreciation for his efforts would not come amiss, frankly. Admittedly he had missed the birthday and that was bad. Possibly unforgivable. But she should be able to forgive. The reason behind the lapse was honourable enough: wanting to do a good job to safeguard his family's future.

And on the subject of work, had she any idea of what *he* had to put up with? *His* capricious employers? The pirates of the printed page under whose yoke he toiled were an infinitely more tricky proposition than that bunch of hormonal singletons she worked for.

And she was wrong about him never making any

effort with their son. He did, but the efforts he made always misfired. Take yesterday. He had offered to take Arthur to nursery but that had all gone wrong once Sophie checked the baby's spare-clothes bag and found Mark had mistakenly packed a pair of his own navy boxer shorts instead of Arthur's little navy tracksuit bottoms. 'Imagine the nursery staff finding these!' Sophie had thundered, waving the offending garments. Mark had nodded meekly, uncertain whether her rage was because of the mistake in the first place or because the boxer shorts were raggedy and old. His underwear collection did need replacing—he'd probably had some of them since school—but there always seemed something more urgent to address.

The evening had continued along this unpromising course until Mark, in the bathroom cleaning his teeth, saw his wife's reflected head appear round the door.

'Sorry,' she mumbled, mouth crumpled, eyes wide with remorse and trying desperately not to notice the spatters of toothpaste Mark habitually left all over the mirror. 'I overreacted. I didn't mean it. I know you're under pressure at work and . . .'

She paused. This was Mark's cue to say he knew she was under just as much pressure, but as he didn't believe it, he didn't say it. Sophie swallowed with the effort of ignoring this omission, then spoke again, her tone conciliatory and aiming for brightness. 'I've been thinking. What we really need to do is spend more time together doing nice things. How about this weekend? We could go for a walk or something. With Arthur. Go to a pub. In the country . . .'

Mark, who had been nodding at this, jerked his chin up at the word 'country'. Bells pealed wildly in his mind. Oh God. Something else he had forgotten among the million and one things he had managed to remember.

The weekend's Charlatan sales conference. He could not imagine a worse time to tell her, nor could he imagine how it had slipped his memory, except that everything not requiring his immediate attention just seemed to, these days. He felt dispirited at the thought of the conference, from the Midlands country hotel in which it was being staged to the collection of very canny book buyers it would be his job to try to sign up for huge quantities of the Charlatan autumn list. But most of all he felt dispirited at Sophie's likely reaction to being told that, yet again, she was being left alone with Arthur.

He sought for the right tone, the right words. But this was diplomatic negotiation at its trickiest and the hour was late. He was tired and his nerves were worn. As he spoke and her face paled with anger, he reflected that Kofi Annan probably couldn't have saved him from this one.

'You've got a sales thing this weekend?' Sophie gasped, disbelieving. 'In a country house hotel? You'll be away from first thing Saturday morning until Sunday evening?'

They had gone to bed in silence. A foot of unoccupied mattress had divided them; never before, Sophie thought miserably, had they slept not touching in some way. Mark, for his part, lay blinking unhappily into the dark. He was about to roll over and embrace her but then exhaustion overtook him and he slipped into unconsciousness. Typical, Sophie thought angrily, listening to his snores. What does he care?

*　　　*　　　*

At work, Sophie tried to concentrate to the exclusion of all else, especially her current problems with Mark. The country house hotel weekend was just the last straw. She found it impossible to believe he really had forgotten to tell her. But what other explanation was there? Why else would he suddenly need to spend a weekend away? It was not a thought Sophie wanted to pursue. Unfortunately, every feature she worked on suddenly seemed to contain uncomfortable personal messages. The current zeitgeist touchstone, the latest in the 'Your Emotions' series, for example, was on the horribly apt subject of Self-Doubt.

Certainly, after chewing over the subject with Dr Martha Krankenhaus, Sophie's doubt was absolute.

'Let me just get this right, Dr Martha. You just said, um, that you believe many of the new paradigms to be incomplete and that a bio-psycho-social-spiritual approach is necessary to address the whole person.'

'Correct,' confirmed Dr Martha from her treatment room in Brooklyn.

Sophie frowned. She had no idea what Dr Martha meant by this. But—oh—did it really matter? Written up and in the context of the piece it would probably read perfectly well. If people got that far, that was. 'Well, thanks, Dr Martha. And goodbye.'

'Hey, wait, I got some news for you. I'll be in town soon. Maybe we can meet up.'

'In town?' Sophie repeated. 'You mean—my town? London?'

'Yeah. I'm coming over for my book launch.'

'You've published a book?' Sophie wondered why she was surprised. Obviously Dr Martha was publishing a book. That was what therapists did. Books with titles like—Sophie thought for a few seconds—*Be So There for Each Other: Marriage Management Made Easy*. She smiled, amused at the thought of something so far-fetched.

'That's right. It's called *Be So There for Each Other: Marriage Management Made Easy*.'

Marriage management made easy. Would it explain where she was going wrong? Perhaps, Sophie thought glumly, she should read it. Unfortunately she had not caught who it was being published by.

*   *   *

That afternoon, Sophie was as usual late for the nursery. A gaggle of casually chatting, perfect mothers turned and stared as Sophie, red-faced and sweating, hurried to the nursery front door.

She passed the valleys between the canyons of high-rise four-wheel drives, where more impeccable mothers were loading impeccable children. As usual Sophie wondered at the fact she could hardly get one coat on Arthur while these other children submitted without protest to puffa jackets with hat, glove and scarf sets, all matching and unlost. Their faces were pale and clean, their noses dry. Most astonishingly of all their unhassled mothers were even relaxed enough to hold conversations with each other.

'It's just marvellous,' breathed one doll-faced beauty whose hair was a sheet of perfect blonde. 'Connor—he's only two, as you know—is already asking for things in French!'

A couple of SUVs away, two women with lowlights and high heels bared very white teeth at each other '. . . yup,' one was saying, 'Hamish is hosting a black-tie dinner for three-year-olds—we thought it would be just the thing to get them to understand how terribly important it is to give to charity . . .'

'Absolutely,' chimed in the other in tones of deepest sincerity. 'Brilliant idea. Evie will love it.'

Sophie shrivelled inside. All this intense social networking already. But the worst thing about it was that Arthur wasn't included in any of it. Which must be her fault; she wasn't giving off success vibes, she looked a mess, she was a failure. She probably radiated hopelessness. At work, at marriage, at motherhood.

After snatching up Arthur—he was as usual the last in his class; a visual rebuke which never failed to churn Sophie up with guilt—she rushed out and bumped straight into someone. Looking fearfully up, gasping apologies, she saw to her relief that it was Helen.

'Hey, this is great!' Helen exclaimed with a genuine pleasure that was balm to Sophie's sore soul. 'I've been meaning to ask you. Would Arthur like to come to Teddy's birthday party next Saturday? Bit short notice, I know, and obviously, if you're doing something . . .'

'No, no, God, no,' Sophie shouted, desperate to grab and nail down this first indication that Arthur might not be the social misfit she feared. Then, realising this might be construed as over-reaction, she took a deep breath, smiled into Helen's fresh, friendly face, took the invitation offered with a calm hand and said, 'Yes. We'd love to. And no, we're not doing anything.'

Apart from everything, that was, she thought as she walked rapidly towards the Tube. As Mark was going away, Saturday morning would be an unaided struggle around Sainsbury's trying to do a week's worth of shopping while preventing Arthur either staging a hysterical tantrum at the sight of sweets, or grabbing glass jars and throwing them on the floor. And had this invitation not come up, on Saturday afternoon she would be masking-taping drawing paper to the kitchen table to allow free rein to Arthur's artistic urges while causing minimal damage to the décor.

'That's great. I'm thrilled you can come. Will you be bringing Mark?' Helen smiled. 'I'd love to meet him.'

'Actually, he'll be away working,' Sophie confessed, trying not to sound cross about it. 'It'll be just us, I'm afraid.'

'That will be *lovely*.'

Pushing Arthur home, Sophie's thoughts raced ahead to what to wear, bearing in mind the possible presence of yummy mummies from the nursery. Something trendy yet straightforward. Something that would as far as possible convince Helen that she was normal, attractive and someone she wanted to develop a friendship with. Above all, she thought, looking down in despair at the navy blue trousers which Arthur had, as usual, managed to smear, something *clean*.

*   *   *

'It's all right for some. Weekend away in a posh hotel. Don't think about me . . .' Sophie's words rang in his ears as Mark drove through a pair of impressive park gates. A large sign in scrolled letters declared him to be entering the grounds of Winterton Hall, Country House Hotel.

'But you're taking Arthur to a party,' he had pointed out.

It irritated her, the way he made it sound as if she were going to the Oscars. 'A one-year-old's birthday bash?'

It irritated *him*, the way she clearly couldn't see just how lucky she was. 'God, don't you think I'd prefer to take Arthur to a party than go on this bloody sales thing? I *never* see Arthur.'

'You're telling me,' Sophie's lips had twisted. 'No, just you go and enjoy your suite, spa, fluffy bathrobe, Penhaligon's toiletries . . .'

Her initial fury at the arrangement had subsided into an effort to be humorous about it, but he hadn't been fooled. Her resentment was as obvious as a lamp through net curtains.

Mark braked outside the hotel's grand, grey-stone entrance. As always on these occasions, he felt defensive as a liveried flunky appeared to drive his battered car to wherever the garage was. His conveyance thus taken away from him, nervous and alone, he strode into the hotel's hall, where a real fire leapt playfully in the grate and the light reflected from numerous silk-pleated lampshades

65

blazed on the polished wooden floor.

As he contemplated this effect, a pair of highly polished black shoes inserted themselves into his field of vision.

'Sir?'

Mark straightened and found himself staring into a dark orange face whose eyes popped and whose features strained with apparent willingness to oblige. A chill, slim palm was laid on Mark's.

'Jeremy Hetherington-Spence. I have the great good fortune to be the manager of Winterton Hall. You must be Mr Brown.'

How plain and unadorned his name sounded, Mark thought, beside the peacock splendour of Jeremy Emery—what was it? And how scruffy and creased he felt beside this impeccable man, with his astonishing tan, whose pinstripe suit fitted like a glove and whose shirt collar competed with his teeth for dazzling whiteness. Possibly the teeth had the edge.

'Come this way,' said Jeremy Hetherington-Spence, clicking away down the hall.

Mark hurried after him down a series of corridors, all white-panelled and carpeted in pale yellow with small dark blue dots on. They went up and down some stairs and at one point crossed a small garden courtyard in the centre of which stood a sundial. They went back inside and down some more corridors and finally came to a stop before a pair of white double doors on which the name 'Don Juan' appeared in swirling black letters.

'You will know, of course, that Winterton Hall has a literary theme to the names of its bedrooms.' The hotel manager smiled.

66

'Oh, right.' Mark supposed that explained the name on the double doors that were next down the corridor: 'Lady Chatterley'.

'Winterton Hall has a long history of literary association,' the hotel manager was explaining. 'The diarist The Revd Thomas Popplewell, author of *Highways and Byways*, was a close friend of the Bracegirdle family, one-time owners of the Hall.'

Mark tried to look impressed while he frantically scrabbled through his mental card index. The Revd Thomas Popplewell? *Highways and Byways*?

Jeremy Hetherington-Spence grasped two round brass handles and opened both double doors simultaneously. The expanse thus revealed astounded Mark. Don Juan was less a room than an apartment. He followed the hotel manager into a hall hung with a riotous mixture of prints and Regency striped wallpaper, passing, to his right, a large and brilliantly lit marble bathroom. The hall swelled out into a huge bedroom whose wall-height windows were covered with at least four different fringed chintzes in contrasting patterns. All restrained by a plaited pink and yellow rope of a thickness that could have held the Queen Mary. Opposite this impressive display of fenestration was a no less massive and decorative bed which reminded Mark of *The Princess and the Pea*. It was canopied, piled with soft furnishings and the level of the mattress was on a par with his shoulder.

'The Don Juan is one of our most luxurious suites,' Jeremy was saying.

Mark wondered what in that case, he was doing in it. He was staff. The people who required the best rooms were Charlatan's important customers.

Or Bella Langley, the author whose about-to-be-published novel *Love At First Site* was one of the main reasons they were all here.

Publishers often invited their liveliest authors to sales conferences. And pretty blonde Bella was probably Charlatan's most presentable. She was the publishing house's most recent signing and Mark had met her only briefly. But she seemed to fit the conference bill, as well as having a book to promote. Bella represented the fledgling publishing house's first foray into the lucrative chick-lit market. She had achieved a reasonable level of success with her former publishers but had been enticed away after Lance had met her at a party and discovered how corrosively jealous she was of her more successful stablemates. He had promised with his usual lack of caution that Charlatan would take her far beyond her rivals, then, also as usual, unhesitatingly passed the responsibility for making this a reality on to Mark. The weekend at Winterton Hall was an important step in this direction.

But already, Mark thought, the familiar waves of panic were beginning to show their foamy tops, it was going wrong. Persephone had made a complete mess of the room bookings, for a start. He, mere sales director designate, was in what amounted to a presidential apartment. So where the hell had she put Bella?

'. . . finest linen sheets with a thread count of . . .' Jeremy was saying somewhere round the other side of the bed. It was only now that Mark realised how much taller he was than the hotel manager, whose brightly polished exterior effectively drew attention from how little of that exterior there actually was, perpendicularly speaking.

He opened his mouth to ask Jeremy about Bella. But the hotel manager had moved on, now whisking about the bedroom's adjacent massive sitting room and drawing his attention to the fine details. 'Being a gentleman of taste, sir will undoubtedly appreciate the magnificent cigar humidor with its burr-walnut interior fashioned by no less a personage than Viscount Linley, nephew of Her Majesty the Queen.'

Mark stared, distracted, at the royal cigar box. Cigars made him feel ill, and the House of Windsor had much the same effect.

Jeremy Hetherington-Spence had now dived into the blindingly white bathroom. This, it seemed, contained even more wonders than the sitting room. 'Each towel has an official fluff factor of twenty. That is, twice the fluff factor of ordinary household towels. No one of these individually finely hand-milled soaps is exactly the same as another. The mirrors are all hand-bevelled by monks from the Venetian island of Murano . . .'

Mark's mind was racing. He was now worrying about the buyers. Surely sense had prevailed and Persephone had put them somewhere decent.

Jeremy was now opening the marquetry front of a cupboard that turned out to be the minibar. Finally, he had Mark's full attention. 'Just look at the attention to detail on these coasters,' he said, waving the lace-edged paper discs at the salesman in whose hard-pressed breast the rows of miniature bottles of spirit had awakened sudden, passionate longing. 'Typical, I have to say, of the sense of style that underpins every aspect of the service at Winterton Hall. And nowhere in Winterton Hall more than here in the Don Juan Suite. The only other suite in the hotel superior to Don Juan is the next door suite, Lady Chatterley,' Jeremy added as he led Mark back into the bedroom and plumped up a cushion. Like all the cushions in Don Juan it did not require such attentions, being already so fat as to be clinically obese.

'And who's in Lady Chatterley at the moment?' Mark asked immediately. An important customer or Bella, hopefully.

'A young lady,' Jeremy replied, twitching his lips as he fussed with one of the layers of curtainage.

Mark felt a rush of relief. 'The writer, is it?'

Jeremy was now mussing up a vase of yellow roses. 'Writer? Very possibly. She works for the publishing company. Very pleasant young lady. The one who has been handling all the bookings.'

The realisation hit Mark like a fork of lightning. 'Persephone?' Could the head of PR really have awarded herself the best suite of all?

'Miss O'Rourke, yes,' Jeremy Hetherington-Spence confirmed. 'She's here too, in fact, arrived just before you did.'

'Is that so? Actually, I'd rather like a word with her.' Mark moved grimly towards the double doors of Lady Chatterley.

'Oh, Miss O'Rourke is not in her suite at the moment. She just popped to the spa. I believe she decided on one of our Top to Top All Over Body Champagne Pampering Packages. A very wise choice, if I may say so.' The manager flashed his teeth. Mark felt his breath coming thick, fast and hot through his nose. She'd gone to the bloody *spa*?

'Now.' Jeremy smiled manically at Mark,

70

clasping his hands together. 'Does sir require anything else? Afternoon tea, perhaps? Winterton Hall offers a choice of finest blends, ranging from ylang ylang—'

'No, thanks.'

As, finally, the double doors shut behind Jeremy Hetherington-Spence, Mark shot over to the minibar, grabbed a vodka and emptied it down his throat straight from the bottle. Then he grabbed another. After the third—which was gin, the vodka having run out—his anger and tension gave way to utter misery. He sat in one of the many patterned and overstuffed chairs thinking black thoughts about Persephone.

*   *   *

A few hours later, he was sitting in a different chair in Winterton Hall's hysterically patterned dining room thinking black thoughts about Bella Langley.

The evening had started reasonably well. Once, that was, he had recovered from the fact that Persephone had indeed put all the major buyers into single rooms in an annexe called The Dovecote, which sounded distinctly unspacious. Bella Langley was in something called The Priest Hole, which sounded less promising still. Worst of all, there was apparently nothing to be done about it. It was impossible to move anyone because Winterton Hall's computer system had chosen this crucial moment to break down. Mark had immediately demanded to see Jeremy Hetherington-Spence, only to be told he had been called away to deal with a family emergency.

As everything unravelled around him, Mark

71

accepted what he could not change and focused on the dinner being a success sufficient to compensate for the accommodation. He soon realised that here, too, he was pitted against dark forces he could not hope to control.

Bella Langley had seemed to be everything he had hoped—at least to begin with. She had wide, eager eyes, a ready smile and lots of long blond hair. For one of that mad and capricious breed otherwise known as authors, she was, Mark thought, unusually pleasant. Her ego was not the usual rampant, untameable beast. As, during the champagne reception, she chattered amusingly about some of her more embarrassing experiences as an author, she seemed, if anything, delightfully devoid of vanity.

It wasn't until the starters that Mark, overhearing Bella dejectedly confide in an important buyer that she was in despair about her latest novel, that alarm bells started to ring. The buyer was, as Mark well knew, a woman of steel in business and one of the hardest negotiators he had come across. Nothing less than utter confidence and one hundred and ten per cent enthusiasm would incite her to put her buying power behind an author.

'Oh God, I mean, it seemed such a good idea at the time,' Bella groaned as the remains of her crispy duck salad was taken away. 'A romance about two archaeologists called *Love At First Site*.'

'Well it is a good idea, isn't it?' the buyer said encouragingly. 'People are very interested in excavation and the ancient world. Post-*Gladiator*, post-*Jurassic Park*.' She had, Mark realised with a glow of self-gratification, swallowed his sales line whole. And why not? It had been a good one.

'No, it's just stupid,' Bella groaned, looking in anguish from between two curtains of yellow crinkly hair.

'Really?' the buyer asked, a strange expression in her eyes. Mark leant over, seriously annoyed. Did Bella not realise the crucial difference between the ability to laugh at oneself and self-loathing so savage it seriously threatened sales?

'But the characters are great,' he said encouragingly. He hoped they were. Mark had not in fact read the book. There had been no time. He had, in the past, relied on Sophie's assessments of the works he was selling but things had not been sufficiently relaxed to ask for her help recently. He sensed that if he presented her with a book she would explode with indignation and demand just when the hell he thought she had time to *read*.

'*Are* they?' Bella's face blazed with tremulous, desperate hope. 'Do you *really* think so?'

'What are the characters like?' enquired the buyer.

Bella launched into a speech of nervous, machine-gun rapidity. 'Well there's this palaeontologist called Julius who's very sexy and arrogant, in fact everyone calls him Julius Six Heures because he's supposed to be able to keep going all night long . . . from midnight to morning. *Six Heures*, get it?' Her eyes welled with tears. 'Oh God, what a pathetic pun, and there are loads like that, people are just going to hate it . . .' She took a gulp of champagne and looked desperately round. 'Excuse me, I must just go to the loo.' She stumbled off, hair and heels thrashing in her haste to escape.

73

Mark shot into her seat to reassure his customer. 'Look, she's just nervous. You know what these highly strung creative types are like. Don't believe in their own, er, genius. The book's great. Getting some *fantastic* reactions from the trade and the press.' He looked wildly around for Persephone to support the latter wild assertion, and saw to his surprise that she was actually approaching him. In the right place at the right time for once.

'Houston, we have a problem,' Persephone announced loudly as she reached the table. 'I've just been in the loos and Bella's in there sobbing hysterically and saying her book's crap and she's crap and we're all crap as well.'

Oh God, thought Mark. Wake me up from this nightmare. The evening was running away from him like a ball down a mountainside.

Five minutes later Bella had been extracted from the loos and given a hissed stiffening speech from Mark about the vital importance of the occasion. 'And now I'm going to take you to sit next to the most important customers,' he added. 'All you have to do is be nice to them. Be yourself.' She stared back at him as if he was sending her to Death Row.

He had assumed Bella was incapable of doing much more damage. Fifteen minutes later he realised he had assumed wrong. She was smoking now, and blowing it at another crucial customer who, Mark knew, had just quit with difficulty and whose arms were probably plastered with nicotine patches under her glittering evening blouse.

'Obviously you're expecting this novel to do well,' the buyer was remarking, eyes slitted against

74

Bella's smoke.

Bella drew mournfully on her Marlboro. 'You must be joking. My sales are always shit. This Charlatan lot can't do worse, I suppose.' Amid the reams of smoke she now emitted, her eyes widened, glassily hopeless. 'Or maybe they can.'

With a bounce and energy summoned up from the last, dry depths of desperation, Mark strode over to Bella and the intended large-scale buyer of her books.

'To be honest, I don't think they're expecting me to do very well,' Bella was confiding as he approached. 'My last publishers used to give me rooms with four-poster beds at dos like this. But here I'm in a sort of boiler-room over the kitchen.'

Several hours later, utterly spent and full of resentment and alcohol, Mark stumbled to bed. As he clawed his way up the cliff of padding that was the bedside and hoisted himself on top with Edmund Hillary-like effort, he thought longingly of home. How much he hated being here, how much he wished he was there and how infinitely better a time Sophie must be having with only Arthur to worry about rather than the entire future of a publishing company, not to mention his own. Lying there in darkness rendered sickly sweet by some violently pungent pot pourri, Mark felt annoyed that Sophie didn't see it that way, did not realise at all how much more fun her life was than his.

CHAPTER SEVEN

Pushing Arthur's buggy into Helen's street, Sophie was surprised at how nervous she felt. She reminded herself that it was only a party for one-year-olds. But she had expectations of it, nonetheless. She desperately wanted Teddy and Arthur to be friends.

And then there was herself and Helen. The distance and unavailability of Mark was increasing her need for an alternative friend and confidante. Helen lived close by. They had so much in common. This afternoon would be an important opportunity to take their friendship a step further.

And yet Sophie doubted her ability to make the most of what lay ahead. Her nerves were shattered. The morning had been ghastly. Arthur had staged his worst-ever tantrum in the supermarket, predictably by the toy section as Sophie tried to decide on the right gift for Teddy. As she searched for a combination of tasteful, educational and not obviously from Sainsbury's, her concentration was shot by Arthur trashing the bottom shelf of toys, to the obvious disgust of an old couple on their way to the bleach section.

'These single mothers . . .' the old woman muttered.

Sophie glanced immediately, defensively, at her wedding ring. Was the old bag blind? The finger, however, was bare. She remembered Arthur playing with the ring at some stage in his bombsite of a bedroom. That she had not yet got round to finding it was probably significant in the context of her current marriage troubles.

'Can't keep their kids under control for a minute,' the old man muttered back.

Yanking a lurid green net full of huge plastic spiders off the shelf, Sophie bundled herself and Arthur to the till.

Now, outside the party, clutching the neon arachnids in their wrapping paper, she worried about the choice she had made. Something tasteful and wooden from a traditional workshop in the West Country would have been infinitely more suitable. That she had done the best she could in the circumstances no longer seemed like a valid excuse.

The outfit she was wearing was not the best choice for the occasion either. Her planned outfit was currently sitting in a heap in front of the washing machine after Arthur threw his lunchtime bowl over it. Scouring her wardrobe for a replacement, the best Sophie had been able to do on the casual chic front was a white T-shirt combined with maternity jeans. While not being quite as bad as it sounded—the jeans apparently being designed for those who when pregnant had stomachs the same size as normal people—it was hardly *Vogue* cover material.

Helen's front gate was freshly painted in a fashionable shade of eggshell. Her husband, Sophie reflected, was obviously as wonderful at DIY as he apparently was at everything else. Helen lived in a gentrified terrace much like their own, but differing in that the exterior looked cared for, with windowboxes and shining panes behind which showed wooden-slatted blinds.

A doll-faced blonde opened the door. She was

dressed entirely in unstained white and her make-up was immaculate. Held in her arms was a child, possibly a boy, with long fair hair, a beautiful, vacant face and huge lips. Despite being less than two years old, he stared at Sophie coldly.

Sophie, half recognising the pair from Little Explorers, felt a sting of betrayal at this evidence that Helen was friends with some of the perfect mothers. Then she felt a rush of reassurance as Helen shouldered her way through the people blocking the hallway. 'You've made it!' she grinned with every appearance of delight. 'I'm so glad. Come through.'

She pulled Sophie through a blur of lipsticked mouths all shouting at each other. In the sitting room Helen took Sophie's coat, gently put Arthur down next to Teddy on the floor, and pushed a glass of wine into her hand. Sophie, feeling better already, looked around.

As its exterior implied, Helen's house was comfortable and fashionable: white walls, sisal floor, paintwork of a calm grey-green, lots of big sofas, good pictures, bookshelves and a real fire securely railed off behind a big club fender. It was tasteful but unthreatening, very much like Helen herself, Sophie thought. The guests, however, were another matter. The large sitting room with its big, light windows seemed to Sophie to be an enclosed, carpeted version of the nursery car park, full of intimidating mothers all talking to each other. She went to look for Arthur.

'You know a lot of people,' she remarked nervously, encountering Helen at the point where the sitting room gave on to the dining room.

The hostess grinned. 'I didn't expect so many to

come,' she confided. 'A lot of them live down this road and they wanted to see what the inside of our house is like, I think. John knocked through lots of walls, did all sorts of things. We had skips outside for months. Let me introduce you to him, anyway.' She pulled at Sophie's wrist.

Sophie cast a nervous backward glance over her shoulder. But Arthur seemed happy enough next to Teddy playing with a pile of wooden bricks.

'Darling, this is Sophie. I've told you about her. From the nursery.'

John's dark, floppy, very clean hair shone in the sunlight streaming through the large window. He was dispensing wine and chatting easily to a number of fashionable-looking fathers. He raised his glass and flashed Sophie a big, white, sincere smile. 'Nice to meet you. Glad you could come.'

Sophie found herself blushing slightly. John was handsome—tall, broad-shouldered, and athletic, if slightly simian in appearance. Teddy had the same look, all his features at the front. It was obvious John was Teddy's father, but you could see that anyway, from the look he exchanged with Helen. It was secret, loving and sensual. You could tell, Sophie thought, that they were potty about each other and that where John really wanted to be was not crushed into a corner by a collection of alpha males, but upstairs with his wife, probably making another Teddy. She tried hard to feel glad, not envious.

'Husband here?' John asked.

Sophie shook her head. 'Working, I'm afraid.'

John pulled a face. 'Shame. Maybe another time.'

Sophie fumbled for the neon spiders. 'I've

brought Teddy a present. I'm afraid it's not very much, and it's actually rather horrible, but . . .'

'But how lovely of you,' Helen exclaimed.

They were now interrupted by the doll-faced blonde. Her whites were still immaculate although she had put down the vacant-faced child.

'Sophie, this is Harriet,' Helen said hurriedly, before being pulled off by someone else to do something else. 'She has a son, Lysander, at Little Exp— yes, OK, I'm coming.'

'You have a child at Little Explorers as well?' Harriet asked sharply.

Sophie nodded. 'Arthur. He's over there.'

Harriet looked in the direction indicated. 'Oh, so that's Arthur is it?'

'You know about him?' Sophie was delighted.

'He bit Sander last week.'

Before Sophie could defend her son, another yummy mummy from the nursery appeared. Sophie had noticed this woman's way of dressing in tight, shiny, Chinesey skirts and even tighter gaudy tops. She had a lank, dark bob and Sophie had never thought she looked particularly clean.

The woman, whose name turned out to be Ruby, greeted Harriet and looked Sophie rudely up and down.

'Hello.' Sophie smiled. 'Great party, isn't it?'

Ruby rolled snake-like green eyes beneath plucked eyebrows. 'If you say so. Frankly, I could do without my husband mentally undressing everyone in sight.'

Sophie was not sure how to reply to this.

'Your husband here?' Ruby asked Sophie.

'He's working.'

Ruby looked sceptical. Sophie thought anew

80

how much she disliked plucked eyebrows.

'They all say that,' Harriet now remarked, unexpectedly.

'Say what?' Sophie asked.

'That they're working. Men who are up to something. It's a favourite line of my husband's.' Harriet began what was presumably an imitation, but to which her flat voice and frozen face could convey no distinction. 'Darling, got to dash over to Amsterdam this weekend. Last-minute thing just came up.'

Ruby cackled bitterly. 'Yes, and we can all guess *which* last-minute thing had come up.' She jerked her brocade-clad pelvis suggestively and took a swig of wine from the glass she held with dried-blood-coloured nails.

An icy, buzzing feeling had gripped Sophie's feet. It was so strong that she looked down at the floor to make sure she wasn't standing on a toy. The feeling crept up her legs to the back of her knees. She was simultaneously aware of a dryness in her throat and a churning in her stomach. What were they implying? A thought she had never dared even frame herself. That Mark, somewhere, in a hotel in the countryside, was . . .

Harriet, mercilessly quick, had noticed her expression. 'Don't look so shocked,' she said, lips pursed with triumph. 'It's quite normal.'

'They all do it.' Ruby smirked. 'Where did your husband tell you he was going?'

Sophie could only answer in a whisper. 'To a country house hotel.'

'*That* old chestnut.'

'On a sales weekend. He works for a publisher.'

'Publishing!' chortled Ruby. 'The *very* worst,'

she added with relish. 'You're quite sure there *is* a sales weekend?' she demanded, her snake eyes suddenly very close to Sophie's.

Terror and fury simultaneously gripped Sophie. 'Yes!' she cried. 'The PR woman he works with rang up to ask him something about it the other night.'

Harriet and Ruby looked at each other. *'PR woman!'* they chorused triumphantly.

Sophie froze. She felt her systems shutting down. If she did not move, and allowed in no further impressions, nothing of what had just been said would stick. It would be meaningless, it would go away.

She sensed a rushing in the air, like butterflies. 'Sophie, you look a bit pale,' came Helen's warm voice. 'Come away from the door, it's cold.'

Ruby and Harriet had turned towards each other and were whispering. As she allowed Helen to bustle her away, Sophie heard them laughing.

She felt her bottom lip tremble and willed it to remain still. She took some breaths.

'Oh darling, you're crying, oh what's the matter?' Helen gasped softly, leading her out into a small passage by the kitchen door.

Although it was not cold, Sophie shook and her teeth chattered. 'My fault,' she muttered, trying to smile. 'Should've known better than to come. Birthday parties haven't exactly been lucky for me lately.' She wiped her streaming nose with her hand.

'Oh don't say that! Teddy's thrilled Arthur is here. But what's the matter? Did Harriet and Ruby say something?'

Sophie stared at Helen with brimming eyes and

82

nodded. 'But what?' Helen demanded.

'That Mark's having an affair,' Sophie ground out from the base of her throat. 'And that's the real reason he's gone away this weekend.'

Helen stared. 'But how do they know? Have they got proof?'

Sophie shook her head violently. 'But they say all men say they're working when really they're . . .'

Helen's lips pressed together, pale with anger. 'But that's *ridiculous*. Absolute crap. Take no notice of them. They're a couple of bitter old bitches. Not everyone's husband routinely shags around like theirs both do.'

Pressure had built in Sophie's throat throughout this speech. Now it exploded. 'But they might be *right*. Mark's been behaving really strangely recently. He doesn't seem to care about me or Arthur at all any more. He never thinks of anything but work. Or maybe someone *at* work . . .'

Closing her eyes against the tears, she felt Helen grasp her shoulders and shake her gently. 'You're tired, that's all,' her friend said firmly. 'A bit down. Imagining things. Look, just stay there,' she ordered. 'Arthur's perfectly OK where he is. You don't need to move, not for a few minutes. I'm going to get you a stiff drink.'

Sophie hardly heard. She was staring unseeing at Helen's dustbins. She knew that she was tired, that her imagination was rioting, but nonetheless, certain things seemed to be making sense now. That PR woman—Persephone—Mark seemed to be talking about her all the time at the moment. Usually to complain, admittedly. But was that a double bluff? One of the symptoms of infatuation was the wish to pronounce the loved one's name at

83

every opportunity.

And the weekend *had* been announced suspiciously suddenly. He'd claimed he had forgotten to tell her, but how often had he done that recently? Forgotten things. Her birthday most obviously. She had been trying to bury the memory, but back it now came and she winced anew at the pain. For him to do that, something—or someone—else really must be occupying his every thought. Which would also explain her oft-felt sensation that Mark, these days, was never really listening to her. Of late his eyes had been glassy, his thoughts evidently elsewhere. Of what had he been thinking? Or whom?

All those late nights at work as well. Even the actual books he was selling. He used to ask her to read them, valued her opinions. But he hadn't brought home any books for her at all lately. She had noticed and had missed it. But it all made sense now. He had someone else to discuss books with. Books and a great deal else.

But was an affair so surprising? Just look at their sex life. The fact that, for all their passionate past, what she now felt strongest about was getting the whole business over as quickly as possible so she could go to sleep. Too exhausted to enjoy it, too guilty to refuse, she had allowed a situation to develop where Mark's advances, once eagerly welcomed and enjoyed, were now tolerated with gritted teeth and the odd dutiful moan.

She had considered confessing she would have felt the same about Brad Pitt, but then doubted that would improve matters.

She gazed at the ground, full of conjecture. Would it really be a surprise if he had turned to someone else? She had never seriously imagined Mark could ever be unfaithful, but then she had never seriously imagined half of the faults now revealed in her husband. It was as if a beautiful blue sea had receded to reveal a beach strewn with rocks and broken glass.

'Here you are.' Helen almost fell out of the doorway in her hurry, the contents of a large glass of wine slopping over her hands.

'I can't. I've got to go. I've got to think.'

'Oh, come on, Sophie,' Helen said in alarm. 'They were just stirring. People like Harriet and Ruby can only get pleasure from making other people miserable.'

'I'll get Arthur,' Sophie murmured.

They were interrupted by a loud, terrified shriek.

Helen shot inside.

Sophie stumbled after her, all thought of Mark's misconduct swept away momentarily by the knowledge that Arthur was in a house where someone was screaming in terror.

Scrambling and pushing, she reached the epicentre of the drama to find Harriet passed out on the stairs, long white-jeaned legs sprawled ungainly and spotless top rucked up to expose a gratifying expanse of Magic Knicker. There was no blood and everyone around seemed unhurt. Some father, who was apparently a consultant surgeon, checked Harriet's pulse. 'She's fine, she's coming round,' he said. Arthur, Sophie was relieved to see, was safely grasped in one of John's strong arms, while Teddy was held with the other.

'What happened?' she asked.

John gestured at Harriet's leather bag,

festooned with that code of buckles, zips and studs that only the truly fashionable could read. The top zip was open and poking out of it were the hairy, black legs of a terrifyingly enormous spider. Sophie's guts leapt up her throat before she realised it was fake. Moreover, that it was one of the toy spiders she had bought for Teddy's birthday. But how had it got there? It seemed to her that Lysander, standing beside his mother, looked a smidgeon less expressionless than usual. He could have looked guilty.

Sophie left as quickly as she could, keeping goodbyes to a minimum and successfully avoiding Ruby, who was squawking with laughter in the window in the middle of a group of men.

Helen followed her to the door. 'Look, just forget all about it, will you? They were being stupid. They are stupid.'

Sophie looked at the floor. 'I'm not so sure.'

*   *   *

Despite being exhausted, Mark was finding it hard to sleep. His veins still pumped alcohol, and lurid images of the evening went round and round in his head. Coffee and liqueurs had been enlivened by Bella Langley sobbing in her brandy glass and saying she was a Nobel brain stuck in a chick-lit body.

Don Juan was horribly hot. But the air-conditioning panel had looked more complicated than a fighter jet's flight deck, so he had left it. Mark tossed and turned, longing to be at home.

A sound disturbed his efforts to sleep. A soft, insistent knocking, that grew louder. He realised it

86

was coming from down the hallway, at the suite's front door. Springing out of bed, Mark felt his body hang in mid air before plunging violently groundwards. He lay stunned in the darkness before recovering sufficiently to understand that he had neglected to factor in the height of the bed before making his manoeuvre.

He opened the door to find Persephone standing opposite him in a pink silk scrap of nightdress. 'Hello,' she breathed, writhing against Don Juan's lintel. 'Here I am, big boy.'

It was with a feeling of clammy horror that Mark now realised that Persephone—the most stupid woman he had ever met and whom he could not have fancied less—was actually suggesting they had sex.

He felt determined fingers attach to his limp hand and pull at it. 'Come on,' urged Persephone. 'You know you want to.'

Mark had assumed his shock at her appearance and the appalled silence that followed to have given the opposite impression. He had, he now saw, been wrong. Persephone's firm, rosy flesh, much of which was exposed mere inches away, was actually the hide of the most obdurate bull elephant. He tore his gaze away from a part-exposed nipple.

He was appalled to find himself wrestling fiercely with brute lust. It proved a stronger opponent than he had expected, especially aided and abetted by the evening's immoderate alcohol consumption. As her predatory red mouth grew closer, he focused helplessly on the pillow-like lips, and tried to shrink back against the doorway.

'I'm not interested, Persephone,' he stammered.

'I love my wife.'

Persephone's plucked brows snapped impatiently together and the red pillows pushed angrily down. 'I'm not suggesting we get *married*,' she snapped. 'Just—you know—keep each other warm.' She widened her eyes and batted her lashes.

Mark thought of the heat billowing out of Don Juan's vast radiators. 'I'm quite warm enough, thanks,' he said determinedly, shutting the door of Don Juan.

Later that night, or rather in the early hours of the morning, Mark awoke to hear faint but regular thuds and the occasional yell. They appeared to be coming from the wall just behind the copiously padded headboard of his four-poster; from the direction of Lady Chatterley, in fact. Persephone had evidently found someone else to overheat with.

CHAPTER EIGHT

The day after his return from Winterton Hall, Mark sat in the bathroom, brooding. He had dreamt last night about seeing a big white mountain in the distance and knowing he had to climb it. It was tall, wide, huge. As he had got closer he realised that the white was not snow but reflected light; the mountain was made of glass. Even the foothills were smooth. Climbing it was impossible. He could make no progress.

He had instantly realised that the mountain symbolised his life. But how had his life become a heap of unsurmountable problems he was unable to get the most basic grip on?

In a word, Persephone. Damn her. She was behind everything bad that had happened recently. That she had tried to seduce him on top of all the other damage she had caused seemed unbelievable.

He was startled from his thoughts by a banging on the bathroom door. 'We're going now,' came Sophie's voice. It yanked open and his wife stuck her head round. In her arms, Arthur stared impassively at his father.

'Why are you looking at me like that?' Mark teased the child.

'He's probably wondering who you are,' Sophie said sharply. 'You've been sitting here for ages,' she added, wrinkling her nose. 'What are you thinking about?'

'Persephone,' Mark muttered.

'Who?' Sophie was shellshocked. He was *admitting* it, then? Since Teddy's birthday party she had worked hard to talk herself down. Away from the poisonous influence of Harriet and Ruby, the idea of an affair had seemed less and less likely.

'Persephone?' she repeated.

Mark shrugged, unwilling to sully the air of the home by saying anything more about her.

But for Sophie, with the firewood already prepared, the renewed spark of suspicion now quickly settled into a small blaze, eagerly consuming the dry tinder of grievance and insecurity. Was Mark *really* seeing this woman? No! It could not be true. She couldn't, wouldn't believe it.

*   *   *

It was late at night in Simon Sharp's glass-sided City office. He sat musing, not on the impending takeover he was supposed to be advising on, but his own increasingly difficult situation at the bank. His lack of wife and family was becoming ever more evident and incriminating as the last of his still-single colleagues stampeded to register offices to save their careers. Or so Simon cynically imagined; certainly it was something of a coincidence that many who had avoided commitment for so long had suddenly found enduring love in the past couple of weeks.

His deputy head of department, for instance, who Simon was almost sure was gay, had last Saturday married a boot-faced Ukrainian academic who, rumour had it, needed a visa. A paunchy middle manager from the legal department, meanwhile, had the week before wed a Filipina fiancée of extreme youth and devastating prettiness. Yes, thought Simon. His last few weekends had been spent at weddings with more than a whiff of convenience about them—a strong whiff in the case of that meeting hall which had been used for one reception and whose cleaners clearly believed in throwing the bleach about the loos.

The result was that Simon was about the only unmarried one left. It was not a situation that could be allowed to continue; certainly not if the Wintergreens had anything to do with it. Just a few days before Simon had suffered an excruciating lunch with the Wintergreen brothers during which they had drunk only water and eaten baked beans

90

while everyone else toyed uncomfortably with lobster. Worse, they had asked probing questions about his personal life.

'You married?' Isaiah Wintergreen had snarled from under his stetson, while Abel, who wore a stamped leather waistcoat, had listened with narrowed eyes.

'No,' Simon had confessed, staring in hunted fashion at the executive dining-room carpet.

'But you got a girlfriend, right?' Abel asked loudly, rattling the spurs in his heels.

Simon looked up helplessly. 'Yes, I've got a girlfriend,' he heard himself saying, utterly untruthfully.

'She purty?' Isaiah demanded immediately.

'Purty? Oh, sorry, *pretty*, you mean. *Purty*, rather. Er, um, yes, she is.'

Part of him wondered why he was submitting to this inquisition. A man of his experience could join any bank in London. In the world, if he wanted. The problem was, he was comfortable here, as were his generous pension, vast bonus arrangements, accrued extensive holiday entitlement—not that he ever took it—and the fact that, given the Wintergreens' track record, if not their personal manner and beliefs, things could only improve. He would be mad to leave.

'You gonna marry her?' Abel demanded now.

'Absolutely,' Simon assured him.

The Wintergreens had seemed satisfied at this, but Simon had left the lunch with the distinct feeling that the subject was not over. He needed to find himself a girlfriend, better still a fiancée, and a 'purty' one, and fast.

It wasn't as if he hadn't tried. He had signed up

with various dating agencies who promised discreet introductions to suitable educated, well-presented, upmarket women. Most of the ones he met, however, were none of that. They were either tarty estate agents called Tara with braying laughs and spray-on tans or else self-deprecating downbeats with big thighs who worked for think tanks. Simon was starting to wonder if he too shouldn't opt for the well-trodden route of his colleagues. His Baltic cleaner Luba was clearly up for promotion, what with her tiny skirts, frequent eye contact and meaningful way of snapping on her Marigolds. She had a way of polishing vertical objects that made him blush despite himself.

Simon let out a snort of frustration. His jaundiced, tired eye rolled across the photograph of Arthur his godson on his desk. A fat lot of good that had done him. Abel Wintergreen had established the true connection within seconds of spotting the picture.

'And who might that be?' he had drawled, pointing a gnarled forefinger at the baby.

'My, er . . .' Simon had muttered, trying to fudge it. He had been hoping for a best-case scenario whereby the Wintergreens noticed the picture and vaguely absorbed this evidence of family connections without wanting specifics. Too late he remembered that the Wintergreens wanted specifics about everything.

Abel's eyes had blazed. 'Your what? Your goddam son? But y'ain't married, are ya?'

'No, no, it's my, er, godson,' Simon had protested in panic, aware that having an illegitimate child, in the eyes of his employers, was even more morally reprehensible than not having a wife.

'Godson!' Abel exclaimed scornfully. 'Boy,' he was addressing Simon, 'if ah put all mah godchildren out on mah desk I'd cover the entire carpet from here to Heathrow. Why you only got one, boy? You got no friends or something? No one trust you?'

Simon had muttered and shrugged his way out of this one. Now he decided to put the photograph away. It had got him precisely nowhere, just as the whole connection with Sophie hadn't. The last time they had met had been that truly horrendous birthday dinner when she had tried—unbelievably—to set him up with that politically correct monster, aptly enough called Cess.

Cess! Simon felt nauseous at the thought of her. Never in a million years! Quite apart from the revulsion she inspired in him personally, she would be a professional liability. Her views on banking and big business would give the Wintergreens heart attacks and they would give him the sack. Besides, she was a mess, and the Wintergreens liked glamorous. They themselves might dress like extras from *Oklahoma!* but their wives, judging from the couple's double portrait in the bank foyer, were trussed-up trophy blondes with huge, fixed smiles, mad staring eyes and very short skirts. They had apparently been Peanut Queens of whatever state they hailed from. Peanuts may have brought them to prominence, Simon reflected, but they sure as hell hadn't married them.

Despite having written Cess off in this fashion, Simon found himself, for some reason, still dwelling on the birthday dinner. He had not thought about it much since it had happened, but now, suddenly, it seemed to strike him as significant in some way completely unconnected with his ghastly fellow godparent. The germ of an idea seemed to be struggling to emerge and Simon was sufficiently confident in his own brilliance to know that any idea he had was worth encouraging all the way.

Carefully, he thought back through the evening. He had not been expecting much of it and had almost refused the invitation. He had accepted eventually and only to keep the avenues for future photographs open, and perhaps to get a more up-to-date one on the night. While he did not especially mind seeing Sophie, what passed for his heart had hit his boots when that politically correct gorgon from the christening had stomped in. The subsequent realisation that Sophie was actually trying to set him up with Cess had been almost laughable. But Simon did not do laughter and so had settled for being disgusted.

The absence of Mark had bothered him a good deal less than it had the women. It was normal. Simon worked in a world where, for all the Wintergreens' emphasis on the family, employees were in the office far into the evening. While Mark had possibly, even by Wintergreen standards, arrived home late, Simon had not until that moment suspected that he was in serious trouble. Sophie's tears and Mark's horror had struck him as both hysterically disproportionate and completely ridiculous. No longer, however. On reflection, now, he wondered if he might have missed an opportunity. The idea gathered momentum.

Connections clicked together in his brain. He realised that until that moment of Mark's homecoming, he had imagined Sophie and Mark happy in that boring, rock-solid way that happy couples were. Their relationship had not struck him as vulnerable. But the birthday row made it clear that there were fissures and cracks. Sophie had been seriously upset with her husband. And now Simon remembered, from the party, Mark's apparent lack of status in the eyes of his mother-in-law. He seemed to be disapproved of as much as, if not more than, Simon himself two decades ago.

He felt glad he had told Sophie he had never found a woman to measure up to her. Of course it had been merely a ruse to change the subject. But it struck him now that it had been a happy turn of phrase. A most useful marker to throw down.

Sophie. The more Simon thought about it, the more perfect she seemed for his purpose. Sophie was a blonde, and a natural one too. Nothing about the Mrs Wintergreens was natural. Sophie was also pretty, if a little overweight, but that could soon be fixed. She also had a ready-made, attractive child. What could not be fixed was the fact that she was married, even if slightly reluctantly at the moment. But one row, Simon gloomily recognised, did not make a divorce, any more than one swallow made a summer. Shame. It would be so convenient. He sighed heavily. There probably was a way to part Mark and Sophie, but he was damned, at the moment, if he could think of it.

*   *   *

Mark had promised Sophie faithfully he would get back from this latest launch party as soon as he possibly could. And he intended to keep his promise. Sophie would, he knew, probably never believe it, but actually he would prefer to be at home with his family than launch something called *Be So There For Each Other: Marriage Management Made Easy*, by some crackpot American relationships expert called Dr Martha Krankenhaus.

He also wanted to spend as little time as possible with the appalling Persephone who seemed utterly unembarrassed by the events of the sales conference, both professionally and personally. She was as brazen as ever, possibly more so. In the interests of transparency he had considered telling Sophie about the incident but the certainty she would make him resign stayed his hand. Being cast back out into a hostile job market just when he was about to reap the rewards of his efforts would be a shame; better, he concluded reluctantly, to keep quiet about it. He decided to try and forget it had ever happened. The only positive aspect was that, so far as he knew, no one else in the company was aware that it had.

He had tried desperately to get out of the Krankenhaus launch. But *Be So There for Each Other: Marriage Management Made Easy* was the centrepiece of Charlatan's autumn non-fiction list, its own attempt to get a piece of the enormously lucrative relationships manual action. It was a launch almost as important as *Red Hearse* and equally impossible that he, Mark, should not be present.

His enthusiasm for the party was further dimmed by the discovery that *Be So There for Each Other* was being launched in the basement of a bar cheesily named La Romantica. Another of Persephone's brilliant ideas.

Having parked the car, he joined the queue shuffling fitfully forward to enter the party. In the distance before him, his least favourite colleague was processing the guests with characteristic inefficiency. Mark watched her with dislike as she tossed her mane of highlights about.

Apparently exasperated by the long wait a small woman with neatly cropped dark hair and swathed in a voluminous black throw broke free of the queue and stalked past the reception desk.

'Excuse me,' Persephone called loudly after her.

The woman turned and flashed a pleasant smile beneath a pair of professional half-moon glasses. 'I'm here for the party,' she said in an American accent.

'Could I see your invitation?' Persephone asked bossily.

'I left it at home,' replied the woman.

'Can't you go and get it?'

'Not really. My home's in Brooklyn.'

Her interrogator flicked her hair and pursed her glossy mouth. 'I'm sorry, but I'm afraid I can't let you in.'

'What?'

'This party,' Persephone declared with throaty officiousness, 'is invitation only.'

The woman opened her mouth to argue. But Persephone got there first.

'This party is for one of our most important authors, Dr Martha Krankenhaus. We can't let just anyone in.'

'Actually, I'm not just anyone. I *am* Dr Martha Krankenhaus. Now can I please go to my own party? Thank you.'

Persephone's face was blank with shock. Dr Martha proceeded onwards. The queue looked after her, some laughing, others, rather more ominously, making notes. Diary editors, Mark guessed, imagining the embarrassing paragraphs that would appear in tomorrow's gossip columns. Another PR triumph for Persephone.

He had been intrigued by his sighting of Dr Martha Krankenhaus. He had imagined a large, wobbly woman in the Andrea Dworkin mould, not someone spry and chic albeit in a rather austere, academic sort of way.

He descended into the downstairs bar to find it heaving with the usual publishing party types. Baggy men in battered tweed suits and large-bosomed, folksy women whose wiry grey hair tumbled messily out of clips at the back. There were also a few younger, intense-looking men and women evidently in therapy—strictly in the commercial sense. From what he could overhear, Mark deduced the place to be crawling with academics, advisers and other workers in the relationships trade.

Everyone seemed deep in earnest conversation. 'Men,' Mark overheard a woman with severe spectacles state to another with spiky red hair, 'have become impoverished and isolated through the loss of the rites of passage and initiations into brotherhood.'

'Separating from our mothers leaves us with an unconscious legacy of resentment and compulsion to control the Mother—both idealising and devaluing her,' a wild-eyed bald man was exclaiming to another with a beard.

'. . . facilitate the journey from conflict or stuckness to relationship potential . . .' someone else was saying to Mark's left.

'Many of us have been deeply wounded by our fathers and the patriarchy, and we want to express this . . .'

Mark pushed through the crowd in search of drink. The pink cocktails he could see in the distance looked sickening, but anything, just now, would do.

'. . . the need to rediscover our sexuality as a tremendously healing and sacred gift . . .'

'. . . refresh, invigorate and renew our Images of Masculinity . . .'

'. . . to provide an alternative to the permissive materialism which has succeeded the repressive age we are emerging from . . .'

After a couple of the surprisingly light and refreshing cocktails, Mark felt a tug on his sleeve. 'You're the sales director, right?' Mark turned to find himself staring down straight into Dr Martha Krankenhaus's eyes, bright and questioning over her half-moon glasses. 'So. How'm I doing? Flying off the shelves? Gathering dust? Tell me straight.'

Mark blinked. After all the psychoblather he had just heard, such shooting from the hip was unexpected. It was, however, clear from the way she now went on to grill him about supermarkets, discounting and market share that Dr Martha Krankenhaus, for one, had her feet firmly on the ground.

'Hmm,' she said, when Mark had told her all he was prepared to. 'So not bad, eh?'

'Great. The orders have been amazing. There's a real appetite for your kind of book.'

The doctor nodded thoughtfully. 'Good. Let's hope there's an appetite for my kind of clinic.'

Mark nodded. 'The one you run in New York, you mean?' He was vaguely aware that she had a practice in Brooklyn. Perhaps she meant she was expanding.

Dr Krankenhaus smiled, revealing white teeth of an amazing size for so small a head. 'No, my new relationships clinic that I'm just about to open here.'

'Here?'

'Sure. I kinda like this country. And it sure needs some help with its marriages.'

Mark looked down quickly. She wasn't wrong there. But he and Sophie weren't at the critical stage yet. It would be all right once these bloody launches were over.

'You mean you're like Relate or something?' he asked.

'Well, kind of more full-on than that. My clinic offers a residential course, not just weekly sessions or whatever. Doctor Martha's Two-Week Marriage-Mending Miracle, it's called.'

Mark grinned. 'It sounds amazing.' It also sounded, he thought, completely mad. 'What kind of couples have you got there?'

'Not couples,' the doctor said. 'My clinic is men only. A School for Husbands. That's what I'm calling it, in fact. Doctor Martha's Two-Week Marriage-Mending Miracle at The School for Husbands. Great idea, huh? You like the sound of it?'

Mark felt panicked. What did the doctor know? There was something very penetrating about those clear eyes over the half-moon glasses. He

100

shrugged. 'Well it's not really aimed at me, obviously.'

Dr Martha looked at him keenly over her glasses. 'You don't have issues within your marriage, huh?'

Mark shook his head with an emphasis that crunched the sinews either side of his neck. 'Our marriage,' he stated, with a suddenly heavy tongue, 'is rock solid.'

'Congratulations. I'm delighted to hear it.'

'Me too,' said Mark, nodding hard. He took another deep draught from his glass. When you'd had a few, these cocktails were really quite moreish.

CHAPTER NINE

Sophie woke to see the sun streaming through the not-quite-closed curtains. She remembered yanking them bad-temperedly together before getting into bed. Alone. Mark had still not got back when finally, crossly, she had fallen asleep. So much for promising he would come back early. She should have realised he had meant the early hours of the morning.

But it wasn't just the curtains that felt wrong. The pillow next to her remained plump and unpressed; the expanse of sheet, as she slid her arm out beneath the duvet, was cold, smooth and empty. Mark had not come home at all.

She lay quite still, absorbing this enormity. Her heart pounded. There was a sick feeling at the back of her throat.

The telephone blasted into the silence. Sophie fought her way through the duvet to the bedside table and snatched it up.

'Sophie?' demanded a rasping, throaty voice. 'It's Persephone here.'

Sophie's eyes narrowed. Her teeth began to chatter. She crouched, as if against an anticipated blow. 'What do *you* want?'

'Mark stayed in a hotel last night,' Persephone trilled. 'He says he'll call you later.'

What? Pouring into Sophie's mind came images of some five-star suite; Mark rubbing Persephone's back with expensive soap in the walk-in shower. Breakfast in bed with a rose in a silver vase. 'Where is Mark?' she demanded, her voice shaking. 'I want to talk to him.'

'Er, I'm afraid that's not possible. Look, I've got to go. He'll call you, er, later.' And with that, the line went dead.

Sophie clutched the phone so hard that it hurt. She struggled to believe what had just passed. Mark wouldn't even *talk* to her. He had got—*that woman*—to do the dirty work. Was he lying in bed beside her as she made the call? Sophie pushed off the duvet with a mighty thrust. The cold air seized her unprotected body but she hardly noticed. One throbbing thought obliterated all others in her brain. The affair! Those women at the party were right. The suspicions she had tried so desperately to suppress were all founded on fact after all. It was true!

*　　　*　　　*

Bugger those pink cocktails, Mark groaned. They

102

were obviously of that sneaky variety that tasted innocently of fruit juice but were more lethal than a quadruple brandy mixed with battery acid. One minute he'd been woozily holding forth about Compromised Masculinity to some bug-eyed woman with aubergine dreadlocks, the next minute his knees had buckled under him. Compromised Masculinity had been about the size of it.

He was hideously hung over. His back ached from the lumpy single bed in the godforsaken travel lodge in which he had hurriedly been found a place when he realised that he was not only paralytic, but lacking his house key. In some eternally optimistic part of his drink-addled brain he hoped that not getting his wife up at half-past two in the morning might go some way to restoring him in her favour. He dared not think of his promise to return in good time.

Persephone had proved, at this stage, unprecedentedly useful, not only sorting out the motel bed for him but volunteering to call Sophie and explain what had happened. Admittedly, this was the very least she could do. One of the many disasters that had befallen Mark was that his mobile had run dry again.

Mark lay in the bed now, squinting at the too-bright blade of sun slicing through the gap in the curtains. His main feeling, apart from nausea and a headache that felt as if an axe was embedded above his right eyeball, was relief. Thank God the two big launches were now over. At last he could— to use that hackneyed phrase, but in the unhackneyed sense that he really meant it—spend more time with his family.

*   *   *

Standing in the kitchen, the cold tiles of the floor burning her feet, Sophie drove a fist into her thigh with frustration. She knew what her rival looked like now. Still in her pyjama bottoms and T-shirt, she had blundered downstairs after the phone call and started scrabbling through Mark's briefcase. What further evidence she expected to uncover she was not certain, but what she had discovered was a battered copy of his company's report and accounts brochure. Inside were photographs of all the staff, including a crumpled but handsome Mark, which had momentarily reduced her to tears. Her eyes had dried, hardened and burned when, a couple of head shots on, they had fallen on Persephone O'Rourke, Head of Public Relations.

The face in the picture was pretty, heart-shaped, hazel-eyed and massed about with wavy black hair. Sophie could easily imagine the body that went with it. Small, slender, gym-hardened and with a perfect all-over tan. Her own baby-ravaged figure could hardly compete. While she steered a determined course away from biscuits and crisps during the day, she steered an equally determined one towards the wine bottle in the evening. And from there, back to the crisps. But the merest glance at Persephone revealed that she and crisps had a very distant relationship. Rather more distant, Sophie thought bitterly, than that she evidently had with Mark.

There was a knock at the door. Sophie started, blinking. Mark? Heart pounding, she raced down the hallway.

'*Ta da!* Hello, darling! Do I look twenty years

104

younger?'

'Mum!'

'Hasn't Dr Carmichael surpassed himself, though?' Shirley trilled. 'I just had to spend last night in the clinic and then they took everything off and here I am!'

'You look great,' Sophie said dully.

Shirley certainly exuded vitality. She trotted into the clutter-strewn hallway, immaculate in her tiny jeans and black high-heeled boots. Her short auburn hair in its trademark bouffant layers, an effect which always reminded Sophie of a chysanthemum, stood proud above a neck remarkably smooth for its age. A crisp white blouse and a pale pink fur gilet completed the look that Mark called 'yummy granny'.

Shirley looked about her in obvious disapproval of her daughter's slipshod interior.

Then she looked at her slipshod daughter.

'You're still in your pyjamas. Is everything all right?'

'Fine,' Sophie said determinedly. She *wasn't* telling her mother about it. She had hardly had time to think it through herself.

'Where's Arthur?' his grandmother demanded.

'Still asleep.'

The one positive thing about this cataclysmic dawn was the fact Arthur had managed to restrain his usual morning bawls.

Shirley clacked upstairs. A chorus of cooing ensued, then she appeared at the top of the landing clutching a dazed-looking Arthur. His cheeks were puce with sleep.

'What's the time?' Sophie suddenly asked her mother. She had lost track of it.

105

'Half past nine.' A flash of Cartier as Shirley checked her narrow wrist.

'God. Is it? Shit. I'm hideously late for work. And Arthur for nursery.' She began to make rapid movements about the hall.

Her mother looked at her strangely. 'It's Saturday.'

'Oh.' Sophie dropped the shoe she was holding, extracted from under a heap of coats that had fallen from their hook. 'Is it?'

Her mother came downstairs with Arthur and strode past her into the kitchen, where an empty bowl, pan and spoon in the sink told of Sophie's lonely supper.

'Mark out *again* last night, was he?'

Sophie hung her head. Her mother was sifting through the evidence at terrifying speed.

'Where is he?' Shirley asked now.

'At work.'

'On *Saturday*?'

Sophie paused, caught in the headlights of her mother's stare. She could not think of anything that might explain this. Her usual defensive reflexes, like everything else, seemed slow to respond. It was like thinking and moving underwater.

'Do you want to tell me what's going on?' Shirley asked gently.

Sophie lifted glistening eyes. 'He didn't come home last night.'

Her mother's mouth tightened beyond anything Dr Carmichael could ever have done. Her hands may have tightened too, as Arthur began to wail.

'I think,' Sophie confessed, 'that he's having an affair.'

Shirley's eyes hardened. 'Come on.'

'No, *really*,' Sophie protested. 'I really think he is.'

'I don't doubt it in the least,' Shirley said grimly. 'I mean come on and pack some things. You and Arthur are coming home with me.'

CHAPTER TEN

Staring out of the taxi window, Mark watched the people congregating outside the bars and restaurants. He decided that, it being Saturday, once he got home he could take Sophie out for a nice long lunch, with champagne, even. Arthur could sleep in his rock-a-tot. Hopefully.

His head still banged agonisingly—it had taken hours to recover even to the extent of being able to ask the motel receptionist to call a cab. Nonetheless, he smiled as he pictured his arrival home in a few minutes.

'Bleedin' maniac!' exclaimed the driver of his taxi as they rounded the corner into Verona Road, narrowly missing another exiting cab. Mark had the vague impression of two women and a baby in the back, but his brain was coursing too happily with plans to take much notice. The big launches were successfully over. Everything had gone well, although exactly how well would not be revealed until the bestseller lists came out. Hopefully both *Red Hearse* and *Be So There* would make the top ten; if so, Lance would have to promote him to Sales Director proper and do some serious investment in the team.

Disgorged from the taxi, Mark shot down the path to the front door, impatient as never before to see his wife and son. He opened the door. 'Soph!' he yelled into the echoing interior of the house. All was silent, however.

Mark frowned. Odd. He had not known of any plans to go out this morning. Although, he reminded himself guiltily, he hadn't exactly kept abreast of Sophie's diary in recent days. Probably she had gone to buy some milk or something.

He walked into the kitchen. It looked untidy, quite normal, but he felt uneasy none the less.

It was now he noticed, on the kitchen table, a face-down white envelope. With suddenly shaking hands, he picked it up. It was addressed to him, in Sophie's writing. Of course, he told himself as he opened it, it could be anything. A note telling him she had to take Arthur to the doctor, say. Yet, as he scrabbled for the note inside, Mark's heart thudded like a panicking rabbit beating the ground with its hind legs.

Dear Mark,

I've had enough and I've gone home with Mum and Arthur. You not coming home last night was the last straw; that and the call from Persephone. I now realise you've been having an affair. I'll be in touch when I've had a chance to think, but don't worry, I'll be reasonable about access to Arthur.

Sophie

He could not believe what he was reading. But he read it again. And again. An *affair*? Had she heard something about the sales conference then? Damn it. He knew he should have told her. Well he would, now. It was all a ridiculous misunderstanding, but equally it obviously needed

108

sorting out.

Sophie's father sounded surprised to hear from him. 'I didn't know Sophie was coming *here*,' he said. 'Shirley went down to London yesterday to see her doctor. I thought the idea was that she called round to see *you* while she was there.'

Having established that Sophie would ring him on his mobile—recharged, unlike himself, in the motel overnight—when she arrived at the Dower House, Mark bowed to the urge to leave the empty house. Not to mention the urge for alcohol. Some hair of the dog might steady his nerves. He decided to go and sit in the bar-café, round the corner. There was nothing serious to worry about, obviously. Once he got to speak to Sophie he could smooth it out in minutes. None the less, he felt concerned.

*   *   *

Sophie had been upstairs in Verona Road packing for Arthur when the telephone in the hall rang. Shirley had picked it up, steeling herself.

'Sophie?' It was a man's voice on a bad mobile line. *Mark*, Shirley thought, her frame stiffening in outrage.

'Oh, it's you. I was rather wondering when *you'd* ring up,' she snapped.

'Er . . .'

'Where were you last night? Why did you not come home?'

'What?'

'You've never been worthy of my daughter,' Shirley stormed. 'This proves everything I always suspected. You'll be lucky if she doesn't leave you

109

over this.'

'*Leave?*' The voice on the other end sounded electrified.

'Yes, *leave.*'

'Is that Mrs Pringle? This is Simon here. Simon Sharp.'

'*Simon!*' In the hallway, Shirley reeled. Blood thundered into her face.

Simon could hardly believe his luck, which had not been good of late. There had been another Wintergreen incident only yesterday. Isaiah had appeared without warning at his desk and barked that Mrs Isaiah Wintergreen and Isaiah himself would be honoured if Simon would attend a dinner for Mrs Wintergreen's birthday.

'I'd be delighted to,' Simon had stammered, relieved and delighted at this unexpected evidence he was in favour. He wondered what Mrs Isaiah Wintergreen's official age was. Thanks to the skill of her surgeon, it seemed to decrease every time he saw her. Her face was about twenty-two at the moment and going down. He calculated they would be celebrating her twenty-first.

Isaiah, whose face was going in the opposite direction and not half so attractively, now thrust it close to Simon. 'Bring your fiancée,' he snarled in a tone which made it clear this was not a suggestion. Simon had the uncomfortable feeling he was being flushed out and that the consequences of appearing solo would be catastrophic. It was with this prospect in mind that he had called Sophie.

It was, he imagined, a long shot. They had probably blissfully made up by now and the birthday row long forgotten. But lack of hope

110

sprang eternal in Simon's cheerless breast and he was clinging to the slight chance that between the parents of his blameless baby godson the fissures of weeks ago had widened into chasms into which he could opportunistically slip.

Miraculously, this was what seemed to have happened. The unfamiliar sensation of pure joy soared within Simon, followed by one of determination to fully exploit this opportunity that had so unexpectedly arisen. He may have missed the chance last time, but he sure as hell wasn't going to now.

'Is everything all right?' he asked Shirley, summoning his most caring voice.

Shirley sighed. 'Hardly.' She glanced furtively upstairs. Simon was Arthur's godfather, Shirley reasoned. He therefore had some stake in the situation. Her interpretation of the last twenty-four hours of Sophie's life, seasoned with a few salty twists of her own, was soon flowing down the line into what she found to be Simon's enormously sympathetic and interested ear.

'It's just so dreadful,' Shirley confided by way of conclusion. 'I just don't know what to do. Mark's behaved appallingly—frankly, he's always been ghastly.'

'Poor you,' said Simon. 'It must be awful, standing by and watching your daughter suffer at the hands of her unsuitable husband.' His heart, not an organ he was usually aware of, thudded with excitement.

'It's all such a mess, Simon,' Shirley lamented. 'If only . . .' She stopped.

'If only what?' Simon pressed, hoping he could guess.

111

All discretion deserted Shirley. 'If only she'd married *you* instead of Mark. There. I've said it. I know I shouldn't have, but . . .' she stopped herself and clapped a horrified hand to her mouth.

'There, there, Mrs Pringle. There's nothing wrong in saying that,' Simon soothed. 'I feel exactly the same.'

'You do?'

'Mrs Pringle, I've never stopped loving her.' His voice dripped with sincerity coloured with the faintest suggestion of tragedy.

'You haven't?'

'No. But of course there's no point me thinking about it any more,' Simon sighed dramatically. 'She's married, and that's that. There's no hope for me.'

'It's such a shame,' Shirley lamented.

In order for this idea to gather force, Simon allowed a brief silence to pass. 'But *need* it be, Mrs Pringle?' he then suggested. 'I mean, isn't there a way out of this? An obvious answer?'

'It would be wonderful if there were,' Shirley agreed longingly.

Simon frowned. The stupid woman was not responding to his promptings. He obviously needed to be a bit less subtle.

'Has the possibility,' he murmured, 'of Sophie divorcing occurred to anyone?'

Shirley, on her end of the phone, started. While the possibility had occurred to her countless times in theory, the practical reality was an entirely different matter. 'Well, I'm not sure . . .' she blustered. 'It's a bit drastic . . .'

'Well, of course it is,' Simon purred. 'But if it meant freeing her up for—' he paused to give due emphasis, 'a *newer, better* relationship? Wouldn't that be a wonderful thing?'

Shirley hesitated. 'Well, yes, I suppose so,' she admitted eventually.

'So what's the problem?' asked Simon, trying not to sound testy.

Shirley sighed. 'But what if there *isn't* another relationship? What if the right man *doesn't* come along?' While she itched to be rid of the social liability that was Mark, a daughter who was a divorced single mother wouldn't exactly raise her stock with Venetia Bothamley-Tartt. 'And there's Arthur to think about as well, of course. Divorce would be an awful upheaval for him. It affects children terribly, doesn't it?'

Did it? Simon neither knew nor cared. 'Look,' he said through gritted teeth. 'What could be better than a powerful and influential man who adores Sophie and wants only the best for her and actually knows Arthur as well? Actually has a role in his life?'

'Yes, that really *would* be perfect,' Shirley agreed.

Simon paused, waiting for the penny to drop.

'But,' Shirley said sadly, 'of course there isn't anyone like that around. Real life doesn't work like that.'

Simon was not given to displays of temper—they rarely had a commercial benefit. But just this minute he wanted to scream. '*Sometimes*,' he said, fighting to lower his voice to persuasive softness, 'sometimes, Mrs Pringle, real life *does* work like that.'

'Does it?'

'Yes. There may, for example, be someone *right*

113

in front of you for whom Sophie is the perfect wife. Who could make her a perfect husband too,' he added hurriedly. 'Someone who is successful and wealthy, with houses in London and the country.'

'I wish there were,' Shirley breathed.

'Who knows Arthur as well. Who would be delighted to take him into his home. *Homes*, rather. And treat him as his own son.'

'Oh, that would be marvellous. If only such a person existed.'

Simon fought doggedly on. 'There *is* someone,' he said through clenched teeth, 'who knows Sophie well. Who has loved her for twenty years. Who has never married, hardly even had any other relationships, in fact, because no woman he has ever met since could possibly compare to her.'

Shirley gasped sharply. 'Oh Simon! You don't mean . . .'

'Me, yes,' Simon said firmly, before the infernal woman could suggest someone completely different. 'Believe me, Mrs Pringle, I'd make her a husband in a million. Millions, even, ha ha. I am, as you may know, extremely rich.'

'So I understand,' Shirley said faintly.

'The merger would,' Simon now pointed out, 'be in both our best interests.'

'Merger?'

'I said *marriage*,' Simon corrected himself firmly. 'Must be this bad line. You must agree this is the perfect solution. You, Mrs Pringle, get rid of a very unsuitable son-in-law. And I get the most beautiful, clever and perfect of wives. Not to mention the most wonderful of mothers-in-law.'

'Oh, Simon,' Shirley sighed, hopelessly flattered and utterly amnesiac concerning their encounters

114

of the past.

'So we're agreed it's a good idea?' Simon pressed, anxious to close the deal.

Shirley felt rather as if she were wobbling on the edge of a diving board. And rather, too, as if she had been prodded there, pushed along by Simon's rather frightening determination and persuasiveness. But there seemed no reason not to jump in, especially as, according to his mother, the pool in Simon's Hertfordshire mansion was heated. *My son-in-law the financier. My daughter's manor in Hertfordshire*. The envious, socially trumped face of Venetia Bothamley-Tartt swam before her.

'What do you say?' Simon prompted, just masking his irritation.

'Well, it doesn't really matter what I say,' Shirley pointed out eventually. 'It's what Sophie thinks that counts. She might not be as keen on the idea of divorce as we are. Actually, I'm not sure she's even considering it.'

Simon had been anticipating this. He had a ready answer. 'But she's *confused*. Upset. She doesn't know her own mind, let alone what's good for her. She needs those who love her, who are concerned with her welfare, to decide for her.'

'I suppose so,' Shirley admitted.

'And you, of course, are making decisions for her already—making her leave London, for a start,' Simon pointed out swiftly.

'Well, she can hardly stay here, the dreadful state she's in.'

'*Exactly!* And she can hardly stay in her dreadful marriage the state *that's* in. And just as you're helping her out of London, you can help her out of

115

being stuck with Mark.'

'Me?' Shirley gasped.

'Yes, you,' Simon said firmly. 'You owe it to her to make the right decision for her now. Only you can make it happen, and only by helping me. Are we agreed on that?'

'Er . . .' Shirley said, bewildered and feeling rather trapped. And yet wasn't there sense in what he was proposing? Why, in that case, did something urge her not to commit immediately? 'I'll have to think about it,' she murmured, starting with guilty shock as Sophie and Arthur appeared at the top of the stairs.

At his end, Simon screwed up his face and free fist in fury. Think? The woman obviously lacked two brain cells to rub together. As she had just abundantly demonstrated by failing to recognise a good thing when she saw it. Christ, talk about leading a horse to water. 'I'll ring you tomorrow then,' he said in strangled tones.

It was not until later, in bed, after the whirl of coming home with her daughter and grandson, appraising James of the dramas, preparing bedrooms and feeding people that Shirley once again had the opportunity of reflecting on Simon Sharp's amazing proposal.

Lying against her smooth linen pillows, her husband James snoring beside her, Shirley put down her Jackie Collins and stared at the shadowy ceiling. Could she really join forces with Simon Sharp, champion his cause as Sophie's suitor and compel her daughter to divorce her husband? It did not seem a terribly ethical way of going about things. She glanced at her own husband. This was not something she could discuss with James. He

116

would not countenance her involvement in such a scheme for a second.

And perhaps he would be right. But on the plus side, Shirley thought, there were all the advantages to Sophie that Simon had spelt out. Not to mention some to herself quite besides those of being mother-in-law to a multi-millionaire.

The devil, as is well known, makes work for idle hands and Shirley's hands, at the moment, were idler than most. To put it bluntly, Shirley was bored. Very bored.

Shirley was a woman whose considerable energies needed an outlet and since, some five years ago, she and Sophie's father had retired and moved from their old village to the grander one of Chewton Stoke, there had been outlets aplenty. The first and most obvious had been herself. Retirement, Shirley had decided, would be for her an opportunity to fully indulge her lifelong interest in grooming. Tanning, gym, weekly hair and nail appointments and, of course, frequent visits to Dr Carmichael were admittedly absorbing at first.

After a while, though, Shirley began to realise that her wrinkles were better filled than her diary was and began to look beyond her waxings for distraction.

She decided on gardening. Everyone who was anyone in Chewton Stoke gardened, as well as, regrettably, many who weren't anyone at all. Moreover, it was an area whose image, previously muddy and staid, had become newly upmarket and glamorous. For those reasons, despite being a far-from-committed plantswoman, Shirley duly applied herself to her acre. She chose the modernist route because this allowed lots of gravel and slabs; nice, clean and orderly compared to plants with their insect-infested leaves, which always needed spraying, staking or other tedious attentions. Yet gardening and Shirley did not, as it were, grow together. She worked conscientiously but wincingly; hating the feel of the soil under her manicured nails and in particular hating insects. What made her finally fall out of the limited love she had felt for the whole undertaking was the spider that dropped into her bra and bit her in the armpit.

As a result, she turned from improving her own house and garden to improving the village in general. The problem here was that Chewton Stoke was almost as well-preserved as Shirley herself. It was a smart collection of Coach, Dower and Manor Houses all restored to within an inch of their lives and encircling an unassuming medieval church like overbearing guests at a cocktail party crowding a diffident host. The villagers were proud of the fact Chewton Stoke had been mentioned in the Domesday Book and possibly even prouder of the enormous sums demanded when any houses in it came up for sale.

Nonetheless, Shirley threw herself enthusiastically into the task of gilding this particular lily. Hers were the freshest ideas in the Anti-Velux Windows Collective, hers the most thought-provoking interventions at the Gibbet Preservation Trust; she rallied the Tasteful Exterior Paintwork Society, the parish council, Stamp Out Dog Poo! and the Wind-Chime Action Group to new heights of achievement—or objection. She actually formed a Vulgar Housename Eradication League. And she hoped, as a by-product of all this application, to penetrate the village's highest social echelons. In this she was doomed to disappointment. Although she had enjoyed their hospitality at gatherings of Villagers Against Leylandii Hedges, the Bothamley-Tartts had not yet welcomed her into their inner circle.

The village's first family had lived in Chewton Stoke since, as Sir Vaizey Bothamley-Tartt liked to put it, the village was 'a couple of huts and a hanging tree.' Sir Vaizey and his wife, Venetia, owned the Manor House, which the Dower House adjoined. They had coats of arms on their teacups and a son who banked in Hong Kong. And, it seemed, no interest at all in Shirley.

James Pringle had had considerably more success than his wife in hitting on a hobby. This absorbed him to the exclusion of all else, including Shirley. But this was not the reason his new pastime annoyed her. It was, so far as she was concerned, as common as bird watching and trainspotting or following football, and possibly worse than all three.

James's new passionate interest was genealogy. He had become fascinated with the whole process of tracing his ancestors, an undertaking that made Shirley shudder as it advertised the fact that he had no idea who his ancestors actually were. It seemed to Shirley to emphasise the distance between herself and the Bothamley-Tartts, whose lineage from Sir Roger de Tartt, close friend of William the Conqueror, was clearly advertised on framed vellum on their drawing-room wall.

James, incredibly, did not seem to care. His hours were spent either poring over microfilm registers in the local library or at home on the internet consulting genealogy sites. Night after night Shirley would glance through the glass door of the small cubbyhole office next to the kitchen to see him at the computer, his face suffused with the light of ancestral revelation. He would thump his desk if some especially satisfying link had been made. As he had got further into the subject, these had become more frequent.

'I've found a direct ancestor,' he excitedly announced the night before Shirley had gone to London.

Shirley raised her eyes ironically to the ceiling. 'Who is it? Elizabeth the First?'

'Better than that!' James's eyes glowed behind his glasses. 'A pigkeeper in Huddersfield.'

'*Pigkeeper?*' Shirley repeated in horror. '*Huddersfield?*'

It was worse even than she had imagined. The thought of the Bothamley-Tartts getting wind of the pigs subsequently kept her awake at night.

But now something else altogether was disturbing her sleep. Shirley shifted on her linen pillows, excitement churning in her shrivelled chest. The more she thought about it, the better Simon's idea seemed. What drawbacks could there possibly be?

Shirley, as members of her various committees knew, and often to their cost, could be a very persuasive person. Now she turned all her powers of persuasion on herself. Helping, she thought, yes, *helping* Sophie towards this way out of her marital problems would settle her daughter and grandson's financial future and have the useful, though naturally merely incidental, side-effect of boosting Shirley's own social standing in the village. *My son-in-law the multi-millionaire. My daughter's mansion in Hertfordshire . . .*

The Bothamley-Tartts' Hong Kong banker son could, after all, hardly compete with a City superstar like Simon—wasn't there some derogatory saying about financial people in the former colony, anyway? FILTH, that was it— Failed In London, Try Hong Kong. Ha ha, thought Shirley. Yah booh sucks.

But there was more. Simon's idea also represented a marvellous new project to get her teeth into. An important one at last. One she could really throw everything into. Allying her daughter with a wealthy banker. It would be a rewarding hobby, in every sense. She closed her eyes and smiled. Yes, when Simon Sharp rang tomorrow, she would have good news for him.

*   *   *

Caffé Toscana, Mark saw, was full of the usual Saturday lunchtime families. Fashionable mothers in faded jeans. Handsome fathers free from the City and half concealed by the Saturday *Telegraph*. The air resounded to maternal cries of, 'Milo! Leave Anya's portable DVD alone', and 'Violet, darling, your crostini have arrived.' Mark sighed. The metal outside tables blazing in the sunshine were making his headache worse. He gestured in vain for a waitress—the only one available was placating four three-year-olds all loudly wanting each other's food—and stared at his mobile, willing it to ring and have Sophie on the end of it.

One particular couple caught his eye, a smiling blonde with a gentle face and a tall, dark, simian man. They were showing a very fair boy holding a bag of toy spiders how to dip croissants in cappuccino. They seemed quieter and less showy than the other families. Watching them, Mark's heart twisted with longing for Arthur and Sophie.

The child's bag of spiders, he now saw, had slid to the floor. Absorbed in the cappuccino game, neither parent seemed to have noticed. Mark got out of his chair and went to pick it up.

'Thank you,' said the blonde, turning on him a delighted smile.

Mark shrugged. 'No problem. I didn't want him to lose them. I've got a son that age and it's exactly the kind of thing he loves.'

The blonde nodded. 'What's your son called?'

'Arthur.' Mark was unprepared for the excitement this provoked.

'Not Arthur who goes to Little Explorers?'

'That's it.'

'Then I know your wife!' said the blonde. 'Sophie, isn't it? She came to Teddy's birthday party. You were away, working, I think.' Her brows had knit slightly, Mark noticed. She was still smiling, but in a concerned sort of way. He nodded. 'That's right.'

'Mark, isn't it? I'm Helen, by the way. Er, Sophie not with you?' A definite note of strain was now underpinning her friendliness. She was really staring at him, Mark realised, as if she knew something, as if she was trying to make up her mind about something.

'Sophie's visiting her mother in Hampshire,' he said in as relaxed a manner as he could muster.

At that moment, his pocket trembled. The mobile.

'Excuse me,' he muttered, drawing it out and seeing a country number. He gave a huge grin of relief. Sophie. At last. Now he could explain everything and get a grip on the situation.

He rushed outside the café. 'Darling,' he said urgently into the mobile.

'A bit too late for that, don't you think?' Shirley said stiffly.

'Oh, hello, Shirley.' Mark felt instinctively that he should act as if everything was normal. 'Could I speak to Sophie, please?'

'I'm afraid that's not possible.'

'Not possible?' He could not help his voice shaking slightly. 'Why not?'

'She doesn't want to talk to you.'

'Could I speak to *my wife*, please?'

The other end sniffed. 'Your *wife*? That's a little up in the air at the moment.'

A javelin of ice thudded into his heart. 'Just what the hell are you talking about?'

'I may as well tell you that Sophie is considering divorce.' Shirley had been uncertain about delivering this whammy immediately. Especially as Sophie had not even been consulted. But Simon had been insistent that, to have the advantage, they must take the initiative. Never let Mark and Sophie talk, and attack, attack, he had urged her a mere few minutes before she had made this call. Simon had insisted she call Mark immediately to fire the first volley. The faster and more conclusively the enemy was weakened, the sooner they would get what they wanted. And to get what they wanted Shirley must be firm. Ruthless, even. It was for Sophie's good, in the end.

Mark gasped. '*Divorce?*' It wasn't just his voice

123

shaking now. His hands were shaking too. His bowels felt dangerously loose and his forehead and back, clammy. 'Please let me speak to Sophie,' he begged.

'Sophie does not want to speak to you. And when she does, it will probably be through her lawyers.'

He had never heard Shirley sound so steely.

'But what about Arthur?' Mark gasped. 'He's my son too.'

'He'll be staying here with us.'

Panic swirled behind Mark's eyes. He felt a tightness in his chest. 'But I want to see him,' he burst out. 'I have a right to see him.'

He was dimly aware that the nearest lunchers were silent and rigid, obviously listening.

'You have no rights to anything at the moment.'

The phone went dead. The call was over. Mark shoved it back in his pocket, went back inside and groped for a chair. He sat down heavily and blinked into the cruelly bright light. He felt as if a breaker's ball had smashed into his head.

A sharp pain seared his nose. Tears pushed. Sophie really had left him. But it was impossible. He loved her. He depended on her absolutely. Life without her and Arthur—Mark quailed before the total horror and emptiness of such a vision.

CHAPTER ELEVEN

Having retrieved the car from outside La Romantica—how long ago Dr Martha's launch seemed now—Mark drove immediately to

Hampshire.

The Dower House, Chewton Stoke, did not look like a lion's den. It was the type of genteel eighteenth-century box whose sale might occupy a half-page ad in *Country Life*. Mark waded across the thickly gravelled drive to the front door and banged on it with his fists. There was no one at home.

He returned to the car and pressed his head against the steering wheel. Inhaling the faint smell of spilt milk he gradually fell asleep.

He was woken by a sharp tapping noise. With a start, he opened his eyes to see a nightmare vision. His mother-in-law was glaring at him through the driver's window.

'. . . exactly do you think you're doing here?' she was demanding in tones that, even through half an inch of tinted glass, sounded icy.

Mark sat bolt upright and rubbed his face. He could see Sophie some distance away, standing behind her father as he fumbled for the front door key. A subdued-looking Arthur, clutching a teddy in one hand, held on to her with the other.

Shirley clawed at his windscreen again. 'Just go away,' she mouthed furiously at him. His sudden arrival was nothing less than a nightmare. She stood in danger of losing the initiative, Sophie had not yet been persuaded into any definite course of action.

Mark got out of the car, slammed the door hard and strode purposefully towards his wife. A panic-stricken Shirley scurried in his wake.

Sophie peered at him over the circular box trees flanking the front door.

'Oh,' she said, clearly flustered. 'It's you.'

125

'Yes, it's me.' Mark was determined, whatever the provocation from Shirley, not to allow his voice to sound anything other than reasonable, low and calm. Arthur was there—hurriedly bundled into his grandfather's arms by his grandmother—and to see his father agitated might upset him.

'How dare you just turn up here?' Shirley demanded, remembering Simon's instructions to attack at all times. 'After everything you've done . . .'

'Can't we, well, talk at least?' Mark asked Sophie over Shirley's teased-up burgundy highlights. His father-in-law, meanwhile, with whom he had generally got on rather well, was clearing his throat and fumbling determinedly at the keyhole. His entire being radiated absolute horror of being involved. The door swung open and he took Arthur inside the house.

Sophie looked at Mark. But before she could say anything, Shirley butted in.

'There's nothing to talk about,' she declared. 'You and Sophie could have talked any of those nights you left her on her own with—how did you put it, darling? Oh, yes—a million TV channels and nothing on any of them while you went off to do God knows what with God knows who. Although,' she added darkly, 'we know perfectly well who.'

'You *can't* mean Persephone. You can't seriously believe that?' He was appealing to Sophie, but it was Shirley who answered.

'On the contrary. We do mean Persephone.'

'But I *wasn't* having an affair with her. Absolutely not. I couldn't think of anything worse. There's been some misunderstanding. That phone

126

call . . . it was late . . . I'd lost my key . . .'

'A likely story,' snorted his mother-in-law.

'Look,' Mark pleaded, to Sophie. 'I'll show you. I'll *prove* it to you.' He fumbled for his mobile and flicked through the electronic address book until he found the number he was looking for. Please answer, please answer, he prayed, pressing the dial key.

'Yah?' yawned a throaty female voice.

'Persephone?' Mark put her on to speakerphone. 'Look, sorry to bother you, but it's Mark here.'

'Mark? Hey!' Persephone gave a conspiratorial chortle. 'You feeling any better? My God, how lashed did you get last night?'

Shirley harrumphed in triumph. Sophie looked away.

'Er, Persephone,' Mark interrupted before she could continue down this unpromising path, 'I'm ringing for a reason.' Acquainting Persephone— nay, involving her—with the most intimate details of his troubled marriage was an appalling prospect. He could only contemplate it because the sacrifice of his privacy would force Shirley and Sophie to accept the truth.

'I'm here with my, er, wife and mother-in-law.'

'You're ringing to tell me that?'

'I'm ringing so you can tell them what happened last night. What happened to me, that is,' he added hastily, in case Persephone launched into some uninhibited account of post-party sex with one of the reps.

'I've already told your wife what happened,' Persephone said, rather frostily. 'But she cut me off.'

127

'Well, I'm not sure you made it very clear,' Mark sighed.

Horror was mounting within Shirley. The disgraced son-in-law was attempting to publicly redeem himself.

She stepped forward. 'Is this really necessary?'

'Er, yah, well, here goes,' Persephone yawned. 'There was a party for this nutty American marriage quack. With some pink cocktails. Vodka ones. Called Love and Passion or something . . .'

'Love and Passion indeed,' snorted Shirley.

'Go on,' said Mark, impatiently.

'. . . and you drank a lot of them, Mark. Stacks of them, in fact. Practically the whole bloody lot—' Persephone hooted.

Sophie sighed.

'Can we move on to what happened after?' Mark asked tersely.

'After you drank the cocktails? Did you say your ma-in-law and your wife are listening?'

'Yes. And they're very interested in knowing what happened later.'

'You're sure? Fine, whatever turns them on.'

Shirley was starting to calm down. It was obvious from Mark's face that this interview was not proceeding as expected.

'Well, you got drunk, obviously,' Persephone continued. 'Thoroughly ratted. Absolutely shitfaced. Utterly steaming. Completely pissed . . .'

'Er, Persephone . . .' The answer he had had in mind—the all-important answer and most salient fact—was that he had gone to bed alone. But the publicity supremo was on a gleeful roll.

'Hammered! Tight! Wasted! Wrecked-bombed-Brahms and Liszt . . . I've never seen anyone so—'

'Yes, thanks, Persephone,' Mark shouted over her. There was no need to look at Shirley's face. 'But what about after *that*?'

'Well, you fell over. There you were, lying on the floor, scrabbling about in between everybody's legs—'

'I think we've heard enough,' Shirley said, trying to sound as disapproving as she felt relieved.

'No, Persephone, wait,' Mark pleaded. 'Look, we didn't sleep together, did we?'

Persephone was silent for a second or two. Then came a screech as if from a maddened macaw. '*Sleep* together? Me and . . . *you*? You are joking, aren't you?'

She was laughing now. 'Ha, ha, sorry, Mark, but that's just too funny. Me and you . . . well, darling, you're hardly my type—'

Mark stabbed frantically at the off button. 'Well, I hope that clears that one up. No affair, OK?'

If he expected his mother-in-law to look impotently back at him, her firepower suddenly gone, his expectations were confounded. 'To be perfectly honest with you,' Shirley told Mark haughtily, 'I'm not sure it really matters whether you had an affair or not. The fact you might have done was merely the last straw for Sophie. The main problem is that you're an absolutely dreadful husband on every possible level.'

It still felt odd, this frank and full avowal of everything Shirley had ever thought about her son-in-law. But Simon was right. It was all for Sophie's benefit in the end. For all their benefits.

'But I'm going to be better,' Mark addressed his remarks to his untypically silent wife. Sophie's eyes were trained on the ground. She looked as if she

129

wished she were anywhere but there. 'I'm going to change,' Mark added. 'I'm making arrangements with work and everything.'

'Come on, darling,' Shirley cut in loudly, ushering her daughter towards the house.

'Sophie! ' Mark shouted. He was unable to believe that this face that he knew so well, that had smiled at and kissed him, that had woken up beside him on countless precious, ordinary mornings for years and years, now refused even to look at him. 'Isn't there,' he pleaded, 'somewhere we can go alone? To talk?'

'No, there isn't,' Shirley snapped, clutching Sophie's arm tightly. 'You've done quite enough damage. The best place you can go is away.'

Mark turned on her. 'Why don't you just get out of our faces?'

'Don't speak to my mother like that!' Sophie exclaimed suddenly.

'Well, how should I speak to her?' Mark howled. 'She's taken you and Arthur away. How do you think that makes me feel?'

'*You* feel? What about how *I* feel?' Sophie flashed back immediately. 'My mother took me away because she wanted to look after me. Which is more than you ever did.'

'But—'

'Oh, just go away,' she muttered. 'It's over. From now on we talk through our lawyers.'

'Lawyers!' Mark exclaimed.

Inwardly, Shirley rejoiced. Up until this point she had been unable to get Sophie to even talk about divorce, or legal intervention of any kind. Mark, however, had just done her work for her. Turning up unannounced, making ridiculous

130

phone calls, attacking her in front of her daughter. He had moved the whole process along marvellously.

'But I haven't got a lawyer,' Mark said pathetically.

'Then may I suggest,' Shirley smiled glacially, 'that you get one?'

CHAPTER TWELVE

Mark got a lawyer. Archibald Ptarmigan came highly recommended by the much-divorced Lance, who, after crushingly criticising Mark's recent distracted performance at work, had finally had to be told what was happening. Unfortunately the lawyer was not exactly coming up with the goods. They seemed to have been talking at cross purposes for much of this first meeting.

Mark gazed at him in fierce dismay. 'But if *I* don't want a divorce,' he argued, frowning, 'how *can* our marriage have irretrievably broken down?'

Ptarmigan placed the tips of his fingers together and looked at Mark over his glasses. 'Your marriage,' he intoned, 'has broken down because your wife doesn't want it to continue. She has consulted a divorce lawyer and her grounds are unreasonable behaviour.'

'So I just have to go along with it, do I? Lose my wife and my son as well? Whose side are you on, exactly?'

'I'm here to support you, of course,' Archibald Ptarmigan said calmly. 'And there are positive aspects. You have it in writing—for instance, on

131

the note your wife left at your home address—that she means to be reasonable about access to your son.'

Access! Mark hated the word, with its vile implications of Sophie and Arthur living somewhere else, not with him. 'But she *can't* want to end it.' He shook his head, as if to shake the thought out. 'Sophie knows I love her. It goes without saying.'

'That rather seems to have been the problem. Or one of them. Along with career-obsessed, domestically negligent, uncaring . . .' He started to tick the points off on his fingers.

'Yes, yes,' Mark interrupted, not wishing to hear this depressing litany again. Ptarmigan had gone through the charges against him at the start of the meeting. 'So I really can't do anything about it?'

The lawyer sighed. 'Defending a divorce usually fails. Judges tend to think that if one party to a marriage feels strongly enough to issue a divorce petition it has irretrievably broken down.'

'But they're wrong to think that!' Mark restrained an urge to stamp and scream like a toddler in a tantrum. He looked despairingly out of the nearby floor-to-ceiling window. The office of Archibald Ptarmigan formed part of the sheer upward glass thrust of one of the City's more recent skyscrapers. The view was impressive, except for the fact that the higher you got the more air-conditioners you could see, and that rather detracted from the grandeur.

He could see himself reflected in the glass. The sight was not an uplifting one. It constituted a visual inventory of all the care lacking now that Sophie had gone. Having run out of shaving foam—it had been she who always bought it—he had not shaved. His shirt needed an iron and his shoes a shine. Looking at himself, Mark couldn't see a single reason why someone who had left him might want to come back.

'But if I could somehow prove to her what she means to me,' he groaned, 'show her that I love her and how sorry I am. If there was something I could do . . .'

'Mmm,' said Archibald Ptarmigan doubtfully, looking down at his desk.

*   *   *

Thirty-eight floors down in the foyer, half an hour later, the mobile in Mark's pocket burst into life. He snatched it out, wildly hoping, as whenever his phone rang, that it was Sophie. Saying that she had changed her mind, it was all a stupid mistake.

'Are you sitting down?' came Lance's gleeful tones.

'Er, no,' said Mark. 'I'm just leaving the building after seeing my divorce lawyer. *Your* divorce lawyer, actually. I can't say he was much help.'

'What, old Ptarmy?' Lance said gaily. 'I thought he was rather splendid at wife-dumping myself. He helped me get shot of three of the buggers.'

'Wife-dumping?' Mark felt a wave of revulsion. 'But I don't *want* to dump my wife. The opposite, in fact.'

'Don't *want* to? Oh. Well, that's probably why you're not getting much joy from Ptarmy then,' Lance breezed. 'Anyway, hang on to your hat, I've got great news!'

Even from his end Mark could hear him dancing

133

about the office. He waited glumly to be put in the picture.

'*Red Hearse* is Number One. In the fiction charts.'

'Oh.'

'And get this. *Be So There for Each Other: Marriage Management Made Easy* is Number One too. In the non-fiction charts. We're top of both charts, old chap. Double whammy. King of the hill.'

'Right.' Mark felt precisely nothing. Or, rather, he felt that this once-dreamt-of professional triumph—about which he had ceased to think or care—was nothing compared to what it had cost him.

'Is that all you can say?' Lance demanded incredulously. 'Aren't you pleased?'

Pleased? If Mark could have shaped words to his thoughts he would have said that the width of the Grand Canyon, as well as millions of years, separated him from the way he might have felt once and the way he felt now.

'It's fantastic,' enthused Lance. 'An incredible achievement for a small firm like us. You did a terrific job, old boy. All that hard work paid off.'

'It ruined my marriage,' Mark said flatly.

Lance made a dismissive noise. 'Hey. A woman is only a woman. But a double number one is— well. A double number one! And as a result— *taran-tara*—I have great pleasure in confirming you as Director of Sales! How about that, then?'

'Great.'

'Hey, come *on*. I'll give you some decent staff too. We can afford it now.'

'Thanks.'

134

'Aren't you *pleased*?' Lance demanded. 'You should be. God knows, you've been banging on about it long enough.'

'I'm thrilled, obviously. It's just that my wife has left me. My son . . .' Mark stopped, suddenly unable to go on.

'You'll get over it. You might even end up with something better. It took me three wives before I finally got lucky with Portia.'

Rage soared through Mark. He took a deep breath and tried to speak calmly. 'Lance.'

'Yes, old boy? So what about it, then? You can have one new full-timer and one part-timer. I've worked it all out.'

'You can shove it all up your arse. I'm resigning.'

*   *   *

Immediately afterwards he rang Archibald Ptarmigan.

'I've resigned!' he exclaimed triumphantly.

'I'm sorry?' the lawyer asked calmly.

'Packed my job in,' Mark said, exultant. 'I can't be accused of being career-obsessed if I've given up the career, can I? That job left me no free time at all, so I've dumped it. I want to prove to Sophie that I'm serious about a new start.'

'I see.' He could hear the lawyer's steady breathing. 'I rather wish you had consulted me before taking this step.'

'Why?'

There was a brief pause. 'I would remind you,' the emotionless tones continued, 'of two things. One, that you are likely to have alimony and child support to pay, and also that, should you take the

135

course of contesting custody of Arthur, the courts are unlikely to favour the unemployed parent.'

Mark slumped against the nearest wall. He could see instantly that Ptarmigan was right.

He could see, too, how tiredness and misery had fatally eroded his common sense. He had become a creature of disastrous impulse. Rushing up to the Dower House had been one example. And now this. If he had been a fool to work for Lance, he was a still greater fool to sack himself in such a fashion. He was wifeless and childless, and now he was jobless.

The mobile rang again. Eagerly Mark pulled it out, desperately hoping it was Lance ringing to persuade him to take his job back. Although, after the ripe expressions that had been aired on both sides, this seemed unlikely.

'Hey there!'

It was Dr Martha Krankenhaus.

CHAPTER THIRTEEN

'I've been trying to get a hold of you,' Dr Krankenhaus told him.

'Why?'

He felt vaguely amazed anyone still wanted him for anything.

'To say how pleased I am of course. *Be So There for Each Other*'s a number-one bestseller. Thank you *very* much.'

Mark's eyes widened, surprised. No author had ever before thanked him for his efforts.

'So I guess I owe you one,' the doctor added.

'What can I send you? A case of Krug rosé?'

Mark felt revulsion at the mere thought. Had it not been for pink alcohol . . . Among the many secret vows he had made was never to touch drink again until he had won Sophie back. It was more difficult to stick to than he had imagined, even though there was no beer or wine in the house. There had been some nights when Galliano, Tia Maria, Tabasco sauce and aftershave cocktails had seemed like a good idea.

'Well, what then?' asked Dr Krankenhaus. 'What *do* you want?'

'Nothing, Dr Krankenhaus. Really.'

'Call me Dr Martha. So you don't even want anything for your wife or son?'

'What wife and son?' asked Mark, bitterly.

He hadn't really meant to say it. After the disastrous phone call to Persephone, he had no intention of advertising his torments to any other near-strangers. But somehow it had just come out.

'That's too bad,' Dr Martha said, immediately all sympathy. 'I'm really sorry to hear about it all.'

All? 'You *know* about it?' Mark gasped.

'Well, someone may have mentioned something . . .'

Lance. The gossiping *bastard*.

'It's just too terrible,' Dr Martha sighed. 'Tell me, Mark, how do you feel?'

'Awful, to be honest.'

'You must feel pretty bad.'

'I do.'

'That's pretty bad, Mark.'

'Yes.'

'So, where's your wife actually *gone*, Mark?'

'To her mother's. She wants to divorce me, but I

137

don't want to divorce her.'

'That's pretty bad,' Dr Martha tutted soothingly. 'I guess right now things seem pretty impossible.'

'You could say that.'

'Can't think of a way out, right?'

'Er, no.'

'Feeling miserable, huh?'

'Yes.'

'Everything looking black?'

'Er . . .' Mark wondered how he could end the call. The sympathy was nice, but it was hardly lightening his load.

'Mmm.' Dr Martha sounded thoughtful. 'This is all very interesting.'

Mark bit back the temptation to point out other adjectives might be horrible, miserable, nasty, depressing, lonely, exhausting, heartbreaking, messy, humiliating, self-loathing, regretful, stressful, uncertain and threatening to one's reason. She was only trying to be nice.

'You know,' the doctor added, 'I *may* have mentioned my School for Husbands.'

'How's it going?' Mark asked politely, despite not really caring. Dr Martha and her mumbo-jumbo, her head-farm for the hopeless, belonged to another life. His old life.

'Great guns,' Dr Martha enthused. 'Matter of fact, the school's pretty much full already.'

'Full?' Already? He supposed that *was* rather amazing. 'How many, er, pupils have you got?'

'The classes are very small and personal. Getting close to the individual, really thinking round a person and his problems, getting to know him and how his situation of emotional and marital stuckness has evolved, finding solutions accordingly, that's what we're all about.' Dr Martha paused her soliloquy to draw breath. 'At the School for Husbands—that's a trademark, by the way—we take a holistic approach to husbandry. We're committed to treating the whole person. The whole husband.'

Although, on the surface, Mark was suspicious of touchy-feely excess, and privately thought of Dr Martha as yet another speculator in the emotional problems gold rush, within his tired, dejected brain, a connection was struggling to be made. *Marital stuckness . . . finding solutions*. Could there be something here for him? 'What are the courses and projects exactly?' he heard himself asking.

'Impossible to say exactly. It all depends on the husband, what his issues are, what sort of help he needs. We structure each course differently according to the requirements of the group and the individuals within it. Our treatment methods utilise my own experience of twenty years as a very successful qualified relationships therapist advising husbands and wives with togetherness issues towards new definitions of successful coupleship. My motto is to be personal, practical and to the point.'

'I see.' Mark felt increasingly swept along by Dr Martha's ready rhetoric. *Personal, practical and to the point*. He had rather imagined the psychology industry, of which this was obviously an offshoot, to be the exact opposite of all these things.

'Mark.' Dr Martha's voice was low and earnest. 'We really believe our husbands *can* come through their troubles to resolution and reaffirmation. And we *can* help them to the other side.'

She was so damned convincing, that was the thing. Mark felt that, just now, someone believing he could get to the other side of anything—the road, the supermarket, anything—was exactly what he wanted. 'Remind me. How long does it last, this course?'

Dr Martha chuckled. 'What the School for Husbands uniquely offers is Dr Martha's Two-Week Marriage-Mending Miracle.'

'Two weeks? You can mend marriages in *two weeks*?' Mark spoke doubtfully. But then a fantastic soaring hope overtook his scepticism. What if it really *were* possible? She was, after all, qualified. Presumably she knew her onions.

'You betcha. The complete compact cure. The ultimate highly effective relationship-rebuilding package.'

Individually tailored courses, small classes, unique solutions. A complete compact cure. It sounded good. It really did. He paused and thought. Then, abandoning all pretence of not being interested, he asked, 'How much does it cost?'

Dr Martha named an astronomical sum. Mark felt satisfied. Sanity returned. That ruled the whole wild idea conclusively out. There was no way on God's earth he could afford that. 'It may sound a lot,' Dr Martha acknowledged, 'but it's a hell of a lot less than even a small divorce. Some guys have to pay out *billions* when they split. Look at it that way, and it's an investment.'

Mark thought about this. There was, he saw, a lot of truth in it. His and Sophie's assets amounted to comparatively little; nothing when measured

140

against anyone who was seriously wealthy. But even Verona Road amounted to much more than what Dr Martha was asking for. And that was only the financial worth of the marriage. The value of having Sophie and Arthur with him in one happy unit as of old . . . how could he put a price on that?

More to the point, how was he to get them all back into the happy unit? It wasn't as if answers to his plight abounded. So how was the marriage to be rescued? He had no ideas himself and, as Archibald Ptarmigan had pointed out, his legal position was a non-starter. Seen in that light, the School for Husbands was making more and more sense. He took a deep breath. 'Count me in,' he said in a rush.

'Sorry?' said Dr Martha.

It was not the reaction Mark had been expecting. Perhaps she had not understood his muttering. 'I said, erm, well, I'd like a place. At the School for Husbands. For your Two-Week Marriage-Mending Miracle.'

'Oh, but Mark.' She sounded genuinely appalled. 'I thought you realised. It's full.'

'What—*really* full?' He had assumed she was exaggerating about the numbers and the subsequent descriptions of the school and its treatments had been effectively a sales talk.

'Demand has been *insane*.' She chuckled self-effacingly. 'I guess there are a lot of guys out there who need my Two-Week Marriage-Mending Miracle.'

Thanks for rubbing it in, Mark thought grumpily. He was bitterly disappointed and rather frightened. The sudden withdrawal of this possible salvation increased his desire for it a thousandfold.

He felt absolutely sure now that the School for Husbands and the Marriage-Mending Miracle would work for him. That it was, in fact, his only hope.

'You're sure there's no way you can fit me in?' he gasped.

'I'm sorry, Mark.'

'But you've got to help me. You're probably,' Mark pleaded, 'the only person who can.' He could not believe now he had ever thought of Dr Martha as a cynical peddler of mumbo-jumbo. Quite obviously she and it were all that stood between him and the lonely, miserable rest of his existence.

'We-ell . . .' Dr Martha said doubtfully.

'*Please,*' he implored.

There was a sigh from the doctor's end. 'Oh, well. Maybe—just maybe—we can. As it's you. I owe you one, after all. I might—repeat might—be able to find you a place as a special favour.'

'Oh God, that's fantastic. You really mean it?' Mark yelped, hardly able to believe this reversal of fortune.

'Sure. Except for one thing.'

'Which is?'

'Obviously, I'll have to increase the fee to cover late incorporation costs.' She named a new figure that made Mark swallow hard.

'OK,' he said weakly.

'Great. You're in, then.'

'*Thank you*, Dr Martha.' He felt like a drowning man unexpectedly tossed to safety by a friendly wave.

'That's OK, Mark,' Dr Martha said brightly. 'You can give me your credit card number over the phone now to secure the reservation. Which must otherwise be considered tentative. Otherwise, all we need is you and some basic ID to prove you're not wanted by Scotland Yard or anything. Oh, and the agreement of your wife, obviously.'

'Agreement of my wife?' He had not bargained on involving Sophie.

'To supply the school with information for assessment and treatment purposes in which she outlines her own major issues in relation to the marriage. This can take the form of either a video or a written testimonial.'

'But . . .' Was Dr Martha joking?

'She also needs to agree something else,' Dr Martha interrupted smoothly. 'To delay divorce proceedings while you complete the School for Husbands course.'

Mark's heart sank like a stone. Given his reception at the Dower House, there was less than no chance that Sophie would contemplate agreeing to either. Much less her mother.

*   *   *

Sophie was oblivious to both the machinations of her mother and desperate manoeuvrings of her husband. All she wanted to do was keep her head down and try and maintain a routine for Arthur, not to mention herself. She had insisted on keeping her job, despite Shirley's puzzling insistence that she should leave it. London was within commuting reach and, anyway, where did her mother think the money to support herself and Arthur would come from if she resigned?

For Sophie fully intended to support them both, to make a new life eventually. The Dower House,

143

she vowed, was a temporary stopping point; a port in a storm while she scraped together the shards of her life. She felt as if she had been at the centre of an explosion and the din still reverberated in her ears. She could hardly bear to think about the future, and strenuously avoided thinking about the past.

And as ports went, the Dower House was more comfortable than most. Bed and board were just the start of it. She had help with Arthur, and the washing, cooking, shopping and ironing were all done, if not exactly by Shirley herself, then at least by Shirley's cleaner and ironing woman, the formidable Mrs Brund. More comforting even than all of this was the moral support she received. Her mother's unflattering views of Mark, so unwelcome in the past, were now eagerly sought and gratefully heard.

Only an incredible degree of self-delusion, Sophie was persuaded, had enabled her to remain with Mark for as long as she had. She had not known the real man. Shirley—primed by Simon— harped on constantly about the need for divorce. And Sophie knew she should act, but, having made the exhausting physical split and organised everything that went with it, she increasingly lacked the energy for anything further. While sometimes—generally after one of Shirley's broadsides—she wanted fervently to cut all ties and cast Mark into the outer darkness, she mostly just wished it would somehow all dissolve or go away by itself.

Or, at least, not come back. Mark's unexpected, horribly embarrassing appearance at the Dower House had made everything worse. The memory of the ghastly encounter still had the power to wake Sophie in the night, her stomach churning, beads of sweat on her brow. Thank goodness her mother had been there to protect her and make him go away.

Yet, for all this help and encouragement, there were drawbacks. Waking up every morning under her parents' roof, Sophie would at first feel the vague oppression of being eighteen again. Then she would remember and feel the much worse oppression of being thirty-seven and a prospective divorcee.

However, with Mark presumably living in the London house, other options were limited. She did not feel ready—financially or spiritually—to rent a place of her own just yet.

Living in the magazine-perfect surroundings of her mother was nonetheless difficult to adjust to. Especially with Arthur, whose ideas of finishing touches were of a smeary, sticky nature and nothing to do with Cath Kidston. Shirley's considerable efforts at interior design had resulted in a fashionably muted set piece in a style she thought of as Country Contemporary. This was distinguished by white walls, beige carpets, oak settles and Knole sofas. None of which were exactly baby-proof.

The house also had highly polished wooden floors across which Arthur in his soft baby trousers tended to skid at top speed. There would be sickening thuds as he cannoned into occasional tables and put the ornaments they held firmly and conclusively out of action. 'I'm sorry,' Sophie would sigh to her mother. 'I'm afraid another one bites the dust.'

Shirley would look at her keenly. 'Dust? There is no dust in my house. Mrs Brund sees to that.'

Arthur's feeding habits were another source of tension. The day after their arrival, Sophie had been feeding him mashed potato when he seized the spoon and smeared it all over himself and the nearby wall like some avant-garde performance artist.

'My goodness,' Shirley exclaimed brightly, trying hard to conquer distress at the damage to her decor. 'Arthur, darling. You're making a terrible mess.'

'Cheer up, Mum,' Sophie grinned as Arthur now began hurling yoghurt while simultaneously loudly filling his nappy. 'Just think, if he was twenty years older he'd probably win the Turner Prize.'

But in secret Sophie worried that Arthur's worsening table manners were a negative reaction to his changed circumstances. For him, the upheaval concerned not only his parents—the people he spent mornings, evenings and weekends with—but the place where he spent most of the rest of the time. Now that he, if not his mother, had cut all his connections with the capital, Arthur had been moved to a nursery in the nearest village.

Little Acorns was run by pleasant and efficient staff and seemed to Sophie as good as, if not better than, Little Explorers. Certainly, there were no glamorous mothers to cope with, especially now that Arthur was ferried to and fro by his grandmother. And Shirley could give as good as she got on the grooming front, none better.

It had been a painful sort of pleasure to inform the uppity Little Explorers manager Arthur was leaving and that, by implication, the constant

146

threat of his being expelled for lateness no longer held its terrible power. But telling Helen about their exodus had been a different matter.

Sophie had dreaded it, especially as Helen, knowing the whole drama had been fuelled by her party, would feel upset and guilty. This was one reason why, in the end, Sophie had avoided facing her. The friendship had been neither close nor long-established. A couple of meetings in the nursery car park and a party. All the same, she would probably never see Helen again and felt not only rude, but regretful. On the other hand, she felt regretful about everything.

CHAPTER FOURTEEN

Sophie considered it an achievement of sorts that she had hardly missed a day of work despite and since the upheaval. Even more miraculously, a fortunately timed commuter train from Hampshire meant she had succeeded in making sure neither Penny nor Lisa suspected anything untoward was happening. It was, Sophie thought, rather galling that she got to work earlier now than she ever had when she lived in the same city as the office. Work was, in other ways too, more tolerable than before; her bosses' violent man-bashing, which had so irritated her previously, was now, if not exactly music to her ears, at least more attuned to her mood.

It was therefore a surprise to enter the office one morning and find Lisa's face white with anger. Neither the anger nor the whiteness were the surprise; rather, the cause. Penny, who had not yet arrived, was, it emerged, leaving to get married with immediate effect. She had met someone speed-dating and now they were going to have a speed wedding. 'It was a lock-and-key party,' Lisa spat.

'What's that?' Sophie asked.

Lisa looked at her in contemptuous surprise. 'Never heard of it? The women all have a padlock and the men all have a key. The idea is that they run around finding each other.'

Sophie blinked, feeling suddenly nauseous. The symbolism was direly suggestive enough; the actual event hardly bore thinking about. Was this what life held after divorce? She forced the thought away.

Lisa, however, was able to do no such thing. Bitterly jealous and quite clearly feeling dreadfully betrayed, she lost no time in launching a fusillade of mean-spirited marriage jokes, all directed at her former confidante.

'Why do men want to marry virgins?' she would demand, apparently of no one in particular. 'Because they can't stand criticism, ha ha. Ooh, and what about this one? The morning after the wedding night, the groom turns to the bride and says, "Since I first saw you I wanted to make love to you really badly." She says, "Well, you've succeeded." Hee hee. Oh, and what's the difference between a boyfriend and a husband? Forty-five minutes, ha ha.'

Sophie had not taken any interest in the question of Penny's successor. She had not put herself forward for the job—extra responsibility was not something she sought at the moment. She

148

was aware there had been interviews, and someone appointed, although she had not seen any of the candidates.

The Monday that the new person was due to start, Sophie arrived in the office slightly late but secure in the knowledge that, as her mother collected Arthur, she could stay an extra half-hour in the evening, if need be.

Sophie could see as she crossed the office that the new girl had already arrived. She drew what conclusions she could from the back view: fair hair, sitting up straight, general impression neat. She felt a wave of sympathy. The first day in a new job was never enjoyable, and this poor girl had Lisa into the bargain.

She put the paper bag containing her latte down and the new girl glanced up. Their eyes locked. Sophie gasped in delighted amazement.

'Helen!'

Her friend from the nursery rocked in her chair. 'Hey!'

'I had no idea you were a sub!'

Helen smiled. 'I could say the same about you. I don't think we ever talked about anything as boring as work, did we?'

Sophie sat down, coursing with excitement. A friend in the office! It felt like brilliant sunshine after unrelieved cloud.

'So tell me. I'm dying to hear,' Helen said after a few minutes' more explanation.

Sophie stiffened. Was Helen about to ask how her marriage was going? The last time they had met, after all, was when Sophie's suspicions about Mark had started to harden. The beginning of the end, in fact. She had no wish to go into any of this.

Not now, at any rate. It was hardly morning banter, even as part of a joyful reunion.

'What are you dying to hear about?' she asked cautiously.

'Why you've left the nursery. Did that terrifying manager give you your marching orders or something?'

Sophie relaxed slightly. There was no accusation in Helen's voice, no suggestion that Sophie should have got in touch to explain. 'Something like that,' she confessed, taking the easy way out.

Helen nodded. Her raised eyebrow suggested curiosity was not entirely satisfied. But she did not pursue it. Instead, she changed the subject. 'You'll never guess,' she exclaimed.

'What?'

'I met your husband the other week. He's *lovely*. So kind and helpful and funny . . .'

Helen had met Mark! What had he said to her? Sophie flushed, hot with fear and awkwardness. 'You were away, staying with your mother,' Helen added, only the faintest hint of beadiness in her look.

Sophie nodded quickly, taut with apprehension as Helen related the encounter in the café. 'But then he went outside to answer his mobile,' Helen concluded, 'and we never saw him after that.'

Out of the corner of her eye, Sophie saw Lisa crossing the office towards them. Never had she been so glad to see her. The subject of Mark could now be closed.

And, although Helen tried several times during the day to bring it up again—it was obvious that she had her suspicions—Sophie would not be drawn. She did not want to discuss it with anyone,

150

not even Helen. It was all far too raw, far too complicated and, frankly, no one else's business.

*   *   *

'Mr Hopkins rang today,' Shirley announced when Sophie arrived home.

'Oh.' Mr Hopkins was the divorce lawyer.

'He was ringing up to find out how we—you—' hurriedly, Shirley corrected herself—'want to proceed with things.'

'Oh.'

'Well, we—you—can't just do nothing,' her mother said, looking at her commandingly. Her manicured nails tapped against the oak grain of the table.

'I suppose not.'

'I'll make an appointment with him for you, shall I?'

Sophie murmured something vaguely affirmative and went upstairs to see Arthur. He was asleep now, and looked angelic against the pure white of his pillow. She stroked his hair for a few moments before going back downstairs.

In the kitchen, Shirley was serving supper. Sophie sat down and took the plate her mother passed her. *Spaghetti alle vongole*. It was one of her favourite dishes, which was why her mother had cooked it, but she'd had it so often lately she was rapidly going off it.

'Have you seen Simon recently?' Shirley asked, returning to the attack, to the job in hand. She knew perfectly well that her daughter hadn't seen the banker since the ill-fated—or, from her point of view, fortunate—birthday party. Her task,

151

however, agreed with Simon that very morning, was to arrange a date. 'The poor girl needs to be taken out and given a good time,' Simon had purred solicitously. Shirley had enthusiastically concurred.

'Well, don't you think you should see him?' Shirley demanded as Sophie shook her head. 'You should spend an evening in London together. Go out and do something fun.'

Sophie thought of the last night she spent in London with Simon. The party. 'I suppose so,' she said without enthusiasm. 'To be honest, though, Mum, I don't think I'd recognise fun if it came up and bit me on the bottom.'

You mean you wouldn't recognise a cast-iron, all-singing, all-dancing, golden *opportunity*, Shirley thought, irritated. Was she the only person in this family who cared about its future?

There was a silence, which James broke by introducing the subject of his latest genealogical discoveries.

'It's *fascinating*,' James began. 'Apparently my great-great-great-great-grandfather, Joe Slowitt, worked down the Heckmucklethwaite pit and lived in a slum in Slack Bottom.'

'*Slowitt?*' Shirley gasped. Cavendish, Curzon, Saxe-Coburg, she could have done business with. But slow-wit? 'Slum?' she added, faintly. Sophie hid a grin in her napkin. Her mother's expression superseded Lady Bracknell and Mr Darcy combined.

'Oh, yes,' said James. 'In the West Riding poll book for 1879 the marriages, births and deaths records show clearly . . .'

Sophie sighed. Official records. Marriage birth

and death records. And in her case, death of a marriage records. Her mother was right. She should see Hopkins. The divorce really did need to proceed. It was important for Arthur as well as to her that this state of limbo did not go on for longer than it had to.

*　　　*　　　*

Arriving at the office a few days later, Sophie went to hang her coat on the stand. As she approached her desk, her phone was ringing. With a smile, Helen, who was already there, picked it up.

'No, she's just coming, this is Helen,' she heard Helen saying. Then, to her surprise, she heard an explosion of enthusiasm: 'Oh, *hi*! *Yes*, we *did* meet, remember.'

Sophie blinked. *Who* was ringing her that Helen had met?

'. . . actually, she's just got back to her desk. Lovely to talk to you, anyway . . .'

Helen bundled the phone at her. 'Your husband.' She beamed.

Mark! The shock was like an elephant landing on the keys of a piano. Every nerve in Sophie's body jangled and reverberated. She had successfully ignored his calls several times before; primed by Shirley—who had been primed by Simon—that her husband would certainly try to bother her at work, she had been monitoring her telephone through her voicemail. She had no intention of talking to him, full stop, and particularly with the ever-listening Lisa opposite. But there was no escaping him now. *Thanks, Helen*, she thought savagely.

153

'Hello?'

'Hello.' Mark was surprised and greatly relieved. He had been desperate to get through. The Dower House had obviously changed its phone number and Sophie never seemed to answer at work. Meaning that, with Dr Martha insisting she couldn't hold the school place for much longer, the option of going up to Chewton Stoke to beard them all in the flesh again was looking hideously likely. Thank God for the nice blonde he had met in the café, who had literally handed him over to his wife.

'What do you want?' Sophie asked sulkily.

'To ask you to do something, please,' Mark said humbly.

'What?'

'Delay the divorce.'

'Delay . . . ?' Sophie exclaimed. She had, only the day before seen Hopkins the solicitor and been persuaded finally to go full steam ahead. The decision had brought with it a kind of relief. She was set on a definite course, now. It was over. Once and for all. 'You must be joking?'

'On the contrary. I've never been more serious about anything.' Taking a deep breath, crossing his fingers and his knees, Mark explained about the School for Husbands.

After silently hearing him out—anything else would attract attention—Sophie put the phone down. Without looking at her colleagues, she flicked on her computer and started on the first piece of work. As she automatically checked the spelling and listed her queries concerning the content, her mind ran frantically over the scheme Mark had just proposed.

The disturbing possibility that he was going mad now struck her. His appearance at the Dower House had been insane—but this? Lunacy. The idea he could, after everything he had done, just go off to some course and emerge the perfect spouse? Madness. She could not believe he had suggested it.

As the morning wore on she felt the pressing need to confide this latest surreal development. The strain of keeping a lid on her increasingly volcanic private life while in the office was becoming unbearable. And unnecessary, now there was a discreet and sympathetic ear.

'Fancy Wagamama?' she suggested to Helen as one o'clock struck and Lisa headed off for her line-dancing class.

*   *   *

They crossed the road to the noodle bar. A restoring bowl would, Sophie hoped, give her strength for the story she was about to tell. After they had ordered, side by side on the wooden benches, Sophie told Helen everything that had happened.

The noodles were delivered without either of them noticing. The conversations of their neighbours, ringing loudly round the white-painted walls, went unheard. Automatically, untasting, they twisted their noodles round their chopsticks. Sophie talked, occasionally sniffed, and Helen listened.

As Sophie came to an end, Helen put a hand over her friend's. 'I'm so sorry,' she looked abashed, 'I did wonder, obviously. You didn't seem

155

to want to talk about him at all, which rather made me fear the worst, remembering what happened last time I saw you.'

'You mean the party?'

Helen groaned. 'Yes, the party. Horrible Harriet and Ruby, more to the point.'

'But they were right,' Sophie said sharply.

'How do you mean?' Helen challenged. 'He hasn't been unfaithful. You just said so.'

Sophie had to concede this point. 'But he's been such a hopeless husband it almost doesn't matter. Frankly, infidelity would almost have been the least of it. Compared to the rest, it almost wouldn't have mattered.'

Helen bit her lip. 'This idea,' she said cautiously. 'This School for Husbands.'

'Ridiculous, isn't it?' Sophie snorted, stabbing a prawn with her chopstick.

'You don't think it might be worth trying?' Helen toyed nervously with a piece of carrot.

Feeling panic rise within her, 'Trying? Are you serious?' Sophie stared. Then her face relaxed. 'Oh, I get it. You're only saying this because you think everything's your fault. Because of the party.'

Helen had reddened and looked wretched. 'Those horrible women . . .'

'Those horrible women just happened to be spot on,' Sophie said robustly. 'And it's not your fault. It's Mark's. Ruby and Harriet probably did me a favour in a way. I couldn't see what was staring me in the face until then. And now it's all over, thank God.'

'You don't mean the marriage is over?' Helen said, shocked. 'Not really.'

'Yes.' Sophie nodded her head firmly.

156

'What—just like that? You're not prepared to give Mark another chance? That's all he's asking for, with this School for Husbands thing.'

Sophie's eyes blazed. 'Just like that? Give him another chance? Have you any idea how long all this has been going on—not just the affair, but everything else? How many chances I've already given him—and that he's fouled up?'

Helen looked reproachfully back at her. 'But this course is only a fortnight,' she pleaded. 'It's not that much to ask.'

That her supposed friend was battling on her husband's side, not hers, enraged Sophie and stiffened her resolve. 'Look, I've made my mind up and I don't want to unmake it now. I don't want to *encourage* Mark. Sending him to this school, putting the divorce on hold. It will only make him think there's hope, and believe me, there isn't.' As silence fell, she felt a grim satisfaction. She had made it clear that nothing was going to distract her from her chosen course. As her mother kept saying, it was the best for everyone.

Then Helen spoke, her face grave. 'You're probably right,' she said softly. 'I *am* right,' Sophie confirmed.

'But you see, Sophie, it's not just about you. It's about Arthur as well.'

'*Arthur?* Well of course it is, but I've tried to protect his feelings as best I can . . .'

Helen was looking at her earnestly. She was speaking earnestly. 'I'm sorry. I know it's none of my business—but I don't mean Arthur's feelings now as much as Arthur's feelings later.'

Sophie churned with exasperation and incomprehension. 'What do you mean, his feelings

157

later?'

'When he is old enough to know what happened.'

'Oh. Right. I see. Well, I'll just tell him that the marriage wasn't working. That Mummy and Daddy just couldn't live together any more because they had too many arguments and so they decided to end it.'

Helen sighed. 'Yes, but what about the fact Mark obviously doesn't *want* to end it? That he clearly sees the School for Husbands as the last possible hope to save it?'

Sophie shrugged. 'Too late now.'

'But if you don't let Mark go to the school,' Helen calmly persisted, 'you can't tell Arthur that you tried everything to save it, can you? That you did absolutely all you could to make sure he wasn't yet another statistic from a broken home.'

Sophie stared. This was a viewpoint she had not considered. 'Look,' she blustered, 'I did everything I could. I put up with Mark's endless selfishness and thoughtlessness . . .'

'Don't you think *you're* being a bit selfish?' Helen said quietly. 'There's this one last chance and you're going to ignore it. Think about it, Sophie. What's the risk to you? If Mark's as hopeless as you say, nothing's going to improve him, least of all this school, which I agree does sound slightly eccentric.'

'*Slightly* eccentric!'

Helen reached out her hand and took Sophie's again. 'But I think you should give Mark the chance,' she said firmly. 'For Arthur's sake.'

Sophie stared at the floor for a few minutes. The lunchtime chatter in the restaurant swelled into

158

the silence between them.

She lifted her head. 'OK,' she muttered. 'The way you put it, I don't really have much choice.'

Helen exclaimed with delight, and hugged her. 'Don't get too excited,' Sophie warned, 'I'm doing this for Arthur. To show him I tried, as you say. Mark can go to the School for Husbands. But I don't want him back under any circumstances.'

CHAPTER FIFTEEN

That Sophie hadn't even said anything was almost the worst, Mark thought. Just put the phone down on him after he had finished speaking. As if the whole idea of the School for Husbands was literally too ridiculous for words.

And yet it wasn't. It really wasn't. He believed utterly in it now and had striven to persuade Sophie that it really might help them. That she didn't, in fact, want any help and was content to see their marriage founder was something he still could not quite believe. What about Arthur? Then again, what about the pressure Shirley was undoubtedly putting on Sophie? He regretted ever arguing with his mother-in-law about brass bands. He might have known she would revenge herself somehow, although not as extremely as this.

Still, at least he had managed to get through to Sophie, if only in the phone sense. That was something. That nice blonde he had met in the café had played a blinder there. Perhaps she might do it again once he had worked up some more courage. Because he was not giving up, Mark vowed. He couldn't. There was literally nothing else in his life.

He shambled down the road from the café he had sat in during the phone call. He tended to be out as much as possible during the day because home was increasingly too grim a prospect. Not particularly because of memories, although that was obviously a factor. The place was a bombsite and there was nothing to eat.

He was hungry, actually, Mark realised. He supposed he could always go to the pub. There were two in the area: one, the British Lion, was a former old-style corner boozer that had been revamped in a tasteful traditional manner, all sawdust floors, wooden furniture, real ales, fresh-faced staff and a menu featuring designer bangers and mash on big plates. It was patronised by much the same people who went to Caffé Toscana, including the children. The British Lion was family friendly, and served line-caught, hand-made, mini cod fishfingers to prove it.

The Friend in Need, two streets away, was another world. It was smoky, sticky and overtly family hostile, patronised almost exclusively by postmen and career drinkers with large bellies. Mark had, many times in the past, looked with scornful amusement at the pub's sign. It was of an anguished, oilskin-clad boatman bearing a strong resemblance to Trevor Howard. He was steering a small rowing boat in the teeth of an epic storm whilst simultaneously rescuing several people.

Now, however, Mark couldn't see anything funny about it. If anyone was a drowning soul, it was him. He was no longer the kind of attractive, successful, confident person who breezed in to the

160

British Lion. He was now of the ilk who crept furtively to the Friend in Need.

Entrance to the establishment was via a thick red plush curtain one had to push aside. Presumably it was there to protect the Friend in Need from the draughts outside, although the reverse could easily be true. It was very chilly in the pub.

'Pie and chips, please,' he ordered from the menu.

'Coming up,' the landlady boomed back. She was a large, cheery woman with dyed hair and a grey tooth Mark found it impossible not to stare at. She wore a bright purple dress rioting with improbable black vegetation. It did strange things to Mark's eyes as she moved away towards the deep-fat fryer to the strains of 'Octopus's Garden'.

Half of Parcel Force seemed clustered round the darts board. Mark took a seat as far from them as possible, opened the plastic file containing the various legal papers Ptarmigan had given him, and started moodily to sort through them. The lawyer had kept the original of Sophie's letter but there was a copy here, which Mark did not wish to read again. But he could sense it in the pile, festering like an ulcer. The misery of his situation slammed into him again. He felt his eyes burning and welling in a way that was becoming all too familiar.

'Pie and chips!' said the landlady, crashing a huge plate down on the table in front of him.

Mark now realised the buzzing sensation he had been for some seconds dimly aware of was the mobile in his pocket vibrating. He pulled it out. The number was one he recognised. One he had just recently dialled himself. His heart thumping

161

painfully in his throat, Mark pressed the answer button. His hands were shaking. At last, it was the call he had been waiting for. It was Sophie.

'H . . . h . . . hello,' he croaked.

His wife wasted no time with salutation. 'I'm just ringing to say OK, you can go,' she informed him shortly.

Mark's back shot up, ramrod straight, from the semi foetal position he now realised he had adopted. 'To the School for Husbands? You mean it? You'll delay the divorce?'

'I'm only doing it for Arthur,' was Sophie's uncompromising reply. 'Don't get your hopes up. There's no way I'm taking you back. But I suppose I have to show him that I tried everything.' So saying, she cut him off.

Mark stared, dazed, at the mobile. She hadn't sounded terribly friendly, it had to be said. But she had agreed. He was going to the School for Husbands. There was hope, after all.

Joy, unfelt for many weeks now, surged within him. He leapt to his feet and punched the air. 'Yessss!'

'Watch out, mate!' chorused the postmen as a dart whistled through Mark's hair and thudded into the bulls-eye behind him.

*   *   *

Simon sat complacently sipping his champagne.

His secretary, Polly, whose celebrity and glossy magazine obsession knew no bounds, had been staggered to be asked by her chilly and distant boss to book a table for two at whatever the capital's most sought-after eaterie was. Simon was uninterested in Polly's surprise, or anything else about her. He was not the sort of boss who yearned to be loved and as a consequence wasn't.

Sophie watched happily as the waiter came round again with the bottle of pink champagne. Agreeing to this night out with Simon—which she had done only to shut up her mother—had been a good idea after all. The effort he had made was touching. He had gone to extraordinarily extravagant lengths to cheer up someone no more significant than his godson's mother.

He had organised things beautifully. He had been waiting, as promised, outside her office to meet her. He had whipped out an umbrella to protect her from the lightest of showers and walked on the pavement's outer side as he ushered her to his car. The car had been a revelation, not so much because of the way it looked—a Mercedes convertible, all rich dark blue on the outside and cream and walnut on the inside—but the way it smelt. Of leather and aftershave, not nappies and sour milk and all the other unguessable, invisible, under-the-seat horrors familiar to parents of young children.

Relaxing now, after dinner, in the fashionable restaurant's even more fashionable bar, Sophie luxuriated in the sense of being thoroughly looked after. It certainly made a change from another night in at the Dower House, with her father uncovering links with more grave-diggers and pig-farmers and her mother nagging her endlessly about divorce.

Simon, for his part, felt it was time they got down to business. It was what they were here for, after all. He picked up his brandy glass and looked

163

Sophie straight in the eye. 'It's wonderful to see you tonight,' he announced, features rigid with sincerity.

'And you, Simon,' Sophie cried, her face shining with gratitude. 'You *are* a love. I can't believe you went to all this trouble just to cheer up an old mate.' She drained the rest of her champagne, wanting the delightful, whirling feeling to last for ever.

Simon's brow wrinkled slightly. Old mate was not quite the effect he was hoping for. But it was early days yet.

'How's my godson?' he enquired smoothly.

'Arthur?' Sophie felt a mixed rush of joy and guilt. 'He's fine, thanks.'

Simon opened a smooth black leather wallet with gold-tipped corners. Sophie was almost dazzled by the array of platinum cards thus revealed, not to mention the finger-thick wodge of notes.

He drew out the photograph, formerly resident on his desk but now removed because of the trouble it had caused. He handed it to Sophie, who gasped with delight as she found herself staring into the face of her beloved son. It was a particularly endearing photograph; Arthur on his christening day beaming a merry, toothless smile.

'He's so, er, cute,' Simon remarked, attempting warmth.

Sophie was woozy with drink and gratified mother-love. 'That's so *wonderful*, that you carry his picture about with you.'

'He's a boy in a million.' Hopefully several million. Arthur was the key to all future prosperity.

'He's a bit naughty sometimes,' Sophie felt obliged to confess.

164

Simon smiled indulgently. Naughtiness did not worry him. He had no plans for closely concerning himself with the upbringing of his children or stepchildren. That job was Sophie's and whatever nannies she chose to engage.

'He waves his spoon about in his high chair as if he's conducting the LSO . . .' Sophie lifted the champagne glass again, to steady lips that were suddenly trembling. What was Arthur doing now? Was he asleep? Was he awake and calling for her? She glanced at her watch. 'Perhaps . . . it's time I . . .'

'Went?' Simon interjected smoothly. 'Oh, come now. You can't go yet. Anyway, I'll drive you to the station. The night is young.'

'Not that young.' Sophie frowned at her wrist. 'It's ten. Definitely late middle age.'

Simon flailed for a subject. 'I haven't yet told you . . .' his voice dropped seductively, 'how absolutely devastatingly beautiful you look tonight.'

Sophie was surprised. She was wearing her usual navy work clothes.

'Amazing,' Simon assured her of her M&S jacket and the make-up partially applied on the tube that morning. 'Stunning.'

Had he, she wondered, been hitting the brandy harder than she thought? 'Thank you. And thanks for this evening. It's been great, but I really should—'

As she made a little half-bob upwards, Simon put out a hand to restrain her. They still hadn't even mentioned the divorce. He racked his brains for a way to introduce it. 'I'm so glad,' he breathed, 'that you had a good time tonight. That you're still

165

able to find enjoyment in things. After the recent unfortunate events with *Mark*,' he pronounced the name with distaste. He looked at her expectantly. 'The divorce and all that,' he prompted.

Sophie rolled her eyes. 'Oh. Do we really have to talk about it?'

Yes, thought Simon. He maintained his expectant pause.

Sophie sighed. 'It's just that it gets more complicated all the time. For instance, I'd just got the divorce under way at the solicitor's . . .'

'Great move,' Simon said. 'Far better to cut the ties as soon as possible when the relationship is so obviously dead and utterly without any hope of revival.'

'Except,' Sophie sighed, 'that Mark thinks there still is hope.'

Simon cackled with contemptuous triumph. 'After the way he treated you. His appalling behaviour at your birthday party—'

'Oh, don't,' Sophie cut in, uneager to relive the experience.

'He thinks there's hope?' Simon scoffed. 'Who does he think he's kidding?'

'Oh, don't.' Sophie took a deep breath. 'Anyway he's persuaded me to put the divorce on hold and let him go to this thing called the School for Husbands.' She shook her head, regretting her folly yet again. Many times since the conversation with Helen she had felt she had been mad to be persuaded. She had not yet dared tell her mother about it.

Simon, who had been until then lounging complacently back on a chaise-longue of pale blue leather, now sat bolt upright and choked violently into his brandy. He felt he had been hit by a runaway car transporter. 'Wha-at?' he spluttered. 'You've done *what*?'

*   *   *

'You've got to do something about it!' thundered Simon. 'She's delaying the divorce! Letting him have therapy, for God's sake.'

Shirley was utterly bewildered. She had absolutely no idea what Simon was talking about. It was late at night and Sophie was still out, although expected back any moment from her date with Simon. As she was later than expected, Shirley had imagined the evening must be a great success; she had, in fact, started to cherish hopes Sophie might spend the night in Simon's flat. That would move things along beautifully. And then, just five minutes ago, he had called in an absolute fury.

'Don't you understand?' Simon howled. 'I thought we'd agreed she was going to marry me?' His fury and frustration were such that he felt he was about to have a heart attack. Either that or explode. He had a meeting with the Wintergreens tomorrow at which he had to give details and a photograph of Sophie to get the pass which would allow her through the Fort Knox-style security system at the Wintergreen mansion near Regent's Park. The dinner party was looming. He was committed to bringing Sophie, and she had to come as his girlfriend at least. He would have to fudge the fiancée bit somehow.

Nothing could be allowed to go wrong now, even though everything was. He had no idea whether

167

she could even make the date. The news about the School for Husbands had so shocked him that he had completely forgotten to ask her. His life was falling apart, and it was all Shirley's stupid, stupid fault.

'How the hell has this happened?' he bawled. 'Right under your nose as well.' Although in point of fact he was uncertain whether Shirley's nose was her nose in the sense of being the original. She could have had surgery; she'd had plenty elsewhere, although admittedly nothing on the scale of the Mrs Wintergreens. They had had so much replaced they were probably now entirely different people to the ones they had been born.

Shirley pressed her fingertips to the skin beneath her eyes. It was puffy and unrested, and no wonder. This phone call was the final straw of a day that had already tested her to the limit. First Mrs Brund had spilt Windolene on the Knole. Then Venetia Bothamley-Tartt had cut her dead as she crossed the churchyard. And just to round everything off beautifully, James had found some ancestors who had run an abattoir in Preston.

And now this. Her brain buzzed with the horror of it. 'I'll talk to her,' she promised, panicked.

'Confront it head on and put a stop to it *immediately*,' Simon ordered, slamming the phone down with a force Shirley could feel fifty miles away.

'Why didn't you talk to me about it?' Shirley demanded of her daughter when Sophie finally arrived home.

Sophie burned with guilt. She should, she knew, have mentioned it. It was the least she owed her mother, after all the help that had been freely

168

given. But how had her mother found out?

'Well, um, Simon told me,' Shirley was forced to confess. Such was her horror and confusion, she hadn't seen that particular query coming.

'Simon?' Sophie stared. She had been puzzled at the dramatic effect the news had had on the banker. He had recovered but had obviously been shocked. She supposed his concern was touching. But to call her mother seemed a bit extreme. She was a grown-up, wasn't she?

'He rang *you*? Why?'

'Because he's very concerned about *you*. He's worried, as am I, that you don't know what you're doing. That you're confused and making mistakes. Terrible mistakes, that will affect your whole future, and that of poor dear Arthur too of course . . .' Shirley sniffed. She was ricocheting between tears and anger. A top City banker for a son-in-law. The mansion in Hertfordshire. Was it all to come unstuck now? She looked at her daughter miserably.

'Don't worry, Mum,' Sophie said, touched by the pain in her mother's eyes and feeling guilty. 'It'll be fine. Mark's bound to make the most enormous mess of the School for Husbands. It's supposed to improve his husbanding skills, but as you know he doesn't have any in the first place.

'He hasn't even written to me, after all. He said he would—'

'*Absolutely*.' Shirley cut in in the most condemnatory tones possible.

'But absolutely nothing has come.'

'You've not got any letters, no,' Shirley agreed in what was less an endorsement of the facts than a subtle correction of them. She had been initially

169

very reluctant about intercepting Mark's letters. It had seemed a step too far. But what other option had there been? Simon had been insistent that the end justified the means and to drive his point home had suggested terrifying consequences if Sophie received any letters from her husband.

'So,' Sophie finished, 'the divorce will be going ahead. It's just a slight delay, that's all.'

The post slapped on to the hall floor just at that moment. 'I'll get it,' Shirley yelped, throwing herself at the doorway with what, had her daughter noticed it, might have seemed almost like panic. But Sophie, grateful for the distraction, had made the front door ahead of her mother. She crouched over the scattering of envelopes on the sisal.

'Any letters?' Shirley croaked behind her, her heart pounding, and not with physical effort alone.

'One for Dad and, *ooh*,' Sophie said, pleased. 'One for me.'

Shirley swallowed and slumped against the hall wall. She had tried her best. But he had slipped past her's and Simon's best efforts in the end. Damn Mark. The flurry of Sophie's excited tearing seemed the ripping of all her hopes. The silence that followed, as Sophie read what was no doubt a marital *cri de coeur* expressed in the most moving terms imaginable, was as deep as the grave.

'*Wow*,' Sophie exclaimed eventually. 'That explains *everything*!'

Her worst fears realised, Shirley felt sick. 'What everything?' she asked faintly, steeling herself for the agony to come.

'About Cess.' Sophie looked up, her face shining.

'*Cess?*' repeated Shirley, bewildered. 'You mean

. . . Cecily? Your friend the headmistress?'

'She's got married!'

'Married!' Shirley echoed her daughter's amazement. It was not exactly an expected outcome for Sophie's dowdy, fat friend.

'An impulse thing, she says,' Sophie frowned at the letter. 'He's called Bryce and he's an Australian. She met him in the Sustainable Foodstuffs chatroom, apparently.'

Shirley could not imagine what that was, and cared less. Relief was thundering in her veins. She had never imagined a circumstance in which she might be grateful to the person she considered the most charmless of all her daughter's university chums. Nonetheless, here it was. Cess had written. Not Mark.

'It's incredible.' Sophie reread the letter yet again. Cess could hardly know anything about the man. On second thoughts, though, what was wrong with that? She herself had lived with Mark for seven years before realising she didn't know him either.

'She sounds very happy,' Sophie mused. 'She says it's the best thing she ever did and that Arthur and I are to come over to Sydney and see her as soon as we can.'

'Well, I hope you're not thinking of doing so soon,' Shirley interrupted firmly, having now recovered herself. Sophie was going nowhere until the Sharp situation was progressing smoothly along its intended path.

Sophie rolled her eyes. 'Hardly, Mum. It's not as if I can afford to, for a start.' Her brow creased as she stared at the letter. 'It's a shame, though. I'd rather hoped to set her up with Simon . . . he seems to be so lonely and I'm sure Cess could win him over in the end. Mum?' This as Shirley began spluttering and coughing helplessly. 'Are you all right? I'll get you a glass of water.' And off she went, with Cess's letter and the one addressed to her father in her hand.

It was now that the cleaner chose to make her entrance.

' 'Scuse me,' Mrs Brund barked. 'But what you yer want me to do wi' these? I've just found 'em under yer bed.'

Shirley's choking redoubled as she saw that Mrs Brund held in her hand a number of unopened letters. She knew without having to examine their envelopes that they were addressed to Sophie in Mark's hand.

Shirley took a deep, controlling breath. 'Oh!' she trilled, in tones of the utmost insouciance. 'I've been looking for these everywhere. Well done, Mrs Brund.' She swooped across the kitchen floor, grabbed them, and stuffed them into both her trouser pockets.

Suddenly, James rushed out of his study, waving the letter, and followed by Sophie with the glass of water. 'You'll never guess!' he exclaimed excitedly, 'There's a message from someone researching the same branch of the family! He thinks he's related to the sewer-building side as well . . .'

CHAPTER SIXTEEN

The cab that had brought Mark from Leeds station drove away. The driver had followed Dr Martha's map without difficulty and dropped him off where it instructed, at the specified time. So far, so straightforward.

Mark now stood at the head of a long drive. Lined with impressive trees, it stretched away in a green tunnel towards a large building of dark stone topped with turrets. While obviously Victorian, it had medieval fortress overtones that made Mark feel nervous.

Possibly because of Dr Martha's being an American therapist, he had imagined a building in the tradition of the celebrity drying-out clinics in various American deserts. Large, blocklike, modern and with a pared-down funky adobe look, as if some simple Mexican peasant folk had just got together and decided to build an all-singing, all-dancing state-of-the-art multi-purpose therapy and treatment centre. But the School for Husbands was nothing like this. It looked, oddly enough, exactly like a school. A forbidding, old-fashioned, boarding school.

He forced himself into a lighter frame of mind. He had wanted so desperately to come here. Now that the law had failed him it was his last hope of reconciliation. Whatever it looked like, it was the gateway back to happiness, to the land of lost content. He picked up his bag and walked towards the front door.

Inside the hall, it took a few seconds to see in the gloom. What eventually emerged from the shadows was a room of the sort one might expect a tweedy colonel with a salt-and-pepper moustache to stride through swinging a brace of recently shot partridge. It smelt of furniture polish. It had wood-panelled walls, a wide wooden staircase, a mock-

Tudor fireplace and stained-glass windows.

'Name?'

Mark turned around in surprise to find himself looking at an old man in a battered petrol-blue jacket and an ancient tweed cap rammed over clumps of grey hair. His eyes glistened in the gloom. One hand dangled a vast clump of keys, like the ghost of Jacob Marley.

'I'm Briggs.' He flashed some twisted teeth.

'Hello,' said Mark firmly. 'I'm Mark Brown.'

'Aye, we've been expecting thee.' A chill went down Mark's spine at the words. 'Thee room's ready.' Briggs bent with evident difficulty towards Mark's bag.

'Oh, no. Let me do that,' Mark protested.

But the old man had gripped the handles with a skeletal yet iron fist. 'This way,' he ordered through a throat choked with phlegm. Mark followed, half scared, half wondering what a Gothic relic like this was doing in Dr Martha's employ. He seemed to have wandered in from *Wuthering Heights*.

He longed for a stiff drink and a lie-down. He had been told by Dr Martha, however, that alcohol was strictly forbidden at the School for Husbands. Along with any reading matter not directly supplied by the school itself.

They passed a grandfather clock that struck him as having a sinister tick. Ahead was a gloomy corridor with a stained-glass window glowing dimly at the end. There was a feeling of faded grandeur. Very, very faded grandeur.

'What was this place?' Mark asked curiously. 'It looks a bit like a school from outside.'

The cadaverous servant gave another of his

174

hideous grins. 'It were school. A boys' school.'

Mark was struck by the aptness of this. From boys' school to School for Husbands. 'That must have been a long time ago,' he remarked pleasantly. About a hundred years at least by the look of it. As they passed a wide fireplace set into the corridor wall, he imagined Tom Brown being held against it by the bullying Flashman.

'I used to be t'caretaker,' Briggs croaked through the phlegm. 'I've lived 'ere ever since.'

As he coughed long and horribly, Mark looked at him in astonishment. Caretaker? How the hell old was he?

'So when,' Briggs gasped, having partially recovered, 'yon doctor took t'place on a short lease, I were thrown in as a job lot, like. This is thee room,' he added abruptly, shuffling to a halt before the last door next to the stained-glass window. He extracted the keys from his pocket with a deafening roar of metal and fitted one into the lock. The door creaked and shuddered open with apparent resentment and reluctance.

Dumping the bag on the floor like a sack of potatoes, Briggs now disappeared.

Mark looked around. The room continued the theme of the cheerless Victorian decor outside. It was tiny and its main features were an iron bedstead covered with a dun blanket, a long, narrow window and a small oak desk with an oak chair.

Mark sat glumly down on the chair. Of course, he was here to learn and improve, not enjoy himself. And while sybaritic it wasn't, clean and tidy it was, which was more than could be said for home at the moment. Mark recalled the scene of

175

devastation he had left in Verona Road and reflected that the washing-up alone would have by now grown enough penicillin to supply the NHS for a year.

There were, anyway, he noticed with a lifting heart, some books at the back of the desk. He stared at the titles and his heart sank again. But he was in a relationships clinic and so should not be especially surprised to see *Why Men Drink Beer and Women Clean Bathrooms* by Dr Arnhem J. Fossum. Or *Find the Love You Want* by Cindee Z. Strumpfhosen, Ph.D., with its companion volume, *Keep the Love You've Found*. As Cindee Z. Strumpfhosen, Ph.D., was billed on the second book as Cindee Z. Strumpfhosen-Cruse, Ph.D., it seemed she'd found some love herself in the interim.

Others offered for his perusal were *Coupleteamhood* by Dr Diddley Squat and *Men Are From Arse, Women Are From Penis: It's All About Sex so Let's Face It* by Dr Terence T. Goole. And, of course, was *Be So There for Each Other: Marriage Management Made Easy* by Dr Martha Krankenhaus.

Mark sighed, and looked around the room again. He opened the plain wooden cupboard that was presumably a wardrobe. Inside, folded neatly on a shelf, was a pile of dark blue T-shirts and a matching baseball cap. Mark shook out the shirts. They each had a white heart printed on them, with the logo 'Hey! I'm One of Martha's Marriage-Mending Miracles™ arranged round it in a circle. The same logo appeared on the cap.

A sheet of paper was lying on the bed. 'IMPORTANT INFORMATION', it announced.

176

Besides details about bathrooms, meals and laundry facilities, Mark learnt the following. Daily Marriage-Mending Miracle™ classes were to be held in the Great Hall. Evenings were to be spent on what were described mysteriously as 'Interactive Pursuits'. Uniforms were to be worn at all times and cost £50 for the cap and £75 for the T-shirt. All the books in the rooms were also for sale at £20 each; if not bought, grubby copies would have to be replaced by the room's occupier. Cheques were acceptable and to be made payable to Dr Martha Krankenhaus Enterprises Inc.

Mark looked out of the window. He had expected some sort of view but as there was a tree pressing into the pane, all he could see was a mass of leaves. He listened. There was none of the accustomed hum of London. Rather, a stillness he found ominous, punctuated by the occasional wail of a dejected-sounding bird.

He had just pulled on the T-shirt and fixed the baseball cap on his head when there came a knock at his door. He jumped at the unexpected sound. Opening the door, he found himself peering, not into the expected, grizzled visage of the ancient retainer, but the bronzed and smooth complexion of someone he vaguely recognised. Another few seconds, and he'd placed him.

'You!' Mark exclaimed in astonishment. 'You're the bloke from that hotel. What was it called—Winterton something or other?'

'Hall,' Jeremy Hetherington-Spence confirmed. He looked wistful. 'Paradise lost. How I wish I was back there now.'

Mark was still absorbing the surprise. To find him in the School for Husbands was a double

177

shock. He had not for one moment supposed Jeremy to be straight.

The hotel manager was peering into Mark's room. 'Gosh, your room's actually *worse* than mine,' he remarked in awe. 'I really didn't think that was possible.'

Mark stood aside as Jeremy minced in, his bronzed arms goosepimpled where the sleeves of his Dr Martha T-shirt ended. 'Isn't it *freezing*?' the hotel manager exclaimed. 'This place isn't a school. It's a gulag.'

'I was trying to think of it as bracing,' Mark confessed.

'And the decor. Well!' Jeremy flicked a disgusted hand at the cotton curtains. 'You can tell Philippe Starck has been nowhere near *here*.'

Mark hid a smile. 'No Lord Linley cigar boxes either,' he added teasingly.

'No,' Jeremy agreed mournfully.

'As for the fluff factor of the towels.' Mark looked at some piled on a shelf. 'Minus one, I'd say.'

'Oh don't. Don't remind me. Have you *seen* those communal bathrooms?' Jeremy looked as if he might burst into tears. 'And I am literally *quaking* at the thought of what the food's going to be like. Free of Gordon Ramsay's personal involvement, *that* much is certain.' He looked disconsolately around. 'You'd have thought, at the prices we're paying, there might be a minibar in the rooms at least.'

'No alcohol,' Mark reminded him, 'It's the clinic's most important rule, remember. It said so on all the enrolment stuff.'

'Quite the goody-two-shoes, aren't we?' Jeremy

looked rebellious for a moment. Then his face fell. 'It's just that,' he added pathetically, 'a glass of pink Roederer would make things *so* much more bearable.'

'Look.' Mark could contain his curiosity no longer. 'I mean, I'm sorry if it's a rude question and of course you don't have to answer it if you don't want to, but—'

'Why Roederer and not Moët?'

'No!'

'What am I doing here?'

'Well, yes.'

Jeremy sighed. 'It's a long story. Basically, my wife thinks I've become over-obsessed with work. The hotel. The quest for excellence in general.' He raised his chin and flared his nostrils. 'I could never persuade her that the pursuit of the perfect is the most noble pastime to which Man can aspire.'

Mark remembered the tour round Don Juan and Jeremy's obsessive drawing of his attention to the thread count and the minibar coasters. He remembered, too, the unavoidable family emergency that had made it impossible for Jeremy to disentangle the room reservations fiasco. And which, indirectly, had led to the disintegration of his marriage and his being here. As it had for Jeremy, as it turned out.

'Yes, the unavoidable emergency was my wife threatening to leave me,' Jeremy confessed. 'I'd just, rather helpfully I thought, pointed out that her tights were a different black to her dress and she suddenly announced that she was sick of me criticising her and was it right that I had more beauty products in the bathroom cabinet than she did?'

'Oh dear,' Mark sympathised.

'But actually, I don't want Julia to leave me. She helps run the Hall with me, for a start, and is awfully good with the business side of things, which isn't my strong point at all. Anyway, my solicitor had heard about this place and I accepted that a bit of suffering might be necessary to get back into Julia's good books. Although I *never* expected suffering like *this*.' Jeremy looked down at his front, his face twisted with repulsion. 'This T-shirt! *Such* a bad cut.'

'I didn't realise T-shirts had cuts,' Mark confessed. 'I thought they were, well, T-shaped, I suppose.'

Jeremy regarded him in amazement. 'Yes, but there are an infinite number of T-*shapes*. Big Ts, small Ts. Loose, flowing Ts, Tight, shape-defining Ts.' He brushed a manicured hand down his front in disgust. 'And horrible, unflattering Ts in bad material, like this one. And these baseball caps. So unstylish. But one can never take them off because of the state of one's hair underneath if one did. One is caught between a rock and a hard place, stylistically speaking. And frequently,' he sighed, 'a Hard Rock place, to judge by all the tragic fiftysomethings who come into my hotel wearing headgear from that infernal establishment.'

'I thought your type of clients wouldn't wear baseball caps,' Mark remarked.

'My dear boy, the richer they are, the worse taste they have. I considered at one time having a no-baseball cap rule until I realised we wouldn't have any customers.'

There was a short silence. 'Oh well,' Mark said.

'It'll all be worth it if Dr Martha can help us.'

Jeremy picked up the sheet of instructions. 'What *are* these Interactive Pursuits we're supposed to spend each night doing anyway? I've brought the whole of *Upstairs Downstairs* to watch on my portable DVD.'

'Hey, you guys!' Both men gasped as Dr Martha suddenly appeared at the door.

Dr Martha looked as brisk and businesslike as ever. Her big, very bright, very wide brown eyes looked enquiringly over half-moon spectacles. Beneath her short dark crop swung a pair of large silver hoop earrings. Her small, wiry figure, as usual, was entirely clothed in black.

'I hope you've settled into the campus,' she cried enthusiastically. 'Great place, isn't it?'

'Great,' Mark lied. After all, Dr Martha was the key to his whole future. It would be silly not to be polite to her.

'Couldn't be better—if you're a deathwatch beetle,' muttered Jeremy.

Dr Martha heard this. 'Sure,' she said, smiling. 'The facilities *are* simple. And that's deliberate. Simple is *good*. Simple is calm and uncomplicated. Simple gives you space to reflect on what really matters in your life. Like the place you are in and the place you want to go *to*.'

Jeremy folded his arms. The gesture implied that the place he wanted to go was one with minibars and a towel fluff factor well over forty. 'But everywhere's so dark,' he complained. 'The corridors are absolutely pitch-black.'

'Jeremy!' Dr Martha shook a smiling head. 'Jeremy. Half the darkness you see is in *yourself*, you know. The darkness of despair. You may *think*

181

you want more light in the corridors, but the light you *really* want is that which enables you to see your way back to your relationship. And that's one bulb we're *definitely* gonna switch on, don't worry.'

Dr Martha extended her arms out. 'And have you looked round the *grounds*? Have you *seen* what a fantastic setting this place is in? You know, you're all going to draw such *incredible* strength from the view. From the grace, the power, the amazing amazingness of Nature, all around you.'

Mark felt concerned. The view was obviously a crucial part of the therapy and he could hardly see a thing. He raised his hand. 'There's a tree in front of my window.'

Dr Martha beamed disarmingly at him. 'I know. It's there for a reason. You see, Mark, you've got issues blocking your relationships vision. That tree is a visual metaphor for the state of stuckness you are in.'

'Oh. I see.'

'No, Mark, you *don't* see. That's the point. Not yet, at least. But, Mark, I want to promise you something. As the Marriage-Mending Miracle gets to work on you, you'll notice that you'll be noticing that tree less and less.' She finished the speech with another brilliant beam.

CHAPTER SEVENTEEN

Dr Martha's Marriage-Mending Miracle™ was about to start in the Great Hall. Mark and Jeremy had yet to find it.

They headed down a sequence of gloomy

corridors. 'Lord knows, I'm no fan of über-bright lighting,' the hotel manager grumbled. 'Terribly unflattering. But some forty-watt uplighters round here would make a real difference. Between staying alive and breaking your neck, for instance.'

After exploring more dark and cheerless passages, they came across a set of double doors behind which a familiar American voice could be heard.

'The Great Hall,' Mark exclaimed, relieved.

'I don't see what's so great about it,' Jeremy muttered as they pushed open the door to reveal the quintessential old-fashioned school hall. The walls were wood-panelled until halfway up, where they became stark white plaster. Set in the plaster were the type of large, high Victorian windows that required a hook on a stick to open them.

Dr Martha sat, in the middle of the room, at a small trestle table surrounded by a small group of men in regulation garb. The gathering looked minuscule in the context of the large and echoing room which was clearly built to take assemblies of hundreds.

'Come and sit down,' the therapist urged them.

The group sitting at the trestle table looked heavy-eyed, no doubt because of their lack of success in sleeping on the narrow, lumpy beds. Mark had found oblivion so elusive he had eventually resorted to Cindee Z. Strumpfhosen-Cruse, who hadn't significantly improved matters.

Dr Martha, on the other hand, looked habitually fresh and purposeful in black trousers and a white shirt, red lipstick and flashes of silver at her wrists and ears being the only colour in her trademark monochrome palette.

183

Fizzing with an energy that made Mark feel exhausted, she looked brightly round at the group.

'The first thing we need to do, guys, is—' she lifted an emphatic fist—'Get rid of 'em. Put 'em all on the table.'

The men looked uncomfortable. Mark felt alarmed, even though he had expected nothing less. Relationships therapy was famously all about revealing private problems in public, airing issues, putting intimate personal details 'on the table'. He swiftly looked away. While he might have to participate sooner or later, he would not be the first to respond to this demand for collective emotional unburdening, for a catalogue of self-accusation.

'Come on,' Dr Martha urged. 'The sooner you rid yourselves of them, the sooner you free yourselves of the things that dog your marriage. The things that let you down, that betray you, that drive your wives to distraction.'

Still the men hesitated.

'Oh dear.' Dr Martha peered in mild exasperation over the top of her fashionable glasses. 'We're not getting very far, are we?' She held out two pleading palms. 'Come on, guys. Surrender.'

No one moved.

'Give me your mobile phones,' Dr Martha ordered sternly.

'Mobile phones?' repeated a handsome man with longish dark hair underneath the baseball cap he wore back to front. 'Mobile *phones*? What for? I mean . . . I *need* mine.'

'Charlie.' Dr Martha looked at him sternly. 'You have come here to save your marriage to Angie, have you not? She wants to divorce you. The School for Husbands may be your last chance of preventing this.'

'Yeah, but I've got people ringing me.'

Dr Martha's gaze, over her glasses, was suspicious. 'What people?'

'People,' Charlie repeated sullenly.

Dr Martha put her head on one side. 'Women, Charlie?' she cooed. 'Ladies?'

Charlie did not answer.

Dr Martha cleared her throat and beamed. 'Well, Charlie, congratulations on being such a great study aid. You've pretty much made my point for me. You're a walking, talking illustration of why the School for Husbands' number one rule is: no mobiles.'

'How do you mean?' Charlie muttered, clearly not enjoying his moment under the spotlight.

'I mean,' Dr Martha whooped, 'that mobile phones are death to marriage. They're more dangerous to husbands than the most conniving temptress. They have no morals, no capacity for guilt. They enslave and addict husbands, then let them down appallingly, developing flat batteries just as the wife's trying to get through, or just as they're trying to call the wife. And flat batteries, guys, mean flat marriages. They encourage clandestine relationships because they promise discretion, but then they fan suspicion, revealing secret calls by means of their bills. And then they betray, sending private text messages to the wife's phone by mistake.'

Charlie's weatherbeaten features coloured a deeper red at this. Mark wondered if Dr Martha had hit on something.

185

'Make no mistake,' Dr Martha added, producing a slim silver clip of a phone from her pocket and waving it about. 'These things can be useful in business. But for any kind of personal business, they're bunny-boilers, pure and simple. They want to split up your marriage and destroy your happiness. And they do. A report in the *US Relationships Journal* found that out of the five million divorces in America last year, four million involved mobile phones. Texts being sent to the wrong person, incriminating bills, redial buttons being pressed by the wrong fingers . . . you know the sort of thing.'

Charlie reddened still further. He clearly did, Mark saw, know the sort of thing.

'So gentlemen,' Dr Martha addressed them, 'the first thing you've got to do at the School for Husbands is get rid of those troublemakers. Go cold turkey on the texting. And if you want to get in touch with your wives while you're here—and you should, on a daily basis—then *write*.'

Mark nodded. As a matter of fact, he planned to do this anyway. Part of his sales pitch to Sophie about the School for Husbands had been the promise that he would call her every day and update her on what he had learnt. She had been unenthusiastic, especially when he suggested the mobile as the means, but had grudgingly accepted when he had offered to write. They would, Mark vowed, be the funniest, most loving, most moving missives she had ever received, Masterpieces, no less.

'You mean there's not even a callbox here?' Jeremy gasped. 'I never thought such basic facilities could exist in a civilised country. My

186

human rights are being infringed.'

Slowly, reluctantly, the men rummaged in their pockets and dragged out their mobiles. They made an interesting collection: Jeremy's, predictably, was tasteful, slim and rather feminine; Charlie's more hi-tech macho. Mark pulled out his own unremarkable black number—scratched from various encounters with Arthur. He suppressed a sudden lump in his throat at the thought. A tall, long-nosed man with narrow eyes and his cap placed very straight on his head contemptuously placed down what Mark recognised to be the top executive model of a leading phone firm—Lance had the same one and was very proud of it. Someone further along the table, whose pale eyes and sharp nose gave him the air of a twitching, whiskery creature, produced an ancient and chunky model from the dawn of mobile time, complete with pull-out aerial.

'Jesus,' said Charlie. 'Where'd you get that? The British Museum?'

The final member of the group, a multi-chinned scruff with wire-wool hair beneath his baseball cap, produced a phone whose plastic cover sported the familiar red and white livery of Arsenal Football Club.

It was, Mark thought, easy to guess why he, at least, was seeking help at the School for Husbands. A sports nut, obviously. His thumbs twitched restlessly as if missing their usual fan of remote controls, and what could be seen of his face had the grey pallor of one who habitually fell asleep in front of the late-night football channels.

With the mobiles all on the table, Briggs stepped forward with a small cardboard box. He proffered

187

it first to Charlie, who ran a regretful, caressing finger over his phone before placing it in the box with a care that was almost loving.

The other men followed suit. 'Well done!' Dr Martha said, smiling round encouragingly. 'You dealt with that very difficult situation very well. Now we move on to the next stage, which is assessment. This gives us all some idea of what we're in here for.'

Mark felt a clutch of fear. This, then, was the confession bit. He stared worriedly at the floor.

Dr Martha opened a red file and took out a piece of paper. 'In order to facilitate the assessment process, I am delighted to present you with a piece of research patented by myself. Ten revealing questions for husbands I have honed and developed over a quarter of a century in the field of expert interpersonal marital-relationships therapeutics.'

Mark's fear grew. Did he want to answer ten revealing questions about his marriage, developed by an expert, in front of all these other men? All about his sex life, no doubt.

'Of course,' Dr Martha added, 'if any of you had happened to pick up Issue Twelve of the *US Relationships Journal* and read the article entitled "Self and Selfishness Within The Modern Matrimonial Structure", first-authored by me and second-authored by Dr Rusty B. Stridgel, these questions would be familiar to you already.'

It was the first time in Mark's entire life that he wished he had read an article second-authored by someone called Dr Rusty Stridgel. It sounded like one of those porn names people used to talk about at dinner parties: the name of your first pet and mother's maiden name combined. His had been Sparkle Bostridge.

Dr Martha looked briefly down at the note she held in her hand. 'First question.'

Mark's eyes nervously raked the ceiling, the floor, the windows, anywhere but Dr Martha. She was bound to be asking about the clitoris. Didn't all therapists?

'Where is the iron in your house?' Dr Martha asked. Mark raised his gaze gingerly upwards. To his relief the therapist was addressing the Arsenal fan. 'Andy,' she added.

'The iron?' Andy repeated in surprise, lifting his cap and scratching his messy mop of hair.

'It's a simple enough question, Andy,' Dr Martha pointed out. 'Where is the iron in your house? Where is it kept?'

Andy's flabby face shone grey with fear. 'The iron?' he asked cautiously. Mark suspected he thought it was some kind of euphemism. For clitoris, possibly. 'That you iron with?' Andy probed.

'The iron. That you iron with.'

'Er . . .' Andy stared helplessly. 'I don't know.'

'On the shelf above the washing machine,' the doctor informed him, 'if you know where *that* is.'

Andy looked uncertain.

'Next question,' Dr Martha announced. 'Explain how the dishwasher's automatic unloading and restacking function works, Charlie.'

Charlie's rangy, athletic shoulders flinched in surprise. 'A dishwasher's *what*? But it doesn't unload or stack itself.'

Dr Martha smiled brightly. 'Interesting that you've reached that conclusion, Charlie. Because

189

most husbands apparently believe that it does.'

Mark stared. He'd expected G-spots and the finer points of comparative X and Y chromosome psychology. Not a plan of the utility room.

'What,' Dr Martha now asked Jeremy, 'is the correct answer to the question, posed by your wife, "Tell me, honestly, how do I look?"'

Jeremy pursed his lips. 'It very much depends on what my wife is wearing. I'd never encourage Julia to wear anything exposing her upper arms immediately after Christmas. And her bottom *can* look pendulous in bikinis. Certain haircuts work best when her face is thinner—'

'Whoa there,' Dr Martha cried, throwing up both hands. 'Wrong answer.'

'But you said she's asking me to be honest,' Jeremy bleated.

'True. But the only circumstances in which you should ever answer this question honestly is when your wife is looking absolutely spectacular. And tell me this. How often do you see absolutely spectacular-looking women?'

'Not often,' Jeremy admitted.

'Exactly. So what do you think most women's husbands are telling them? Not what you've just said, that's for sure.'

As the class absorbed this. Mark felt more puzzled. When were the big subjects coming?

'What, Graham,' the therapist asked, 'is the correct answer when your wife asks you, in a restaurant, the following question: "Can I have one of your chips?"'

'You should have ordered some of your own,' said the ratty man with the ancient mobile as indignantly as if the scenario was actually

190

occurring.

'Wrong answer!' sang Dr Martha. 'Women do not routinely order fries, but they routinely expect to be able to help themselves to their husbands'. Ditto pudding. It's one of marriage's unwritten rules.'

This was evidently news to Graham. Mark wondered when his question would come. He was not looking forward to it.

'Rupert,' Dr Martha now addressed the man with the executive mobile. 'Tell me, if you can, the correct answer to the question, posed by your wife, "Can we go away on holiday this year?"'

Rupert looked annoyed. 'Impossible at the moment,' he said testily. 'There are a number of mergers under way and it's a very sensitive time for me to be leaving the office.'

The therapist's hand was up. 'Wrong! The correct answer is, "Of course, darling, it would be wonderful to spend some time away together. What about the Maldives?"'

Rupert looked horror-struck. 'The *Maldives*! My BlackBerry would never work there.'

'And it would cost a fortune,' Graham added. 'I looked into it last year after Mary said she'd like a change from camping on the Isle of Man.' He shuddered. 'In the end I persuaded her to go to the Malverns.'

Dr Martha folded her hands and looked at him calmly. 'Which was possibly not such a great move, Graham, because look at where you're currently spending your time off. Here. A holiday in the Maldives would be cheap compared to what a divorce will cost you. Both of you.' She looked from Graham to Rupert.

It was now that Mark saw Dr Martha's bright brown eyes swivel in his direction. His buttocks tightened with tension. His heart hammered as he watched her lips begin to move. 'What, Mark,' they asked, 'is the correct response to the question, "We've run out of tonic. Do you think the off-licence is still open?"'

Mark relaxed slightly. He was on familiar territory here. It was uncanny, but Sophie had asked him just this during a particularly fraught evening the previous month. He answered now as he had answered then. 'Probably not,' he said apologetically. 'But we've got some lager. Fancy a can of that instead?'

Dr Martha sighed. 'I'm not sure, darling, but why don't I go out and have a look. And if it is shut I'll hop in the car and nip to the twenty-four-hour supermarket. I understand that when a girl wants a gin and tonic she *really* wants a gin and tonic.'

'Sorry?' Mark was confused.

'I was giving you the correct answer,' Dr Martha said. 'Let's try again though. What's the right response to this next question, also posed by your wife.'

Mark looked indignant. Two questions in a row! Was that fair?

'Do we have any chocolate?' the therapist enquired sweetly.

Mark reddened. He remembered that the last time Sophie had asked this, exhausted after a particularly strugglesome bathtime with Arthur, he had confirmed that they hadn't. This had not gone down well. 'Er . . .' he mumbled, hanging his head.

'Wrong answer. The right answer,' Dr Martha said firmly, 'is "Yes, actually, darling, there is some. I'll just go and get it." ' She paused. 'You see, guys, every husband has a duty to provide chocolate for his wife. But not in huge boxes with ribbons on—that'll just make her feel guilty. Or, worse, that she has to hand them round so everyone else gets the best ones first. No, the chocolate that really counts, the chocolate that maintains marriages, the chocolate that a husband hides for emergency purposes so he can produce it late at night, after the shops shut, after the wife has hunted around a bit and thinks all hope is gone.' She smiled. 'Men may be from Mars, to quote one of my well-known colleagues. But if you ask me, they can be from Twix, Snickers and KitKat with equal success.'

There was a pause. 'Can I just ask you something?' Charlie asked, frowning.

Dr Martha gave a dazzlingly obliging smile. 'How can I help you, Charlie?'

Charlie spoke in a rush. 'Look, don't take this the wrong way, right, I mean, I appreciate you've got all that research and whatever behind you but, look, all this isn't what I expected, exactly.' He stopped and folded his arms defensively.

'Go on,' Dr Martha said gently. 'What isn't what you expected?'

Charlie sat forward again. 'Well, chips, G and T and all the rest of it. I was kind of expecting that you'd be explaining the reasons behind the *big* stuff that causes marriages to go tits up. Sex. Money. Affairs. Whatever.' He shrugged.

There were a few murmurs of assent at this; Mark's among them.

Dr Martha smiled calmly at her interrogator. 'I'm so glad you've asked me that, Charlie.

193

Because that, in a nutshell, is what my Two-Week Marriage-Mending Miracle is all about. The small things *are* the big things. That's the whole point. I've counselled—'

'Yeah, I know,' Charlie interjected. 'Literally thousands of couples over twenty years. I know, I know. But . . .'

Dr Martha held up a hand. 'That's right, and what I've found with these troubled marriages is that—guess what—it's the small things every time. The small things going wrong that makes the big things go wrong. It's the last-straw theory. For instance, you might think your wife's divorcing you for a one-night-stand with someone else. And of course, that's a contributory factor. But nine times out of ten, what she's really divorcing you for is ten years' worth of hair you've left in the bathplug. Ten years of throwing your clothes on the bedroom floor. Ten years of not putting milk back in the fridge, of forgetting the most important things on the shopping list, of using all the petrol and not filling the car up, of refusing to say sorry, ever, of leaving the bathroom mirror spattered with shaving foam.'

While Charlie continued to look sceptical, a great bell seemed to be ringing in Mark's head.

But Dr Martha had not finished. 'And if your wife leaves you for another guy? Believe me, it's not because he's great in bed. Or not only that. It's also because he takes the trouble to colour-sort the washing. Because he not only empties the pedal-bin but puts a new bag in afterwards. You don't have to be Brad Pitt to be sexy, you see. You just have to make an effort. You see what I'm saying?'

Mark stared uncertainly down at the surface of

the trestle table. It was old and bore the gouged-out initials of what were presumably past pupils. It was, he thought, all rather Dotheboys Hall. Or, perhaps, Dothehusbands.

*   *   *

'I wonder whether I might tempt you out,' came Simon's flat and nasal tones.

'Er, no, sorry, but thanks all the same,' said Helen. 'Here's Sophie. I think the switchboard put you through to the wrong extension.'

Sophie, reddening, took the receiver. After listening for a few seconds she interrupted, 'I'm so sorry, Simon, but I just can't. I'm really tired and I need to spend some time with Arthur.'

'But he's in bed anyway when you get home, surely.'

'Well—yes.' Sophie sighed. She hardly needed reminding. To go from a position of knowing every aspect of Arthur's home and nursery environment to one where she and her son were merely ships that passed in the morning was taking some getting used to.

She remembered this morning, as she bent to Velcro Arthur's shoes together and kiss him goodbye. Holding his solid little body snuggled in her arms, she felt a rush of regret, the wild urge to stay and look after him, not slog off to London to spend the day under the beady, bitter eyes of Lisa.

'So what's the problem, then?' asked Simon.

'I can't leave my mother with him all the time. It's too much responsibility.'

'But she *loves* looking after him,' Simon said confidently. 'She worships the ground he toddles on.' He tried to amend his tone to sound less incredulous.

'I know,' Sophie admitted. 'She really has been amazing with him. But I can't take advantage of her.'

'Why not?' asked Simon, whose entire career had been built on taking advantage of people.

'It's Covent Garden,' he pressed. Neither had he got where he was by giving up easily. 'I thought you liked opera.'

'I do,' Sophie admitted.

'It's *Madame Butterfly*,' Simon said, saving the best until last.

Sophie gave a longing groan. *Madame Butterfly*. She had seen it once, years ago and still remembered how it had lumped her throat, filled her eyes and sent her out into the night reverberating with the emotion of it all.

Shirley had remembered too, not that she had been present. But her recollection of Sophie talking about it was why Simon was making the offer. It had come to her in a moment of rare inspiration and Shirley hoped it might redeem her, in the narrowed eyes of Simon, for the disaster over the School for Husbands. Shirley, who had been made to feel entirely to blame over the episode, could not know that things in Simon's camp were marginally better of late. The Wintergreen dinner had been cancelled on account of Mrs Wintergreen's sudden illness, which Bella, who had inside information—literally in this case—translated as one of her silicon implants breaking loose and going on the internal rampage. The date had yet to be refixed—presumably it would be when Mrs Wintergreen was. In the

196

meantime, Simon was keeping up the pressure.

'Another time, perhaps,' Sophie said firmly.

'There won't be another time,' Simon said even more firmly. 'This is the last performance. I practically had to kill to get the tickets. I thought,' he added in hurt tones, 'that you'd be pleased.'

Sophie hesitated. Simon had been so good to her, so generous. And here he was again, thinking he was giving her a wonderful surprise. And here she was, turning him down flat.

It would be rude beyond measure to refuse. And, after all, it was terribly flattering that someone wanted to cheer her up so much. That someone was, after all, Arthur's godfather, with whom she needed to preserve a relationship.

'Of course I'd love to,' she sighed.

'This Simon,' Helen mused, after the receiver had been replaced. 'Tell me to keep my nose out if you like, but who is he, exactly?'

'Simon's a friend, an old friend,' Sophie stressed firmly. 'He's Arthur's godfather, that's all.'

'That's all?' Helen was smiling, but her eyes were uncertain.

'Helen! He's a dry-as-a-bone banker I've known since he was a spotty youth. He's not interested in me and I'm not interested in him. Not in that way, anyway.'

'If you say so. Don't forget about Mark though, will you?' Her tone was light but disguised, Sophie sensed, serious meaning. She sighed. Why could Helen not accept what was obvious?

'Look, my marriage is over. Mark's only at the School for Husbands so I can tell Arthur that I tried. As you suggested, remember? Or . . .' her eyes widened, as the idea suddenly struck. She turned to Helen, amazed. 'Did you think that if he went there I might actually take him back?'

Helen pulled a wry face. 'Guilty as charged, your honour. I thought anything that delayed the divorce was a good thing, yes. But I did think it had that advantage for Arthur too. It wasn't just a front.'

Sophie shook her head in wonder. 'And all this on the strength of one meeting with Mark. He obviously did quite a number on you.'

'He was very charming,' Helen confessed apologetically.

'He could certainly turn on the charm.' Rather to her surprise, Sophie found herself recalling a few examples. Surprise bunches of flowers. Unexpected bottles of champagne on dull midweek evenings. She forced the thoughts away. That was all a long time ago.

Helen spoke hesitantly, as if aware she was treading on the thinnest of eggshells, 'I just hoped that, if you had some time apart, you might see everything more in perspective. And you really don't know what he's learning in there. It really might make the most enormous difference. Therapy does, you know.'

Sophie felt resentful. It was all very well for Helen to say all this, with her perfect John. The last sentence made her pause, however. Was her friend speaking from experience? She looked speculatively at Helen, whose eyes were now carefully on the floor.

'Well, OK,' she conceded. 'You're right, I suppose.'

Helen looked up, her troubled face cleared.

'You're right that I don't know what he's

learning,' Sophie said gloomily. 'He said he'd write every day and tell me about all the wonderful improvements to his behaviour. But he's failed on that promise as well. Or he's forgotten. Or he can't be bothered. Frankly, I don't believe he's changed at all.'

CHAPTER EIGHTEEN

Briggs was dragging a large and peculiar object, which he negotiated with difficulty through the hall doors. It was a large box on wheels, the size of a telephone kiosk but half the height, completely surrounded by black curtains. Nothing could be seen of what the curtains were concealing.

When the box reached a position level with the trestle table at which everyone was sitting, Dr Martha strode forward and placed her thumb and forefinger on a drawstring operating the curtains.

'Gentlemen,' she said, looking at her class gravely, 'the causes of marital difficulty are many and varied. But in my experience, few causes of relationship stress are quite as widespread as the behavioural impact issues arising from . . .' she jerked her hand on the drawstring, '. . . this.'

Mark stared. On the castor-mounted box before them was an ordinary white lavatory, complete with chrome handle and upturned black plastic seat. Its enamel gleamed in the overhead lights.

Dr Martha smiled and tapped the enamel. 'Sanitary equipment, gentlemen. A big subject. A big *big* subject. I could probably run a school for

199

husbands on this topic alone.'

No one contradicted her. Mark slid a glance around. Rupert looked scornful and Charlie mildly amused. Jeremy's burnished face, meanwhile, bore an expression of deep disgust.

'My research and experience over twenty-five years in the field of marital therapy show that bathroom issues can cause huge strain within a close partnership situation. I might add,' Dr Martha added, 'that in the information received from your loved ones, negatively impacting body waste removal unit behaviours presented in almost all cases.' She smiled. 'So this morning we are going to get to the bottom of this business.'

She approached the gleaming loo, then turned to address them. 'The gender-specific automatic response situation of most males to a flush-waste facility is to leave a component part in a place-inappropriate position. Like so.' Dr Martha gestured at the upright black plastic lavatory seat and lid.

'The School's response to this,' she added, 'is to utilise cognitive behavioural treatments with regard to addressing and challenging wrongness in regard to these and similar units.' Seizing the seat and lid, she moved them downwards to a closed position. 'So that's the theory. Now I want to see you put it into practice. Everyone line up, please. One by one.'

The class shuffled to its feet and filed past its instructress, who lifted the lid and seat before each person so he could put it down.

'*With feeling!*' commanded Dr Martha. 'The key to this is to seal the facility with *real* commitment, as if you never intend to leave it up *ever again* . . .

yes, Andy. Like that. Charlie, you've slammed it down much too loudly. Excellent, Mark. A very good, confident gesture! *Excellent!'*

When the last man had replaced the lid, Dr Martha beamed round at the class again. 'Congratulations. You have all made significant progress. Moreover, you have shown real willingness to reverse your hygiene-unit-cover-related preconceptions. You just need to keep it up, that's all. Or, rather, down.'

There was a dutiful snigger.

'And now we move on to explore a notorious marital flashpoint, Severe Extended Hygiene Facility Occupation Syndrome.'

'Whatever is that?' demanded Jeremy.

'Put in layperson's terms, Severe Extended Hygiene Facility Occupation is the clinical name for the syndrome whereby the male half of a heterosexual partnership disappears into the bathroom with a newspaper only to emerge half an hour later to discover that his wife has made all the beds, dressed and fed the children, loaded the dishwasher or done half a pile of ironing. You understand?'

'Retraining and redirecting to a non-relationship-threatening level of Hygiene Facility Occupation requires constant assessment, commitment and dedication,' Dr Martha warned.

*   *   *

After the class, as was customary, Dr Martha swept out and Briggs staggered in with the hot food trolley. As, having parked this and plugged it into the wall, he pushed out the lavatory on its castors,

201

Charlie stared after it and remarked that he may as well have left it, as after lunch they would be needing it anyway, and not for the purpose Dr Martha had intended.

The food at the School for Husbands was every bit as vile as Jeremy had gloomily predicted. Dinner was the contents of a portable serving unit so ancient it could have dated back to the days when the building actually was a boys' school. It was manned by Briggs, who definitely did. Gazing into the dollops of cheese mush in whose glutinous depths half-submerged bits of colourless tomato floundered like drowning men, Mark felt a sense of awe that any cooking in the world was as bad as this. It was worse even than his own.

There were metal jugs of water on the trestle tables, but then he had seen, at the end of the serving station, a table bearing a geometric arrangement of attractively packaged bottles. 'Marriage Water' declared a small sign printed in flowing script and propped against the front of the display. 'Blessed by the Archbishop of Canterbury. Guaranteed to put you in Marriage-Mending Mood!' Deciding it looked more fun Mark took a bottle.

'That'll be five pahnd,' growled Briggs.

Mark stared indignantly. 'I thought the food was included in the fees.'

'It is. But that water costs five pahnd.'

Mark had not opened the Marriage Water. It was staying sealed in his room, reserved for emergency purposes. And an interesting souvenir, once he got out of here.

*   *   *

The evening yawned ahead of them. Or, to be precise, Interaction Time yawned ahead of them. Dr Martha had been firm on the point that disappearing to one's room was forbidden for two hours after dinner. This period was designated Interaction Time, 'intended to de-introduce the practice of flopping in front of the television all night and to re-introduce the principle of communicating with and entertaining one's female partner,' as Dr Martha had put it.

The de- and re-introduction programme was to take place within the austere confines of the Great Hall. The idea, in line with Dr Martha's general hyper-practical approach, was that if you could amuse yourself and others there for two hours, you could amuse people anywhere.

Last night, Briggs had led them in a game of Monopoly. The only other options had been conversation. 'Remember that?' Dr Martha had teased. 'Talking? Pointing your face at your wife and letting words come out of that hole below your nose? You need to get those chatting muscles built up again.'

As, now, he watched Briggs bringing in the tiddlywinks box, Mark decided to take the latter option. He pointed his face at his neighbour, Charlie, and racked his brains for something to say.

'Hello.' It was hardly original, but it was too short to be boring.

Charlie nodded. 'How's it going, mate?'

'Fine. Er . . .' Mark felt the conversation battery within him sputtering. Chatting about nothing was harder than it looked, particularly without alcohol.

He must think of another question fast. Charlie, however, was there first.

'What do you do, then?' he asked Mark.

'Er, actually, I'm between jobs at the moment.'

'Oh.' His neighbour raised his eyebrows. 'I'm a builder. Own a building business, I mean.'

He looked the type, Mark thought, with those shoulders and muscles. It explained the tan as well, and the general air of exuberant fitness. He felt pasty, weedy and ill by comparison.

'Why're you here?' Charlie asked.

Mark flinched slightly before remembering he may as well be honest. As Dr Martha never tired of saying, they were here to share. This was not a place for squeamishness.

'I neglected my wife,' he confessed. 'Stayed at work too late, never rang her, forgot things, acted as if I was still a bachelor and not the father of a toddler. She got fed up with it.'

'Blimey,' observed the builder. 'That all? Doesn't know she's born, by the sound of it. My wife got sick of me because I had so many bloody affairs.'

'Oh, well, Sophie thought I had affairs too,' Mark seized this extra justification.

'She just *thought*? You mean you didn't play away?'

'Er, no.'

Charlie snorted. 'That's bad luck, mate. You're carrying the can and you didn't have any fun.'

'Actually,' Mark explained, 'I don't see it like that.'

Charlie gave him a puzzled look. There was a short silence.

'Um, do you regret *your* affairs?' Mark asked.

Charlie gave a short, cawing laugh. 'I bloody well did after Angie found out, let me tell you. She made sure of it. I've still got the scars. And I regretted it when my solicitor told me I had to come here.'

'You didn't want to come here, then?'

' 'Course not. Who in their right mind would?'

'Well, me,' Mark admitted quietly.

'You what, mate?' Charlie shook his head in slow wonderment. 'Blimey.'

'Didn't you want to save your marriage?' Mark asked him.

Charlie's laugh was incredulous. 'Save my marriage? I'm here to save my money, mate. My building firm's worth a fortune and I've got no intention of handing half of it to Angie if we split.'

'I see,' Mark said slowly.

'So what about you?' the builder prompted. His eyes had a teasing look which made Mark feel even more uncomfortable.

He paused, scraping together the courage. 'I'm here to try and show my wife I'm sorry. Persuade her to take me back.'

Charlie stared. 'Blimey,' he said again.

CHAPTER NINETEEN

Dr Martha pressed a button on her laptop DVD player. The screen lit up.

A thin, dissatisfied-looking blonde of about forty was sitting on a large, red, clearly expensive brocade sofa. Her long, slim legs were elegantly crossed and her hands were folded composedly in her lap.

'I am married to a supermarket,' she began brightly. 'And actually, if I were a multi-outlet retail facility, I'd get approximately one hundred per cent more love and attention from my husband. Or perhaps if I were a packet of ice-blasted prawns. Rupert, you see, is chairman of one of the largest frozen-food retail groups in the country. He spends more time with the women on his checkouts than he does with me. Or in his office, where he works until all hours video-meeting, conference-calling, you name it. Oh, he's a whizz with computers is Rupert. Do you know,' she added, leaning forward into the camera with an impish smile, 'he speaks fifteen different computer languages! But hardly ever says a single word to me!'

Mark's eyes slid to Rupert. He sat bolt upright at the trestle table, he looked as if he were receiving a particularly unwelcome piece of performance news from a regional manager. Mark knew the expression. It was one he had had to fight against employing on his own regional managers. When he had had them.

The on-screen blonde reached over to a side table, removed a piece of paper and held it up. 'This is a little play called *My Marriage To Rupert*.'

Rupert coughed. 'Annabel,' he remarked drily, 'is a leading light of the local amateur dramatic society.'

'Act One. Scene One,' continued Annabel. 'The setting is the master bedroom suite of a Surrey commuter belt mansion. Annabel and her husband Rupert are in a contemporary four-poster bed with mood lighting, digital radio and built-in plasma screen TV. Despite all these distractions, Rupert is keying away into his BlackBerry and oblivious to everything else, especially Annabel, who is attempting to have a conversation with him.'

Annabel: Would you like to hear about my day, darling?
Rupert: Mmm?
A: They're opening a lapdancing club in the village. They're advertising for trainees in the church newsletter. Do you think I'd be any good at it?
R (absently): Oh, absolutely.
A (trying a new approach to the conversation): I thought I could be on top this time. You know, when we start our six-hour-long nightly sex marathon? But let's hold the white chocolate sauce, shall we? It makes the sheets so sticky.
R: Mmm.
A: I'm thinking of training to be an astronaut.
R: Mmm.
A: Rupert, do you love me?
R: (distractedly): Mmm?
A: I want a divorce.
R: Um.
A (Louder, insistent): *Did you hear me, I want a divorce!*
R (Now listening, genuinely shocked): What? A divorce? Why?

The screen faded into darkness. Mark forced himself to look serious. Annabel had impressive timing and a sure comic touch. It was easy to believe she was a star of the local drama society.

Poor old Rupert, though. Video evidence was so embarrassing. He felt almost grateful that Sophie had refused to speak to Dr Martha—not that she knew it was Dr Martha, she had taken so little interest. Her submitting evidence in writing to ensure the lowest possible level of involvement with school staff had, Mark thought, been a fortunate decision. In as much as anything about his current situation was fortunate.

Rupert, meanwhile, was looking thunderous. As Dr Martha laid a soothing hand on his wrist, he started back as if touched by the National Grid. 'It's important that you hear your issues articulated,' she advised him. 'It's a crucial part of the process of acceptance and correction.'

Rupert looked sceptical.

'Rupert, cases like yours have an abnormal view of themselves,' Dr Martha said gently. 'People like you can appear remote and chilly—'

Rupert leapt to his feet. 'Now, look here. I didn't sign up to this school just to be insulted.'

'Hey, cool it. Calm down,' Dr Martha smiled. 'Relax. What I was about to say was that even though you may appear remote and chilly . . .'

Rupert jerked his chin up angrily.

'. . . issues presenting like yours—distance from your wife, an inability to give and receive emotional commitment—are actually easy to tackle. You remember I told you that my take on relationships therapy is to concentrate on the very small and simple things?'

Rupert jerked his chin down.

'The answer to your problems,' Dr Martha explained gently, 'lies in three very small words. The three words every woman wants to hear.'

'I'm a millionaire?' quipped Jeremy, who seemed in ebullient mood this morning.

'It can't be that,' Rupert said crossly. 'I'm a millionaire many times over, but that doesn't interest Annabel any more.'

Dr Martha smiled. 'Quite. I'm talking about something completely different. These words. They're inside you, unable to get out because you're emotionally constipated. Bunged up, big-time. And so I'm going to give you a great big bowl of bran.'

'*Bran?*' Rupert looked appalled.

'I'm speaking therapeutically, of course,' Dr Martha said patiently. 'What we need to do is get you in a verbal emotional release situation.'

Rupert looked wary. 'What does that mean?'

'I love you,' said Dr Martha, passionately.

Rupert did not look as if this intelligence was welcome.

'I love you,' Dr Martha repeated. 'The three simplest, most wonderful words in the language. Nothing more, nothing less. Just say them.'

Rupert swallowed. His face contorted. 'Er . . .'

'Hey! Come on. Roll the words round your tongue. Feel them. *Taste* them.'

'I love you,' Rupert repeated stiffly to the centre of the opposite wall.

Dr Martha clutched her ears in despair. 'No, no, *no*. Sound as if you really mean it. Imagine I'm your wife. I'm Annabel. You're desperate not to lose me.'

'I love you,' repeated Rupert, with no perceptible increase in warmth.

'Not like that. Like *this*.' Dr Martha stood up and beat her skinny breast. She thrust her face into

209

that of Rupert, for whom Mark was now beginning to feel a definite flicker of sympathy. 'I love you!' she declared desperately.

'I love you,' Rupert responded dutifully.

'Tha-at's better! Now tell everyone.'

'Everyone?'

Dr Martha nodded. Her eyes had a messianic gleam.

There were a few moments of laden silence. 'I love you,' Rupert said to Mark, who nodded and looked hard at the floor, flustered and embarrassed for them both.

'I love you,' Rupert told Charlie who leant forward, clapped him on the arm and croaked, 'I love you too, mate.'

'Very good,' commented Dr Martha approvingly.

'I love you,' Rupert told Jeremy, who looked delighted. 'Awfully nice of you to say so,' he replied. 'I must say, it's marvellous to be appreciated.'

Rupert rolled his eyes. 'I love you,' he sighed at Andy, who looked doubtful.

'Where are your appreciation response skills, Andy?' Dr Martha chided. 'Rupert's freely giving you an emotional present which you've got to freely accept. It takes two to love, you know? A big part of being loved is believing you *can* be loved. Believing you're *worthy* of love. So—*receive!*'

Andy tried to look as worthy of Rupert's affections as he could manage.

'That's better!' Dr Martha exclaimed. 'And you're a natural, Rupert. You're *full* of love, you see. It just needs unlocking.'

Rupert did not reply. His face, however, said a

lot.

'Now you've got the idea,' the therapist smiled, 'all you need to do is practise. The more you say it, the easier you'll find it. The more you tell people you love them, the more love you'll get back, from Annabel and everybody else. Won't that be great?'

Rupert nodded abruptly.

'So what I want you to do now,' Dr Martha said, 'is just tell everyone you meet you love them. *Everyone*. Don't be embarrassed. Just say it. Get used to hearing those words.'

Rupert's face was an impassive mask. Mark felt sorry for him. He was a strange, stiff creature, but his was a hard and difficult fate. Telling everyone he met that he loved them! Jesus.

'*And* the rest of you,' Dr Martha added.

There was a silence.

'You mean,' Charlie's eyes narrowed with disbelief, '*we've* all got to tell everyone we meet we love them as well?'

'Absolutely. According to your wives, you've all got acute emotional interactivity issues. All of you must learn to participate in creating emotional opportunities.'

'But where?' Graham asked. 'There's only us here.'

The therapist's face lit up. 'I'm so glad you asked that, Graham. As you so rightly point out, there is indeed only us here. Which is why I've arranged a school trip out to the nearest village this afternoon.' She raised her arms melodramatically. 'Go forth and spread the word of Love.'

* * *

After lunch, the group climbed reluctantly into a minibus whose front seat was occupied by Dr Martha. Behind the steering wheel was Briggs. Now Mark realised that the only conveyance he could imagine the wild and grizzly caretaker piloting was a closed carriage with lamps aflame, pulled at reckless speed by headless horses.

They drove down country lanes for some time before arriving in a small village. A sign at the end of the straggly main street advertised it as Upper Grimside, which did not seem to Mark to augur especially well. It seemed unlikely that the inhabitants of a place thus named would respond positively to spontaneous displays of affection. Still, he reminded himself, at least they had Dr Martha with them. Her manic enthusiasm and absolute indifference to criticism should be more than equal to the worst the villagers could throw at them. If, indeed, there were any villagers to throw anything. As they dismounted from the bus, Mark looked cautiously around. There was no one in sight.

'Well—good luck!' Dr Martha smiled at them. 'We'll be back in a couple of hours. See you later.'

The group looked aghast. 'What, you're just *leaving* us here?' Charlie demanded.

'Why not?' Dr Martha smiled. 'You're big boys. Grown-ups, or so you'd like your wives to believe.'

They watched the minibus splutter into the distance. 'What now?' Graham asked, his tone despairing. A light but insistent drizzle had begun.

Charlie looked about him. 'There's a pub over there,' he pointed out.

The pub was called the Butcher's Arms, which

seemed to continue the village's theme of unpromising names. It was dark, low-ceilinged, completely silent and empty apart from an old man, who could have been dead, and a quivering Jack Russell, both of whom sat so near a small, sullen fire as to be practically in it. Andy stared round, hoping, Mark guessed, to find a TV tuned to Sky Sports. His face fell when there was none.

The landlord seemed friendly enough. He served the others pints, and Mark—remembering his no-alcohol-until-reunion vow—an orange juice, and asked them if they were from the minibus that had been reported pulling up in the village.

'Yes,' said Mark in surprise. 'Don't you get many minibuses, then?'

'Don't get many vehicles of any sort,' rejoined the landlord cheerfully. 'Although last week there were two white cars came through only half an hour apart.' His eyes widened in fearful wonder. 'That were strange, that were.'

'Right,' Mark said, arriving with the drinks at the table Graham had chosen. It was by the window, but afforded views only of condensation and drizzle. 'We need to decide on a plan of action. Dr Martha said we had to tell someone we loved them every half hour. So what we probably need to do is go outside, split up, do the deed and then come back here and wait for the bus.' Everyone nodded gloomily apart from Charlie, who was staring at Mark with a face alight with mischief.

'It's about half an hour since we got here,' he said, brandishing the watch on his wrist and looking meaningfully over at the bar and the fireplace. 'Is that an emotional interactivity opportunity I see before me?' he asked mockingly.

'If not two?'

The men looked at each other. No one moved. Then slowly, reluctantly, his heart sliding to his shoe soles, Mark stood up. 'I'll do the barman,' he said to Jeremy, 'if you do the bloke by the fire.'

Jeremy looked at the old man in horror. 'He looks disgusting,' he shuddered. 'What if he *smells*?'

'Love conquers all, remember,' grinned Charlie.

Swallowing hard, Mark walked across the acres of dusty floor to the bar where the landlord was polishing glasses. 'Excuse me,' he said unsteadily.

The landlord put his tea towel down, placed a hand on the beer pump and smiled. 'And what'll it be this time, squire? Another orange juice?'

Mark drew a deep breath. 'I love you,' he said, gazing furiously at the floor.

There was a short silence. As he raised his head, blushing furiously, Mark was surprised to see the host looking relatively unperturbed. 'Well now, that's nice to hear,' said the landlord. 'It's something customers say from time to time, I don't mind admitting. Along with stuff about me being their best mate and all that. Have to say though,' he said, looking hard at Mark, 'they don't usually say it when they're on soft drinks. Goodness me, what's all that shouting?'

The shouting was Jeremy's professions of endearment. The old man, who was not dead but deaf, was sitting up and staring at the dapper hotel manager, one hand cupped under a quantity of straggly white hair which presumably contained an ear. 'What's that you say?' he was yelling.

'Don't know what you're laughing at.' As he returned to the table, giddy with relief, Mark

214

grinned at the sniggering Charlie. 'It'll be your turn in a minute.'

Charlie's smile vanished. 'No, it won't. If you think I'm going around telling Royston Vasey that I love it, you've got another think coming. Nah, mate.' He settled back, pint in hand. 'You go ahead and enjoy yourselves.'

'But you have to,' Mark protested. 'It's part of the therapy.'

Charlie shook his head.

'Come on. You've got to. We've all got to. We're all in this together.'

Charlie met his eye with mocking obstinacy. 'Leave me out of it, World's Most Fabulous Husband. I'll stay here and keep the seats warm.'

With an effort, Mark ignored the jibe. It stung, however. But, as Charlie clearly had no intention of co-operating, cutting his losses seemed the only option. There was no point in arguing; the exercise was about love, after all, and the others were demotivated enough.

'Come on,' he urged his fellow students. 'The sooner we get on with it, the sooner it's over.'

As they bowed their heads to exit under the low door, Charlie raised an arm. 'The best of British to you,' he called in a mock-patrician accent.

'Traitor!' snapped Rupert.

Half an hour later, Andy was being chased down the street by a furious little old lady, Rupert was being drawn into the church porch by a vicar thrilled at his grasp of the Christian message, and a young woman who had been reading a letter on a bench with an air of lonely tragedy was looking up at Graham with a face full of hope and wonder.

It was a relief when the bus finally rounded the

corner. Never had Mark imagined he would be so glad to see the caretaker's grizzled face. He wondered whether he would ever again look at the hour and half-hour points on a watch without dread.

'That,' said Rupert, looking back through the bus window at the cheerfully waving vicar, 'was a bloody nightmare. Saying "I love you" to every Tom, Dick and Harry. I've never done anything as difficult or embarrassing as that.' He snorted in disgust.

From the front seat, Dr Martha turned round and beamed. 'Exactly, Rupert. That's the whole point of the exercise. Just think how much easier it's going to be saying it to your *wife*.'

*   *   *

It was the end of *Madame Butterfly* at Covent Garden and Sophie was wrestling with her feelings. Her insides felt twisted and her throat swollen and aching with the effort of not crying. Part of this was due to the plot: the story of the wife betrayed by Pinkerton, the husband she adored, for whom she had waited so long and so faithfully to come back, but who ultimately had betrayed her, never failed to move her.

Sophie could not help remembering, too, the first time she had seen Puccini's powerful opera. It had been a birthday surprise from Mark, in the days when he had thought of romantic things like that. He had met her from work, then walked her to the great white pillared façade of the Royal Opera House, a place she had never been inside but had always longed to.

And then, quite suddenly, she was. He had walked her across the road, through the opera house's heavy glass doors and into a mirrored, gilded, red velvet-lined world of swirling music and high emotion. She had been speechless all the way home, her throat the hard lump it was at the moment. She was worlds away now, hardly noticing even the fact she was walking, with Simon, along the red plush carpet from the auditorium. Thoughts of Mark, how happy they once had been together, kept pushing through her efforts to concentrate on how miserable he had recently made her.

Simon, oblivious to the turn of her thoughts, felt satisfied. She had obviously loved every minute and was clearly overwhelmed with emotion. This struck him as amazing. He could not imagine being overwhelmed by feelings for anything not containable in a bank account.

And while it was incomprehensible that her eyes had been riveted to the stage, it was also fortunate. She had not noticed him yawning his way through the first and second acts and sleeping through the third.

He tried to hurry her along. He needed a drink. Simon had never been to an opera before and the sheer length of the production had been a shock. Assuming it was over, he had, in fact, tried to leave at the interval.

There was a champagne bar somewhere in this cavernous building, he knew from the programme notes. Sophie had assumed he was reading the plot, as had the woman on his other side, a flint-faced brunette accompanied by a man who looked as bored as Simon. 'It's all about men being bastards,' the woman hissed at Simon, looking meaningfully at his programme. 'Culture in a nutshell, if you ask me,' she had added, shooting a huffy glance at her companion.

'It would never have happened,' Simon remarked, once they were in the bar with flutes of boiling bubbles in their hands, 'if Chow Chow whatsername . . .'

'San. Cio-Cio-San.'

Simon pursed his lips. He hated being corrected or interrupted. '. . . had had a good solicitor.'

Sophie, in mid-sip, spluttered into her glass. 'What?'

Simon raised a grave eyebrow. 'A simple pre-nuptial agreement would have ensured that Butterton . . .'

'Pinkerton.'

Simon's lips pursed again. 'Well, whatever he was called, if she'd made him sign a proper pre-nup she wouldn't be in the position she finds herself in now.'

Sophie's eyes were large and shining. 'But she loved him. She trusted him. And he betrayed her.'

'Absolutely,' Simon agreed, spotting a cast-iron opportunity. 'Just as Mark betrayed you.'

Sophie sighed. 'I suppose so.' She turned a troubled gaze on Simon. 'The thing is, though, being back here again, seeing this opera, reminds me Mark had his good points.'

The banker stiffened in horror. This was precisely the reverse of the effect intended. Shirley had suggested he take her daughter to the production not only because Sophie liked it, but because, according to Shirley who had pretensions to culture, it was about the worst husband in opera.

218

It was intended to ring vengeful bells with Sophie, not exhume happy memories. Sophie's remarks constituted dangerous talk, especially with the divorce on hold and Mark at a School for Husbands.

He thought fast. 'Surely it reminds you of how awful Mark was. All that hanging around Madame Butterfly does. Waiting for that guy who never turns up. Remind you of anyone? A certain birthday party?' he prompted.

A dark cloud passed over Sophie's face. Simon had a point. She felt her heart hardening against her husband. 'Let's not talk about it,' she said sharply. 'Let's talk about the opera instead.' Her eyes grew dreamy again. 'Such wonderful music. And so, so sad. Didn't you think her suicide was tragic?'

Simon didn't. Madame Butterfly, in his view, had no one but herself to blame and the fact she had not sought legal advice meant he was unable to feel an iota of pity for her. And, after sitting through some madwoman shrieking in her dressing gown in Italian for the past two hours, his sympathies were with the chap who had deserted her. He had every reason to, in Simon's opinion.

As he explained this, Sophie stared at him in bemusement. Then her eyes creased. Her shoulders started to shake. She clutched her glass for fear that she would drop it.

'Are you all right?' Simon asked, perplexed.

'Oh, Simon!' Sophie gasped for breath between fits of giggles. 'You *are* funny.'

Was that, Simon wondered, a compliment? Comedy wasn't something that particularly appealed to him. The only thing that made him laugh were the failures of his competitors.

Sophie was really laughing now.

Simon relaxed slightly. Even if he hadn't quite got up to speed with Sophie's sense of humour, he had to admit the evening was on the whole going well. 'More champagne?' he suggested, settling his elbow more comfortably on the bar's designer sweep of a counter.

'Yes, please.'

Spreading within Sophie, fuelled by the champagne, was an increasing sense of well-being. It was so wonderful to be taken to see something so stirring. And to spoil her with champagne as well! Dear Simon. She gazed at him fondly. He really was good to her. But Helen was completely wrong; that there could be anything but friendship between them was ridiculous. And that Simon wasn't interested either was obvious, anyway. There was not one single spark of sexual chemistry.

Simon, passing her another glass of bubbly, eyed her speculatively. Might this be the night to make a serious move towards permanent commitment, to get her into bed, in other words?

'It's very late,' he murmured, as suggestively as he could manage.

Sophie glanced at her watch and yelped. 'I'm really going to have to rush to make the last train.'

Simon could have kicked himself. He hasn't been trying to encourage her to leave, rather open negotiations for her staying in his luxury apartment. It was certain to impress her. A fashionable gated warehouse conversion with an inbuilt garage where the tyres of his Mercedes squeaked on the shiny floor. An aluminium lift direct to the apartment which played muzak. The flat itself was a retina-dazzling expanse of white space, acres of oak floorboards and a glass-brick breakfast bar upon which he had had the forethought to position two tall champagne goblets, just in case. For the same reason, a bottle of Laurent Perrier chilled in the vast steel fridge.

'But you won't get home until God knows what time,' he protested.

Sophie looked determined over her champagne glass. 'I have to be there for Arthur in the morning.'

Simon, personally, couldn't imagine anything worse than a screaming toddler after five hours' sleep—after any amount of sleep, frankly. But there was no understanding this motherhood business. He tried one last time. 'Sophie,' he murmured in his best persuasive tones, 'you really should stay in London tonight.'

Sophie shook her head, shuddering at the thought of the house in Verona Road, so full of memories, some happy, most not; yet empty now Mark was away and Arthur in Hampshire. She imagined it, dark apart from the orange streetlight sloping through the windows; silent apart from the occasional siren or ambulance heading for the estate. She could not imagine ever returning. 'I don't want to go home.'

'I'm not surprised,' Simon snorted. 'Horrid little poky place like that. And that street's possibilities are distinctly limited, I'd say.'

Sophie felt a sweep of indignation. 'It's not that bad. I used to quite like living there, in fact.'

'You could do better,' Simon said shortly, deciding to get to the point. 'A lot better. Stay in

221

the absolute lap of luxury if you like.'

'I can't afford a hotel,' Sophie said.

'I didn't mean a hotel. I meant you could, um, stay with me.'

'With you!' Her eyes, as she stared at him, were wide with amazement. Simon tried not to notice that the thought had clearly never even crossed her mind.

'Yes. There's lots of room in my place. It's big. Gated warehouse conversion, all mod cons, built-in stereo in the power-shower, cinema projector in the bedroom.'

'Cinema projector in the bedroom?' Sophie repeated, mystified. 'What for?'

'Oh, so you can show films on the wall if you want,' Simon said dismissively. It wasn't a facility that had ever interested him. He had never had time and he didn't like films. But all this was digression and was wasting time. Before she left he had to get her to agree to another date. The relationship had to develop fast. The Wintergreen dinner may have been cancelled but that didn't mean the brothers weren't on his case in a hundred other ways.

'Look,' Sophie said. 'I'm sorry, but I've really got to get home.'

'OK,' Simon sighed, 'I'll drive you to the station.'

*   *   *

'Now this morning,' Dr Martha smiled at the group, 'we move on to one of marriage's most central issues, and one over which a great many relationships break down.'

222

The men looked at her expectantly.

'I speak of the correct way to screw,' Dr Martha said, without batting an eyelid.

There was an explosion from Charlie. Rupert looked disgusted and Graham terrified. On the whole, Mark thought, he was with Graham.

'We'll also be looking at the whole issue of squeezing,' Dr Martha added brightly.

Mark had known that, sooner or later, sex would rear its problematic head. He had dreaded Dr Martha probing into everyone's intimate secrets in her brisk, matter-of-fact manner. Even more ghastly, he imagined, would be her practical suggestions to tackle whatever issues came up, as it were. He imagined himself being forced to improve his kissing by snogging the ends of milk-bottles. Or worse humiliation, that he could not even imagine.

He stared apprehensively down at the small white tube on the table before him. A similar one sat before every other member of the group. What, he wondered, was in that tube? And what was Dr Martha going to ask him to do with it?

'Gentlemen! Could I now ask you to remove the caps from your tubes?'

Mark's fingers had turned to butter. He was sure it was lubrication jelly. Or worse. Miserably, he scrabbled at the small red plastic tip.

'Great.' Dr Martha was folding back some sheets on an easel. The image revealed was a large illustration of a similar tube and cap to those held by the class. The tube was marked B and the cap A.

She gave her trademark dazzling smile. 'Gentlemen, could I ask you all to manually connect A to B? Like this?' She flipped over the sheet on the easel to reveal a tube with the top attached in the recommended manner.

'Fantastic!' she encouraged as everyone obliged. 'Apart from . . . oops, Andy, I think you might have got your threads crossed there.'

'It wouldn't be the first time,' Andy said glumly.

'*Fantastic*! Very good!' Dr Martha praised the class. 'Hold them up and show them to each other.'

The class raised their work obediently.

'Now remove A from B,' Dr Martha encouraged.

The class unscrewed the caps.

A hand went up in the air beside Mark. 'Can you tell me,' Rupert demanded of Dr Martha, 'why we seem to be putting the tops on toothpaste tubes?'

Dr Martha trained on him her laser beatific smile. '*You* might call it putting the tops on toothpaste tubes, Rupert. But the term we utilise at the School for Husbands is Dental Preparation Packaging Disorder.'

'Dental Preparation . . . ?' Rupert blustered.

'Packaging Disorder, Rupert,' finished the doctor. 'My work for twenty-five years in the field of marital therapy has shown time and time again that factors with an ostensibly negligible irritation level, such as the failure of husbands to replace toothpaste caps and persistent underachievement in squeezing the tube from the bottom, can in fact be significant contributors to relationships breakdown.'

She looked around the group. 'Hands up everyone who has experienced friction in this area.'

Everyone raised a hand except Andy. He stared at the floor defensively, exposing acres of unshaved neck. 'Ah yes,' Dr Martha murmured. 'Your toothpaste issues are of a slightly different nature, of course.' Remembering how yellow Andy's teeth were, Mark felt suddenly queasy.

Dr Martha smiled. 'Yes. There are a few grooming issues about. But we'll be tackling that in the next class, don't worry.'

CHAPTER TWENTY

The Dower House had been a port in a storm, to be sure, but now life seemed to have reassumed some semblance of routine, Sophie was starting to wonder about running her own affairs again. Having her washing done, being cooked for and not having to even think about cleaning was admittedly wonderful, as was all the help with childcare. But there were drawbacks; the commuting, obviously, but most notably Shirley's ceaseless nagging that she finished what she had started and rid herself of Mark permanently.

'Just divorce him. Now.'

'But, Mum, of course the divorce will go through. I've only agreed to put it on hold while he's in this School for Husbands.'

Shirley rolled her eyes in exasperation. 'It's just ridiculous. What is he supposed to be learning in there anyway?'

'Not how to keep promises, certainly!' Sophie sulked. 'There still haven't been any letters.'

'No,' Shirley agreed quickly, looking down to hide the guilt in her eyes.

Sophie sighed. 'I'd been rather looking forward

to them. He used to write such great letters. Really funny . . .'

Praise for Mark! Shirley's stomach surged in horror. Sophie had to be persuaded off this track, and fast. 'Well he's obviously forgotten how to now, or more likely can't be bothered,' she said sharply. 'Typical, if you ask me . . .'

Sophie felt a surge of defensiveness towards her husband. Shirley's constant attacks were having the unintended effect of making her feel more sympathetic than she would have liked to be towards Mark. This was another reason Sophie wanted to leave the Dower House. She had made up her mind about the divorce and did not want to unmake it. Taking him back was out of the question. He had hurt her very badly and would no doubt do so again if she let him. The way ahead was forward, not back. Forward with Arthur.

'Mark never made any effort, unlike wonderful, dedicated, hard-working Simon who took you out for such a wonderful evening . . .' Shirley was saying.

Sophie stretched her eyes. Why was her mother always banging on about Simon? He was another bee she had in her bonnet, and one that buzzed almost as loudly as the divorcing Mark one.

Arthur was another worry. He had not seemed to have settled as happily in his new nursery as hoped, although Shirley was doing her best to play this down, for some reason. She had been behaving quite strangely with Arthur in general.

That she loved her grandson was not in question. But his constant proximity seemed to have brought out Shirley's inner duchess to a ludicious extent.

226

'Don't you think you should decommercialise Arthur a little?' Shirley had asked her only last Saturday.

'Decommercialise?' Sophie blinked. 'I'm not sure I'm with you, Mum.'

'*You* know. Thomas the Tank Engine pyjamas, Bob the Builder jackets, Postman Pat wellies. When I take him out for walks in the village he looks like a Formula One racing car, completely covered in brands.' Shirley looked fastidiously pained.

Sophie pulled her open lower jaw back up to join the top. 'But he *likes* Thomas the Tank Engine.'

'Ye-es. But the overall effect, darling, if you don't mind me saying so, is a little bit *common*. Much better to have nice plain clothes, don't you think? It's not as if those particular characters he's plastered with offer much of a role model either. Bob's a *builder*, after all. And Pat's only a postman. And although Thomas seems like a perfectly pleasant sort of an engine, if a little silly at times, I'm not really sure that a career on Network Rail or whatever it's called at the moment is what Arthur should be aiming for.'

Sophie sighed. 'I see what you're saying, Mum. But I'm not sure that Bob the Brain Surgeon or Thomas the Top International Art Expert yet exist.'

'Well, I hope they're on their way,' Shirley sniffed. 'Parents are very aspirational these days. There's a definite gap in the market.'

*   *   *

227

Yes, putting some space between herself and her mother was a good idea, Sophie decided. But if she returned to London it would not be to Verona Road. It was too soon, too painful. Perhaps there were some properties she could rent for now.

She mentioned the plan to Helen at lunchtime. But if she had expected her to be pleased at this evidence of coming back to life again, of making decisions and plans, she was disappointed.

Concern flashed over Helen's face. 'You don't want to go back to Verona Road?' Sophie shook her head. 'Not yet, while everything's in the air. But hopefully I'll get the house once the divorce goes through.'

Helen bit her lip. 'You're still set on that then?'

'Of course.' Sophie nodded. 'Nothing's changed. And, if anything's changed with Mark, I haven't heard about it.'

'Still not written?'

Sophie shook her head. 'There's been nothing from Mark but a big, black void. Not that,' she added waspishly, 'there's anything new in *that*.'

Helen could see there was nothing to be gained from pursuing this line of argument. 'Hey, I've just had an idea!' she exclaimed. 'Teddy would love to see Arthur again. Why don't you bring him down this weekend? We could have lunch or whatever and then John could look after the boys. Maybe we could look at some properties to rent, to get you a base until things are, er, settled.'

'Great idea. Except that . . .' Sophie had clapped a hand to her forehead. 'Damn. I'd completely forgotten. I'm seeing Simon on Saturday.'

'Again?' Helen's disapproval rang clearly in her voice.

'Why not?' Sophie felt defensive and irritated that Helen seemed still to object to Simon, who had been so kind. It was as ridiculous as it was none of her business. 'So what's wrong with that?' Sophie pressed, as Helen did not answer.

Her friend bit her lip. 'Well, he was once your boyfriend.'

'About a thousand years ago!'

'And he seems to have been spending an awful lot of money on you.'

'Well, he's got a lot of money. It's nothing to him.' Sophie turned her attention fiercely to her computer to signify the exchange was at an end.

'Just be careful,' Helen beseeched.

'Careful about *what*?' Sophie groaned.

'Well, you're in a bit of a complicated situation, what with the divorce, and Arthur. You don't want to make it any worse . . .'

Sophie rummaged her hands through her hair in annoyance. What was especially irritating about all this was that she didn't even want to go to Simon's house. But he had been absolutely insistent after the opera, and in the face of his generosity then she had hardly been able to refuse.

'We're just friends,' she repeated. 'He's Arthur's godfather.'

'Yes, I know. But what I was wondering was— does he see it as friends too? He hasn't got anything . . . well . . . *else* in mind?'

Sophie summoned up what little patience she had left. 'Of course he hasn't. And neither have I. I'm not lucky in love and I don't want anyone else. The only man in my life now is Arthur. OK?'

*　　　*　　　*

While not quite what he had imagined in content, Dr Martha's curriculum far outstripped what Mark had anticipated in quantity and intensity. Every day he added a further pile of notes to the heap on the desk in his room. He was sure he was making progress. He tried desperately hard—to Charlie's obvious amusement—in every class, in the hope of favourably impressing Dr Martha. Increasingly, he could see the point of her philosophy. See, too, where he had been going so badly wrong for so long. His nights—the only time he was free to think, away from the pressure of self-improvement—were full of recrimination. What an idiot he had been. What a rank fool. He was going to show Sophie how sorry he was. When he got out of here, he would be every bit the reformed character the institution intended. He was counting the days. He missed his family desperately. What, he wondered about every five minutes, were Sophie and Arthur doing now? Had she enjoyed his letters? He had tried to make them as amusing as possible and added lots of funny drawings for Arthur. Yesterday's lesson had offered plenty of scope for both.

On entering the Great Hall, the students had been greeted by Dr Martha holding up, with an expression of fastidious distaste, a pair of large, saggy, and clearly ancient grey boxer shorts.

'The Intimate Garment Deterioration Ratio Theory.' Dr Martha's lips had pressed together. 'It's one of my more important discoveries. During twenty-five years of marital therapy I have proved and demonstrated many times there are few more accurate snapshots of the state of a union than a quick look at the husband and wife's knicker drawers. Any damage, neglect, discolouration and loss of shape within a marriage is invariably reflected in its underwear.' She shook the saggy boxers. 'Found in the school laundry this morning. I won't name names. For academic purposes, these are the Smalls of the Unknown Husband.'

Mark felt a nudge. 'Not all that unknown,' Charlie whispered, grinning, nodding his head over towards where Andy had flushed a deep purple.

'As I explained,' Dr Martha added, 'the disintegration of a relationship is echoed in its underwear. The corrective to this situation is to buy clean white boxer shorts in bulk and subject intimate garments to the same constant vigilance as the rest of the relationship.'

* * *

'Where are we going?' Rupert asked suspiciously a short while later. The group were back in the minibus, with Briggs, once more, behind the wheel.

Dr Martha smiled brightly. 'For some location-based therapy, utilising skills and equipment not readily available within the central campus situation.'

Jeremy sniffed. The sniff eloquently conveyed his view that very little equipment was available within the central campus situation, and none of what there was was up to the standards he would expect.

From the country roads, the bus entered the outskirts of a small town. It seemed to Mark a smart, busy little place with prosperous-looking shops of the butcher-baker-greengrocer variety.

The minibus halted beside an expanse of black glass which bore the repeated motif of a cowskull with horns and, beneath it, in Western-style lettering, the words 'Jon Wayne Grooming.'

Five minutes later, the six men were seated in brown leather bucket seats in a reception area with ginger suede walls and a black sheepskin rug on the floor. Dr Martha had left them and they had been asked to remove their baseball caps, which made Mark feel oddly vulnerable.

'Well, let's get cracking,' grinned the salon owner who had chivvied them in, a cherub-cheeked individual with tangled blond hair, a flowing white shirt exposing acres of blushing plump chest and leather trousers held up by a vastly studded and hugely buckled belt. 'Ready for a full and frank assessment, guys?'

He strode over to Rupert on heavy, clumpy heels and fingered his thinning dark strands. 'This kind of scrapeover look fools no one, basically. You know what the Japanese call it, don't you?'

Rupert looked thunderous.

'A barcode. Because it looks like one from above. Thought you'd have known that. You're the supermarket bloke, aren't you?'

Mark blinked. The assessment was both fuller and franker than he had imagined. He wondered what the dividing line between it and plain insulting was. Charlie had obviously reached the same conclusion.

'Blimey,' he interjected. 'Don't hold back, will you?'

The salon owner put his hands on his hips and stared at the builder. 'Hey. This is Jon Wayne Grooming. I'm Jon Wayne, right? *Me*, salonista. I

232

shoot from the hip. I tell it like it is.' He produced from his leather pockets two pairs of silver scissors, he hooked his forefingers through one loop of each and revolved them like a pair of pistols.

'Huh,' snorted Rupert, still furious about the barcode remark. 'I bet you've never handled a gun in your life.'

'And you have?' challenged the salonista.

'At corporate shooting weekends and suchlike, yes, certainly I have,' replied Rupert stiffly.

'Bully for you.' Jon shrugged. 'But do me a favour, yeah? Just accept you're going bald and go for a cool crop instead. Let's have a look at your skin.' He leant close to Rupert's face and squinted. 'Broken veins everywhere. Stress and overwork, mate, that is. Jesus, I could go potholing down some of those pores.'

Jon moved over to Andy and pulled gently at his wild thatch. 'I mean, don't get me wrong, mate, but how long is it since *this* saw a pair of scissors? Or even a pair of shears, ha ha. Make a great rug, this would. Are *you* hairy! Basically, you could go to a fancy dress party as a gorilla without having to hire a costume. Of course, body hair is a matter of taste. But it's not a taste most women like.' Andy looked utterly miserable.

Mark now saw the bulging blue orbs swivel in his direction. The heels of doom clumped over. 'Blimey, look at you. More shadows and black bags than a dustbin at midnight. Hair's not too bad though,' he added, pulling at Mark's crown. 'Apart from the dandruff, that is, the dirt, and the fact you obviously haven't rinsed it out properly for years. You just dunk it in the bath after you've washed, am I right?'

233

Mark nodded guiltily. 'I never seem to have the time to do anything else.'

Jon snorted. 'Excuse of the slob, that is. Do you think your wife has time to put all her slap on and do her hair? Of course she bloody hasn't. She *makes* time, doesn't she? More often than not to make an effort for you. And so can you. For her.'

Mark did not argue. He was quite prepared to believe grooming could improve his appearance, and that Sophie thought so too. Why else had she bought him that tube of smart moisturiser last Christmas, which had languished unused in the bathroom cabinet apart from the occasions it had deputised when he ran out of Brylcreem?

Jon was ruffling his hair again. 'Basically, the only proper finish for the hair is a rinse in Evian. Makes it lovely and soft.'

'Evian!' spluttered Graham. 'Just to rinse your *hair*? What an *incredible* waste of money.'

Jon turned on him. 'Waste of money! I'd think of it as a rock-solid investment if I was you. Those eyebrows, man. They need some serious attention. A tree surgeon, possibly. Talk about a wild bush. You got Sleeping Beauty in there somewhere, have you, mate?'

Graham stared, astounded. But Jon was now looking sorrowfully at Charlie, shaking his head. 'Skin like sandpaper, spider veins, fingernails full of concrete, where do I start?'

Charlie, who did not take kindly to having his status as group hunk undermined, flushed with fury.

Jon sighed and turned to the group in general. 'Basically, you all need resurfacing.'

'Resurfacing?' Charlie exclaimed. 'Like a road,

234

you mean?'

Jon beamed. 'If you like. But the road to new opportunities, mate. The road back to marital happiness.' He rubbed his hands together. There was an uncomfortable silence. It was Charlie who eventually put into words what the rest of them were thinking. 'Do you mean to say,' he demanded, 'that you know? About us and our, er, um, *challenges*, as Dr Martha calls them?'

'Well, yeah,' Jon said easily. 'You're wearing T-shirts and holding baseball caps with "The School for Husbands" plastered all over them.'

There was a nervous silence.

Jon shrugged. 'Look, guys. I'll give it to you straight. None of your wives think you look any good any more. You need to clean up your act. Literally, in some cases.' He parked one leather-clad buttock on the arm of Mark's bucket chair and grinned round at them all. The class stared nervously back. 'Relax. Enjoy yourselves. We're going to have a lot of fun together today.

'You'll have a facial massage to rub off dead skin cells, then we zap your wrinkles with a laser. You'll look ten years younger by lunchtime.'

'Wrinkles?' repeated a shocked voice. 'I'm not aware of having any.'

It was Jeremy who had spoken. Jon Wayne immediately clumped over. 'I was coming to you,' he said, looking him doubtfully up and down. 'While grooming is vital, there is such a thing as too much of it. You, basically, are one of the Pumpkin People.'

'Pumpkin People?' gasped the hotel manager.

'You look like some kid could scoop your insides out and stick a candle in your guts. Gone

235

overboard on the old fake tan, mate. And the hair?' He ruffled Jeremy's short, shining crop. 'Bit *too* black, if you know what I mean.'

'Thanks very much,' Jeremy huffed.

'Look, guys.' Jon moved back to the centre of the room, his leather trousers creaking with the effort. 'I'm not just insulting you for the fun of it.'

'Are you sure?' Rupert asked crossly.

'No, mate. Believe it or not, I'm trying to help you.'

*   *   *

As he lay on a ginger linen bed, his face pressed into a towel-covered pillow, Mark tried to remember if he had ever known agony like it. The masseur, a weedy-looking boy of about twenty, turned out to have the strength of Mike Tyson. 'Did you know you had a lot of pore blockages on your back?' he asked Mark. 'It's really quite spotty, to be honest.'

The powerful fingers probed mercilessly into the knots in his neck and pitilessly squeezed the tenderest parts of his shoulders. 'Ooh, you're *very* tense,' remarked his torturer, sticking a hard thumb into the top of his spine. Mark bit the towel to stop himself screaming in pain, and wondered what exactly about this was meant to be relaxing.

Worse was to come, however.

Rupert's eyes bulged as Jon told them exactly what. 'Look,' he protested. 'I come from a long line of distinguished generals. None of them ever went in for chest-waxing . . . I mean, I just couldn't.'

Jon shrugged. 'Up to you, mate. I can't make

you.'

'You most certainly can not.'

'Like I say, it's up to you. But believe me, women love it. All the top blokes are doing it. Film stars. Footballers. More waxed chests on the A-list these days than at Madame Tussauds. Male waxing appointments at this salon are, well, waxing. And guess who's making the bookings?'

'Masochists,' muttered Rupert.

'Wives, that's who.'

Rupert looked thoughtful.

Rupert's chest was, Mark noted, surprisingly hairy for one with so little on top. There was, he realised, a form of inverse proportion at work here; his own thick head thatch, for example, found but a faint echo in the patchy scrub of his torso. While a handmaiden worked on him, a handman slathered warm green wax over Rupert's nipples.

The handmaiden smiled. 'Don't worry,' she told Mark. 'Lots of men say that it's like coming to the dentist, but it's not that bad once you get here.'

Mark wondered if dentists assured clients that root canal work was like having your chest waxed.

'Right, just a minute or so for it to set,' the handmaiden announced. 'Fancy a shot of single-malt whisky, an ice-cold beer from the boutique or something?'

'Do you do general anaesthetic?' Mark asked.

Across the room, Rupert's wax had evidently set. The handman now prepared to remove it.

'Just relax,' he advised.

'Are you joking?' snorted Rupert. 'Now that I'm about to have my chest hair agonisingly ripped off?'

Jon, passing, snorted. 'Oh, it's the pain that's bothering you, is it? Thought you said you came from a long line of generals.'

Rupert muttered something inaudible.

Mark's handmaiden now returned and removed the wax with the ease of one pulling a roll of loo paper. Mark, on the other hand, felt as if his skin was being forcibly removed. On the adjacent bed, Rupert was roaring in agony.

'Very good,' said Mark's handmaiden. 'Bit of a reaction, but not much.' Mark stared down at the florid inflammation rising on his breast, and tried to imagine what could look worse. Bubonic plague, possibly.

Thirty minutes later, they had all been resurfaced. A woman with a tongue stud had waved a laser over him like a wand and finished by shoving a small jade roller up and down his cheeks as if she was mowing the lawn. Now he was busy trying to follow what Jon was saying about skincare. Charlie had been prescribed antioxidant moisturiser with age-reversing penetration.

'Age-reversing penetration?' Charlie challenged.

'George Clooney swears by it,' asserted Jon briskly. 'And you,' he was saying to Graham, 'should be using sea kelp to cocoon your epidermis and immerse it with energising marine ingredients.'

'Where do I get sea kelp?' Graham asked.

'It's special stuff, Graham. Sea kelp is harvested only once a year in specific regions of San Diego. The wealth of antioxidants in the formula helps combat environmental stressors.'

Graham looked very stressed. 'And how much does *that* cost?'

Jon shrugged. 'Upwards of ten thousand pounds for a treatment, basically. But you only need one of those three times a year. Now what *you* need,' he told Mark as Graham slumped, horrified, back in his chair, 'is a skin-firming lotion to protect against free radical damage.'

Graham revived. 'Did you say free? Why didn't you mention anything free to *me*?'

'This isn't the kind of free you want,' Jon said abruptly. 'A skin-firming lotion with rhodiola,' he added to Mark.

'With what?'

'Rhodiola. It's a super-herb with anti-fatigue and immune-enhancing properties.'

'Sounds like I should be taking it, not putting it on my face,' Mark remarked.

Jon nodded. 'You have a point, mate. It used to be a prized secret of the Soviet military. It works on a cellular level, enhancing energy and reducing signs of stress . .'

Mark wondered about the Soviet military secret aspect. While he could well imagine that organisation had many things to hide, he had never envisaged skincare on the list.

Two hours later, Mark's hair had now been cut and the grey bits discreetly 'tinted'. His eyebrows had been shaped, his nosehairs removed and his fingernails and toenails trimmed, buffed and rubbed with cuticle oil—'to make you even more of a cutie,'—the handman quipped. His teeth had been bleached—a hideous process during which, in a tongue restraint reminiscent of Hannibal Lecter, he had dribbled copiously as his teeth were painted with peroxide. 'We might not be able to get rid of all the stains,' the technician remarked doubtfully,

239

'but we'll do our best.'

But for all this and Mark's smarting chest and aching back, the improvements were not only noticeable, but dramatic. Now, as they all gathered back in the reception area, Mark could read the extent of their transformation in the satisfied eyes of Jon Wayne. Not to mention all the mirrors. The ones he looked in told him that his skin looked clearer and some wrinkles had definitely disappeared. His teeth, to his secret relief, were not Hollywood fluorescent; rather, just white enough. His hair, meanwhile, looked shorter and sharper, but tousled and trendy at the same time. Jon Wayne, much like Dr Martha, may have an unorthodox approach, Mark reflected, but he sure got the results.

Andy was the most unrecognisable. Cleaned up, de-bushed on top and with all orifice hair removed, he looked half the size and twice as pleasant. Rupert's closely shaved cranium made him appear quite unexpectedly trendy, while underneath Graham's shaggy brows, it turned out, a pair of really rather attractive green eyes had been lurking. Charlie, who was handsome anyway, looked more handsome than ever—and even more pleased with himself. Smoother, more polished. Only Jeremy looked almost exactly the same.

'There's nothing much we can do about that colour,' Jon told him. 'It'll fade in time. Although dermabrasion is an option if you're in a hurry. Basically, you take a revolving wire brush to your skin and grind the surface off. But it grows back beautifully—not to mention the right colour.'

'I think I'll wait,' Jeremy gasped.

'Well, for the moment you'll have to,' Jon told

him. 'You're done. But the rest of the group,' he looked round with twinkling eyes, 'have one more treat in store . . .'

Mark, Graham, Rupert, Charlie and Andy eyed him warily.

'The Jon Wayne Spray Tan Experience. Clients love how natural the effect is, with no streakiness or orange-peel issues to worry about.'

'What's the issue with orange peel?' Andy asked mildly. 'I quite like oranges.'

*   *   *

'Hey, guys.' They were on their way back to the School for Husbands. Dr Martha turned round from the front seat of the minibus. 'What's the great smell?'

'It's redolent with the very first stirrings of spring,' Charlie rolled his eyes ironically. 'Earthy notes of an early morning garden after rain and turned soil, vetiver and the stalk of the Angelique. My sort of smell, according to Jon.'

'It's lovely,' Dr Martha said, sniffing appreciatively. 'Too many men just don't realise how important it is to smell. Nice,' she added quickly. 'What's yours, Andy?'

Andy frowned. He could not remember what Jon had said. 'Notes of blackcurrant . . .' he began. Sandalwood and birchwood, was it? Something to do with birch and sandals. Essence of Birkenstock? Surely not, that was what his wife had complained about in the first place.

Mark wondered about his own bespoke scent. Kaffir lime, vanilla pod and coconut would, Jon promised, deliver 'ultimate tranquillity'. The

241

phrase worried Mark. Wasn't death the ultimate tranquillity? Hadn't Freud said as much somewhere?

He crouched at the back in the semi-darkness. While he felt much improved in appearance generally, the fake tan had been something of a setback. The handmaiden operating the tanning booth had passed him a card displaying the various positions to assume to ensure all-over coverage. Once inside the box, however, the size and shape of an old-fashioned telephone kiosk, Mark had realised he was too tall for the spray to reach his face. He had had to crouch, which had fatally compromised the efficacy of the positions. There he had huddled, stark naked, flailing intermittently about in order to catch the colour as it flew, with predictably disastrous results.

It had added insult to injury that Jeremy, whose tan was deep, possibly crisp, but at least even, had openly sniggered when, after hiding in the booth for as long as possible, Mark had emerged.

'Don't laugh,' Mark had snarled.

'I'm not.' Jeremy protested. 'Your tan's great, really. The bit that's worked is a fabulous colour.'

CHAPTER TWENTY-ONE

On Saturday morning, Shirley appeared just as Sophie was buttoning Arthur into his coat.

'What are you doing?' she enquired in a bright but strained voice. Shirley wondered what Sophie had on under her own coat. From the evidence of the battered blue trousers beneath it, nothing exactly fitting the occasion of a future chatelaine's first visit to her manor.

Sophie looked up and smiled. 'Getting ready to go to Simon's. We're getting the train to the nearest station and he's meeting us. Come on, darling,' she urged to Arthur. 'Stop squirming. We're late enough as it is.'

'We? Us?' Shirley asked in panic. 'You mean you're taking Arthur after all? I thought we'd agreed he was staying here and doing some baking.' It had been a sacrifice, this suggestion. She adored her grandson, but not the idea of him flinging cake-mix all over her immaculate kitchen with its pristine surfaces and shining utensils. However, if it enabled Sophie to be alone with Simon in his mansion it was worth it.

Sophie smilcd apologetically. 'I know, but I've hardly seen him all week. I miss him so much. And he *is* Simon's godson.'

Shirley willed her face to remain a mask of calm. Inwardly, however, she panicked. Simon had called her expressly to instruct that the boy should be kept at home. 'Are you sure,' she asked carefully, 'that that's a good idea? He's got a slight cold, after all.'

'I know,' Sophie admitted, 'but it's only a sniffle.'

'I tried,' Shirley sighed to Simon down the phone when Sophie and Arthur had left for the train, driven by James, who had an urgent appointment at the County Record Office. 'But I'm afraid Arthur's coming.'

Cold fury swept through Simon. The boy would be a distraction from the business of the day, which was very important indeed. Buoyed up by the success of the opera evening, he had decided Sophie's visit to his house would be the occasion on which he paid her the ultimate compliment of asking her to be his wife. She would think it precipitate, undoubtedly. She had only just started divorce proceedings. But there was, she knew, such a thing as instantaneous attraction, as love at first sight—or second, in their case. Which is what Simon intended to tell Sophie, even though the only instantaneous attraction he ever felt was towards his bank account. He also planned to point out that in this world one had to take opportunities as they came. And one look at his house, at what he owned, would undoubtedly suggest to Sophie the inadvisability of letting this opportunity, however suddenly it had arisen, pass. Simon, certainly, could not afford to let it pass. The Wintergreen dinner, which had been cancelled, was now back on. Isaiah's wife had apparently located and reinstalled in its place the rampaging rogue implant. 'Apparently she had some amazing cleavage on her ankle,' Bella had sniggered.

The Wintergreen dinner was not only rescheduled, but had changed in a sinister way. It was now to be a dinner dance, which struck Simon as the inner core of the seventh circle of hell. He hated dancing and had no co-ordination. This latter failing threatened to be on full view as the dancing in question was of the sort most calculated to expose it.

Yesterday, Isaiah had stopped by his desk and paused. He fixed Simon with a gimlet eye from under his bushy brows. 'You and your purty li'l gal good at line dancing?' he asked suddenly, making some presumably illustrative, stamping

244

movements.

'Line dancing?' Simon repeated, playing for time.

Wintergreen's eye glinted coldly. 'Yuh can't line dance?'

Simon was horribly conscious that millions might hang on his answer. 'Of course I can,' he assured the other man smoothly. Inwardly, he wondered frantically how long it would take to learn it. The party was in a fortnight's time.

This was the other reason he had called Shirley. 'I need,' he told Sophie's mother now, 'to ask you a very important question.'

'What?' Shirley quaked. She could tell from his urgent tones that it was something difficult. She worried, after the Arthur business, that she would have to disappoint him again.

'Do you happen to know,' Simon intoned, 'whether Sophie can . . . line dance?'

'Line dance?' Shirley clutched the receiver in amazement. It was the very last thing she expected to hear. *Line dance?* What was that exactly? That ghastly thing that lower-class people did in big hats and boots, while some council estate Dolly Parton yelled 'Yeee hah!' How could Simon possibly think that Sophie—*her* daughter—had an interest like *that*? It was a terrible slur. As Shirley took a deep breath to enable furious denial, Simon spoke again.

'It's quite important that she can, you see.'

Can? Shirley's brain reeled and skidded unhesitatingly into reverse. Yes, she thought, Sophie could line dance. She could bloody Morris dance if Mark required it. She could do whatever sort of dance was necessary to seal this union once and for all. Especially as Mark would be coming out of that wretched School for Husbands in an alarmingly short space of time. 'I think so. Yes. She's very fond of line dancing,' she assured the banker.

'Good,' said Simon.

He met Sophie and her son at the station in his leather-lined Mercedes.

'Oh,' Sophie exclaimed in dismay as they walked towards the gleaming machine. 'I thought we were walking. I don't have Arthur's carseat with me.'

Walking? Simon thought in amazement. No one successful walked anywhere. Didn't she realise that? She had a lot to learn if she was going to make a satisfactory Mrs Simon Sharp. Fortunately, he didn't mind teaching her.

'Don't worry about the carseat,' he said magnanimously opening the back of the car.

His initial frustration that Arthur was coming against his own wishes had vanished when an opportunity to exploit it had occurred to him. Simon was particularly proud of this example of what a generous and considerate stepfather he could be.

To Simon's satisfaction. Sophie now gasped. 'Wow, Simon. Thank you. That's amazing. So incredibly considerate of you.'

Fitted to the immaculate back seat of the gleaming, costly vehicle, was a baby throne of almost comparable luxury and almost comparable expense.

She felt amazed at the expense and trouble he had gone to on her behalf. And guilty that she had not anticipated the trip with more pleasure. Simon was doing his best.

She shot a glance at Simon's off-duty look: too-tight jeans and a burgundy V-neck T-shirt that did nothing for his Adam's apple. On the whole, she felt the suit she usually saw him in was preferable.

Arthur, unfortunately, did not share her guilt or gratitude. Least of all her enthusiasm for the child seat. Forcing him into its unfamiliar embrace, Sophie felt what remained of her nails split against the straps and buckles.

Simon came to help and stared, appalled, at the screaming, thrashing child. 'Strong, isn't he,' he remarked disapprovingly as Arthur was finally restrained.

From the squashy pale leather front seat Sophie looked around with interest as Simon sped through winding country lanes fringed with copper autumn hedges. The countryside glimpsed between them was pretty and rolling. As she began, finally, to relax, she looked forward to the nearing prospect of Simon's famous mansion.

She imagined what the house would look like: a pillared, white-painted entrance, fanlights, a redbrick front foaming with wisteria and two rows of five tall windows marching elegantly across the front. There would be a pretty formal garden with a fountain, which eventually gave way to lawns. At the side, a walled garden whose Gothic arched doorway would be slightly open to give a glimpse of brick pathways bordered with lavender. Her own idea of the perfect country manor, in other words.

'Here we are,' said Simon, as they turned into a wide driveway with a pair of imposing gateposts.

*   *   *

247

Mark yawned. He was exhausted. Last night he had lain awake, longing for Sophie and wondering again why she never answered any of his letters. Surely he had given enough detail of his good intentions and efforts to improve to merit an encouraging postcard, at least? To this disappointment had been added the agony of missing Arthur.

Mark could hardly bear to think about his son. Growing, no doubt, all the time. His hair would be longer. His face bigger. Where, Mark agonised, did Arthur think his father was? Probably he had already passed from the stage of wondering to not wondering at all. Children forgot so quickly, or so it was said.

Fathers didn't, however. Especially fathers forced to be absent. Thoughts of Arthur lurked to spring out at the most unexpected times. Mark could hear his low chuckle in the sound of the birds or the wind. The smell of soap in one of the school's Arctic bathrooms would remind him of Arthur after his evening bath, damp and snuggly in his towel. Whenever his foot struck something unexpected on the floor he was immediately back at the Verona Road house, stepping on a particularly knobbly part of Arthur's toy railway. He would have given anything now for the agony of standing barefoot on the Fat Controller's level crossing. It hadn't been long since he had last clasped Arthur's small, solid little body to his, but he was increasingly tortured by the possibility that he might never do so again. The fortnight's course would soon be over. Had he learnt anything? Had he improved? Would Sophie take him back?

*　　*　　*

'Halright!' sighed the thin-faced Frenchman in the tall white hat. 'We 'ave run through ze 'elf and safety, ze hequipment and all that. So I reckon we can finally start.'

The group from the School for Husbands was assembled round a large, tile-topped block in the centre of a large basement kitchen. It was that of a hotel which had probably once been the pride of the small town in which it was situated; the same that contained 'Jon Wayne Grooming'. But this establishment had none of the scissor-toting salonista's self-confidence. There was an air of langor about the place, and about the head chef too, who had presumably seen better days himself. At least Mark hoped he had.

Around the block at which they were receiving instruction, the hotel's various other chefs continued about their business. Charlie, Mark noticed, had already caught the eye of a grim-faced blonde working along a rib of a large animal with an enormous cleaver. As he winked at her she brought the shining instrument down with more force than was strictly necessary. Charlie and Mark winced.

The head chef, whose name was Anton, looked dolefully around. He looked as if he had not slept for days. The eyes above the bags were big, dark and melancholy and the moustache drooped, as did the long, thin mouth below it. He gestured wearily at the pile of vegetables in the centre of the block. 'Can you—Andy ees it?—start by chopping up ze courgettes?'

249

There was no movement from Andy's end of the table.

'The courgettes, please, Andy,' sighed Anton.

There was still no movement from the addressee. Now his bush of hair was no longer there to protect him, Andy looked hunted and uncomfortable beneath his spray tan.

'What's the matter?' Anton asked. Andy murmured something inaudible. 'What was zat?' demanded the chef, putting a hand behind his ear.

'Er, he says he doesn't know what a courgette looks like,' Graham translated. Jeremy guffawed.

Anton looked horrified. 'Mais, Andy, that ees impossible.' He rolled his eyes in agony. 'Unbelievable. Martha told me some of you were a leetle bit dim about cooking, but . . .' He shook his head. 'To theenk that once I cooked for Presidents. And now . . .' He looked tragically round at the assembled faces. '*Thees*,' he waved a shining green column at Andy, 'is a courgette. We are going to be making ratatouille with it.'

'Rat—what?' demanded Rupert in disgust.

'Ouille. Wee. *Oo-ey*. It's a mixture of tomatoes, courgettes and aubergine. I will explain about aubergine,' Anton added hastily as panic flashed in Andy's eyes. 'Eet's a Mediterranean vegetable dish that's very seemple to make and is wonderful with chicken. Eet's one of the arsenal of basic recipes Martha has asked me to teach you.'

The sentence had an electric effect on Andy. 'Arsenal?' he repeated, looking enthusiastic for the first time Mark could remember.

The group worked conscientiously through the day. The plan was to prepare an entire meal from beginning to end and serve it to Dr Martha.

250

'Much better,' sighed Anton mid-afternoon. The kitchen, which Mark guessed was never exactly frantic, was almost completely quiet. 'Your wives are going to be—'ow does Martha say?—blown away. Blown away. Your *wives*,' he added meaningfully to Charlie, who was once again looking longingly at the blonde, who was the one member of staff remaining. She was torching a *crème brûlée* with gusto.

Anton picked up a glass of cooking brandy from one of the steel surfaces nearby. He swigged it thoughtfully. 'You know, guys,' he murmured 'in my experience, if you can cook for a woman, you can do anything with a woman. You know, they love to see a man in full control of a *batterie de cuisine*. As a tool of seduction, eet is unparalleled. Look at Gordon Ramsay and Jamie Oliver. Neither of them are 'andsome, but 'ave you seen their wives? Beautiful . . . *mon Dieu* what ze hell ees that?' He had leapt over to where Mark was pulling something out of a big steel industrial oven.

'It's the chicken,' Mark said.

'I am a chef!' Anton snorted angrily. 'I know eet is a chicken. And I 'ope Andy does too,' he added, looking uncertainly over in his direction.

'Oh, he does,' Mark defended in a gesture of inter-husband solidarity. 'Matter of fact, it was Andy who put this chicken in this roasting tin . . .' He faltered. Perhaps Anton had a point. Something about this beast was decidedly not right.

'Which explains, I suppose, why eet's in upside down,' Anton groaned. 'With its legs in the air like a dancer at the Moulin Rouge.' He pressed both hands to his eyes. 'I used to cook for ze crowned 'eads hof Europe . . .'

Mark patted him on the back. He was beginning to feel sorry for Anton.

Eventually, all was ready and Dr Martha descended into the kitchen. 'Hey guys! Smells good! I love fish.'

'Zat,' sighed Anton wearily, 'is the 'addock Mornay for tonight's main course in ze hotel restaurant. A big favourite with ze regulars, because they don't 'ave any teeth,' he added, anguished.

'Oh, OK,' said Dr Martha amiably. 'So what have you guys got for me then? Am I hungry!'

The meal began with the nibbles Graham had been working on. 'They're called *Amuse Girls*,' he informed the therapist soberly.

They were named aptly, Mark thought. Dr Martha was evidently trying not to laugh as she took one of the bullet-hard baked balls with a frazzle of cheese on top.

The meal proper then began.

'Anton says,' Charlie told Dr Martha, 'that you can't go wrong with a simple shellfish starter.'

'Although I theenk,' Anton muttered as the doctor looked doubtfully down at the prawns drowned in pink sauce, 'that Charlie has.'

'Never mind,' said Dr Martha, bravely tucking in.

The chicken and ratatouille, for all its earlier difficulties, emerged unexpectedly well. Andy and Mark looked on proudly as the therapist made appreciative remarks.

It was now Jeremy's turn to shine. He minced away and returned with what looked like a brown curly wig on a plate.

'It looks delicious,' Dr Martha said cautiously. 'What is it?'

'Chocolate mousse,' explained Anton unhappily. 'It didn't set and he has put far too many chocolate curls on it. I try to explain that less is more.' He opened his hands like a tragic Christ.

An earsplitting bang interrupted proceedings, followed by a shower of warm, wet brown speckles. Dr Martha leapt to her feet.

'It's hot ash!' exclaimed Jeremy in terror. 'Oh my God, it's like . . . like Pompey or something.'

'Pompeii,' corrected Andy gravely. 'Pompey is the popular term for Portsmouth Football Club.'

Anton, who had wandered off to investigate, now returned with Rupert, whose hair and face were almost entirely covered in the brown stuff. From their dark surroundings his eyes blinked white and shocked. 'There was a bang,' he whimpered. Mark remembered he was descended from a long line of generals 'I don't remember anything else,' Rupert moaned. 'What happened?'

Anton sighed. ' 'E was making the coffee in the mocha and ze top exploded. He not screw eet on properly.' He looked despairingly at Dr Martha.

She smiled back at him reassuringly. 'Never mind, Anton. I did ask you to show them how to blow their wives away. It's a start, even if there is room for improvement.'

'Just don't ask me to do ze himproving,' groaned Anton, reaching for the cooking brandy again.

CHAPTER TWENTY-TWO

The gates of Simon's country mansion, while every bit as big and wide as expected, struck Sophie as rather more modern than she had imagined. There was also a name plaque on one of them. She squinted, then frowned. Was the house really called 'Swaying Willows'? She realised she had imagined something more like 'The Old Manor House' or 'The Hall'. But she supposed there was nothing wrong with willows.

As they proceeded up a winding tarmac drive Sophie craned for her first sight of the mellow historic front. But it was difficult to see anything. A long, low, grey building that reminded her of an airport terminal seemed to be blocking all the view. Probably the garage. Very big for a garage though, Sophie thought. More of a hangar, really. But it must be the garage because Simon had stopped outside it.

'Like it?' An indulgent smile played at the corners of Simon's thin mouth.

'Oh, I'm sure I will,' Sophie smiled. 'When I see it.'

Simon frowned. 'You're looking at it.'

Her mouth dropped open. The grey box was Simon's historic country mansion? She looked at the building in disappointment. Its walls were completely featureless, flat and grey, interrupted only by large, flat, featureless windows.

They got out of the car. The sleeping Arthur, unbuckled, now stirred and opened his eyes. He looked around in surprise for a few seconds then burst into noisy tears.

'He's not well,' Sophie explained, soothing her fractious son. 'He's got a bit of a cold.'

Simon raised his eyebrows. He had no sympathy with illness in other people, however young. Business lost billions of pounds a year through malingering. He was never ill himself.

'It's very modern,' Sophie remarked at length. It had been a struggle to comment on the architectural avant-garde whilst simultaneously placating a child.

'I wanted modern,' Simon stated.

'It's just that I'd imagined somewhere . . . well . . . a bit *older*, I suppose.'

Simon looked amazed. 'But why? Old houses are a complete pain. If it's not damp, it's rot. The joy of designing your own is . . .'

'You *designed* this?' The only explanation she had been able to imagine was that he had got it cheap from the previous owner.

He nodded proudly. 'Yes. So I had absolute control from the start. I specified everything I wanted. Swimming pool complex, office suite, CCTV room, panic room . . .'

'Panic room? Is that where you go when the share prices fall?' Sophie giggled.

'It's in case of a national emergency. A secure strongroom at the heart of the house. With its own supply of oxygen. You go there, lock yourself in, activate the oxygen and wait for the police to arrive.'

As Sophie absorbed this, realising with a shock that he was serious, Simon looked speculatively at the still-bawling Arthur. Perhaps the panic room had other uses too.

'The house is split level,' Simon raised his voice over the din as he ushered her to a front door that was a funereal slab of black wood. 'It has five double bedrooms, three bathrooms, five loos . . .'

A lot of loos, Sophie found herself thinking. Perhaps very rich people went to the toilet more.

The hall of Swaying Willows could not have been further removed from her fantasy mansion. The marble-floored hallway she had imagined, with grandfather clock, statues and a light staircase in pale grey stone tripping gaily to the upper floor, was nowhere to be seen. Ditto the pale grey walls enlivened with classical alcoves and pedimented doorways offering tempting glimpses into other downstairs rooms.

The hall of Swaying Willows was entirely black marble. Its mausoleum effect was increased by its circular shape. In the centre of the floor was a large concrete tiger poised to leap, its mouth drawn back over its fangs. It seemed to Sophie a strange sort of welcome. But it had, at least, the effect of silencing Arthur. He stared at the animal in amazement before crawling over to it, making appreciative noises as he did so.

As they moved on to a white-carpeted sitting room as big as a barn, Sophie suddenly found herself wishing Mark was there. He would have thought it as bizarre as she did. She squashed the thought. Mark was not there, and would not be again.

In the sitting room, three brown leather sofas huddled in a C-shape in the centre and seemed lost in the space. 'It's very . . . er . . . *warm,*' Sophie remarked, at a loss for what else to say. The room had no other particular characteristic.

'All underfloor heating,' Simon said with satisfaction. 'The latest technology. You don't need to take up space with radiators.' As if space was an issue in this vast building.

Arthur had started to cry again. The sound boomed round the empty house with its hard, reflective walls. Sophie picked him up, but the child continued to complain. She thought of the emergency chocolate digestives in her bag, then looked nervously at the snowy carpet. She guessed that Arthur found the stark atmosphere of the house oppressive, as indeed she did herself.

'Why don't you show us the garden?' Sophie suggested brightly. After all, on the other side of the characterless windows, the sun was shining.

The garden was as featureless as the house. Swaying Willows squatted in an Astroturf-effect pool of brilliant green lawn. Groups of manicured bushes crouched here and there, and there were, she noted with surprise, even a couple of palm trees dotted around a small pond. She had not realised palm trees grew in Hertfordshire. Perhaps it was global warming.

There were no willow trees that she could see; possibly the swaying referred to the positions they sank into as they were cut down.

The three of them walked around; Arthur, pacified now, staring about with his big brown eyes. Sophie was touched and amused at Simon's awkward but determined attempts to talk to his godson, even if he did it in the manner of someone addressing a board meeting. It struck her that perhaps they would get on better if she left them for a few minutes. They had hardly ever been alone. It would be good for them to spend some

257

time bonding.

'Er . . .' Simon was dismayed when she suggested this. The bonding he had planned was not with a nine-month-old infant.

'Don't be shy,' Sophie said, putting Arthur down and holding him upright by his hands. 'You can walk him around like this if you hold on to him.'

Simon practised gingerly. Arthur seemed amused at his amateurishness. When he had got the hang of it to Sophie's satisfaction, she decided to beat her temporary retreat. 'I'm just going to the loo—the loos, rather.' She grinned, turning back towards the house.

'Don't forget the front-door code,' Simon yelled as he grappled with the baby's wrists. 'It's 020305.'

Sophie stopped. 'But that's the date of Arthur's birthday!' she exclaimed in delight. 'Simon, how *sweet* of you!'

Simon inclined his head graciously. He had not got where he was today by missing details. It had been a useful thought to change the code this morning.

*   *   *

Back inside the sepulchral silence of the house, Sophie decided the loos could wait. Surely Simon wouldn't mind her exploring a bit. He was obviously so proud of this strange house.

Every room, she noticed, had a sign on it as in an office building, denoting its function. She paused before a black door on which a shining metal nameplate read 'Library'. Her spirits rose slightly. There was some culture here, after all. An entire room, devoted to books. She pushed the

258

door open to reveal a room empty apart from two tiny bookcases facing each other across more gleaming marble. The one nearest her held, so far as she could see, mostly sports biographies.

Next, she explored the kitchen. Its marble worktops seemed to contain every gadget imaginable, from bread-makers to cocktail shakers. Yet, apart from a few expensive-looking packets of black-squid-ink pasta in the cupboards, there was no food. Nor was there anything in the huge, humming, stainless-steel-fronted fridge but milk and a row of bottles of champagne. Did Simon ever eat? Were she and Arthur intended to, either? Her stomach grumbled. It was approaching lunchtime, after all. She was sure lunch had been mentioned in the original invitation.

There was no evidence of it here though. She could not help noticing that the oven was not only not switched on, but seemed very small, and the dishwasher tiny. The sink was similarly minute and lacked a draining board. She raised her eyebrows. Simon had five double bedrooms, five loos, palm trees and a swimming pool complex. But he didn't have a draining board.

She looked for the stairs, and soon realised there were none. There were, however, pairs of aluminium doors set into the walls of each room. Perhaps the stairs were behind those. Sophie went to the doors in the dining room and pressed a button. The metal slid back to reveal a lift.

After a smooth zoom of a ride, she stepped out into a circular hallway, the same shape as that of the entrance it was presumably above. The walls and floors were covered with black carpet-like material, the doors were black ash with brushed-steel handles and the whole, despite presumably being the bedroom level, had the same officey feel as the rest of the house. Sophie looked around, expecting to see large, illuminated green exit signs and signs directing the visitor to meeting rooms, lavatories and Reception.

She entered the nearest room, which appeared to be Simon's bedroom. The bed was featureless and huge, big, square and white. That the bedside tables were innocent of books was hardly surprising, given the library, although there was, Sophie noticed, a small pile of CDs on one of them. Anticipation rose within her at this window into Simon's soul and interests.

30 Line-Dancing Greats. Well, it was unexpected, put it that way. Underneath was another compilation: *These Boots Are Made for Line Dancing* and, at the bottom, *Grandma Chrissie's 25 Yee Ha Floor-Filling Favourites*. Sophie raised her eyebrows. For all its impersonal appearance Swaying Willows was revealing some astonishing aspects of its owner. Sophie stepped back into the lift.

A short ride later, the doors slid open. But not, as Sophie had expected, on to the ground floor. Instead, she walked out into a large light room where a big pale blue sheet of water lay unmoving. The famous swimming pool at last!

It was indeed a handsome pool. She imagined Simon doing his lonely laps, his head full of the finer points of usury.

Outside, she could hear Arthur yelling with delight at something Simon was doing. She glanced back at the swimming pool, thinking how much her son would enjoy it. What a treat it would be, a whole pool to himself. A change from the jostling, penned-up, lifeguard-hectored municipal experience of public swimming with babies in London.

She walked to the window and looked down. On the zinging green grass, against which Simon's pastel jeans stood out startlingly, he and Arthur appeared to be getting on well. Simon was swinging him gently around amid cries of delight from the child.

Arthur's yells seemed to be very loud. He was obviously having a wonderful time with Simon. She listened harder, twitching to catch every nuance of the sound. With a hot rush of horror, she realised that Arthur was not laughing now, or even shouting. He was screaming.

*   *   *

This morning's class with Dr Martha was about shopping. 'Although not clothes shopping,' she had reassured them. 'Most wives are realistic enough to know that's a complete lost cause. What I'm going to explore this morning is the thorny marital area of Retail Environment Temporary Personnel Loss.'

'What's that?' Graham asked tentatively. He had, Mark sensed, been worried from the start of the lesson. Shopping inevitably implied spending.

'Retail Environment Temporary Personnel Loss. Otherwise known,' Dr Martha told him, 'as Husbands Buggering Off In Tesco's.'

A surprised snigger greeted this. Dr Martha put her hands on her hips and looked at them sternly. 'This is no laughing matter. If you could hear, as I have heard, the number of wives who cite the way their husbands vanish the moment they enter large retail outlets as one of the more annoying aspects of a generally annoying relationship, believe me, you would take it seriously. Especially now you can actually get divorce advice packs in some supermarkets. It gave one of my clients an idea, I can tell you. She lost her husband by the cheese, saw the divorce packs next to Stationery and by the time they finally met up again in Household she'd filled the form in and was demanding a split.'

Mark was trying his best to concentrate but found his attention wandering. As the days and lessons went by, he was finding that the question of what happened next, after the course, was increasingly worrying him. Dr Martha was always encouraging, but had made no concrete commitment to any of them. Had he, Mark wondered, cut the School for Husbands mustard, and if so how, where and when was the reunion to be facilitated with Sophie? He resolved to ask Dr Martha when the class ended. There was usually a five-minute window between subjects.

He shot to her side as soon as the lesson was over. 'Dr Martha. There's something I need to ask you.'

She looked at him kindly over her very clean half-moon glasses. 'Yes of course, Mark. What is it?'

'Am I a better husband?' Mark burst out. Dr Martha smiled reassuringly. 'You have grown greatly as an individual, Mark,' she replied. 'Your individual improvement ratio evidences a positive response to therapeutic intervention promoting an enhanced understanding of issues surrounding your relationship-specific role and the resolution of former negative impact situations.'

She was praising him, as far as he could tell.

'It's my assessment,' Dr Martha added, 'that you have evidenced reversal, refocusing and renewal of certain core values, changed attitudes and behaviours, experienced spiritual growth and learnt personal emotional truths concerning fear, trust, honesty and dependency.'

'So does that mean,' Mark asked, his heart beating hard with excitement, 'that I've passed?'

Dr Martha beamed. 'You're well on the way to graduating with honours. You're my star pupil. I'm delighted with your progress. You have tried harder than anyone, listened to everything that was said to you, participated willingly and intelligently . . .'

Her assessment, Mark thought guiltily, would have amazed the teachers at any other school he had ever attended. If only his mother could have heard it.

'. . . Never once broken the rules of no alcohol, no mobiles . . .'

There had, Mark knew, been lapses on the part of most of the others. Andy had shambled into a recent lesson with a slobby day's beard growth, Jeremy had been spotted further deepening his already-too-deep tan in some unseasonable sunshine and Rupert had been seen obsessively devouring the business pages from a three-day-old copy of the *Daily Mirror* Briggs had left about. Charlie, most heinously of all, had been caught on a mobile he had borrowed from someone delivering milk. The someone had been pretty and female into the bargain and Charlie had not passed

263

up the opportunity to flirt. There had, Mark gathered, been harsh words for them all from Dr Martha, although they had just about managed to hang on to their places. Only he and Graham had kept a clean sheet; Graham having no intention of wasting a course which had cost so much money. And Mark, of course, was desperate to be reunited with his family.

'. . . So yes, all is set fair for you to complete the course successfully.' Dr Martha smiled. Mark felt he wanted to hug her.

'So what about my wife?' he asked. 'Will you let her know?' He wondered how Dr Martha would handle this.

Dr Martha nodded. 'At the right time. Just leave it to me. I have my procedures in place. Tried and tested over twenty-five years of marital therapy with . . .'

'Literally thousands of couples,' Mark finished, grinning, happy to leave the finishing touches to Dr Martha. She, after all, was the expert. He felt a surge of pure, triumphant happiness. All his hard work had paid off. Success was assured.

'One word of warning, though, Mark.'

Fear clutched at him. 'What?'

'You're not there yet,' Dr Martha reminded him gently. 'There are a couple more days to go. Anything could happen.'

'Like what?'

She shrugged. 'You have to complete the entire course, remember. There could be a problem. A module you find impossible for some reason.'

'Never!' Mark declared stoutly.

The doctor chuckled. 'So keen! It's wonderful. And of course it's very unlikely anything will go wrong at this late stage. You're doing so well and I'm proud of you. Now let's get on with the next class. If you'd all just wait in the corridor for a few minutes, Briggs and I need to do a little preparation.'

Beaming, almost dizzy with delight, Mark filed out with the others.

'What are you looking so pleased about?' Charlie demanded, still sore after the rocket he had received about the milk lady.

'Nothing.' It would hardly to diplomatic to tell him, Mark thought. On the other hand, he itched to celebrate somehow. Alcohol was of course out of the question. Perhaps now was the time to break open that bottle of Archbishop of Canterbury-blessed Marriage Water that was still in his room from the first night.

And with that answer he had had to be content.

*   *   *

Now, the School's director stepped forward out of the gloom to begin this morning's module. The Great Hall looked different. It was, for a start, much darker than usual. The reason for this, Mark saw as he looked up, was that the windows were covered with heavy black curtains. The room also looked emptier than usual as all the furniture had been pushed back against the walls. Dr Martha looked different too. Exactly how, it was too dark quite to make out. Something to do with her clothes.

'Next,' she announced, 'the class will be exploring and challenging their automatic responses to a proven relationship danger area.

265

Take it away, Briggs!'

There was a burst of violently loud disco music. Everyone jumped in shock at the sound. In one corner of the hall, a flashing red strobe now illuminated what was possibly one of the strangest sights Mark had ever seen. Behind a console whose fascia flickered with coloured lights, Briggs could be seen squinting at the record decks as, with hands that even in this light were clearly shaking, he lowered a CD into position.

Dr Martha was shouting over the din. Mark strained to hear what she was saying. '. . . defined as Male Relationship Provider Socio-Musico-Physical Inarticulacy Syndrome.' The class's expressions were uncomprehending, or possibly, given the sound levels, unhearing. '. . . facilitate therapy for individuals with movement underachievement issues impacting on social fulfilment . . .' she was bawling now.

'You mean husbands who can't dance?' shouted Charlie.

Mark felt his heart sink. It was true that he was bad at dancing. Sophie had always said so. But he didn't want to be good at it. He hated discos. Waving his arms and legs about made him feel silly.

The ceiling of the Great Hall was now whirling with alternate red and blue strobes. Dry ice was billowing up from somewhere. As, after some initial scratching and spluttering noises, 'Stayin' Alive' began to pulse through the vast and echoing room, Dr Martha bounced into the middle of the empty floor and began to execute some dance moves. It was now that Mark saw he had been right about her clothes. Dr Martha wore a hot-pink strappy top and tight gold trousers. Her face

266

contorted in a manic smile as she gestured to the class to join her on the floor. 'Come on!' she yelled. 'Throw some shapes!'

Jeremy looked appalled. 'Throw what?' he shouted. 'Grapes?'

After some more thumping and screeching feedback the music changed to 'I Will Survive'. The expressions of the class, however, seemed to be begging to differ. Graham looked incredulous and Rupert's purple features were contorted with horror. No one had yet moved.

Dr Martha gestured at Briggs to lower the music. It stopped as suddenly as if it had been cut off at the mains, which perhaps, Mark thought, it had. That Briggs had not quite mastered the volume control was evident from the shattering din so far.

'The music interaction programme,' Dr Martha explained gravely into the ringing silence, 'is designed to assist non-movers to work through their own socio-musical inadequacy issues and assist in the development of functional grooving processes and dance-floor coping mechanisms. It is,' her voice grew sterner, 'a *compulsory* element of the school's general refocusing and reprocessing programme.'

The class stayed where it was.

'So come on,' commanded Dr Martha. 'Grow, explore and discover together! Work through old traumas and humiliations. Heal together!' She jerked her body wildly as she spoke. The music began again. Keeping up an energetic foot-to-foot jig to the thumping beat, Dr Martha urged her class on to the floor. Mark, accepting the inevitable, was the first one to obey. The dance

267

class could not be allowed to be the impossible module, the one that stopped his progress. Not now Dr Martha herself had confirmed how brilliantly he was doing. Now success was virtually assured.

*   *   *

Apart from a slight worsening of his cold, Arthur seemed to have survived the shock of falling into Simon's garden pond. His misery and discomfort, in Sophie's view, had been compounded by the ridiculous inconvenience of having to dry all his wet clothes on Simon's heated marble floors, the lack of radiators making any other means of doing so impossible after it had been established that the clothes dryer in the purpose-built laundry at Swaying Willows did not, in fact, work.

Simon was apologetic, but not as much as Sophie would have expected. He had, in fact, gone so far as to hint that he imagined Arthur might be able to swim, or at least be taking lessons. His views about what babies were capable of seemed insanely wide of the mark. The accident had apparently occurred while Simon was explaining to Arthur the life-cycle of the tadpole.

She tried to persuade herself that the episode had a positive outcome in that Helen, Sophie had decided, was absolutely right after all that she should stiffen her resolve to leave the Dower House. To which was now added a new resolve; to see less of Simon Sharp. Like her mother, he had been very supportive in her hour of need, but what she needed now, Sophie felt, was to gather her forces and find a base of her own. Especially as

268

Mark would presumably be leaving the School for Husbands soon.

*   *   *

As he saw them off on the train, Sophie pale with shock and Arthur still sobbing, the possibility that the visit to Swaying Willows had not been an unqualified success had occurred to Simon Sharp.

It was an uncomfortable and unusual feeling to know that everything he had planned had gone wrong. He had pictured himself leading an excited Sophie about the hi-tech splendours of Swaying Willows, impressing her with the pool, astonishing her with the size and luxury of the bathrooms. And, finally, out into the pristine garden where he planned to ask her to marry him.

But it hadn't happened. And that idiot of a child was entirely to blame. He had, Simon reflected bitterly, been rightly apprehensive about Arthur coming. The foolish infant had fallen into the pond and Sophie, after reacting with disproportionate hysteria, had called a cab to take her to the station. The lift he had offered had been rendered impossible by Arthur's screaming uncontrollably whenever Simon came within a few feet of him. A few minutes after Sophie's cab—and the magnificent new carseat—had disappeared down the drive, another car had come up it.

Simon's heart had lifted slightly until he realised it was the delivery van from the Michelin-starred gastropub from which he had ordered his and Sophie's expensive lunch. Gloomily he had unpacked truffled pigeon and goat's cheese ice-cream and reflected that none of it had got him

269

any nearer the result he sought.

Simon did not like to lose anything, and this was especially bad. Not only was there the matter of the Wintergreen hoe-down—as Isaiah had chillingly described it—but, according to Shirley, that timewasting loser Mark would be graduating—if that was the word—from the School for Husbands in a mere few days' time. He would be at large again, in the community.

How was he to tackle it, Simon wondered. Sophie, if not firmly committed to himself by then, must obviously be removed from anywhere Mark could get at her. This would not be easy, especially as there was Arthur to consider. The added problem was, of course, that he could not keep the two of them apart for ever, not if Mark was as determined to see his wife as Simon imagined he would be. Only someone desperate to rescue a relationship would sign up for a fortnight of marriage therapy.

Simon paced the garden. Of course, at this moment, Mark was still at the School for Husbands. Was there not an opportunity there, then? Could he not foil Mark's progress? Sabotage his studies? Ruin whatever he had managed to achieve in the School? Get him expelled and discredited in the eyes of his wife?

He was thrilled by this stroke of genius. Classic Sharp, in every way. But he was also appalled at its lateness. He should have thought of it a week ago. But there was still time, just about. There were a few days of the course left to run. He had time to find out what the rules were and determine where Mark could yet come unstuck. Shirley had the address of this place because she had what sounded like a tower of letters to Sophie from Mark. Thank God he'd told her to intercept them.

All that remained now, Simon decided, was to put a certain someone he knew on to the case, someone who had come in handy many times in the past where industrial espionage was required.

CHAPTER TWENTY-THREE

The figure carrying a bag headed along the passage to Mark's room. As always at this hour of the night the place was silent, supper over, Interaction Time finished, and every pupil in his room.

The figure walked quickly, with purpose, and paused before Mark's door. It was not quite shut. The figure peered cautiously inside and backed swiftly away when it spotted Mark inside, lying on the bed. It melted into the shadows of the corridor, waiting for its opportunity.

Inside his room, Mark was feeling exhausted. The day had been devoted to Communication. They had entered the Great Hall that morning to find a table set with a pink cloth and candles.

'It isn't a restaurant table,' Dr Martha had informed them. 'Or rather it is, but what you must learn to see it as is an Interaction Enhancement Facility.'

'A what?' Andy had echoed.

'An opportunity to talk to your wife in pleasant surroundings,' Dr Martha had explained patiently.

Andy had paled.

'You may think,' Dr Martha told him, 'that you

are incapable of talking about anything but the Premier League, but I am about to help you surprise yourself, not to mention your wife.'

Andy paled further.

The lesson began with strategies for successful conversation opening. These were what Dr Martha called the Cheersome Threesome. 'You look great,' 'Have you lost weight?' and 'I love your new hair!'

There's no wife who won't respond positively to one of those,' she assured them. 'Learn them, but make sure you don't get them muddled up. 'Have you lost your hair?' is unlikely to gain you points, as is 'I love your new weight.'

Dr Martha had then tackled what she referred to as Oral Retention Failure. This loosely translated as Not Listening. Each member of the class had to read out a shopping list and ask the person sitting next to them to repeat it. The exercise was then performed again with a list of social dates.

Then had come the therapy Dr Martha called Silent But Deadly. Each member of the class in turn had to launch in on any subject of conversation that interested them—football and business excepted—during which any lapse of more than three seconds was indicated with a loud, farty-sounding buzzer. It was designed, Dr Martha told them, to encourage formation of sentences more than three words long. Afterwards the subjects passed from class member to class member who then had to continue the train of thought. This was called Picking Up And Running With The Conversational Ball. Both were, Mark felt, exhausting. He had found continuing with

272

Caesar's Wars in Egypt, the topic inherited from Rupert, particularly tricky, but not as tricky as Andy had found The Life of Yves St Laurent, as passed on to him from Jeremy.

The last session of the day had been a Gossip Module. Mark, along with the rest of the class, had been presented with a copy of *Heat* magazine, told to peruse it in detail and practise bringing up at least one item from its pages for every ten minutes of conversation.

As he lay on his bed, Mark let an arm hang down and felt about on the floor for the magazine. He may as well, he decided, strike while the iron was hot. But he was tired and the bright pictures and busy type made his eyes ache, as did the effort of trying to work out who most of the people featured were. But he knew Dr Martha was right about reading it. Mark was aware that his lofty lack of interest in and knowledge about the world of celebrities had always annoyed Sophie, who enjoyed trivia about the famous.

'Did you know Jennifer Lopez is planning to buy a hotel in the Lake District?' he muttered. 'And apparently Scarlett Johansson hates snakes.'

He lay back and shut his eyes. 'Where do you fancy for a holiday this year?' he asked the empty air, recalling a central plank of the How To Converse With Your Wife in Restaurants Module. 'I thought Tuscany. I know it got a bit over exposed in the Nineties with the Blairs and all that, but it's coming back into its own now and apparently the wine is fantastic.'

'Love the new hair!' 'Have you lost weight?' Damn. What was the third of the Cheersome Threesome?

273

Oh, sod this. He was going to have a nice, relaxing bath. He got off the bed and headed to the bathroom.

As soon as he had gone, the figure slipped inside, removed the bag's contents and placed them on the desk. It seemed about to leave when it paused, an idea apparently striking it. It retraced its steps and picked up a plastic bottle whose label bore the legend 'Marriage Water Blessed by the Archbishop of Canterbury'. Breaking the seal and unscrewing the top, it then crossed to the window; after a brief, intense struggle eased it open and emptied the contents of the bottle into the blackness outside. Then it turned to the object it had brought with it. A few minutes later, its business done, it left the room.

Mark, meanwhile, was in the bath. He had taken to having baths as often as possible recently, having once read somewhere that hot ones were good for depression. He had found it to be true; a real scalding tubful distracted the mind from whatever was troubling it. Perhaps the borderline agony was the reason.

The school's bathrooms, in addition, were unexpectedly cheery places. They were elderly, admittedly, and patched with damp. But they were also high-ceilinged and full of Edwardian high-specification ablutionary equipment: vast square sinks, copper piping and claw-foot tubs. They had a certain stirring majesty.

They were always freezing cold on entry but soon warmed up once the bath got running. The hot water seemed limitless and came gushing into the vast tub through huge taps, filling the room with steam and giving Mark a quite convincing

274

facsimile of a sauna.

Lying in the hot water tonight, Mark's mind rolled back over the day's classes. What stuck in his mind most was the art therapy. Everyone had been urged to draw images of what they most longed for. He had produced, with difficulty, having never shone at the subject, a stick man, a stick woman and a stick child inside a stick house. Dr Martha had stood and pondered over it for a long time.

'Now this is really revealing,' she had remarked eventually. 'What you're saying here is that you want to be back in your own house with your wife and your child.'

He moved his hands about in the bathwater, the noise and movement echoing the turmoil of his feelings. He longed to see Sophie and Arthur again. These few weeks way from them had been an eternity. Thank God there were only a few more days to go before he graduated, hopefully with honours, and Dr Martha's mysterious good offices would intervene between him and his wife. He had still not established how this would be achieved but he had no choice but to do what Dr Martha suggested; trust in her and his own ability to complete the course.

He got out of the bath. Swathed in towels like a Roman senator, his limbs lobster-red and full of the slightly stunned well-being that a very long hot bath brings, Mark made his slow way back up the corridor.

He noticed that there seemed to be activity at the far end. In the vicinity of his door, in fact. Figures were moving about. They looked like Briggs and Dr Martha.

Strange. What were they doing outside his room

at this time of night? Surely Dr Martha gave them enough to think about during the day without imposing herself in the evening for unscheduled extra tuition? And why bring Briggs?

When he arrived at his door it was to find that Dr Martha's expression was far from its usual one of benevolent interest. She looked profoundly sad. Strangely, she was holding in one hand the bottle of Marriage Water blessed by the Archbishop of Canterbury that he had bought to accompany his supper that first night at the school. And which he had never opened; the cost transforming it from mere beverage to a sort of souvenir.

'What's the matter?' Mark asked.

Dr Martha held up the bottle and shook her head. 'Oh, Mark. Why didn't you tell me you had these kinds of problems? I had no idea. Sophie never mentioned it in her written Spousal Assessment, even.'

'What kinds of problems?' That he had been gullible enough to fork out a fiver for a bottle of plain old H2O?

Dr Martha looked at him in apparent anguish. Her eyes shone with what seemed like genuine tears. 'Mark. You were my star pupil. Why have you thrown it all away?'

'I don't follow,' Mark said, rather nervously now. Something serious was obviously afoot. 'What have I thrown away?'

'Everything!' declared Dr Martha dramatically. 'Oh, Mark. How could you?'

'What? How could I *what*?'

Dr Martha shook her head sorrowfully.

'I was alerted by means of a note slipped under my door. It said you had forbidden substances in

276

your room. I got Briggs and we came here and found . . .' she waved the bottle, 'approximately *half a litre of vodka.*'

'*Vodka!*' Mark exclaimed. No wonder the Marriage Water had been more expensive than expected. He wondered briefly what that said about the Archbishop of Canterbury's take on the state of holy matrimony. 'But I don't get it. Alcohol's banned in the school.'

'Exactly!' wailed Dr Martha. 'You've broken one of the school's most important rules.'

'But you sold it. In your dining room.'

'Mark! Why are you pretending not to understand?' Dr Martha chided. 'The water has been substituted for alcohol.'

Mark screwed up his eyes, trying to follow what was happening. He was never at his sharpest after a hot bath. 'Substituted! But why? And you said you were *alerted*? Who alerted you?'

'The note was anonymous.'

Anonymous? This was like a bad dream. There had to be an explanation.

'But I didn't swap the water,' Mark protested. 'I've never had alcohol in my room. Not even aftershave. Someone must have put it here. Just now. While I was in my bath.'

Dr Martha shook her head sorrowfully. 'I'm afraid that explanation just won't do, Mark. You've been caught red-handed, you see.'

Mark stared at her in horror. Was it possible she didn't believe him?

'You know, of course, that anyone found drinking alcohol or in possession of alcohol faces instant dismissal from the school,' Dr Martha now said.

'But, Dr Martha. It wasn't me.' He was, Mark knew, looking at disaster. Ejection from the institution he had pleaded so hard to be allowed to enter would confirm Sophie's worst suspicions. The divorce would go through, he would never see her or Arthur again . . .

'You should have thought of all that before you did this,' was Dr Martha's sad response. 'School rules are school rules. I can't make exceptions under any circumstances. Much as I would like to.' She turned away and began to walk down the corridor, Briggs shuffling beside her.

'Please! Dr Martha . . .' Mark screamed after her. 'You can't do this to me!'

But her retreating back said that she could. And would. There would be no mercy. He was out on his ear. After having wanted so much to be admitted, worked so hard whilst enrolled, and made definite progress, he had now been expelled from the School for Husbands. But how had it happened? Who had planted the vodka?

*   *   *

The day after the visit to Swaying Willows, Sophie had been too occupied with Arthur and his sniffles to give Shirley the news about her decision to leave the family home. But Monday morning, the day after that, was a perfect opportunity. Arthur seemed to have improved and any histrionics Shirley might throw could be curtailed by the necessity of Sophie having to leave for work. She dressed, got Arthur ready and went downstairs with her son in her arms. Her mother wouldn't like it, but there was no doubt it was the best for

278

everyone.

'Hello, darling,' smiled Shirley, coming into the hall. 'Or darlings, I should say.' She planted a loud kiss on Arthur and tried to look as normal as possible. Shirley did not feel normal, however. Sophie's account of the trip to Swaying Willows had made her blood run cold. Simon's own rendition, delivered some hours afterwards by telephone, was, on the other hand, coldly furious. Listening to the barrage of complaints and blame the banker had directed at her, Shirley wondered why, exactly, she was putting up with it. Thank goodness she had, as yet, been able to conceal her involvement with Simon from James. He would have been apoplectic—or as near to it as he ever got—to hear how Simon spoke to his wife. But James was now far too immersed in his family tree to take any notice of what his real-life contemporary family was up to. He was away now, at a Genealogy Weekend Workshop.

Listening to Simon's sneering, contemptuous tones as he berated her for not preventing Arthur coming, Shirley had wondered whether she really wanted Simon Sharp as her son-in-law. Mark had been lazy and insolent, but at least he had never been nasty. Nor did he bully her as Simon was able to.

Shirley's stomach churned at the thought of Simon Sharp now. He was interfering with her sleep and coming between her and her appetite. She was beginning to regret ever having got involved with him, but it was too late now.

Take this new, latest plan he had bullied her into facilitating. The idea, he told Shirley, was to get Sophie safely out of the way while Mark came out of the School for Husbands. It seemed precipitate to Shirley, by whose calculations Mark would not be emerging for several days yet. 'Trust me,' Simon had snapped. 'I think we both know who's the best at maths, don't we?'

Shirley did not look at all normal, Sophie thought. She was standing by a window and of course the strong morning light did no one any favours, but even so, Shirley looked drained and depressed. She looked thinner than ever and her normal bouncy uprightness, reflected in everything from her hair to the collars of her crisp white shirts, seemed to be lacking; her hair looked limp and obviously free of the attentions of the heated brush and today she wore a T-shirt under her gilet, not an ironed blouse. There was, Sophie thought, something defeated about her and she knew instantly what that thing must be. The strain of coping with herself and Arthur, especially the latter.

She looked defeated herself, Sophie knew. The speed with which she normally dressed never usually left time for lengthy scrutiny of either her figure or her face—the need to sort out Arthur and get to the station made sure of that. But today she had really noticed, as her trouser waistband slipped to her hips, how much weight she had lost in the last week. It was perhaps less surprising that her face had lost the rosy look it had had previously—the misery of a broken marriage had seen to that. But that she was quite so drawn—grey under the eyes, the lines pulling unhappily downwards either side of her mouth, the loss of weight adding years—had been an unpleasant shock. The fact there had not been time or opportunity for a haircut did not help—she was now at the stage of shoving it all back into a ponytail, a look that worked if you were twenty-one or Kate Moss, but being thirty-seven and Sophie Brown, it just looked scruffy. Especially as a good deal of regrowth had appeared. She could, Sophie thought grimly, show her father everything he wanted to know about the family roots.

She looked tired and weak, and felt it. Divorce had been meant to be empowering but had turned out to be the exact opposite: the most enormous emotional and physical, not forgetting financial, drain. Thank goodness she was leaving her parents'. With what little resources she had left, she had to get her life back on the rails.

She pecked her mother on the cheek. She felt completely in control about the leaving speech she was about to make.

She was surprised, now, to notice the neat, new suitcase standing in the middle of the floor. 'I didn't realise you were going anywhere.'

'*Me* going anywhere?' Shirley gave a puzzled smile. 'What do you mean, darling?'

Sophie pointed at the suitcase. 'That.'

'Darling, that suitcase isn't mine. It's *yours*.'

'*Mine?* I've never seen it before in my life.'

'That's because I've just bought it for you. A present. Yours was a bit—well—*battered*, if you don't mind me saying so.'

'Oh.' Sophie tried to look pleased. But she was puzzled. Everything she owned was battered. What made her mother think she needed a new case more than she needed anything else?

'I've packed for you as well,' Shirley offered.

'*Packed?*' Sophie frowned. Then she smiled too.

281

'Oh. I *see.*'

The relief was enormous. She would not, after all, be obliged to hurt feelings and make excuses about leaving the Dower House. Shirley must have been thinking along exactly the same lines—that her daughter needed to regain her independence. She had hit on the new-case ruse as a way to sugar the pill. Sophie blinked in admiration of the deftness displayed. Such subtlety was a first for her mother.

'Yes, you're absolutely right, Mum.' Sophie smiled, cuddling Arthur happily. 'I've got to move back to London. I mean, I just need to find somewhere to live until the divorce goes through and I could easily find another nursery for Arthur, and . . . what's the matter, Mum?'

Shirley's precision-applied lipstick framed an 'O' of horror. 'Move back . . . to *London*?' Oh no. This was not the plan. This was not Simon's idea at all. Shirley felt panic rise. She didn't think she could bear another of his acid condemnations.

If her mother had had the same idea, why did she look so shocked? Sophie nodded at the case. 'Haven't you bought it for me to take back to London?'

Shirley's head was shaking so hard it seemed likely to come off. 'It's not for London,' she spluttered. 'It's for Paris.'

'Paris?!' New starts were admittedly on the cards, but she didn't know anyone in Paris, and her French was, frankly, pathetic. What on earth was her mother thinking of? At the prearranged signal from Shirley—a discreet tap on the inside of the front door—Simon, on the other side of it, now knocked hard.

Sophie gasped as he was ushered in. Things were complicated enough this Monday morning, without him too. What was he doing here? And why did he look so pleased with himself? His eyes seemed to burn with something she couldn't quite identify. Purpose, perhaps. Intent.

She had never thought of Simon as a particularly big person, although he was tall. But now he seemed taller than before, his shoulders in their overcoat seemed to stretch and fill the hall. He had always been focused and in control but now he stood there positively radiating confidence; there seemed something hugely powerful about him that made Sophie feel tireder than ever.

He immediately chucked Arthur under the chin. Confronted by the tall, dark and frightening figure, whom he possibly still associated with a sudden plunge into icy and blurry depths, Arthur clung to his mother and started a snuffly wail.

'Simon!' Sophie exclaimed, bewildered. 'What . . .'

'Am I doing here?' Simon rejoined smoothly. He assumed his most inviting voice. 'Hoping to persuade you to come on a little surprise trip to Paris with me!' He slipped a hand in his pocket and produced some Eurostar tickets. 'They're first class, obviously. They give you champagne and a three-course breakfast.'

'Paris?' Sophie frowned, thinking that champagne was the last thing she felt like. She looked at the suitcase and then at her mother. 'So this is what this case is for. But *you* knew about it, Mum?'

Shirley tried to smile eagerly, but her lips just wouldn't go that far. She was trying to remember the official version of how exactly she was involved, but was too overwrought, confused and tired. She hoped Sophie would not ask anything difficult.

Guessing the situation, Simon steamed smoothly to the rescue. 'I had to let your mother into the secret,' he said silkily. 'I needed someone to get everything ready so I could just whisk you off.'

Arthur coughed. Sophie soothed him and wiped his streaming nose. He whimpered.

Simon eyed the child with irritation. The boy was such a ham, always acting up and distracting its mother at vital times like this. Yet he had no intention of letting anyone divert him from his purpose. He had to get himself and Sophie out of the country, both to avoid any risk of her meeting her newly freed husband and any suspicion attaching to himself that he was involved in the circumstances which had freed him. Simon had been called early that morning and informed that the agent he had hired to scupper Mark had done the job as directed. And while this was intensely satisfactory, it was only half of the task. He could tell from her face that Sophie had not yet been persuaded to go to Paris.

'I thought,' Simon smiled, 'that you might prefer to be in Paris today rather than at boring old work. Don't worry,' he held up a hand. 'I've fixed everything with your boss. I spoke to her just now, in fact.'

'You spoke to *Lisa*?' A man not her husband had called the world's nosiest and ill-natured woman and asked permission to take her away on a surprise trip to the world's most romantic city. Lisa must have near-spontaneously combusted with what this implied about Sophie's marriage.

'Yes, luckily she was in the office early. A very hard-working woman,' Simon said approvingly.

Sophie did not enlighten him as to Lisa's usual reason for arriving before anyone else: to snoop about the desks of her colleagues.

'Very obliging and accommodating, I must say,' Simon added appreciatively. 'She was very interested in the whole idea.'

'I bet she was,' muttered Sophie, trying to soothe the fractious Arthur.

Simon smiled, showing his small, pointy teeth. 'So, come on. What do you say?'

'Go on, darling,' Shirley pressed brightly. 'I've packed your suitcase for you. You'll see it's full of lovely things. All new. You deserve a treat.'

Sophie clutched her son. 'I'm not sure. I don't want to leave Arthur. He's got a nasty cold. It's definitely worse than it was.' With difficulty she resisted adding, 'Since he fell in your pond.'

With even more difficulty Simon prevented his features from contracting into a thunderous frown. That bloody child spoilt everything. Well, it couldn't be allowed to. Sophie had to come to Paris, and not just for the reasons associated with Mark's being thrown out of the School. The Wintergreen dinner was rapidly approaching and he had to get Sophie on side once and for all. He had to return from Paris with a clear commitment from her, or all would be lost. He trained a laser beam glare on Shirley, who, he sensed with satisfaction, was frightened of him. 'Sort this out,' the glance ordered.

'It'll be fine, don't worry,' Shirley assured her daughter jumpily. 'Children are always getting colds. It's no reason not to go on this lovely trip.'

285

Sophie looked doubtful. She loved Paris, but did she want to go there now with Simon? On the other hand, did she want to face Lisa after Simon's call? The office would be seething with speculation. If she went in, the obvious fact she had split with Mark would be compounded by her appearing to have split with Simon as well. The prospect was excruciating.

Feeling herself wilt under Simon's expectant stare, Sophie looked helplessly at her mother. 'I just don't think I can . . .' she faltered.

'Go on, darling,' Shirley begged. 'Arthur will be fine with me, I promise. I looked after you for long enough; I know what I'm doing with babies!' She tried to sound bright. 'And after all, darling, you were happy to leave him here today while you went to work. Paris isn't that much further.'

'Good point, Shirley,' Simon cut in, pleased. It was almost the first intelligent thing he had heard the woman say.

It was a good point and Sophie felt her resistance melting. Her mother obviously wanted her to go; could she not grant her this last favour after she had been so supportive?

She shot a timorous glance at Simon standing in the hallway, dominating both her and Shirley, and felt both helpless and resentful. But the Paris trip, annoying though it was to be railroaded into it, was at least the perfect opportunity to tell Simon that, grateful though she was for all his efforts, she had decided to manage without his help as well. She wanted to see less of him from now on. A lot less.

CHAPTER TWENTY-FOUR

The hotel was certainly impressive, all glittering gilt and mirror. The necklaces on sale in the foyer display cases were as vast and sparkling as any oligarch's wife could wish. Uniformed flunkies whisked away the smart packages Sophie had allowed herself to be bought, more to humour Simon than because she really wanted an azure ostrich-skin passport cover and a pair of violet marabou-trimmed mules. Up they went in the suite's personal lift. She was beginning to think of elevators as Simon's leitmotif.

Yet, for all the splendour, she was miserable. The thought of Arthur tugged on her heart. She had been all but wrenched away from him.

The suite they were now shown into could have housed a small aeroplane comfortably; the carpet was like wading through a cornfield, albeit one printed in swirling pink and yellow flowers. There was a special designer mixer tap in the dazzlingly bright marble bathroom that stretched the width of the tub and looked like the mouth of a chrome fax machine. A hi-tech telephone was positioned right next to the lavatory; a faintly disgusting juxtaposition in Sophie's view. And outside the bathroom door, above the enormous minibar, was a small shop unit selling honey allegedly produced by the bees who lived on the top of the Paris Opera. Sophie thought that she would far rather have sampled what was produced below the roof rather than above it.

She glanced apprehensively at Simon, who was

frowning at the financial channel on the widescreen television that he had uncovered behind two vast burlap doors within seconds of arrival. He had spent much of the train journey on the mobile which, while rude, had at least saved her the effort of having to make conversation. Some difficult piece of business was in motion, she had gathered.

She took a step towards him. Perhaps this was the time to gently suggest that, grateful though she was for his friendship and support, she could stand on her own feet from now on.

The doorbell rang. A buttermilk-jacketed waiter appeared with a bottle of champagne in a silver bucket which was accompanied by a vase containing a pink orchid. Sophie's spirits lifted at the sight of alcohol.

Simon happily passed her a foaming flute. He was feeling triumphant. He had foiled Mark spectacularly and could not be suspected himself. And now, the icing on the cake, a complex takeover he had been working on for several weeks had finally overcome its difficulties and was going well. It had cost him valuable time on the journey; time he should have spent charming Sophie. But that could not be helped. He looked speculatively at Sophie. She seemed contented enough, anyway. And now, Simon thought, it was time to complete the other important takeover he planned. The one of Sophie.

He watched approvingly as Sophie emptied her glass. He filled it again. She was obviously enjoying herself. This was encouraging behaviour, no doubt about it. More encouraging still was the fact she had not remarked on the one double bed in the suite's adjoining bedroom. What further proof did he need that she had accepted his advances and was willing to surrender? Tonight was going to be the night. This whole tiresome, time-wasting courting business was about to move up a level. And not before time, frankly.

Sophie, meanwhile, had walked over to the vast windows and the huge view of a magnificent winter sunset over Paris. Its beauty made the guilt she felt well-nigh unbearable. She quelled the notion that the same sun would be reflecting its dying rays on Arthur's nursery wall. She grasped the refilled glass that Simon passed her. Surely he would be glad to hear she felt independent enough to lead her own life from now on? That he need not spend every weekend supporting her.

'Simon.' She turned to him with a smile. 'There's something I wanted to let you know. It's about you and me.'

'And there's something I want to tell you,' he butted in, excitement that she seemed to return his intentions removing any caution. 'You're a fabulous woman, Sophie.' It was extremely satisfactory. They could get their own terms and timetable agreed and he could get back to the takeover. 'And a wonderful, intelligent, caring person,' he added. He had been intending to add 'fantastic mother' as well, but did not want to risk dragging the whole boring Arthur business up again.

Sophie stared at him, puzzled. 'Thanks, Simon.'

'And very beautiful . . .'

Embarrassment surged within her. Where, exactly, was this conversation going? Not where she had intended it, she suspected.

She looked out of the plate-glass penthouse window. The view was glorious. Over to the west, the sun was now sinking into a curtsey of billowing flame clouds. The intense tawny light lit the trunks of the leafless trees far below them in the Tuileries Gardens. It was set to be a clear and possibly frosty night. Above the sunset, the duck-egg sky was darkening and the first star could already be made out. Or was it a planet? Sophie didn't know, although she would have liked to. It was the kind of thing Mark was good at. He had had a small boy's enthusiasm for astronomy, although a grown man's scorn for the newspaper horoscopes she herself could never resist. She felt her lips press together in a rueful smile.

'Is that Venus up there?' she asked Simon abruptly. It would be wise, she thought, to move on to a topic other than her own personal charms. She realised immediately the choice had been unfortunate.

'The planet of Love,' Simon intoned rapturously. 'I'm sure it must be.'

'Or Mars,' Sophie interrupted, hastily. 'The planet of War.'

Simon turned to her. 'Winter,' he breathed, 'is such an exquisite season.'

'Isn't it?' Sophie agreed nervously.

'It reminds you,' Simon skewered her with a meaningful gaze, 'that it's not all just about the blaze and fanfare of summer.'

'I suppose it does.'

'It reminds you that it's never too late.'

'Yes,' yelped Sophie nervously. 'What time is dinner, exactly?'

'I'm so glad, my darling,' breathed the banker,

suddenly moving close and clasping her hand. 'You'll be the most perfect mistress of Swaying Willows.'

Sophie's head seemed suddenly full of noise. With shattering suddenness, everything crashed into place. Helen's suspicions about Simon had been spot on. That she herself had not realised before could only be due to colossal self-delusion and wilful ignorance. It *was* more than friendship, was more than the simple wish to cheer her up. Simon wanted to marry her! He wanted her to live at Swaying Willows.

She pulled her hands out of his in horror.

'You can do whatever you like to Swaying Willows, you know,' Simon added, in a rush of generosity.

Sophie fought for words. Swaying Willows was possibly the most hideous, soulless house she had ever seen in her life. The only thing she would want to do to it was knock it down. 'I couldn't possibly . . .' she gasped.

'Well, I suppose it *is* perfect as it is.' Simon smiled complacently.

Sophie forced back a loud exclamation of disgust. Swaying Willows, with its marble halls, its sterile lifts, was a house so disgusting it made her think with warmth for the first time in ages about the house in Verona Road. Scruffy it might be, with dust-clouded windows and with paintwork sporting more chips than Harry Ramsden's, but it had soul at least. With pictures and proper books. Music, too. There had been no music at Swaying Willows. Apart, of course, she recalled with a fresh stab of horror, from the line-dancing CDs.

Her mouth opened and closed. It was

impossible, embarrassing, awful. How could he possibly think she would want to marry him? Her just-ended marriage lay in smoking ruins around her. She had a child. Was Simon Sharp mad?

It was now that, through the open door of the bedroom, Sophie noticed the large double bed. The one and only double bed. There were no other doors in the suite, and therefore no other bedrooms. Why had she not noticed this before?

Simon's eyes followed hers. He had watched the procession of emotions across her face and entirely misread it. Now he mistook the leap of horror in her eyes for one of excited anticipation. His teeth gleamed in a smile of victory. Slowly he leant towards her and pressed his lips to hers. He felt a thrill of triumph. At last. He'd got her.

'Simon!'

To his amazement, he felt hands at his throat. But not pulling him towards her as he might have expected. These hands were pushing him away.

'Simon! What the hell do you think you're doing?' She pushed again, hard. 'Get off me, for Christ's sake!'

She looked desperately around for an aid to her predicament. Her glance fell on the champagne ice-bucket. While she continued to push him away with one hand, she lunged at it with the other. With the tips of her fingers, she seized its chilly, slippery metal rim.

As the icy cascade suddenly swamped his head and shoulders, Simon screamed. Shock ricocheted round his veins like a pinball. When the water cleared from his eyes, the world looked blurred and lopsided. One of his contact lenses had washed out, damn it.

The room was silent, apart from Simon's subsiding gasps. Sophie adjusted her clothes, feeling horribly foolish, frightened and guilty in equal measures. Now he had declared his intentions, they were always obvious. Only she had been too preoccupied to notice; rather, had never imagined it possible that anyone could be so crass.

'Look,' she said, agonised. 'I'm sorry. It's all been a misunderstanding.'

Simon stared at the part-fuzzy image that was Sophie. His body twitched with panic even more than with cold. He had put so much into this takeover bid; time, money, ingenuity. And the Wintergreen hoe-down was, like the Deadwood stage, coming on over the plain. Fast. He could not allow all his effort to end in failure. His entire future depended on its success.

As he extended imploring, dripping arms a lump of ice slid from his head, down his nose and into his groin. 'Please,' he begged Sophie. 'You're my dream woman. Come on. Think of what I can offer you and Arthur. Financial security . . .'

Sophie's insides twisted with shame. And surprise; she had no idea he had felt so strongly. That he was capable of such Mediterranean displays of passion. She searched for a way to let him down gently. 'It's very flattering,' she lied. 'But there's no way I'm your dream woman, Simon.'

'Yes, you are!' he shouted.

'No, I'm not. We've got virtually nothing in common.'

'That's not true!'

'Yes it is.' Sophie paused. 'Simon, let's be honest. We don't share any interests. You don't like the theatre and I do. Your idea of a nice house

293

isn't the same as mine . . . not at all.' She remembered the bedside tables at Swaying Willows. 'And you like line dancing and I hate it.'

Simon's expression changed. His brows drew together, his mouth turned down. Beneath the melting ice, his eyes froze. 'What?' he rasped.

'You like line dancing,' Sophie repeated. 'I saw some CDs on your bedside table.' Perhaps she shouldn't have snooped. Certainly, Simon did not look very pleased. He looked very angry, in fact.

'And you don't?' he growled.

'No. It's not my thing, I'm afraid. I've never done it. I wouldn't know how to.'

Another sound now echoed in the room—that of the telephone. Simon's soggy spine jerked upright. The takeover. Had to be. The only people he'd left the hotel number with were business contacts. Apart from Shirley, that was, at Sophie's insistence, but it was hardly likely to be her.

He had to answer. Everything else—he shot a burning look at Sophie—would have to wait. Dripping but determined—there were billions at stake here, after all—he rushed into the loo, where, as Sophie had noted earlier, the nearest phone hung on the marble wall by the lavatory. But the voice at the other end was not, as he had expected, the monotonous, well-fed tones of the corporation's lawyer. It was the sparsely fed and obviously hysterical tones of the co-architect of the personal takeover he was handling at the moment.

'Simon!' gasped Shirley.

*   *   *

It had, Shirley thought, been the day from hell.

First there had been the early-morning strain of persuading Sophie to go with Simon to Paris. Then with the post had come the discovery that she and James had not, after all, been invited to Venetia Bothamley-Tartt's sixty-fifth birthday party. Talk of it had buzzed about the village for weeks. From her bedroom window, which overlooked part of the Bothamley-Tartt demesne, Shirley had watched the marquee being erected. Her misery as to the whereabouts of her invitation was only slightly alleviated by the sight of the group of strikingly young and muscular tent-builders whose presence reduced the average age in the village by a good decade.

The party was to be held on the Saturday night. As the Saturday morning post came bringing nothing but a gas bill, a letter for James and a flyer from the local supermarket about reductions on beef joints, Shirley was despondent but not yet entirely defeated. There was most of a day to go, at any time during which Venetia might, with a horrified clamp of a hand to the mouth, realise her omission and rush round with a gold-edged stiffy.

'I don't know why you're worrying,' James had said on his return from his Genealogy Workshop that lunchtime. 'We hardly know her anyway.'

'What do you mean?' Shirley demanded, stung at hearing her worst fears expressed so baldly. 'I've met her at meetings of the Gibbet Preservation Trust. And I've had Anti-Velux Windows teas there several times.'

James shrugged and turned his attention to the letter that had arrived for him.

Shirley stalked out into the kitchen and stared out of the window. Far away, at the end of the

295

garden, the gracious beeches in the Bothamley-Tartt garden could be seen swaying in the early winter sunshine. There seemed to be something mocking about the movement. Venetia, Shirley reasoned, would never have not invited her if she had had a son-in-law who owned a manor and was a millionaire banker to boot. But did she now want one anyway? She thought worriedly about Simon and Sophie in Paris. Did she really want such a frozen bully—however rich—for her daughter? Not to mention her grandson. There was a heavy feeling of dread in her stomach.

James suddenly burst into the kitchen. 'You'll never believe it!' he cried excitedly.

Shirley turned. Seeing that he was waving something in his hand, the hope fluttered within her that the longed-for invitation had finally arrived, perhaps slipped under the door by a red-faced Venetia. 'Is it . . . ?' she gasped.

'Yes!' James shouted. 'He *is* my cousin once removed after all.'

Shirley realised that what James was waving was a limp piece of paper, that looked very like the recently arrived letter.

'*Who* is your cousin?' she asked icily.

'That chap I was telling you about. I tracked him down through the Internet site, remember?'

Shirley did not remember. There had been many such chaps, many such sites. 'He's related to me via Ezekiel Heckmondwike, who was a grave-digger in Halifax.'

'Oh God,' Shirley groaned, pushing past her husband. 'Let me out of here.'

'Oh, but I haven't finished yet,' James cried. 'He's coming down here this weekend.'

296

She turned, electrified. 'What? You've invited him to *stay*? Here?'

'No need,' James beamed. 'He's coming down already. Family visit to someone who lives nearby, or something. We've arranged to meet!'

Shirley nodded wearily. Just so long as she didn't have to meet him, that was all. 'I'm going upstairs to check on Arthur,' she announced.

The fact that their grandson's cold had suddenly worsened again had cast a further shadow on Shirley's gloomy day. She felt Arthur needed to see a doctor but this was not something the hard-pressed receptionist at the local health centre seemed to be able to accommodate. On the understanding that he probably had nothing worse than flu, Arthur had eventually been booked in for half-past five and had spent the afternoon so far in bed. Shirley had dithered about the matter of calling Sophie. If it was only a bad cold, she didn't want to disturb her. Still less the terrifying Simon Sharp.

In Arthur's room now, Shirley discovered that her grandson's wheezing had worsened. Everything, frankly, had worsened. The little boy lay on his pillows at a drunken angle. He was hot and sweating.

Terror swept Shirley like a blowtorch. Something was wrong. Very wrong.

'James!' she screeched, flying out to the landing.

An ambulance was called. Then, swallowing hard, with trembling hands, Shirley stabbed out the number of the hotel in Paris.

'Well, I'm rather glad you've called, as it happens,' Simon said petulantly from the looside. 'There appears to have been something of a

297

misunderstanding about Sophie and line dancing.'

'Bugger that!' shrieked Shirley. 'Give me Sophie. It's *urgent*. It's *Arthur*. He's *ill*!'

CHAPTER TWENTY-FIVE

'Goodbye then.' A lump concentrating all the disappointment and frustration he felt rose in Mark's throat as he stood before his old classmates. Nearby, a waiting taxi revved its engine.

Jeremy was the first to skip forward. 'Chin up, ducky,' he said, airkissing Mark on both cheeks.

Andy, clearly uncomfortable, shuffled forward and muttered his goodbyes.

'Goodbye, old chap,' grunted Rupert, giving him a manly hug and clapping him hard on the back.

Graham twitched unhappily. 'It's awful,' he burst out. 'I mean, who could have done it? Not one of us, that's for sure.'

Mark nodded. 'I know.' Although, inevitably, immediate first suspicion had been that one of his fellow students had been behind the set-up. But who? They all got on very well, increasingly well, give or take the odd fracas over Cluedo. Interaction Time, from being a burdensome bore, had in fact become one of the most eagerly looked-forward-to periods of the day. All the men had, Mark thought, made great strides in amusing themselves and each other. Even if Graham could get very heated over Monopoly. 'Oh, build a five-star on Park Lane if you want to,' Jeremy would sniff. 'See if I care. Hotels, schmotels. I get

298

all my kicks these days from Buckaroo.'

The only vague possibility of betrayal, following the letting-the-side-down incident in the Upper Grimside pub, was that Charlie could somehow have let the annoyance with Mark he had displayed that afternoon fester into destructive hatred.

As it happened, it *had* been Charlie. It had been he who went to Mark's room while he was in the bath, filled his water bottle with vodka and then wrote a note to Dr Martha. Or so Charlie had claimed to the head of the School. Unfortunately, Dr Martha had not believed him and had established with frightening speed that Charlie had an alibi. In the end, Charlie had been unable to deny what Briggs could confirm: that at the time the vodka was being planted he was engaged in a death-or-glory Jenga battle with Andy. With obvious regret, but equally obvious determination, Dr Martha had confirmed her decision that Mark had broken the rules and had to leave.

Failed effort though it had been, Mark had been astonished by Charlie's heroic willingness to sacrifice himself. It was as bizarre and unexpected as the planting of the vodka. Why would Charlie— at the school, like himself, to save his marriage— do something so impulsive and self-destructive? But there had been no opportunity for him to ask or for Charlie to explain. Once his guilt had been conclusively re-established, Dr Martha had wanted him out as soon as possible.

He clasped Charlie's hand as, now, the builder came forward to say goodbye. 'See you,' he muttered.

'Good luck with everything,' Mark said. He was sincerely trying to put all envy of his classmates and resentment at his fate behind him. But now that the means of saving his own had been abruptly removed, expressing hope for the unions of others took effort. 'Hope it all goes well and you get back with Angie.'

'You shouldn't to have to go,' Charlie muttered. 'We've none of us been perfect at sticking to the rules. But you're the only one who gets chucked out. And it's not your fault.' His face darkened with anger. 'If I ever find out who did it . . .'

'Send him my way,' Mark said ruefully. 'Anyway, if Dr Martha had believed you, you could easily have been thrown out instead, and that would have been the end of your marriage.' Or your money, rather, he thought, remembering Charlie's own frank revelation of his motives for attending the School for Husbands. That had been on the first day. How many years ago it seemed now.

'My marriage!' Charlie snorted, but resignedly rather than bitterly. 'It's down the toilet. Has been for ages, if I'm honest. Angie and I never were all that suited, right from the start.' He grinned at Mark. 'So sticking up for you wasn't as much of a sacrifice as you might think.'

Mark shifted uncomfortably. 'Sorry to hear that.'

'Don't be.' Charlie shrugged. 'Just the way things are, that's all. It was what you said about *really* wanting to get your wife back that first made me realise. And watching how hard you've tried in the classes ever since. You want it so much more than me. Hanging on to the money's a bit pointless if I'm also hanging on to a wife who doesn't love or trust me. We'd both be better off with other people.'

Mark looked down at the grey gravel drive. There was no reason to think, even if he had graduated *summa cum laude*, that Sophie loved or trusted him any more either. What he was facing—now his marriage was finished—was something he may have had to face anyway.

'So what are you going to do now?' Charlie asked.

'Go back to London, I suppose.' Mark thought briefly, reluctantly, of the empty house in Verona Road. At least, he presumed it was still empty; that Sophie was still at her mother's. 'I need to get a job,' he added. 'I'm pretty skint.' Looking on the bright side, the only positive aspect to the curtailment of his instruction at the School for Husbands was the accompanying curtailment of part of the bill. He was grateful to Dr Martha for being fair about this, if nothing else. He had been relieved to take off the baseball cap and T-shirt. After all, he very emphatically was not one of Dr Martha's Marriage-Mending Miracles™. The doctor herself had sadly admitted this when shaking hands with him in the hall ten minutes ago. 'I had such high hopes for you, Mark,' she had said, her eyes moist behind her glasses. 'It's very sad to see such a promising student fail to fulfil his potential. But rules are rules.'

'But everyone else has broken rules too,' Mark pointed out desperately, remembering Charlie's observations.

'Not such serious ones. I had no choice, Mark, and I hope you can understand that.'

'Goodbye, Dr Martha,' Mark had muttered. There was no point reiterating his innocence. He had tried to countless times. There was nothing to be gained from a further appeal.

'What about your wife?' Charlie now asked.

'Well, if that isn't the sixty-four-million-dollar question,' Mark admitted with as much of a grin as he could manage. But he was sure about one thing. Heading straight for the Dower House would be a tactical disaster. He was determined to make no more mistakes. Desperate though he was to see his wife, and to see his son in particular, Mark sensed that another miscalculation, another hysterical, unscheduled appearance, could be terminal for any faint hopes he could fan into being.

'Well, I hope it all works out, mate.' Charlie spoke with such warm sincerity it made Mark's eyes prick. 'You deserve to get your wife back, you really do. If I see her, I'll tell her.'

'Thanks.' With a final squeeze of the builder's supportive hand, Mark lowered himself into the taxi. As it headed up the drive his conviction grew that the whole undertaking, far from being the answer to everything, had been one enormous waste of time.

He felt sick and frightened at the thought. He had to find a way of drawing himself, Sophie and Arthur together once more. There had to be a way. It was unimaginable that there wasn't. There had to be hope. There was always hope.

*   *   *

After speaking to her mother, Sophie flung the receiver against the wall of the Paris hotel bathroom. It dangled drunkenly, scraping against the marble, as she stumbled about the bedroom. Arthur was ill. Very ill, from what her mother had tremblingly, tearfully said. Her entire being was focused on the one thing that really mattered, a small boy in an ambulance—he would, please God, be in the ambulance now—hundreds of miles away.

Simon, too, was reeling. But not from the news about his godson. Arthur's apparently endless illnesses were nothing compared to the life-shattering earthquake of Sophie's last words. He could not believe that the entire weekend—and the weeks of ardent effort before it—had been based on false pretences. The disaster was conclusive. The wreck was total. Sophie did not line dance.

And then, even as he knelt there, still dripping in icy water, the idea struck him. She could learn! They could learn together! Quickly, with all speed. All was not lost after all. He looked up, eyes blazing with feverish hope, at Sophie rushing out of the suite. He sprang to his feet. 'Stop! Wait! We can do it. There's time.'

Sophie, her head rioting with travel possibilities and trying to decide which was fastest, screeched to a halt at the door. 'A taxi and Eurostar,' she panted. 'It's the only way.'

Simon flapped his hands agitatedly. 'Not that, not that. Line dancing. We just need to take some lessons.'

It took some seconds for this to sink into Sophie's brain. 'Line dancing?' she echoed faintly. 'My son's dangerously ill and you want to stick on the Country and Western?'

'He'll be fine,' Simon breezed. 'And it's not as if there's anything you can do. You're not a doctor.'

Sophie's wet eyes hardened and blazed. 'No, I'm

303

not a doctor. I'm Arthur's *mother*, Simon. Does that register, at all?'

Simon wasn't sure that it did. He was not especially fond of his own mother. The only effect of her charging up to his hospital bedside, he was sure, would be to make him a good deal worse. He started to say this, then watched in amazement as Sophie slammed out.

'Where are you going?' he yelped, diving after her, aware that if she went out of the room his further chances of professional advancement went too.

'Home!' Sophie snapped. 'Where do you think?'

'Now hang on a minute. What about me?'

'*You?*'

'You can't just leave me,' Simon complained.

'Why not?' Sophie howled. 'I just left Arthur.' She wanted to beat her fists against him, against Shirley, against everything that had conspired to make this moment. Herself most of all. But that would take time and be pointless, and time for pointless things was no longer a luxury she had.

'But . . .' Simon blustered, 'we've got dinner booked at a top Michelin-starred restaurant tonight. You can't let me down. I can't cancel at this stage without invoking a charge of fifty per cent on my credit card—'

He did not finish the sentence.

'Simon. Fuck your credit cards,' Sophie screamed as she raced down the corridor. 'I don't care about them. And, let me make this clear once again, I don't care about you, either. Not in that way. And frankly, after everything you've just said, not in any other way. You don't need me, Simon. You need psychiatric help.'

304

Simon, left alone, marched crossly into the bathroom in search of a towel. He thought furiously of Shirley and her line-dancing lies. She had sworn Sophie could do it. Could he, he wondered, sue?

In the smelly velour cocoon of the taxi, edging through the traffic to the Gare du Nord, Sophie whimpered with fear, praying with more fervour in the cab than she ever had in a church. Her location agonisingly exacerbated the helplessness she felt. One never felt more at the mercy of circumstance than in a cab. And never more so than now.

On the train, frustrated to screaming point as it loitered to leave, she resisted getting out and physically pushing the vehicle. Every second she waited was a second less of Arthur. And who knew—the idea sprang directly from the dark centre of her terror—how many seconds Arthur might have left?

Against the window, staring rigidly out into the darkness, Sophie bunched her fist into her mouth. A silent scream sounded within her like an unending whistle. She summoned the face of Arthur, her lips moving as she whispered to him, concentrating fiercely, as if he were a flame that would go out if she looked or even thought away.

*   *   *

Mark walked up to his old home feeling rather as he imagined a released prisoner must. Not so much delighted by the liberation as oppressed by the challenges ahead. It was strange, he thought, how the house in Verona Road looked rather as it always had. He had half expected its period of emptiness to result in smashed windows, blankets of creeper, doors hanging open, rubbish in the garden. More rubbish than was customary, that was. Sophie had had plans to build a pond once in the garden, or pave it over Italian-style and fill it with pots of herbs. That would obviously not be happening now.

Admittedly, it was less than a fortnight since he left it, but a period so tumultuous it seemed certain the house would in some way mirror the damage suffered by its owners. But the house looked the same as ever, albeit empty. The possibility that Sophie would be there had always, of course, been an unreal one. She was obviously still at her mother's.

He noticed with surprise that even the car was still outside, apparently unscathed, or at least scathed only by himself at ill-judged moments in the past.

He felt the chill edge of the car key in his pocket, and those of the keys to the house, and eyed the front door of number 82 with apprehension. The thought of pushing open the door into an empty hall was a miserable one. He dreaded the ghost of the many evenings he had pushed this same door open to hear Sophie upstairs singing—admittedly through gritted teeth of late—to Arthur as she bathed him.

He steeled himself, took a deep breath and approached the gate.

'Hello there!'

He jumped at the voice. Its friendliness was a shock.

'Mark, isn't it?'

He found himself looking into the open, pretty

306

face of the friendly blonde who worked with Sophie. The one he had met in Caffé Toscana about a million years ago. He nodded. 'That's right, er . . .'

'Helen.'

'*Helen*. Of course.'

'So, how's the School for Husbands?' Helen asked cheerily. 'Just graduated, have we?'

He stared at her, shell-shocked. 'How the hell . . .'

'Do I know about it?' She smiled. 'Sophie told me. I thought it was a great idea.'

He nodded ruefully. 'So did I.'

He was determined not to reveal his failure to the blonde. He had yet to come to terms with it himself.

'So,' Helen asked brightly. 'How was it? Tell me, I'm dying to know. Are you a better husband?'

Mark hesitated. Dr Martha had told him he was. But then she had thrown him out. He wasn't sure where that left him.

'It's difficult to know,' he said truthfully.

She looked, to his surprise, very disappointed. He was filled with the urge to please her. She had been helpful after all. It had been she who had passed the phone to Sophie on that crucial occasion.

'I'm sure,' he added, more cheerfully, 'that some of what I learnt was useful.'

But Helen still looked troubled.

'There's just one thing.' She bit her lip. 'Why didn't you write to Sophie from the school? Bit of an own goal, that, wasn't it?'

'I *did* write,' Mark said indignantly.

'But Sophie said she never got any letters . . .'

'I sent them. I sent them to the Dower House . . .' He stared at Helen as the dreadful suspicion came into focus. But no. He didn't like his snobbish mother-in-law, but deceit on this level was surely beyond her. She was meddling, but not mendacious. She could not, surely, have intercepted his carefully, lovingly composed letters. After all the effort he had put into them! They had been masterpieces, nothing less; manifestos for a new start. No. It was impossible. But what other explanation was there?

'Are you going to see Sophie?' Helen interrupted his thoughts.

Mark shook his head, remembering his resolution. 'Not yet. I have to think about the best way to approach her.'

'Fast,' Helen said immediately.

Shock shot through Mark. 'What do you mean?'

'I'm not saying this is true, because it was mentioned by one of the subs whom you never can trust really . . .'

'What was mentioned?' Mark demanded.

'Well, according to her, Sophie's gone to Paris.'

'Paris? What? To *live*?' It was worse than he had thought. Visions of international custody battles exploded in his head.

'No. Just for a couple of days. A romantic trip, the chief sub said.'

'*Romantic?*' screamed Mark. 'With *whom*?'

'Someone,' Helen sighed, 'called Simon Sharp?'

Mark staggered against the rickety fence of number 82. It leant dangerously inward and then cracked and splintered with a deafening finality, depositing him amid the wreckage of his garden. He looked up from the rubble. 'A romantic trip with . . . *Simon Sharp*? You're joking.'

'I wish I was,' Helen groaned.

CHAPTER TWENTY-SIX

'Come *on*, darling!' Sophie tried to speak without her voice shaking. But the sight of the antibiotics drip suspended above his tiny arm made it difficult. She confined her field of vision to what she could see of his eyes through the distorting plastic of the oxygen mask. Closed, his eyes terrified her, although his frightened expression when they were open was almost as bad.

When, as was frequent, the doctors and nurses came to the cotside, they were sympathetic. But no one could tell Sophie what she really wanted to know. To learn it was pneumonia had shaken her to the core. Not a fatal illness for most adults. But for the very old and the very young . . .

'It's a severe case,' the consultant paediatrician had told her. 'But we're doing our best, believe me.'

Sophie had stared into the young woman's sincere face. She unhesitatingly believed her. But would belief, and their best, be enough?

The consultant had no doubt that Arthur falling into Simon's pond had exacerbated the cold he had already. The pneumonia had not developed immediately, but gradually and unevenly, before eventually taking a lethally firm hold. When I was out of the country, hundreds of miles away, Sophie berated herself endlessly.

On the other side of Arthur's cot sat Shirley in

equal agony of remorse. In vain had Sophie tried to persuade her that what had happened had not been her mother's fault. She had acted as quickly as she could. 'If it's anyone's fault it's mine,' Sophie pointed out, 'leaving him to go with . . .' she hesitated before groaning out the fateful name, '*Simon*.' She had not discussed the strange events in Paris with Shirley yet. She was not sure she ever wanted to discuss them with anyone.

But Shirley was determined to blame herself. In the few hours since Arthur had been admitted to hospital, she had sat unmovingly by his bed, her make-up messy with tears, her hair unbrushed, her clothes creased. It was this more than anything that illustrated to Sophie the depths of her mother's despair.

Feeling churned and sick, Sophie continued to stare at her son, holding his hand, willing him on in the fight against the deadly bacteria in his lungs.

Beside her, Sophie's father squeezed her own hand in much the same way as she was squeezing Arthur's. She was grateful for the reassurance, but increasingly convinced that the man sitting next to her should not be James.

That she should once have considered her marriage problematic now seemed more than absurd. The presence of real difficulty in the shape of Arthur's illness made her long for the days when Mark's being late home was the main source of her frustration. In addition, his shortcomings as a husband had withered to nothing compared to her own genuine shortcomings as a mother.

How could she, who loved Arthur so, possibly have allowed this to happen to their son? What sort of care and stewardship of her most precious possession had she demonstrated? What responsibility had she shown? How would she ever be able to explain herself even now, let alone if the worst should happen?

The torture of sitting by Arthur's bed witnessing his laboured breathing was made yet worse by the thought Mark did not know he was ill at all. Perhaps—just perhaps—if both parents were by his bedside, Arthur might rally.

'Do you think,' she tremblingly asked the consultant, 'that it might help if his father was here?'

The doctor hesitated. There was a worried flicker in her eyes. 'It might.'

'I've got to get in touch with Mark,' Sophie said to Shirley as they retired to the waiting room while Arthur was examined. 'I've got to trace him at that school.'

To her surprise, Shirley did not argue. She nodded eagerly. Sophie thought rapidly as she sipped black coffee in a plastic cup. Mark's mobile number had not worked. She would have to try the school itself. 'But I don't have the address, damn it. Mark never wrote to me.'

Her mother put her coffee down on the brown felt carpet by the leg of her chair. 'Actually,' Shirley said, in a low voice, 'Mark did write to you.'

She opened her handbag and silently handed over a thick wodge of letters.

'Mum!' Sophie raised shocked eyes to Shirley. 'What . . . ?'

'It's my fault, all of it,' Shirley sobbed now. 'It was me who first suggested Simon as a godfather. If I hadn't done that, hadn't insisted you went to see him at his house . . .'

Sophie drew a long breath. She could probably guess the rest but it no longer mattered. Nothing mattered but the small boy in the bed next door. And, perhaps, the fact that Mark had kept his promise, after all. Shirley fled, snivelling.

While the doctors murmured over her son in the adjoining room, Sophie opened the letters. Her mother's one, tiny credit in the affair was that she had left them sealed. Each was the same—full of Mark's determination that his sojourn in the school would secure their future.

The letters were often sad and wistful, recalling older, happier, times. Sometimes they were funny, describing with wit and relish some of the pottier classes at the School for Husbands. But Sophie's smiles never lasted long. The misery of missing Mark, the anguished awareness of having misjudged him, would rise within her once again. She had not recognised a good thing when she had it. What she had lacked all along, Sophie now realised, was not a good husband. Rather, a sense of proportion.

Still, at least now she had the address. She could get in touch with Mark. That was something.

Except, heartbreakingly, it wasn't. The School for Husbands address had no number, according to Directory Enquiries. This did not initially dismay Sophie. Buckingham Palace probably had no number according to some directory services. It was only after she had tried them all and met with the same response that she was forced to recognise that there really was no number and Mark was uncontactable.

Where was he? She had asked the same question many times in the past, of course. But

Sophie was horribly aware that, this time, his being unreachable was not his fault. It was hers. She had started this horrible ball rolling; she, ultimately, had caused all this trouble. This whole miserable chain of events, culminating in this worst calamity of all, would never have happened if she, Sophie, hadn't had a hissy fit over a party. *A party!*

James, beside her, now patted her on the hand. 'Your mother and I have to go.' It was the end of visiting time. Only Sophie was permitted to camp on a put-up bed by her son's side and watch him through the endless striplit, swing-doored, murmuring, red-light-winking nights.

Sophie resumed her vigil. She knew that the abyss was deepening and darkening. She had fought the knowledge all day, but there was ultimately no escaping the fact that Arthur's breathing had got worse and his fever seemed heightened. She knew, even without the concerned looks of the nurses, that Arthur was fading. Having lost her husband, was she now about to lose her son?

*　　　*　　　*

Mark sat in the car outside the Dower House, listening to the radio and feeling as irritated now as he had felt apprehensive on arrival. Just where the hell was everybody? It was dark and the house was empty.

Oh, where were Shirley and James? Vile though it was to admit it, only they could help him now. Only they knew where in Paris Sophie—and possibly Arthur too—had gone. Was that ghastly, slimy, slippery cold fish bonding with his son even

313

now?

Sophie, on a romantic trip with Simon Sharp. The news had been incredible. Impossible. Simon Sharp and romance were a contradiction in terms. The only thing the man was capable of loving was money.

In his heart, however, Mark knew that the trip was all too possible. No doubt it also had something to do with the non-delivery of his letters to Sophie. Shirley had never considered him a worthy son-in-law. Someone as obviously successful as Simon Sharp was—now if not when he had originally dated her daughter—much more suitable. The snotty old troll had tried to shaft him. And, for all he knew, might well have succeeded. He had to find Sophie, and fast.

A pair of headlights, swinging into the drive, made him sit up abruptly. He peered anxiously into the night. The car was James's all right, the black Lexus that Mark, an agnostic to all forms of motor-vehicle worship, had tried many times to feign interest in.

The headlights flashed on his car. Mark's stomach tightened into a knot of terror. He had to handle this properly. Everything could depend on it.

An instant later, doors slammed and he could hear feet skidding across the gravel. He had obviously been recognised. Shirley was even now hurtling towards him, no doubt boiling with anger. Spitting fury, possibly. She wouldn't appreciate having her plans for Sophie and Simon interfered with.

Here she was, scrabbling on his screen, her face distended as before. He opened the door resignedly, bracing himself for a torrent of abuse. As she flew at him with her claws, he flinched.

'Oh, Mark! Oh, I'm so glad to see you! Oh, please, come on, come on . . .'

As she pulled hard on his arm, he stumbled out, bewildered. This was not the script he had been expecting. Nor the voice—jumpy and frightened, not grim and vengeful. And now Shirley was hugging him, sobbing, no less, into his arms. He stared across the gravel at James, still behind the wheel of his Lexus.

James leant sideways out of the door. 'Come on, old chap,' he urged. 'There's no time to lose. Arthur's in hospital.'

Arthur! Hospital?

*   *   *

Sophie was slumped on her chair, weaving in and out of not-quite dreams filled with screaming ambulances, Arthur in an oxygen mask and Simon Sharp in the shrubbery. Time after time she jerked herself awake. She must concentrate, for Arthur's sake. Before her, in his cot, the boy lay sleeping fitfully. He seemed no better.

Come on, Arthur. Come on. It's just you and me now. But we can do it. We can do it together.

The boy sighed and stirred. His forehead was flushed and shiny with fever.

The door to Arthur's room swung open. 'Cup of tea?' asked the nurse cheerily.

The inside of Sophie's mouth was already rank with hospital tannin. But she must take comfort from where she could. 'Yes, please.'

The nurse went away. Almost immediately, the

door swung open again. Sophie looked up, curious that the tea had been produced so soon.

But it was not the cheery SRN standing in the doorway.

'*Mark!*'

CHAPTER TWENTY-SEVEN

Sophie walked slowly back down the aisle. The weather outside was sombre but, to the right and left of her, the smiles of the guests blazed like Barbados in August. Everyone had dressed up: the men fresh in pale summer suits, the women pretty in floaty florals. Some, gratifyingly, had gone as far as hats, which looked sharp and colourful against the ancient stone of the walls.

As they walked, Sophie squeezed her husband's hand. That they should renew their wedding vows with a church blessing had been his idea. The suggestion had been the finale to the process of mutual heart-searching that had begun in earnest the day they could at last afford to think about themselves, the day Arthur finally came home to Verona Road from hospital.

The doctors thought the fever might have broken slightly before Mark arrived, unannounced, in the little boy's room, But Sophie, for once, did not believe them. That Mark had saved their child she was certain. As soon as he had leant over the bed, touched Arthur's hand and murmured to him, the atmosphere had changed. Arthur's face had changed. He had opened his eyes—closed for hours up until that moment—stared at his father and given a slight, uncertain smile. And from then on, his progress had been steady.

'But you've never been much of a churchgoer,' Sophie had said surprised when her husband had suggested the renewal ceremony.

Mark had shrugged. 'Well, after what we've survived recently I've definitely got faith in something.' His face became serious. 'We've got so much to be thankful for. It was a near miss, in more ways than one.'

Sophie nodded, biting her lip, her eyes brimming as almost always these days. Tears were never far away. Of relief mostly. 'But are you sure you want to stay married to me? I've been so awful.'

He folded her in his arms. 'You're not the only one.'

'And my mother?' Sophie sighed. She still could not quite believe the part Shirley had played in it all.

'We've all made a complete mess of things. And, strangely enough, we all thought we were doing the right thing.'

'So you can forgive her?'

His eyes twinkled. 'Absolutely. What I went through at that grooming salon gave me a lot more respect for her, as it happens. But seriously, I can forgive anyone anything. Almost.' A shadow crossed his face as he thought of Simon Sharp. The same shadow crossed Sophie's face as she thought the same.

'Anyway,' Mark added cheerfully, 'it would be a good start for my fabulous new relationship with Shirley to give her the mother of the bride moment she's always wanted.'

As she passed her parents' pew now Sophie beamed as her mother, sniffing copiously, smiled shakily back. She had risen to her big moment in an unexpected way. Her suit was unshowy and long-skirted, her hat half the size of the one she had worn to the christening and her make-up more muted than Sophie had ever seen it. The effect was both stylish and dignified, and suited her, her daughter thought, far more than the old tight-jeans-and-fun-fur yummy granny look.

Arthur, sitting happily on his grandmother's knee, clapped his plump little hands in delight.

Sophie felt the tears, yet again, rush hotly to her eyes. Arthur had been fully well for months now, although never a night passed without her and Mark tiptoeing from their bedroom at least once in the early hours of the morning to check on him as he slept.

It was amazing, Sophie thought as a sudden shaft of light pierced the stained-glass window, how much the blessing looked like the christening. The church was the same. Most of the guests were the same. Equally vast amounts of champagne had been bought for the party in her parents' garden.

Yet in other ways, the occasion could not have been more different. Since the last time they had gathered in this building, those at the centre of the ceremony had undergone personal upheavals that could never have been foreseen. The godparents as much as anyone.

Cess had sent her best love and best wishes, but confessed she and Bryce were much too poor to make the trip over. Which was why Sophie and Mark, with Arthur, would be stopping off in Sydney on their second honeymoon.

Less regretfully, Simon was not present either. Sophie had been in touch with him only once since the Paris dramas, to write and absolve him of his duties to Arthur. She had, however, traced his recent actions through a most unexpected turn of events. Incredibly, Lisa, the sour, man-hating chief sub-editor, had suddenly got married. To Simon Sharp.

As the ceremony had apparently been small and private, no one from work had been asked to the wedding. But all had been revealed by Lisa's subsequent zeitgeist touchstone piece entitled 'Never Too Late; My Mid-Life Marriage Miracles'. In this she revealed that their mutual interest in line dancing had been what brought her and Simon together.

Whether even Lisa's departure would ultimately be enough to keep her at the magazine, only time would tell, Sophie thought. But there had been enough upheaval lately without adding a career crisis to the mix, and for the moment she could see no problems working as Helen's deputy. She grinned at her new boss, currently waving and smiling from the third pew and looking softly elegant in a baby-blue suit with a white-waistcoated Teddy on her knee. Beside her, John looked broad-shouldered, clever, friendly and capable. Which Sophie hoped he was; he would need to be if he and Mark were to make a go of the upmarket children's party service they had decided to set up together.

'Everything provided, from ready-wrapped Pass the Parcel to Punch and Judy,' they had told their wives excitedly after emerging from the last of the meetings in which they had thrashed out the

319

details. 'Our USP is games for the parents. You know how bored they always look, hanging about watching their children stuff in the sausage rolls? We'll give them silly things to do, quizzes about how well they really know *Bob the Builder*, how many of what fruit the Very Hungry Caterpillar ate on Thursday, the names of the trains in *Thomas the Tank Engine*, that sort of thing. Entertain the parents, and the children will look after themselves. And of course,' Mark had added, 'keeping the parents occupied means they won't be getting into trouble. Or making any, come to that.' Sophie had thought the idea a good if wild one.

'His fairy cakes, my selling skills,' Mark had reassured her. 'We can't go wrong.' But beneath the banter was a business plan so sound that even Sophie's notoriously careful father James had invested in it. The prospect of a new challenge, working hours he wanted with someone he liked, had energised Mark, Sophie happily recognised. Nor was this the only way in which he looked different.

Unsurprisingly, she had not noticed his new burnished, groomed appearance when first he had burst through the doors of Arthur's hospital room. It was only as the days went by, after it was obvious the little boy's condition was improving, that she registered something different about Mark's hair. His teeth. His eyebrows. His skin. 'You've got a fake tan,' she had remarked in amazement. 'My God. And your teeth are bleached. You look like Peter Andre.'

Mark had surged with embarrassment. He had never been quite certain about the tan himself, especially not once he was out of the school and

320

away from everyone else who had had one. Had all that effort in the Jon Wayne salon really been wasted?

'No,' Sophie assured him after she stopped laughing. 'You look lots better, really. And once the orange has calmed down a bit you'll look fabulous.'

Mark had shrugged good-naturedly. He would have been sprayed green, happily, if it amused Sophie. That it had made her smile at him again made even the chest-waxing worth it.

Some days later, when Arthur's progress had been sufficient to allow them to overnight at the Dower House while he continued to recover in the hospital, Sophie had unbuttoned Mark's shirt and stared in amazement at his hairless torso. Her eyes had widened questioningly, then twinkled with mirth as they had travelled the line of smooth skin leading to where Mark's jeans unbuttoned. 'Have you . . .'

'No!' he had laughed. '*They're* not waxed, thank you.' Even Jon Wayne had not presumed that far.

Sophie was rocking with suppressed glee. That she thought it quite so funny made Mark wonder whether there had been another agenda to the grooming session after all. Was making wives laugh at their husband's touching efforts to please them what the module had really been about? He knew enough about Dr Martha and her methods to realise the idea was far from impossible.

Whatever the truth, he had taken some of Jon Wayne's tips to heart. Being clean and, within careful boundaries, scented made self-evident, unarguable sense. Moisturising and shaving too. The jade face roller he could, however, live without.

'You smell delicious,' Sophie had said as, that night, they made love properly for the first time for what seemed centuries. 'What is it?'

'Essence of Birkenstock,' Mark told her, eyes twinkling.

Sophie smiled, now, at her father. James nodded happily back from his place beside his wife, whose hand, Sophie was pleased to see, he held supportively.

There had, Sophie knew, been serious words in the parental home. James had been horrified over what had emerged about Simon's intentions and the part his wife had played. But he had accepted too, in a guilty, apologetic phone call to his daughter and son-in-law, how his own passivity, obsession with his hobby and habitual wish to avoid conflict had contributed to events.

One benefit of the upheaval, as far as James was concerned, was that Shirley no longer attacked him about genealogy. She had, admittedly, been surprised when what she assumed was a beggar on the doorstep turned out to be James's long-lost cousin once removed. Who, as it happened, was in Hampshire as an invitee to that socially resonant event, the birthday party of Venetia Bothamley-Tartt. Who was the beggar's cousin and therefore James's too. But it was with less excitement than might previously have been expected that Shirley learnt she was actually related to the inhabitants of the Manor House.

A much greater surprise had awaited Mark, arriving at the church for the service. There, just outside the porch, in appearance strangely close to the gargoyles protruding from the church tower,

322

had been the familiar crazed, creased, crumpled sight of Briggs. Who, it turned out, was his father-in-law's cousin, turned up during the latter's forays into family history.

But the surprises, even then, had not been over. Mark, back outside, adjusting the flower in his buttonhole after ushering Briggs into the church, had blinked, then squinted in disbelief to see a small, determined figure with short dark hair and half-moon glasses coming rapidly up the church steps.

'You!' he exclaimed. 'What on earth are you doing here?'

'Of course I wasn't going to miss this,' Dr Martha told him, her eyes dancing. 'You're my first success from the School for Husbands.'

'Success?' blurted Mark. Even for Dr Martha, this was a bit much. 'But you said I was a huge disappointment. A failure. Hell, you *expelled* me.'

Dr Martha put her head on one side and smiled enigmatically. 'Mark. Therapy moves in a mysterious way.'

'I guess so,' Mark conceded, remembering the dancing class.

*   *   *

Outside the church, after the service, Shirley squeezed her daughter's hand. 'I'm so sorry, darling. I've been such a fool.'

'So have we all, Mum,' Sophie smiled.

'But me especially,' Shirley insisted. 'I should go to a School for Mothers, really.'

'Now there,' said Dr Martha, sidling past, 'is a *great* idea.'

323